MAGIC TIME

Also by Daniel M. Klein

EMBRYO
WAVELENGTHS

MAGIC
TIME

Daniel M. Klein

DOUBLEDAY & COMPANY, INC.
Garden City, New York
1984

DESIGNED BY LAURENCE ALEXANDER

Library of Congress Cataloging in Publication Data

Klein, Daniel M.
Magic time.

I. Title.
PS3561.L344M3   1984   813′.54
ISBN 0-385-17452-7
Library of Congress Catalog Card Number: 83-45565
Copyright © 1984 by Daniel M. Klein

For Tom

MAGIC TIME

Prologue

ANYTHING COULD HAPPEN. There was that much promise in the air, that much magic. The whole world seemed an experiment. It was a fine time to be young and a magnificent time to be a young man just a day out of Harvard, ready for life to begin.

Axel Stenhorn was the first of the five to arrive in the Square that evening, as much to make an early escape from his family as to be punctual for Jerry's experiment. Since lunch, Axel's mother had been sighing noisily, wondering aloud what they would do alone in Cambridge that night while their son—for whose graduation they had traveled almost a thousand miles—abandoned them to attend a private celebration. Only his sister, Annalena, had been truly curious about what he was going to do with Jerry Halligan for an entire night. "Is it some kind of stag party, Axe? Naked ladies jumping out of Boston cream pies?" "Worse," Axel had replied, deadpan, while their mother clucked at them both. "Worse than you can imagine."

Axel bounced on his heels in front of Hayes Bickford's cafeteria, his glasses slipping down his long nose. He smiled: Trudging miserably up Massachusetts Avenue with parents *and* grandparents in tow was a fellow graduate—another Ohio boy he realized with special satisfaction. Axel nodded to them gratefully—yes, tonight was a night to celebrate with friends. Like a double confirmation of Axel's thought, Todd Brewster and Greg Gregorian appeared at the corner of Plympton Street, recognizable a block away by the foot difference in their height—the "Mutt and Jeff of Post-Kantian Vaudeville," as Jerry liked to call them. Axel waved.

"The trouble with you, fat man," Greg was saying to Todd as they ambled toward Axel, "your goddamn basic existential problem is that you want all your experiences predigested for you. That's why you had to read Huxley all afternoon. So you'd know exactly what to feel tonight."

Todd grinned down at his roommate—alas, *former* roommate. He felt inordinately happy tonight. There seemed to be such a pleasant order to things: Harvard behind him, a mysterious adventure with his best friends in store for his last night in Cambridge. Stanford graduate school ahead of him. He popped his copy of Huxley's *The Doors of Perception* against Greg's curly-topped head.

"I don't predigest a thing," Todd said. "I swallow everything alive." He opened his mouth wide and growled just as they arrived in front of Axel.

"One day out of Harvard and he's already regressing to his natural self," Greg said. He saw that Axel was offering his hand and hesitated a second before shaking it; Greg was still not used to Axel's oddly formal manners.

"Either of you have any second thoughts?" Axel asked.

"Just one," Greg said. "We should have insisted that Jerry let us bring dates."

"I've had a few doubts, I guess," Todd said, "but I wouldn't miss this for anything. Say, did you have a tough time leaving your folks?"

Axel shrugged. "Not too bad."

"For some it takes a lifetime," Greg said. In fact, Greg had only managed to make an exit from his parents' hotel room by saying that he was being initiated into a very selective Harvard secret society. That had really put a smile on the old man's face and, anyhow, it was not a complete lie, at least the way Jerry told it. Jerry had said that the trip to Newton was going to be the biggest privilege of their lives.

"Well, looks like Debilio *is* bringing a date," Todd said.

David Debilio was crossing from the Yard toward them, one bare and very hairy arm slung across the shoulders of Patricia Beardsley, the girl he was going to marry in just two days. She had insisted on accompanying him to his "clandestine rendezvous," as she called it, although it only made him feel guiltier about not spending the night with her. David had considered begging off from the whole business, but that wouldn't have been fair to Jerry; besides, he had this nagging sense that tonight would somehow give him a jump on the future. It was only a feeling, really, but it was just the kind of feeling Pat said he should pay more attention to.

Greg fell to one knee, pulled Patricia's hand to his lips and loudly kissed it. He squinted at David, working up his mock-earnest Cornel Wilde face.

"I'll be perfectly honest with you, David," Greg intoned. "If you bring this young beauty with us tonight, I can't be responsible for anything I might do."

Pat slipped her hand away from Greg, her cheeks coloring.

"I'm just dropping Dave off," she said. Her voice had the patrician cadences of what they were again calling a "Harvard accent" —JFK had brought that expression back.

"Just tell me one thing, Pat," Greg said. Standing, he was still a few inches shorter than she was. "If you wanted to bring something home that was really going to upset your family, why not an Armenian? Anybody can marry an Italian these days."

They all laughed, although David did not like the joke much. Greg always went a little too far. In his *Crimson* cartoons it was funny, but in person it could be annoying after a while. He hoped Greg wasn't going to keep up this way all night.

A horn sounded five short blasts. Across the street, in front of the Yard portal chiseled with the motto "Enter to Grow in Wisdom," stood a wood-paneled Ford station wagon. The driver's window was down and Jerry Halligan's handsome Irish head leaned out of it.

"Gentlemen," he called. "Welcome to the Transcendental Express."

Jerry waited until they were out on the highway before removing his clipboard from his canvas book bag. He handed it to David.

"Why don't we get this out of the way while we still have some light," he said over his right shoulder.

Axel was sandwiched between Todd and Greg in the back and David was up front with his erstwhile roommate. Jerry was not only the night's ringleader, he was the common link in the group: David had been his roommate since his freshman year; he knew Greg—and hence, Todd—from a short-story writing class; and he'd met Axel just two terms ago in Social Relations 120, "Interpersonal Behavior."

"I think it's pretty self-evident," Jerry was saying. "Kind of a 'before and after' thing. Your life goals as you see them today and then again as you see them tomorrow morning. That's the whole shootin' match."

Axel inched forward in his seat and peered over David's shoulder. The top of the mimeographed questionnaire was emblazoned with the letterhead of the Harvard Center for Research in Personality, including a crimson "Veritas" shield. Reassuring, that. Harvard. Axel sat back.

David had already filled in most of the form. It was the kind of thing he could practically do in his sleep by now—scholarship students were always writing down their *curricula vitae* and goals for some review committee. Immediate plans: Harvard Law School. Long range?

"Be as specific as you can," Jerry said, seeing David hesitate. "Put down exactly where you think you'd like to be twenty years from now."

"Go ahead, put down the White House," Greg piped.

David wrote "constitutional law expert" and left it at that. The last question asked what he expected to get out of tonight's experience. He jotted down "a glimpse into the future" and passed the clipboard to the backseat.

"All those lovely blank spaces just interested in me," Todd said, smiling as he took it. He flipped immediately to the last question— what he expected to get out of tonight—because he had already given it some thought that afternoon while reading Huxley. What Todd hoped for tonight was what he had wanted ever since taking Professor Tillich's course on "Self-Interpretation in Western Thought": He yearned for a truly mystical experience. For once he wanted to bypass the elaborate theological systems he was always reading and get right to the source. Tonight, he wrote, he'd like to have a vision, a visitation—even hearing voices would do. Jerry's other questions seemed trivial after that. Maybe he would teach somewhere after he got his Ph.D. at Stanford; he'd like to get married someday.

Axel passed the clipboard across his lap to Greg. "I'd like to think a couple of minutes, if you don't mind."

"No problem," Greg said. He printed his name and mailing address—"General Delivery, New York City"—and then drew an elaborate squiggle through the space intended for the name of his graduate school. He answered the next question aloud as he wrote: "Twenty years from now I expect to be America's best known playwright. If possible, I'd also like to be six inches taller." As a start, all he asked for tonight was one truly original theatrical idea. He handed the clipboard to Axel.

"What if you aren't sure?" Axel said, picking up the pen.

"Come on, Axel," Jerry said. "These aren't questions any of us can be sure about. I'm just looking for your fondest dreams."

"I mean about immediate plans," Axel said. "What I'm going to be doing next year."

The others looked at Axel quizzically.

"But you're in med school already, aren't you?" Todd said.

"Yes, P & S," Axel said. "But I'm pretty sure I could get them to hold my place open a couple of years if I went into the Peace Corps."

"My God, good for you!" Todd thumped him on the back.

"You are full of surprises, aren't you, Axe?" Jerry said. He lifted his hands from the steering wheel and wrung them fiendishly. "A perfect subject for my experiment."

"But I'm not really sure," Axel said. "It's just a possibility. You know, to break up all the schooling. But that might be a bad idea too." He paused a moment. "I don't think my father would think much of it."

"Put down both possibilities," Jerry said. He was easing the car off the highway onto a suburban avenue. "Either, or."

Axel did and then wrote that he eventually expected to become a general practitioner, perhaps in partnership with his father. He did not honestly think that he had any expectations for tonight.

"How about you, Sigmund?" Greg tapped Jerry on the back of his head. "Don't we get to hear your answers?"

They all knew, of course, that Jerry had declined a very good offer from the Weston Advertising Company in New York City so that he could stay on at Harvard in graduate school. It had been a fairly recent decision, arrived at after a long discussion with his Social Relations tutor. Tonight, actually, was the first experiment in his graduate research project.

"Yes, where do you think you'll be in twenty years?" David said, looking at his friend.

"On Olympus," Jerry answered and winked.

It was twilight now and Jerry switched on the lights as he took a turn onto a tree-lined Newton street.

"There's one question that's not on the sheet," Jerry said, his voice abruptly free of its habitual irony. "Have any of you ever ingested mind-expanding material before?"

They all said no quite quickly, then fell silent as Jerry pulled the station wagon to a halt in front of a white colonial-style house. Suddenly the door to that house opened and they all gazed up at the tall figure in white duck pants and an open Oxford shirt who stood framed in the doorway. With the light behind him, Harvard lecturer Timothy Leary looked like a god.

"That night in Newton"—that is how their experience was known to all five of them thenceforth and forever afterward. Not that they spoke of it often. Over the years, only Greg and David would ever bring it up socially, casually letting it be known that they were in one of the first groups at Harvard to experiment with psychedelics—a hip social credential which Greg sometimes used to encourage women to come home with him or David would employ to win a client's confidence. But neither of them ever *really* told a stranger what happened that night or tried to explain why it would always link the five of them. And not even Jerry would ever be able to make anyone else understand why for the next two decades—even long after the excitement was over—they would all keep tabs on Timothy Leary's life as if he were a twin, trying to interpret their own lives in terms of his, trying to catch the shape of that wildest of hallucinations known as history.

ONE

1960-1963

1

TO EVEN consider postponing medical school was as radical an idea as Axel had ever entertained. Up to that point in his life, he had been a model of consistency, single-mindedly mastering every task of growing to adulthood—from crawling to calculus—as if the slightest deviation would result in a lifelong handicap. By the time he was seven, he already knew that he wanted to become a doctor. He made the announcement to his parents in the airy Stenhorn kitchen one morning just before he left for school, and as the back door closed behind him he heard his mother release a great gasp of laughter. *Such a serious little boy. Not a cowboy or a G-man, mind you, Eric, but a doctor, just like his dad.* Axel's face had burned. The very earnestness she'd praised him for while fussing back the hair from his long, square forehead became a joke the moment he was gone. But it didn't matter. Life *was* a serious business, and anyone who ignored that fact would eventually pay for his lapse. Believing this helped Axel endure a great deal of laughter all through high school.

Harvard had been a wonderful relief. Arriving in Cambridge in the fall of 1957 with his Westinghouse science prize and his National Merit Scholarship, Axel's greatest hope had been to find an atmosphere where he could study free of taunts and laughter. What he found was a whole schoolful of intelligent young men, most of them every bit as earnest and hardworking as he was. He majored in chemistry. He roomed with two physics students from Long Island. He played fourth-chair flute in the Harvard-Radcliffe Orchestra. In his junior year the university obligated him to select one course from the social sciences to satisfy its requirements for a well-rounded education, and Axel arbitrarily chose a survey course called Social Relations 10. His thought at the time was that a little psychology might be useful later on in dealing with patients.

The very first lecture was on primitive rituals and Axel was spellbound. He drank in every detail, as if quenching a thirst that had been left there as a child when he had shunned fairy tales and boys' adventure books to pursue more practical matters. Now he became absorbed with Samoan puberty rites, Peruvian magic, Eskimo spirits. He was amazed by the way quirks and customs varied willy-nilly from one little parcel of geography to another, and he found the sheer arbitrariness of it strangely exhilarating. Suddenly the Harvard rule requiring coat and tie in dining rooms —one he had taken for granted for three years—seemed positively whimsical. A talisman around his neck to merit his mound of mashed potatoes? They might just as well require a stripe of bright red paint across the bridge of his nose. As the course turned to personal psychology, Axel read his assignments in Piaget and Freud with the seriousness he'd once reserved for pure science only. He dissected dreams, charted motives. He sorted through the italicized case histories like a traveler searching for a letter from home. He was studying himself.

All these new thoughts suddenly tumbling around in Axel's brain constituted a minor mental revolution of sorts. Nothing was quite what it had always seemed. And yet nothing had changed. Nothing at all. He studied chemistry. He had dinner with his roommates or alone. He typed out a one-page review of the week's events in stiff, declarative sentences every Saturday night and mailed it home to Akron. The only girl he talked to was the gaunt Radcliffe flutist with whom he shared a music stand at orchestra rehearsals. Perhaps he laughed to himself more frequently than he had before, but it was *to himself.* He was like a man who had changed the prescription in his glasses: The only person he looked different to was himself.

At the beginning of his senior year, as Axel settled himself in for the long haul of his thesis in physical chemistry, he made a last-minute change in his schedule. He dropped "Automorphic Functions"—a graduate math course he'd been preparing for since his freshman year—in favor of Social Relations 120, "Case Analysis: The Interpretation of Interpersonal Behavior." He knew nothing more about 120 than what he had read in the registrar's catalog:

> The aim of the course is to develop the student's understanding of his values, attitudes, and perceptions as they affect human relations, and to improve his observation in interpersonal situations.

Axel thought the course might help him clarify some of the unsolved conundrums of Social Relations 10. He bought a new notebook at the Coop and arrived in the small, third-floor Emerson Hall room ten minutes before the first class began. There was one other fellow there already, a handsome, reckless-looking boy with longish hair in corduroys and tennis shoes, his rep striped tie loosened and flung over one shoulder like a noose that had just been cut from the scaffold in the nick of time. Axel thought he might have seen him before, perhaps in the Yard, but he could not be sure. He was not the sort Axel was even slightly curious about—too slick, cocksure, no doubt intellectually shallow. That was his initial impression of Jerry Halligan.

"Ah, so the first case study walks in. Let me guess—" Jerry scratched his head. "Classical repressed oedipal rage, correct?"

Axel took a step backward. "I think I'm in the wrong room," he blurted.

"That's what everyone says." Jerry burst out laughing, a surprisingly high-pitched, reedy sound—an adolescent laugh. He shot out his hand and Axel automatically took it. "Jerry Halligan, Dunster House," he said. "I take it 'Soc Rel' isn't your field."

"No, chemistry," Axel said. "Premed."

"Just taking 120 for comic relief, eh?"

"I guess."

"Well, I hear it's not too many laughs. I hear Dr. Donlevy really puts you through the mincer."

Axel looked at the door. He wished the others would arrive.

"You aren't Catholic, are you?" Halligan said.

"No."

"Too bad. Confession is supposed to be the best preparation for this. In the department they call it Shame 120."

At that moment a heavyset, bearded man came through the door and plopped his shabby, overstuffed briefcase onto the seminar table. He sat down before he looked at either of them.

"Well, Mr. Halligan," he said at last. "Trying to get in a few innings before the game begins?"

Halligan grinned, but it did not hide the fact that his face was coloring. Then, all together, the five remaining students arrived—three men and two women—and Donlevy began to distribute copies of a case history around the table. He said to take a few minutes to read it before the discussion began.

Axel found himself totally incapable of focusing on the page in front of him. His pulse fluttered in his ears. He was sure he did not belong here. It was a ridiculous mistake. Learn about the world. Learn about ideas. You didn't go to college to be psychoanalyzed. He pushed back his chair and began to lift his notebook off the table when he saw that Dr. Donlevy was looking directly at him. The bearded man wrinkled his brow in an awkward, avuncular half-wink and, leaning toward Axel, mouthed the words, "Give it a chance."

Axel stayed.

The course turned out to be every bit as terrifying as Jerry Halligan had predicted. For three weeks they talked about case histories and then, at the start of the fourth, they began to talk about themselves and each other with a candor Axel could never have imagined. He was embarrassed for every one of them. It was appalling. It was totally pointless. And when he was not working on his thesis, it was all Axel could think about.

At the beginning of the sixth week, the red-haired Radcliffe junior who always sat on Axel's right abruptly turned to him and said, "Aren't you ever going to say anything?"

Axel blushed. He shrugged and managed to say, "Not yet."

"He's too busy judging the rest of us," Jerry said, grinning directly at him.

Axel grasped the arms of his chair tightly in both hands. He had known this would happen sooner or later. He had even guessed that it would be that complacent clown Halligan who would be the first to go after him, and he had spent hours lying in bed preparing his retort. But now, in a voice he barely recognized—it was so calm, so matter-of-fact—he heard himself saying, "Sometimes I can make myself laugh just by imagining my folks listening to all of this."

"What do you think they'd say?" the redhead asked.

"They'd say we should all have our mouths washed out with soap."

Someone laughed and abruptly Jerry scooted out of his seat. "That's a terrific idea," he chirped, halfway to the door. "What's everybody's preference—Palmolive? Ivory?"

"I don't know, Jerry," Donlevy said very slowly, scratching at his beard. "What did *your* mother use?"

Jerry emitted a short, sharp laugh and then he just stood there, looking back at each one of them. They all stared up at his lean, handsome face. It was red and now there were small drops forming in the corners of his eyes. At that moment Axel first realized how very much he wanted to be Jerry Halligan's friend.

That was in October 1960. That same month Axel received an

absentee ballot from Akron, Ohio. Several weeks before, his father had sent him the application for it, along with a letter that went on for three pages about the privileges of a free society and how propitious it was that Axel had turned twenty-one in the same year as a presidential election. Dr. Stenhorn had concluded by assuring Axel that he in no way wanted to influence his vote and that, in fact, privacy was the very hallmark of a democratic election.

On an impulse, Axel loped up to Jerry Halligan after class the next day and blurted, "Who do you think I should vote for?"

"Kennedy, of course," Jerry answered. "He's Irish. He's from Boston. He went to Harvard, for Christ's sake. He's going to be my very own personal President."

Axel smiled. They were walking side by side across the Yard, their ties flapping in the autumn wind.

"Of course, you're probably looking for some more esoteric political reason," Jerry continued. "Like his position on excise taxes or some such. All totally irrelevant stuff, mind you. The only thing that matters is that he's going to lead us out of the yawn of Eisenhower boredom by the sheer twinkle in his eye."

They crossed Massachusetts Avenue and turned down Plympton Street. In fact, Axel's knowledge of the American political scene was limited to what he had gleaned from his father's dining room lectures and from a high school civics course, but it had never caught his interest; to Axel it was in the same class of information as baseball statistics. Even the heated arguments that raged nightly in Kirkland House dining hall about Nixon and Kennedy and Communists and the death penalty seemed to Axel like exercises, an excuse for a little yelling and screaming between bouts of studying in the deathlike quiet of Lamont Library. And so Jerry's reasons for voting for Kennedy sounded just right to Axel. He decided on the spot to do the same. He wished his father could see the way he had arrived at his decision.

"You're coming for lunch, right?"

Axel looked up. They were approaching the corner of Mt. Auburn Street, where he would normally turn.

"You mean to Dunster House?" Axel suddenly felt shy. In three years he had never been invited to eat in a house other than his own, Kirkland.

"That's right," Jerry grinned. "Home of the famous chipped beef *à cheval.*"

In the dining hall they were joined by Jerry's roommate, David Debilio, a swarthy New Jersey boy with serious, dark eyes. David was—much to Axel's surprise—what was known on campus as a "wonk," just like himself. All the telltale signs were there: the checkered shirt and mismatched tie, the pencil holster on his belt, the unwashed hair, the look of furtive intelligence—the complete stylelessness that distinguished him from clubbies, sportsmen, even turtlenecked literary types or anyone with a bit of flair. A wonk, and an Italian one at that, just the opposite of what Axel would have imagined for Jerry's roommate.

"Nice to meet you." David grasped Axel's hand quickly, his other already prodding a fork into his mashed potatoes. "Jerry's told me about you. You're the 'Grand Inhibitor,' right?"

Axel shrugged. He did not much like the sound of that description of himself, yet he could not help feeling flattered that Jerry had mentioned him at all.

"That's my name for the conscience of the group," Jerry said quickly. "Every section of 120 needs one. Otherwise there'd be this mass of primordial ids oozing all over Donlevy's nice oak table. The 'Grand Inhibitor' supplies us with just enough boundaries to give us individual shape."

Axel shrugged again and smiled. "It's nothing I do consciously," he said.

"All the better." Jerry laughed.

"Watch out for Halligan," David said, not looking up as he sawed at the gravy-coated toast on his tray. "He's obsessed with moral types, anyone who even smells of having a sense of purpose. It's because he's Catholic."

"*Former* Catholic," Jerry said, smacking the table but smiling nonetheless. "Ex, as in *excommunicado.*"

"Same thing," David said. He winked at Axel. "So now he thinks that being an *ex*-Catholic is the only true religion, and he goes around trying to demoralize guys like you and me. He's still a missionary at heart."

Axel kept his head bowed. He was not used to hearing people talk like this outside of Donlevy's classroom.

"You make one good point, Davido," Jerry began in a chastened-sounding voice, but as Axel lifted his eyes he saw that Jerry was beaming. "I do admit to favoring the missionary position."

David rolled his eyes and groaned, but he could not resist laughing, and Jerry cackled and soon Axel was laughing too, rolling with it, leaning back his head and letting the sound come straight up out of him. He could not remember laughter feeling so good.

"Enough about me, gentlemen," Jerry said at last. "I brought you two together to discuss politics. Axel, here, holds the pivotal Ohio vote."

David's eyes lit up. He was a government major, prelaw, a member of the Young Democrats. He started right off by telling Axel that he really wished that Stevenson had gotten the nomination—he was pretty sure he could have won this time—but that, given the alternative, Kennedy looked damned good. He quoted to him from Kennedy's voting record in Congress—still baseball statistics to Axel's ears, but David's enthusiasm did sound sincere to him. Axel finally held up his hand, smiling.

"Okay, I'm convinced," he said. "I can guarantee you Kennedy will carry Ohio."

"Great, but wait a minute," David said. "I want to be sure you're voting for him for the right reasons."

Jerry hooted. "Jesus, Debilio, you are incorrigible. No wonder you liberals are doomed."

They all laughed again and then the talk turned to David's girlfriend, a Radcliffe freshman with a surprisingly aristocratic-sounding name, then to the cartoon in that day's *Crimson,* drawn by a friend of theirs named Greg Gregorian, then to Axel's thesis, music, hamburgers, back to politics again—rambling, disjointed talk, totally inefficient and totally enjoyable.

From that day on, Axel rarely took his lunch or supper in Kirkland House. If his roommates noticed his absence, they did not mention it. He ate with Jerry and often with David, and sometimes others of their friends, including two philosophy majors from Adams House, Todd Brewster, a huge, comical-looking boy whom they all teased about being elected to Phi Beta Kappa, and Greg Gregorian, the *Crimson* cartoonist. Something else changed for Axel too: One Saturday evening he came home from an orchestral concert and decided to postpone writing his weekly letter home until the next day, but that day went by too, and then another week, and finally his mother called from Akron. Axel apologized, telling her that his thesis took all his time these days and then, without having planned it, he said that he would have to forgo his Christmas vacation home so he could remain in Cambridge and finish his schoolwork. Mrs. Stenhorn remained silent for several seconds—one moment longer and Axel certainly would have relented—before she said, "Oh, Axel, we'd all so hoped that you'd learn how to have a little more balance in your life once you were on your own."

"I know," Axel said softly, feeling a rare flush of love for his mother. "I'm trying."

On the day that Kennedy was inaugurated, Axel joined Jerry, David, Greg and Todd in the Dunster House common room, where a small T.V. set had been placed on a table beneath a grand, gilt-framed portrait of Henry Dunster, Harvard College's first president. The outsized oil of old Henry made the television screen look even punier than it was—"just to keep things in their proper perspective," Greg quipped as the proceedings began. That was the theme of the day: The inaugural was a Harvard event that just happened to be taking place in Washington, D.C., like an "away" football game. There was Master Finley, from Eliot House, on the screen; and here was Robert Frost, who often came down for high table at Adams House; and wasn't that Professor Schlesinger over there and Professor Galbraith just behind him? It was a family affair, and Axel Stenhorn, wedged between his friends on the folding wooden chairs, was part of that family.

"Poor Jack," Jerry said. "Do you realize he's only going to be fifty-one when he finishes his second term? How's he going to top that? Poor bastard will have nowhere to go."

"He can always become president of Harvard," Axel said, and the whole bunch of them roared.

In March Axel was accepted at all four of the medical schools to which he had applied; he chose P & S in New York. In April he submitted his thesis in physical chemistry. And at the beginning of May, without mentioning it to anyone, he wrote a letter to the newly formed Peace Corps in Washington, D.C., requesting information and an application. When Jerry Halligan asked him to participate in his experiment the day after graduation, Axel agreed immediately, although he knew very little about Dr. Leary and nothing at all about psychotropic drugs. And on the morning after that night in Newton when Jerry passed his followup questionnaires around the breakfast table, Axel had no trouble answering the first question: His immediate plans were to join the Peace Corps. At some point during that bizarre night with his new friends he had decided to do what was not expected of him for the first time in his life.

Jack Kennedy's promise to shake everyone's hand was all they talked about on the Greyhound buses that ferried them from the Rutgers training camp to Washington. They were the honored guests, the President's first special envoys come for punch and watercress sandwiches in the Rose Garden on the day before their mission began.

Their caravan was waved through the iron gates of the White House like ambassadors' limousines. They strolled across the lawn in twos and threes, talking in hushed tones, looking like extras in a drama of palace intrigue. The suppressed excitement could have shattered glass. The President and his wife, Jacqueline, were frighteningly beautiful and yet so familiar-looking that some of the young women could not contain their tears. And Axel was barely conscious of any of it. Yesterday he had been assigned his village in the north of Tanganyika and he had been assigned his coworker, the most extraordinary-looking girl in the Corps—by God, the most extraordinary-looking girl he had seen in his life. No matter how hard he tried to concentrate—after all, he had promised to report to Jerry about meeting his "personal President"—Axel could think of nothing but this girl.

He searched for glimpses of her as she wandered gaily around the grounds in her Greek peasant blouse and flared skirt. Even when the presidential aide caught him by the elbow and guided him to the reception line, Axel went on looking for her. And when, at last, he was face-to-face with the handsome young President, their hands clasped manfully in front of the official photographer, she caught his eye. She was standing just ten feet away from them, twisting a flower from a rosebush, now pinning it in her raven-black hair. The President followed Axel's eyes and smiled just as the camera clicked.

The photo appeared the next day on the front page of the Akron *Beacon Journal* ("Harvard Man Meets Harvard Man"), and a month later one of the copies his mother had sent was hanging from the mud wall of Axel's hut in Udo, Tanganyika. The other copy was doubling back around the world to Cambridge, Massachusetts.

2

"AXEL. Axel Stenhorn." Jerry Halligan waved the envelope under the nose of the pretty young woman with red braids who sat cross-legged on the rug. "You know, he was in the first group, the original vestal virgins. Sweetest fellow in the world, old Axe, but devoutly self-controlled. 'Repressed as a bellhop in a whorehouse,' as me Uncle Seamus would say. But, Jesus, could that boy hallucinate! Hallucinated us all right under the table that night. A regular shaman." He grinned down at the girl. "The surprises that lurk within, eh, Gabby?"

"Can I have the stamp?" the girl replied.

Jerry wandered over to the window seat without answering. The stamp *was* lovely, a brightly colored depiction of two natives in loincloths holding farm tools—a shimmering African Gothic. The rest of the envelope was a maze of postmarks, stamped red arrows, and ballpoint squiggles that charted its travels from Dar es Salaam to Cambridge (one month), and then back and forth across the Harvard campus (three months) until it finally found its way to the Harvard Center for Research in Personality, where someone had pocketed it and brought it back that afternoon to the house in Newton. Jerry opened it.

Dear Jerry,

I bring you greetings from your President.

I am the happiest man in Africa. Details to follow.

How's Cambridge? And what's happening with your research?

Please write.

Ever,
Axel

Jerry gazed out the window onto the street, trying to picture Axel writing the letter. Under a banyan tree—or were those in India? In a tree hut? On an elephant's back? He clicked each possibility past his mind's eye, vivid as Kodachromes, and then he laughed out loud. There really was no need for him ever to travel anywhere himself; he could see it all by a mere twist of his psychic kaleidoscope, just one of the totally new senses he'd acquired this past year through the grace of psychotropic drugs. *But research, Axel?*

In fact, the first seven times he had taken the magic mushroom Jerry painstakingly recorded his insights and "levels of awareness" in a loose-leaf notebook. He'd looked for recurring patterns, drawn up charts, put it all down with a ballpoint pen that was attached to the notebook by a length of string so that he could always find it in mid experiment. But therein lay the utter absurdity of the whole idea. It was all so excruciatingly self-conscious. It was as if he were a helium balloon attached to that piece of string; his mind could only float so high and then it would be snapped back to the mundane business of psychological data. Good Christ, you needed a totally new language to describe each session, and he was keeping notes? At the beginning of his eighth session, Jerry walked over to the fireplace and ceremoniously dropped the notebook on a burning log.

"I am making an offering," he intoned to the others, deadpan. "To the god of psychological data, praisèd be he. May the fumes of my humble sacrifice fog his mind as he has fogged mine."

"Hallelujah!" Gabby bowed her head to the floor like a Muslim.

From then on, if anyone on campus asked Jerry about his research, he would reply with perfect sincerity that the experience *was* the data. "And *I* am the cumulative record of all that data."

Now Jerry noticed that there was something else in Axel's envelope. "Diggitty, diggitty!" It was the clipping from the Akron paper. "Me old pals, Axel and Jack, together at last."

Gabby glided over and leaned against Jerry's back, peering over his shoulder. "How come they aren't looking at each other?"

Jerry squinted. By God, she was right. Axel and President Kennedy were shaking hands, but both their eyes were looking off mysteriously in the direction of a blur of dots next to a piece of shrubbery.

"They must be hallucinating," Jerry said, grinning.

From downstairs someone called, "Magic time!"

Moments later, as they joined the circle in the living room, Jerry noticed something colorful plastered in the center of Gabby's forehead. It was the Tanganyikan postage stamp.

Okay, Saint Paul time. Time to play the all-things-to-all-people game. That had been Tim's word on the way into Harvard. No one had come to Cambridge for a week. Hell, no one had come down to earth for a week. There'd been no reason to, not until the phone started ringing every few hours with the latest Harvard bullshit paranoia: Public Health was snooping, Dana Farnsworth was issuing mental health warnings. Gabby wanted to pull the phone out of the wall—"It's the devil calling," she'd said—but Dick said to cool it. "We can't cut ourselves off from people just because they're ignorant," he said. Not the loving thing to do. Can't teach anyone anything that way. So the game was this: Clean up and look like regular Harvard squares. Winner gets the last glass of Tang. Sheer madness. The Marx Brothers dressing for the cotillion. Clothes flying. Gabby fills buckets with soapy water, says in teeny-tiny voice for all good little children to line up so nurse can get them squeaky clean. Soap bars slipping and sliding over backs, buttocks, balls. Gabby wants her insides cleaned, an orgy of cleanliness. And when they'd finally piled into the station wagon, only Tim and Dick looked vaguely "major university." The rest looked like a ragtag mime troup lost in a road picture: tennis shoes and navy cords, pirate sashes and Gabby's feathers. Tim was pissed. Sitting behind the wheel in his three-piece fantasy, he'd delivered his lecture on people's natural terror of internal freedom, especially at a place predicated on the value of control games and power plays. You don't lead these people out of the cave in a clown outfit. You've got to spread the word in a language they can understand. That's when he'd brought up Saint Paul, looked over his shoulder right at Jerry and winked when he'd said it. Irish Catholic to Irish Catholic, the club within the club.

Breezing into the Yard under the archway inscribed "Enter to Grow in Wisdom," Jerry turned to Gabby, skittering over bricks, feathers flying. "Enter to shrink in consciousness," he said, and they both fell down laughing. There's a metaphor everywhere for those who can see. The sign in front of the MTA says, "En-*trance*" not "Entrance." Deep inside the sign painter knew what he was doing; he's got a magic madman yearning to get out just like everyone else. Too bad he has no idea how easy it is.

The bell in Memorial Church clanged and Jerry stood and pulled Gabby to her sandaled feet. An hour ago she came three times on the end of a bar of Ivory, and now she looked like somebody's little sister playing Indian after school. Presto-chango. Everyone's got a whole cast of characters jabbering away inside his brain, upleveling each other, each one claiming to be the true identity. In front of Widener Library, standard-issue Harvard types sauntered, ties fluttering over shoulders, green canvas book bags swinging ever so casually from one hand like a bag of potatoes, conveying the fine edge of Cambridge snobbery—"Heck, just Kant and Virgil in here, nothing serious." Seeing Jerry and Gabby, they turned their heads and gawked. Baby Face Nelson and his moll. Jesus and Mary. Jerry smiled back.

"Mingling envy and despair," he said, and Gabby nodded.

Everyone knew, of course, that they were Leary people—and it wasn't the feathers that gave them away, either. They could be stitched in tweeds and people would still twitter and stare. By their eyes they shall be known. Eyes that have viewed the cosmic circus never quite look the same again. And they look altogether different from eyes that have been blinking over required reading in the stacks of Widener.

Jerry took Gabby's hand as they bounced up the front steps of Sever Hall, swung up to lecture room A. Her palm was cold, damp.

"Let's go to a movie," she said. She looked frightened.

"Write your own and show it in your head," Jerry said. He led her to a seat in the rear of the lecture hall. "This'll all be over in an hour."

"Too long," Gabby said, eyeing the other graduate students who sat on every side of them.

"We're doing it for them," Jerry whispered, gesturing at the students. "Mom and Dad do so live for our visits, don't ya know?"

Gabby smiled back. She pulled notebooks from her sling bag, handed one to Jerry along with a ballpoint.

"Props," she said.

Jerry opened his notebook. "Theories of Personality" was lettered neatly at the top of the first page, under it "Prof. Bartlet, Tues. & Thurs. 2 P.M." The course was required for first-year graduate students, and on some afternoon in October Jerry had scrawled the lecture note "Personality is defined by the particular empirical concepts which are a part of the theory of personality employed by the observer." What consummate bullshit. It was the only note he had taken in five months. He'd taken an "incomplete" in his fall term, pleading that his graduate research project took up more of his time than he had expected it would. The absolute truth, that. His graduate research project took up all his time, waking and sleeping.

Below, Professor Bartlet lumbered to the lectern, placed his notes in front of him, then surveyed the classroom over the top of his glasses and managed a tight smile.

"Good afternoon," he said. His eyes seemed to linger a moment on Jerry and Gabby, but he immediately looked down at his notes. "Today I'd like to further explore Lewin's concept of the dynamic restructuring of the psychological environment."

Jerry scratched this sentence in his pad. He had to admire Bartlet. Surely the old bird knew that it was all over, this "dynamic restructuring" crap. It had all gone out the window with that first mushroom cap—Freud, Fromm, Lewin, Rogers, all about as relevant now as medieval medicine was after the invention of the microscope. But old Bartlet puffed away, not missing a beat. He had to. He had too much to lose—all this nice dark wood and hightable teas and Faculty Club dinners. He didn't realize he had everything to gain.

"Lewin's notions of personality vectors and valences are, quite simply, figurative ways of conceptualizing the alternating fluidity and rigidity of personality in relation to—"

Jerry stroked his jaw—not an inch of exaggeration in the gesture —but, oh shit, it was just enough to get Gabby going, only a little titter at first, but when the others started to turn their heads with their goodness-gracious stares, she let loose with that deep-throated raucous laugh of hers that was so popular out in Newton.

Professor Bartlet paused only a second, not lifting his eyes, then went on, pitching his voice an octave lower. Brave soul. Jerry did not dare turn his head to Gabby, but he reached out his hand and clasped hers tightly.

"Easy," he whispered.

She jerked her hand away.

"Come on, Jerry," she said out loud. "The emperor is naked. What are we hanging around for?"

That did it. Dead silence as Bartlet stepped out from behind the lectern, pulling off his glasses, deliberately folding them and slipping them in his vest pocket. There was enough earnest blushing going on all around to raise the room temperature.

"Miss Feldman," Bartlet said, staring directly at Gabby. "Did you have some sort of revelation you wanted to share with us?"

Jerry waited just a second, then turned his head. Gabby sat rigidly in her chair, her thin shoulders trembling, her front teeth dug deeply into her lower lip. Jerry stood, grasped Gabby's arm and yanked her to her feet.

"Okay, let's go," he murmured to her.

The students beside them jumped to their feet to let them by.

"Are you leaving too, Mr. Halligan?" Bartlet called. The old fool was really enjoying himself now. "Must you hurry back to your research project?"

A good har-har all around for this. Jerry felt his heart fluttering in his chest, his head swimming. He drew in a long breath, then turned to face Bartlet and threw back his fine-boned head, a marvelous-feeling grin spreading across his face.

"Sir," Jerry said softly, "I would like to share my theory of personality with you."

Jerry could feel every eye in the room on him as he slowly spread his arms, turning up his palms. And then he let out the loudest, most joyful, pure vibrating operatic hoot Sever Hall had ever heard and, trailing Gabby behind him by the hand, made his exit.

They circled the Yard for an hour, rerunning the scene in Bartlet's class a dozen times, Gabby more delighted each time through, saying she had never felt so free in her life, that she had finally cut the academic-oedipal-bullshit-approval noose from around her neck. Tim is right, she kept saying, school is house arrest, students are mental patients. The only lesson worth teaching is how to achieve ecstasy.

Then she got it into her head that she wanted to suck Jerry's cock on the steps of Widener, make an object lesson of it, give all the button-down kiddies a glimpse into the future of academia. "In three years they'll be giving courses in cocksucking here," she giggled, pulling at Jerry's fly. "Interpersonal Enravishment 103, Orgasm 10." But by then Jerry was not with her anymore, tired of

Cambridge and the story and not so sure that Tim would find it all quite so amusing as she did. This was, after all, supposed to be Saint Paul's Day. He told her he had errands to do, that he would meet her back at the center before they all went home.

Walking off, he realized that he had not really been away from any of them in the past six months, no longer than to take a leak, and even then there was usually someone searching for his reflection in the bathroom mirror. Looking up, he saw that he had crossed the MTA tracks and was loping past Cronin's only half a block away from David's apartment. Suddenly the idea of seeing David and Pat seemed like an absolutely perfect idea, a fulfillment of the whole day. He'd tell them about Axel's letter. Yes, they'd want to hear about that. He ran all the way to their apartment door and buzzed, then knocked, then called their names, growing more and more incredulous that they could possibly be out at a time when he wanted so much to see them. Jesus, it was just like Debilio: He was never there when you really needed him.

3

WHEN they were roommates, Jerry used to chide David about what he called his "unreachable center."

"But there is no center," David would reply, looking over the top of his ever-present newspaper. "I'm all surface, Jer. Dull surface. I'm afraid you got the short end of this deal."

It was an answer calculated to madden Jerry, who was obsessed with uncovering everybody's "inner man." But the truth was David knew very well that he been hiding behind a mask of affability ever since he was a young boy. Back then it had seemed the best way to deal with the fact that he was vastly more intelligent than any member of his family.

Sitting around the oilcloth-covered table of the Debilio kitchen, David had taught himself to smile attentively while his father fumbled through a joke he'd heard at the store or his mother contradicted herself two and three times in a single breath. David buried all evidence of his superior intellect as if it were a stolen gun; it was his first lesson in the complexities of inequality.

But throughout David had sustained himself with a single thought: He was going to get out. He had studied alone in that kitchen until two in the morning, invigorated by the idea of leaving Hoboken forever, and he had been rewarded with an acceptance at Harvard on a string of scholarships ranging from the local Rotary's "good citizen" award to a prestigious Harvard Club Scholarship. Then, one month before he was to depart for Cambridge, it had all fallen apart: Lifting a drum of paint onto a hand truck, his father had suffered a massive stroke which left him paralyzed. There was no question: David stayed. For two more years he lived at home and ran the family's paint supply store, waiting for his brother, Dom, to return from the Army and relieve him. They were two years which deepened David in ways Harvard never could have. By the time he finally entered college at twenty, his remoteness was no longer just a shield, it was a perspective.

Being assigned Jerry Halligan as a roommate at first struck David as diabolical, later as inspired. Jerry's manic enthusiasms, his shimmering con-man energy, his total disinterest in the state of the world made him a perfect complement to David, his ballast. They teased one another relentlessly, took potshots at each other's excesses, gaped in wonder at each other's talents. For David Jerry was the bright, challenging sibling he had never had in Dominique, and by the time they moved to Dunster House he loved Jerry with all the nervous ambivalence of a brother.

It was Jerry who discovered Patricia Beardsley—he always spoke of "discovering" people as if their true beauty or brilliance would have languished in obscurity without him. He brought her to their room one Saturday afternoon in their senior year and introduced her to David as "a thinking man's Grace Kelly."

David stood behind his desk, annoyed that Jerry, as usual, had failed to warn him that he was bringing a guest to their room.

"You'll have to forgive Jerry," David said to the girl. "He's going through this stage of giving everyone brand names. He's trying to get into advertising, you know."

The girl laughed, her light blue eyes looking directly into David's. He wished he did not have to leave, but it was protocol to vanish when your roommate showed up with a young woman, announced or not. He began to gather up his books and newspapers.

"He called you the Hoboken Diamond," she said, still smiling at David.

David shot a glare at Jerry but then looked back at the girl and laughed. "Well, at least he's improving. Last week I was the Rhodes Tattoo."

She laughed again and her cheeks colored. She was a delicate, fresh-faced girl and very lovely. David had not moved.

"Jesus, I hope you two are having a wonderful time," Jerry said at last, leaning against the mantel.

David slipped his books under his arm and started for the door. He was aware that the girl had turned and was looking after him.

"Hell, I've got a better idea," Jerry said cheerfully. "Why don't we all have a drink and go out for some Chinese food. I've discovered this authentic little chop suey joint in Central Square."

It was the best of Jerry. He could take as much pleasure in watching two other people fall in love as in falling in love himself. That night, after an uproarious dinner, he broke open his fortune cookie and, pretending to read it, said, "You will take a long trip across water, skipping out on your share of the bill." With that he stood, bowed to them each in best oriental fashion and backed out the door. His instincts were right, of course: At that moment David and Patricia were well on their way to falling in love.

She was as different from David as Jerry was: wealthy and well-bred, brought up in a family of liberal intellectuals who delighted in each other's company. Yet there was none of the brittleness about her that David associated with upper-class Radcliffe girls. She was soft and very eager to learn more about life than she knew she possibly could at places like Putney, where she'd gone to prep school, or at Harvard.

"College is just a way of prolonging adolescence," she said. "As soon as I'm out I'm taking off for Europe with a one-way ticket and five hundred dollars. Duncan"—she referred to her father by his Christian name—"says your education begins when you put your books away."

"My father must be a genius then." David laughed, but already he felt a twinge of pain at the thought of her leaving alone for Europe.

Their hands touched the moment Jerry left, first tentatively above the table, then hotly beneath it, and on their way back to Harvard Square they clung to each other in the swaying subway car like stowaways, too delirious to talk. The following day, after making arrangements with Jerry, David brought Patricia Beardsley back to the room and there, on his narrow metal bed, they made tender, rapturous love.

David was twenty-three then and Pat just eighteen. It was the first time for her and, as David told her afterward, it was as if it were the first time for him. But it wasn't. Unlike most of his classmates, David had arrived at college with a long history of sexual encounters: He'd started at thirteen with a dim-witted neighborhood girl out on an abandoned Hoboken pier; in high school there had been a series of heavy-breasted Italian girls who had spread their legs for him, their fleshy faces turned to one side, half-denying what was happening; and during those interminable two years when he ran the family store he had slept almost every evening with the sad-eyed widow who lived upstairs. But, my God, this was totally different from all that—he was in love.

"Still, I'm glad it wasn't really and truly the first time for you," Patricia said, rubbing her hand across his chest. "I'm sure if you'd been as ignorant as I am we'd have done it all wrong."

David laughed and kissed her hair. She propped herself up on her elbows, supporting her head in both hands.

"I'm serious," she said, grinning down at him. "Do you really think you'd have done it right the first time if no one had shown you how? I mean, it's so out-of-the-way, don't you think? Wouldn't you have tried to put it somewhere else first—say, my belly button."

"No, no, nothing so obvious as that. Maybe your ear or a nostril."

They were both giggling now, their bodies jiggling together on the narrow mattress.

"Oh God, this is all I want to do for the rest of my life, David. Just this!"

By the end of the month they were already planning their summer together, and by spring they decided to marry as soon as David graduated. There seemed no sense in living separately while David went to law school and Pat finished Radcliffe; it would be hard enough to find time for each other. Pat never again spoke of her one-way ticket to Europe, and when she discovered she was pregnant that first winter of their marriage, she decided she would take a leave of absence from college until the baby was old enough for nursery school. It had all happened faster than David had ever expected it would, but he never once wished it otherwise. He felt like he had finally come home.

On that spring afternoon when Jerry hooted in Professor Bartlet's class and later found himself pounding frantically on David and Pat's apartment door, the newly married couple was lying in bed in the Beardsley country home in Vermont, away from Cambridge for their first weekend since Dave had completed—and won—the first round of the law school moot-court competition. They had just made love and now Pat slept curled up like a child, her belly barely showing the child that was growing inside her.

David dressed and came downstairs in his bare feet. There was no one in the living room and on impulse he tiptoed across the braided rug to the sun-room and gazed out at the terrace. Duncan and Margot sat on a wrought iron bench, daiquiris in hand, chatting with Lincoln Ames, a popular civil liberties attorney who also had a summer home in Wolfeboro. In Hoboken David could have never imagined a group of people like the Beardsleys' Wolfeboro friends; he'd always pictured moneyed Yankees as stiff and shallow, preoccupied with their good names and little else. But Ames, like the Beardsleys and most of their guests, was dedicated to culture and liberal causes. Suddenly uncomfortable about spying through the window, David turned and walked quickly out to the terrace. "Pat's still resting," he said.

"Hello, David." Lincoln Ames shook David's hand. A tall man with close-cropped hair and a lean, handsome face, he looked a good ten years younger than his sixty. "I hear you did well in the moot court."

"So far."

"I want to hear every detail," Ames said.

"Really, sir, I don't think there'd be much new in it for you."

"I insist." Ames smiled and gestured toward the lawn.

As they set off at a slow walk, David found he was eager to talk about the case with the older man. Duncan and Margot certainly would never ask him about it—there was a country house rule against discussing work. David quickly outlined the case: Like the Woolworth and Kresge cases, this one challenged the right of the owner of an Atlanta diner to bar Negroes from his establishment. Public right versus individual right. David had drawn the defense of the diner owner.

"Good," Ames said when he heard this.

"But I hated pretending to embrace a position I loathe as much as that one," David said.

"Never mind. The only way to beat the devil is to learn to think like him." Ames smiled. "Anyway, you mustn't have found it totally loathsome. You did win, didn't you?"

"My opponent lost," David said, smiling back. "I confounded him with my surprise precedent, *O'Hara* v. *Tucker's Family Restaurant.* It seems that on a spring day in 1898, a Mr. O'Hara strolled into a restaurant after spending a week in the woods hunting quail and apparently the poor fellow had been squirted by a skunk. The restaurant owner wouldn't seat him, said it wasn't fair to ruin twenty people's meals just to serve one man his. And the State of New Hampshire agreed. I argued that the same principle applied here: A white man brought up in the South would have his appetite ruined by having to eat next to a Negro. It was a perfectly absurd analogy, of course, but it caught my opponent flat-footed. He'd never heard of *O'Hara* v. *Tucker.*"

"Wonderful," Ames said, laughing. The two made a slow arc back toward the terrace. "There's a fever of liberty overtaking this country," Ames said, suddenly serious. "By the time you get out of school, you'll be defending freedoms we can barely imagine now. Your friend, Dr. Leary, says that the control of consciousness will be the major civil liberties issue of the decade. Who knows? He may be right."

"He's wrong," David said. He wished Pat had not told so many people about the night in Newton. "I'm sure the question of where a Negro can eat dinner will always be more important than what drug a college kid can experiment with."

"Perhaps."

There was a cheer on the terrace and both men looked up. Patricia had just stepped out of the house. She wore one of David's shirts, the tails tied calypso-style just above her waist, exposing an inch of milk-white skin. Around her neck was a pale blue ribbon and her hair was piled on top of her head in an elegant knot. David had never seen her look more beautiful.

"Are you cheering for me or Thérèse?" Pat laughed, spinning

around and curtsying to the colored woman who followed behind her in a white serving uniform, a tray of hors d'oeuvres in her outstretched arms.

"We applaud you both," Duncan said, raising his glass.

Everyone laughed and David turned his head, aware that Lincoln Ames was looking at him. The older man was laughing too, but his blue-gray eyes remained serious.

"It's all terribly confusing, don't you think?" he said.

4

"LET'S pretend that Shaku, here, has just taken a bite of a banana." Axel quickly sketched a cartoonlike figure on the blackboard, then turned back to his students, who sat cross-legged on the dusty ground in front of him. "Now what's the first thing that must happen to that banana on its trip to Shaku's stomach?"

"That's easy, Mwalimu," young Ludi called out. "He must take it out of his mouth and peel it!"

They all howled, Axel included. For every piece of information imparted in his outdoor classroom, Axel expected at least two or three good jokes. That was the way of Udo communication—jokes and pranks and rambling, gossipy stories that seemed to ease the sun along its equatorial arc. Axel could barely remember any other way of talking.

"What next?"

"Chew it—if Shaku has any teeth left!"

Another eruption of laughter and a cloud of black flies rose from their faces, then settled back in the corners of their eyes and around their mouths. Axel did not bother to brush his away. Even his reflexes had become African.

It was just over a year since the Peace Corps coordinator had deposited Axel and Despina in this hill village south of Kilimanjaro, but it might just as well have been two years or five. Axel had absorbed the elongated rhythms of village life with the same ease that he had acquired their Chagga dialect. For someone who had felt out of step most of his life, it was a marvelous change.

"You probably have some African genes stashed away somewhere," Despina would tease him.

"I certainly hope so."

The two of them often fell into the ironic banter of villagers when they were alone. They spoke a hybrid of English and Swahili peppered with playful Chagga expressions—it was as if it were a language invented just so Axel could overcome his inveterate shyness of women. He was madly in love with Despina.

She did not know this, of course. At least he hoped to God she didn't. Not now. Now he had the glorious pleasure of her company every day—long evening walks in the hills behind the village, porridge dinners by the fire, late nights at her table, composing letters and Corps reports by the light of a kerosene lamp. He would be a fool to risk any of this for some impetuous declaration of love.

Axel had never before so much as imagined a girl like Despina Delahanty. She was a concoction of Greek and Irish genes, her mother born in Thessalonika, her father somewhere in Cork, giving her hair black as any African's and olive skin that glowed in the relentless sun, while her mineral blue eyes remained clear and cool as pebbles in a Kilkenny brook. She was raised in New York in a place called—appropriately, Axel thought—Queens. There she had put herself through college working in her uncle's bakery rolling phylo dough by the mile.

"Your life sounds infinitely *realer* than mine," Axel once told her..

"Oh God, only a Harvard man would say something like that," she'd laughed. "The rest of the world thinks of working in a bakery as just one more lousy way to make a living."

She had opinions on subjects that Axel had never even considered: progressive jazz and Reichian analysis and even, God help her, premarital sex and marriage. It was her thoughts on the latter subject that got Despina off to a precarious start in Udo. The first question a villager asked any stranger was, "How many children do you have?"

"None," Despina had told Chief Nagomway's wife. "Actually, I'll probably never have any. There's so many other things I want to do instead."

To an Udo woman, even one as worldly as Nagomway's wife,
who had once been to Dar, Despina's answer was as bizarre as
saying that she was thinking of drowning herself in Lake Victoria.
The story spread through the village immediately; by nightfall the
young Peace Corps volunteer who had come to Udo with plans of
starting its first nursery school was known as the woman who
hated children. Despina had no idea why the villagers were so cool
to her and she tried everything to win them over: She traded all
her blouses and skirts for brightly dyed *kangas;* she unpacked her
sewing machine and demonstrated its miracles on a table in front
of Axel's clinic. But in the end it was Axel's mastery of the Chagga
dialect—and Udo gossip—that uncovered the root of her problem.
Axel broke the news to her over their evening porridge.

"All you have to do is say you made a mistake," Axel explained.
"Tell them you're planning on having at least ten kids as soon as
you can find a husband."

"Jesus, I don't want to lie to them."

"Okay, tell them five kids."

That was only the first of many times that Axel saved the day for
Despina. Much as she yearned to become the perfect Udo woman
—she replaced her Greek cross with Chagga trading beads and
went barefoot everywhere—Despina never could completely
slow her own rhythms to match theirs, and the art of roundabout
communication always eluded her. Yet she was forever bursting
with ideas for village projects: nutrition classes and weekly scabies
inspections; even an elaborate scheme for a sewage system. The
selling of her ideas to the villagers was left to Axel.

"We make a perfect team," she often said.

"Indeed we do." It was all Axel dared to ask—to be her perfect
teammate. In time he might be more. And there was an endless
amount of time in Udo.

Axel's students had finally traced the banana morsel to Shaku's
lower intestine when they heard a scream from the other side of
the village. A second later two children came running, shouting
for Mwalimu Axel.

"Mufba is bleeding!" they panted. "The car is on top of him!"

Axel dropped his chalk, hastily removed his glasses and set off at
a run, his students loping behind him. He cut through the banana
grove, drawing in the thick odor of fermenting fruit, then criss-

crossed behind a row of huts and picked up the path at the tobacco shed. Half the village stood in a circle around the Peace Corps Land-Rover. Mufba, the self-appointed village mechanic, lay pinned on his back under the length of the car. The front tires were off and the axle lay just a fraction of an inch above his Adam's apple, trapping him. There was a gash on his left forearm and Despina was pressing a wadded T-shirt against it to stem the flow of blood.

"The jack slipped," she said, seeing Axel arrive. "I told them not to move him until you checked for broken bones."

Axel dropped to his knees just in back of Mufba's head. The young man was conscious and his frightened eyes widened when he saw Axel's face above him.

"I think you're driving this upside down," Axel said, touching his forehead, and Mufba managed a little smile.

Axel felt along the back of his neck with both hands, then crawled around and slithered under the side of the car as far as he could and continued feeling along Mufba's spine. He traced his collarbone, shoulders and arms. There were no fractures, no dislocations. Axel pulled himself out and onto his feet.

"He's okay," Axel said. "Let's get him out of there." He saw the jack lying in the red dust and started to reach for it.

"Let's not tempt the spirits a second time," a voice behind him said in clipped English.

Axel turned. It was Ngoso, the chief's eldest grandson. He had only been back in the village a week after spending years away at the mission school in Dar es Salaam. This was the first time he had spoken to Axel.

"What do you suggest?" Axel said.

"We can lift the car if you think you could pull Mufba out." Ngoso took a step toward Axel. He was a massive man, easily six feet five. His thighs bulged in his British walking shorts and the long muscles of his chest and abdomen were visible through the opening of his unbuttoned khaki shirt. Axel had little doubt that he could lift the car single-handedly.

"Let's do it," Axel said. He quickly fashioned a pressure bandage so that Despina could release Mufba's forearm, then he removed his own shirt and slipped it under Mufba's head, looping the arms under his shoulders as a sling. Ngoso had positioned two other young men on the right side of the front bumper and he stood on the left, wrapping his hands with banana fronds. He hunkered down like a sumo wrestler, braced his hands under the bumper, nodded to the others and lifted. The car rose on its rear wheels, Axel tugged and Mufba slid free. Around them all the villagers began jabbering at once; by dinnertime the episode would surely be an hour-long herculean tale.

Ngoso carried Mufba in his arms like a child to the clinic and set him down on the army cot Axel had appropriated from St. Elizabeth Hospital. The gash on Mufba's arm was not as bad as Axel had expected. He cleaned it with alcohol while Despina fanned away flies, then drew the skin tight with a butterfly bandage. Mufba's wife appeared at the clinic door with maize beer and porridge for her husband. She thanked all three of them. She said she would be happy to wash their clothing. Axel looked at Despina and Ngoso: They were streaked with blood and grease and caked with dirt.

"I think we need more than just our clothing washed," he said.

Ngoso smiled. "Come," he said. "I'll show you where I bathed when I was a boy."

The three of them set off at once for the hill behind Udo, picking up the path along the stream that fed the sisal fields. Halfway up the hill the stream cut away from the path into a dense thicket of bamboo. Ngoso stepped down into the stream bed, reaching one hand out behind him. Despina took it, then reached back for Axel's hand. It might have been at that moment that their glorious alliance began, what Despina would later call the "woolly trinity." They had merely joined hands, but Axel sensed that they were joining together on a great adventure. About a hundred feet into the thicket, the stream suddenly opened onto a clear, sun-dappled pond. Ngoso dropped Despina's hand, threw off his shirt, and fell into the water, grinning. Axel jumped in after him. The water was cool and tingling, an effervescent spring. Axel submerged his head, then bounced up like a dolphin. He saw Ngoso staring behind him and he turned. Standing at the lip of the pond, Despina was unwinding the last turn of her orange *kanga*. She stood there one second longer, her plump, olive-skinned body glistening in a shaft of late afternoon sunlight. Then she jumped in.

5

Dear Todd,

I've been trying for a week to get down to writing this letter. The rainy season has started and I spend most of my time inside listening to the rain drill on that thatch of grass over my head which they insist on calling a roof here. The drops come down sharp as pebbles. The first day they turned the dust to mud in a matter of minutes.

Axel lifted his pen and stared out the open window. Seen through the rain, everything was distorted. It was like living inside a prism.

To tell you the truth, Todd, I didn't know who I was going to write this letter to until today. I've had the most remarkable experience and I need some help understanding it. I thought maybe you would be the one who could help me.

Axel turned up the collar of his shirt and leaned back in his hammock. There was another reason why he had put off writing this letter: It made him feel vaguely disloyal to Despina and Ngoso. This whole confusion had started with them.

One evening after their swim, the three friends had hiked up to a slate outcropping that overlooked the village. Viewed from above, Udo had a striking symmetry: Perfect parallel curving lines of thatched roofs surrounded the oval green. It might have been laid out by a Renaissance architect.

"The first time I saw the village from up here," Axel had said, "I asked your grandfather who decided where each hut was built. And he looked at me like I was a total idiot and said, 'But the huts were always here, Mwalimu!' "

"Ah yes, Nagomway's famous mumbo jumbo." Ngoso laughed. "He doesn't believe that stuff, you know, Axel. He just likes to play the native fool. Years ago he found out he could charm missionaries with remarks like that." Ngoso gazed down at the village, suddenly serious. "The best lesson one learns from the missionaries is how to be deceitful. They march in bartering for our immortal souls—a contract to buy our sisal if they can hold a holy mass in the fields first; a schoolhouse if they can build a chapel beside it. And the clever chiefs, like my grandfather, quickly learn the tricks of negotiation. The very first time they came here, Nagomway realized he had the most to gain if Udo never completely became a Catholic village. Ever since I can remember, it has been on the very brink of conversion."

Despina smiled. She sat with her legs crossed under her, her clear blue eyes fastened on Ngoso's. "I'd say Udo's lucky to have such a shrewd chief," she said.

Ngoso shrugged. He rocked onto his feet, scooping up a handful of slate chips, then skimming them over the tops of the bamboo below.

"I was one of Grandfather's deals," he said at last. "A perfect deal it seemed at the time. The mission was only too happy to get me for themselves for a few years. Once they converted me, Nagomway's grandson, they were sure they could finally claim Udo. The advantage for Grandfather was that it got me out of the village. Oh, he cares for me in his way, but he's always known what I think of his games. He thought I'd never return from Dar—not for more than a visit. He thought I'd find myself a nice civil service job and marry a city girl. As it turned out, I came back sooner than any of them expected." He flung a last stone down toward the village.

Neither Axel nor Despina had moved. It was the first time their new friend had spoken to them so openly and they were both afraid that the slightest reaction might stop him. Ngoso's face looked pained, his brown eyes desolate. He gazed at Axel.

"There is some gossip that even you do not hear, Mwalimu," he said. He drew in his breath and let it out slowly before continuing. "I was expelled from the mission school a year early. Fired by the priests for consorting with criminals, as they called them. Me and four other boys from other villages. We were all secret recruits in the SERA—the Social and Economic Revolutionary Army." Ngoso looked at each of them. "I am still a member," he whispered.

For a long moment no one spoke. Then Despina abruptly burst out laughing.

"Is it that funny?" Ngoso said bitterly.

"Oh Jesus, we were warned about you in Peace Corps training camp, you know!" Despina was on her feet, her *kanga* swinging at her knees, her eyes glittering. "Beware of the SERA, they told us. They are agents of the Communist conspiracy. Those *ujamaa* snakes have a million disguises!" She danced over behind Ngoso and planted both hands on his bare shoulders. "And I had this image in my mind of some kind of Communist guerrilla lurking at the edge of the village carrying a knife in his mouth." She kissed the top of his woolly head. "And all it is is you, Ngoso. Just you!"

Ngoso still did not smile.

"But I do lurk at the edge of the village," he had said at last.

Just before the rains began [Axel wrote], my Peace Corps coworker and I went with an Udo friend on a trip to the most remarkable place I've ever seen. It's a village about a hundred miles south of here called Luhira, and a year ago it didn't exist. A group of men and women simply carved it out of the jungle with machetes. They wanted to start a village from scratch—a village in which everything was shared and all decisions were made communally. They formed an alliance called the Social and Economic Revolutionary Army and they call their movement *ujamaa*—that's Swahili for "family." What they've done down in Luhira is nothing less than create a little paradise.

We arrived there just before noon and there was a bell clanging from a mud tower at the center. In seconds the path began to fill up, first with children and old people, then with the young men and women, in from the fields and workshops, carrying their tools. Luhira is no bigger than Udo, where I live, but in Udo you never see the whole population together in one spot like that. We all crowded into this three-sided building and squatted in a circle, everyone laughing and jabbering, making more human noise than I'd heard in a year. Then bowls of warm porridge were passed around, dipped out of a huge kettle with the bare hands of an old woman. Someone told me that we were in *ujamaa* hall.

Instead of twenty-five fires, they said, we have one fire. Instead of twenty-five cooks, we have two.

That is the way they do everything down there. All the land is owned communally and it is farmed communally. If they sell anything, they have a meeting to decide what to buy with the profits—schoolbooks or water pipes or medicines. They vote on absolutely everything.

Axel found himself smiling as he wrote. On their last night in Luhira there had been an interminable *ujamaa* meeting where they debated the expenditure of what was the equivalent of four dollars and thirty-eight cents. After the vote was finally taken, the fat woman who served the porridge stood and began to sing a slow, wavering song in a southern dialect that Axel did not understand, but the word *ujamaa* was repeated at the end of each verse. Everyone in the hall had joined in and Axel tried his best to follow along. When the song ended, he had turned to look at Despina— her face was streaked with tears.

As you probably remember, Todd, I never had much enthu-siasm for political discussions back at Harvard. Whenever David got started at dinner on the virtues of the two-party system, I'd usually head for Mallinckrodt to mix a few chemi-cals. As usual, I didn't know what was really important. All of which is kind of a roundabout way of getting to my point: I'd like to learn something about political philosophy now if I could. I'd like to see how *ujamaa* fits in with the way the rest of the world does things and if—Axel hesitated here for a second—in some way I don't understand, it really is part of some Soviet conspiracy to take over Africa.

Axel hesitated again. Which dangers did he mean? Could any-one really believe that one idyllic village in the middle of the jungle could possibly be part of a conspiracy?

On the long trip back from Luhira, the "woolly trinity" had decided that somehow they were going to bring *ujamaa* to Udo. They made a solemn vow to one another as they turned off the Morogoro road onto the red clay that led back to their village.

But as Axel pulled the Land-Rover to a halt on the outskirts of Udo, young Ludi ran up to them waving a piece of paper.

"He was here," Ludi shouted. "He waited for you all day."

The paper was from Bouchard, the Corps coordinator in Dar, and his message was short: "I want a full report on your absence."

Despina crumpled the paper into a ball and flung it on the

ground. Then she grabbed Axel by both his hands and danced around him.

"What kind of report shall we write?" she had laughed. "The one about the scourge of African socialism? Or how about the one about the international threat of the village of Luhira?"

If you wouldn't mind [Axel wrote], send a few books that might educate your poor, undereducated friend. Of course, I'll pay you as soon as I'm back.

All my best,
Axel

Axel quickly reread his letter in the dying afternoon light. Somehow it seemed to miss the point completely. The real education he lacked was in the politics of the heart, and there was not one word in his letter about love.

6

GREG GREGORIAN had not fallen in love in over a week and he was beginning to think there was something physically wrong with him. Maybe the New York air was finally getting to him—he had not stepped off the island of Manhattan since he had arrived over a year ago. The fact was he had pledged himself not to even go to Connecticut for a weekend until he had one play produced. Just one, and it did not have to be on Broadway either. The basic problem, of course, was that he had not finished writing one play yet.

During that first year, while he was still living off his Uncle Aram's generous graduation gift, Greg had spent most of his time recording the incredible dialogue of the city in one spiral notebook after another. Fantastic stuff. Astonishing scenes absolutely everywhere: Chekovian playlets of love and betrayal in the subway, heartbreaking family dramas straight out of Miller on street corners, Pirandello in the elevator. Last week when he had telephoned Uncle Aram in Fresno to ask for a small loan to carry him a few months longer, there were thirty-five notebooks crammed full of wondrous theater piled on his desk.

"It's just a question of finding the right vehicle, 'Ram," he said. "You know, giving it shape. My working title is 'Uptown Express.' I figure I can put the whole thing together in a month, two tops."

"It sounds wonderful, Greggy," Aram said. "I think it's time to give Bernie Jacoby a call."

Bernie Jacoby was an old friend of Aram's who had once been his partner in a couple of Fresno movie houses and was now an agent at the William Morris Agency in New York.

"Soon," Greg said. "Just as soon as I have something to show him."

"I'm writing out a check right now," Aram said. "Call Bernie."

How the hell did you explain to an old Armenian uncle that it was precisely places like the William Morris Agency that kept America from producing a Luigi Pirandello?

Bernie Jacoby spoke so softly that Greg had to sit on the edge of his seat with his ear jutting toward him.

"Your uncle Aram is one in a million," he said several times between taking calls from California. "He's wasted in Fresno."

Greg nodded. The only items on Jacoby's desk were a yellow legal pad, a pencil, a telephone, and an intercom. It looked as if it were the first day of business.

"So, I understand you're writing a play," Jacoby said, finally, setting down the phone. "What's it about, Greg?"

Greg stiffened. It was just the kind of simplistic question he had expected. ("And what is *Death of a Salesman* about, Mr. Miller? The insurance business, you say?") He simpered at Jacoby.

"My play is about the roles people play in order to elicit the kinds of responses they want from others," Greg began, shifting into the imperious tones of the honors students he used to parody for Todd in college. "It's about the selfishness inherent in trying to please people. But what I'm doing is using the whole concept of theater as a metaphor for my theme. My working title is 'The Audience.'"

"Sounds interesting," Jacoby said, pressing his fingertips together. "Perhaps a little along the lines of Pirandello. I'd like to see it when you're ready."

"Thank you." Greg could not resist smiling. Jacoby obviously knew *something* about theater. He stood. Just talking about the play made him want to race back to his typewriter. He wondered if he was supposed to sign something that officially made Jacoby his agent.

"How are you planning to pay the rent until we can get something going with the plays?" Jacoby asked, pulling a large manila envelope from a drawer of his desk. The handwriting on it looked familiar.

"Probably drive a cab or something."

"That shouldn't be necessary." Jacoby shook the contents of the envelope onto his desk: It was Greg's old *Crimson* cartoons. Jesus, Aram!

"That's just some college stuff," Greg blurted, his face reddening.

"They're brilliant. Wonderfully visual, just as Aram said." Jacoby hit a button on his intercom. "Get me Bobby Burger, will you, Nan?" He waved Greg back into his seat. "Of course there's nothing much in New York. Never is. But I think I've got something that'll keep you going."

Greg stood again. Goddamn it, if these were the conditions of Aram's loan, he could keep his lousy money. In fact, this was exactly what his play was about—the fascism of generosity. Actually, it might be a terrific idea to set the whole play right here in this office and call it "The Agent."

"Thank you very much, Mr. Jacoby," Greg said. "But I intend to devote all my time to my plays just now."

"Greg, do you have any idea how long it takes to see a penny *after* a play has been optioned? Minimum of a year. Average is more like five."

The intercom announced that Bobby Burger was on line two.

"Burger's a client of mine who's producing a perfectly ridiculous daytime game show over at NBC. He needs somebody to write stunts for them. Greg, you could do the whole job every day before lunch. I can probably get you two hundred and fifty a week."

Greg felt like he was paralyzed.

Jacoby picked up his phone. "Bobby," he said, winking to Greg. "What'll you give me for a Harvard man?"

She had been Greg's third try that night, but, then again, it was clear that Greg had not been her first choice either. It didn't matter. Tonight was a night for making love. She had insisted on turning the light off, but she was soft and very sweet and for several minutes Greg was sure that he was madly in love with her. It was right after he had made love to her for the second time that the inspiration came to him. It was an absolutely brilliant idea. But what was the protocol for this? How did you excuse yourself from bed on the first date?

"I think you're terrific," Greg said.

"So are you. I'm glad this happened."

"Yes." Greg sat up in his oak double bed. "Say, would you mind if I went over to my typewriter for a minute. I just don't want to lose an idea. The light's not very bright."

She smiled and put her hands under her chin like a cherub. "I feel like a muse," she said.

Greg kissed her on the forehead and stepped gingerly over to his desk. The chair felt cold and sticky under his bare behind, but, never mind, he didn't want to lose a word of this. He switched on the lamp and rolled a yellow sheet into his typewriter. He had every word of it down in less than five minutes. He looked up—the girl was snoring softly in his bed. He picked up the phone and gave the operator a number in Palo Alto.

"Hello?"

"Todd. Hi."

"Jesus, Greg, it must be two in the morning out there. You okay?"

"Terrific. I just got a job writing stunts for a game show on NBC. Two fifty a week. Listen, what are you doing right now?"

"I've been snuggling up with my Schopenhauer since dinner, why?"

"I just wanted to try some on you."

"Shoot."

Greg pulled the sheet from the typewriter and read his old college roommate his first page of stunts.

"Funny stuff," Todd said, laughing.

"Sure," Greg said, happy in spite of himself, "but are you sure this is the way Strindberg got his start?"

"Strindberg? Oh, no," Todd said. "He worked for CBS."

7

TODD STOOD in line at the parcel post counter, his package under his arm. He had started with three books—Hobbes, Bentham and Rousseau—but then he had added a collection of lectures by Marcuse and *The Portable Marx*. The box now held seventeen paperbacks. God knows what it was going to cost to send it to Tanganyika. Not that it mattered. Books were for people who did things, people like Axel and Gregg. Todd shook his big head and smiled. By that logic, the last people in the world who deserved books were students. Especially grad students like himself, who sat all day in front of a desk. Maybe he should send his whole library to Africa.

8

LONG BEFORE Todd's package reached Axel, half the village of Udo had been stricken with dysentery and there was time for neither politics nor love. When ten sick children were brought to Axel before noon that first morning, he knew that he had an epidemic on his hands and immediately distributed tetracycline tablets to everyone, sick or not, at a table he set up in front of the infirmary. He sent Despina on a tour of each hut to see that every kettle and bottle was boiled; and he gave Ngoso the impossible task of carting in a fresh supply of water from the stream. In the early evening he met with Nagomway. It was not the first dysentery epidemic the old chief had seen, but it was the worst he could remember.

The children were hit the worst. Ludi lost a quarter of his weight in a week. He was glazed with fever and dehydration; the skin on his fingertips shriveled from loss of potassium and he moaned in a delirium. Axel doubled his dosage of tetracycline, but by the end of the week Ludi could still barely move and three other children were approaching the same condition.

At night Axel pored over his medical manuals and notebooks from his Corps training course in tropical diseases. He read everything he had about dysentery a dozen times while Ngoso and Despina paced silently in and out the door, a parade of helplessness. That afternoon Axel had palpated Ludi's abdomen and back and the boy had yelped every time Axel came near his liver. The evidence was inescapable: This was amebiasis, the most intractable strain. A broad-based antibiotic like tetracycline could never contain it; they needed an amebicide and, more urgently, they needed Flagyl. Axel had to get to Dar in the morning.

"If I can't get a mission doctor to come here," Axel said, "at the very least I'll ask for enough Flagyl for every child who's infected now. I'm going to get an official request from Nagomway—we can't risk any stalling for protocol." Axel looked up at Ngoso and Despina. Neither of them had any symptoms of the disease yet, but they were racked with fatigue and worry. "I'm going up to see Nagomway now. Do you want to come?"

Ngoso stood in the doorway. "This is just what the mission loves best—to have us come begging for their help," he said.

"I don't mind begging," Axel said quietly.

"They'll exact their price, Axel. They don't give anything away for free."

"I can't worry about that now." Axel stood and started around him.

"It will be ten steps backward for all of us—for *ujamaa!*" Ngoso called after him.

Axel turned and looked into his friend's eyes. "Ngoso," he said, "let's get Ludi well first, then we'll think about *ujamaa.*"

He walked on in the darkness, his body aching with tension. He had no strength to argue; he was running on instinct now.

Chief Nagomway had been expecting him. He agreed it was time to go for help. He put one hand on Axel's shoulder at the door.

"I hope you have no trouble, Mwalimu," he said. "Tell the good fathers that I have been praying to Jesus for our children's recovery."

There was just the faintest flicker of a smile on the old man's face when he said this—a smile not unlike Ngoso's, Axel thought. Nagomway's hand remained on Axel's shoulder like a benediction.

"Are you taking my grandson with you?" he asked.

"I think it would be better if he stayed here." Axel looked into Nagomway's eyes. "No one else can calm the children as well as he can."

"The children love him," Nagomway said. There was no mistaking the pride in his voice.

Axel woke frequently during the night, sure he'd heard Ludi moaning in the hut next to his, but whenever he went to the door he heard nothing but the rasp of tree frogs and the occasional thud of a coconut. When he woke again at five he stayed up, washed and shaved and dressed in clean clothes. He ate a banana and set off. Passing in front of the infirmary, he saw his oil lamp still burning in the window and he looked in the door. Despina was dead asleep on the cot, sprawled on her stomach with her *kanga* hiked up to her thighs; on the floor at her side Ngoso was asleep too, his head cupped in his hands as if he had fallen asleep while deep in thought. For a moment Axel considered tiptoeing in and kissing Despina's upturned cheek, but he was afraid of waking either of them. He walked on to the Land-Rover.

It took two hours to get to Morogoro, then four more to get to Dar. He parked by the fish market stalls, breathing in the exhaust of buses and motorbikes. The dissonant cries of seabirds and human voices pierced the air. Axel braced himself against a stall, as unsure of his footing as a sailor set ashore after a year at sea. An Arab woman came by hawking tea from a samovar that hung from a yoke across her shoulders. Axel signaled to her and gulped down two cups while the woman stooped beside him, her black eyes searching for her next customer. There were more people milling about in the fish market right now than in the entire village of Udo. For a dreamlike moment he imagined himself part of that crowd, wandering from market to market, never returning to Udo. He inhaled again and started off at a brisk pace toward Kivukoni Avenue.

As he came to the intersection of Uruhu Street, Axel considered checking in at the Peace Corps office and letting Bouchard know about the epidemic. Bouchard knew everyone at the mission; he might even go over to the hospital with him. Still, Despina had been adamant about keeping Peace Corps people out of Udo business as much as possible while they tried to organize an *ujamaa* movement in the village. Axel stood on the corner. At that moment in this rackety city, all those plans for changing Udo suddenly seemed terribly naive, like some mad high school scheme for turning the tables on the teachers. Maybe after the epidemic was over, Despina could escape with him to Dar for a day and they could think it all through again away from the claustrophobia of the village. For now, though, he crossed the street and continued on to the St. Elizabeth Hospital alone.

Axel entered the hospital and found his way to Dr. Becker's office. A sister said that the doctor was making his afternoon rounds and showed Axel to a waiting room, where he sat under a fan, dozing on and off for an hour. Finally the heavyset German appeared, standing in front of him in his short-sleeved white jacket. Axel had met him more than a year ago when he came to Dar in search of a cot for his infirmary.

"Stenhorn," the doctor said in heavily accented English, "that's a German name, isn't it?"

"Actually, it's Swedish. At least that's what my father tells me." They had had this identical conversation the first time they met.

Axel followed Becker into his office and they sat silently while a boy poured them thick, presweetened coffee. "Well, how is everything in the Peace Corps?" Becker said at last. The way he said it, it sounded like Piss Corps.

"We have a major dysentery epidemic in Udo," Axel said. "Amebic. A few of the children show signs of liver infection."

Becker took delicate sips of his coffee while Axel went on, describing the course the disease had taken in the village. Axel found himself speaking the technical language of medicine fluently. When he finished, Dr. Becker smiled and said, "There is really only one cure for dysentery and that is cleanliness. Clean hands. Clean water supply. A proper sewage system."

Axel nodded.

"How is the sewage system in Udo?" Becker asked.

"Poor," Axel said. "We've been trying to get them to build a new one ever since we came there. Perhaps this will finally get them to change their minds."

Becker smiled. "Nagomway," he said simply, and Axel realized that the doctor knew a great deal more about Udo than he had let on.

"You are absolutely right, cleanliness is the only long-range cure," Axel said hurriedly. "Right now, I think we have a real problem though, sir."

Becker raised his eyebrows, then smiled, crinkling up his eyes. "We'll have to see what we can do then," he said.

"Thank you, sir."

Becker was rising from his chair and Axel stood too.

"What happens now?"

Becker was already at the door. "Exactly what I told you. We'll have to see what we can do."

"Do you want me to wait here?"

"That's not necessary. We know how to find our way to Udo."

"Will you be coming tonight?"

"I'm in no position to answer that, Stenhorn," the doctor said. He was no longer smiling. "I do not make these decisions alone."

"It's urgent," Axel blurted.

"I will convey your opinion to the others." Becker gestured toward the door.

Axel still did not move. The thick odor coming from the wards suddenly made him feel queasy. He touched the side of Becker's desk. There was a pad of prescription blanks in the corner.

"Sir, I—I can't return without at least enough Flagyl to keep those children from abscessing. Just until someone from the mission can get there."

"Mr. Stenhorn, prescribing Flagyl is a medical decision to be made by a physician." He looked over the top of his glasses at Axel. "I expect if you continue with your studies you might make a very fine physician yourself one day. Now, if you'll excuse me, I have patients waiting." He walked out into the hall.

Axel was trembling. For a moment he could not move; then he suddenly rushed after Becker, half-stumbling through the doorway. "Dr. Becker, please. I forgot to tell you . . . Chief Nagomway wanted you to know that he is praying to Jesus for the children's recovery."

A slight ironic smile appeared on the mission doctor's thin lips. "Well, please tell Nagomway that our prayers are with him," he said, and walked briskly away.

Axel was running, his sandals slapping on the wooden floor. Black nuns in white habits held out their hands, signaling for him to slow down, but Axel raced on through the doors and down the steps onto the grill-hot street. He did not stop running until he came to the Peace Corps office on Uruhu Street. He walked up the splintered wooden steps to the second floor and stood outside the door for a moment, wiping the sweat from his face. Then he entered.

Rick Bouchard did not look pleased to see him. Two electric fans swiveled on his desk. An attractive Dar woman in a loose-fitting tunic sat next to him sipping iced tea.

"What brings you to town, Stenhorn?"

"Some trouble," Axel said, catching his breath. "Something pretty serious."

Bouchard scratched his forehead. He turned to the woman and, speaking in the Arabic-sounding cadences of Dar Swahili, asked her to meet him in half an hour at a café on Kivukoni Avenue. She smiled at Axel on the way out.

"Sit down," Bouchard said. Although he was only twenty-six, he seemed much older to Axel. "Now what's this all about?"

While Axel told him about the epidemic and his meeting with Dr. Becker, Bouchard drank the iced tea his woman friend had left on his desk. He tapped his fingernails on the glass for a moment after Axel had finished.

"I'm sure Becker will do what is necessary," he said finally.

"If he understands how urgent the situation is."

"Hell, Stenhorn, they've had dysentery in Africa ever since the first little brown boy took his first shit. You know what they call this part of the world over at CARE? The Turd World." He emitted a short, barking laugh. "Becker's been here thirty years."

"I've got a boy with an abscessed liver."

Bouchard snapped open a ballpoint pen and wrote the word "liver" on his desk calendar. "I'll include that in my report," he said. "And I'll call Becker in the morning to see what's happening." He yanked open a drawer and pulled out a packet of envelopes. He pushed them across the desk. "Might as well take the mail back with you."

There was nothing more to say. Axel stood and started for the door.

"By the way, Stenhorn," Bouchard said, "I still haven't received a report from you and Miss Delahanty about your absence when I was up there. Don't let it drag, will you?"

Axel was already out the door. Minutes later he was on the trash-strewn outskirts of the city—the slums of country villagers who had come to Dar to seek their fortunes. He realized that he hadn't eaten anything solid since he'd left Udo ten hours ago and found a little three-walled store that sold corn bread and salted fish. While he ate, he looked through the packet of letters Bouchard had given him. There was one from Akron. In addition to his mother's five closely written pages, there was a square of note paper "From the desk of Dr. Eric Stenhorn" clipped to a printed sheet. The note read "Sign this and return." It was the first communication of any kind that Axel had received from his father since the day he had told him he was joining the Peace Corps. The attached sheet officially reserved Axel's place that coming fall in Columbia medical school. Axel stuffed everything back into the envelope and stuck it in his pocket. For the second time that day he was momentarily overcome by the fantasy of disappearing in Dar es Salaam.

"Do you have the medicine?"

Axel was still sitting in the Land-Rover when the beam of a flashlight shone in his eyes and he heard Despina's voice.

"They're bringing it tomorrow," he said. He waved his hands in front of his eyes and she lowered the light. "They want everyone seen by Becker before they prescribe anything."

There was a short, rasping laugh and Axel realized that Ngoso was standing beside Despina.

"The fathers were in no hurry to help, were they?" he said. There was something smug in his voice that Axel did not like.

"I didn't see the fathers. Just Becker. And Bouchard." Axel tried to find Ngoso's eyes in the dark. "The hospital was awfully busy," he added, and immediately regretted the defensive tone of his voice. He stepped down from the car. "The doctors will be here tomorrow. Everyone will be all right."

Despina touched his cheek. "You look exhausted," she said.

Axel trudged back to his hut alone. He slept in his clothes. If Ludi moaned in the night, he did not hear him.

In the morning Axel went immediately to his neighbor's hut to examine the boy. He was considerably worse. There was a film over his eyes; his skin felt dry and scaly; he was sensitive wherever he was touched. He emitted soft, murmuring moans with every breath, like an animal that has been caught in a trap for days. Ludi's mother sat on the floor next to him, spooning water into his mouth every few seconds. Axel noticed that over the mat where the boy lay was a bamboo crucifix; he did not remember seeing it there before.

Axel ran down to the infirmary. Despina was boiling water over a fire in the back.

"We've got to get Ludi's temperature down," he told her.

He took a thermometer, aspirin and alcohol from the medicine cabinet and started back with Despina. For over an hour they rubbed Ludi with alcohol, but his fever never dropped below 105 degrees. Axel crushed an aspirin into a spoon of water and Ludi's mother got it in his mouth, but that did not help either.

"Shall we take him to Dar?"

Axel looked at his watch. It was eleven. Bouchard would have called the hospital by now. Surely Becker or another doctor would leave before noon if they expected to examine all the patients before sundown. And if Axel took Ludi, what about Kiti? He had not even seen her yet.

"Let's wait," he said.

At two in the afternoon Ludi's temperature rose to 106. Minutes later a boy ran in with a message from Ngoso: Kiti's temperature was at 105.

"Tell him to take her to the pool," Axel said. "I'll meet him there."

Axel lifted Ludi into his arms. He weighed no more than an infant. His arms and calves swung free like a puppet's. He whimpered as if Axel were crushing him. Ludi's mother and Despina followed silently behind in single file. When Axel reached the stream bed, he walked straight down the bank, then out until the water came to the top of his shorts. He slowly lowered the boy up to his neck in the cool water—a baptism.

The afternoon sun dappled the water like a ring of stars protecting them. The water lapped at the weightless child in his arms. A breeze drifted toward them from the hills, carrying with it the delicate scent of wild orchids. It was exquisitely beautiful here, more beautiful than it could possibly be anywhere else in the world. Axel breathed deeply. There was a taste of salt on his lips. Ludi was cool against his chest. He was dead.

Axel said nothing. He cradled the boy closer to him, turning away from the women, now rocking Ludi, crooning his name softly over and over. Tears streamed down Axel's face, dropped and disappeared into the stream. Sweet child. Sweet Ludi.

Axel did not hear Ngoso until he was beside him with Kiti in his arms. Her eyes were open, sad but clear, and her eyelids fluttered when Ngoso lowered her into the water. Ngoso looked at Axel's face.

"Oh, God, I'm sorry," he whispered.

Axel could not speak.

Ludi's mother insisted on carrying her child's body back to the village alone.

Axel sat on the bank watching Ngoso bathe the little girl. She was responding, flexing her little hands, a trace of a smile appearing as Ngoso bounced her lightly in the water. Her temperature was dropping. After a few more minutes Ngoso carried her out of the water.

"Wait for me here," he said.

Despina came up behind Axel and wrapped her arms around his chest, pressing her face against his back. They rocked back and forth, not speaking.

When Ngoso returned, he sat beside them, silent too for a moment. At last he said, "In the village they are saying they are all cursed. They wonder how they have offended the spirits." He shook his head. "No one's coming from Dar, you know, Axel. They may have promised you, but they are not coming to Udo."

Axel continued to gaze at the water, wanting to hold on to his grief, in all its purity, a little longer before he thought of anything else. Suddenly Despina let go of him and stood.

"Then we'll have to get the medicine ourselves," she said matter-of-factly, looking down at the two young men.

"We've tried that," Ngoso said.

"No, we've asked them for the medicine," Despina said. "Now it is time to go and get it. To take it without asking."

Axel bit down on his lip.

"Don't be foolish," Ngoso said. He threw a stone into the water. "We do not steal."

"What do you propose we do?" Despina said. "Wait until another child dies and blame it on the mission doctors?"

Axel drew in his breath. "Let's take the worst cases to the hospi-

tal today. Right now," he said rapidly. He stood. Neither Despina
nor Ngoso moved. "We'll take Kiti and Mumbai and—"

Ngoso jumped up.

"No!" he said loudly. "Despina is right. We will bring the medicine back to Udo. Why should the children have to move? It is not
stealing. It is ours."

Axel looked from Ngoso to Despina and back again. His heart
was thudding in his chest. He heard a sound below the village,
prayed that it was Becker finally arriving, but it was nothing, a
leopard coughing in the jungle.

"Are you coming with us?" Despina looked straight at him, her
eyes narrowed, strangely cold-looking. She took a step toward
Ngoso.

Axel closed his eyes. He felt dizzy. This was crazy, all of it, a
feverish nightmare. But there really was no decision to make. He
knew he had to follow Despina.

"I left the keys in my hut," he said. "I'll meet you at the car in
ten minutes."

By the time they reached the Morogoro road, the sun had already dropped behind them and Axel finally had to abandon hope
of encountering the mission car along the way. Ngoso sat beside
him and Despina hung over his seat from behind, her chin resting
on Axel's shoulder, both oblivious to the madness of what they
were doing. The way they chattered and laughed as they bounced
along the road one would have guessed that they were on their
way to Dar for a night on the town, dinner in the Twiga Hotel, a
party at the embassy. They were putting Ludi's death behind
them—that Axel knew—but he could still feel the boy's flesh gone
cold in his arms. They could see the lights of Dar in the distance
before anyone spoke about what they were actually going to do.

Despina grilled Axel about what he knew of the layout of the
hospital. All medicines were dispensed from a pharmacy in the
rear barrack—it was next to the storeroom where Axel had requisi-
tioned his cot. The pharmacist was an old German, but Axel remembered that his assistant, a young Dar man, ran the pharmacy
alone from late afternoon until it closed for the night. Axel had no
idea when that was.

"What kind of door does it have?"

"Wooden. Teak, I think. Most of the doors are teak."

"I mean the lock. How does it lock? What does it look like?"

Axel shrugged. "I don't know. Look, you don't think we're actually going to pick a lock like some kind of burglars, do you?"

"How the hell do you think we're going to get that medicine?" Despina said.

"Listen," Axel said quietly. "Why don't we find Becker, wherever he is, and insist he give us that medicine tonight. Tell him about Ludi. Make him understand that he is morally obligated—"

"No!" Ngoso said. "It's too late. Why let him redeem himself now?"

"That's not the point, is it?" Axel raised his voice. He looked in the rearview mirror at Despina for confirmation.

She seemed to hesitate for just a second and then she said, "No, we're through asking."

No one spoke for several minutes. Axel looked again at Despina.

"Well, probably our best bet is to simply act like we're picking up a prescription," Axel said in a voice so cool it amazed even him.

"How do you mean?"

Axel explained that he had seen all types of hospital personnel—sisters, orderlies—picking up prescriptions at the hospital pharmacy. He was pretty sure that medical supplies for outlying missions and villages were dispensed in the same way.

"By God, it sounds easy!" Ngoso cheered.

Despina still looked grim. "Wouldn't that pharmacist's assistant know everyone by sight?"

"Maybe. I don't know."

"And what about a prescription?"

"I think I know where I can find one," Axel said.

"Okay. That's it, then," Despina said.

Axel's pulse jumped. This was no longer a crazy, impulsive gesture, a rationale for escaping in the night from the awfulness and helplessness of Udo. They were on the outskirts of Dar now and they had something of a plan. The reality of it seemed to have struck them all. Ngoso finally broke the silence.

"Do you realize that we can change everything in one night?" he said. "That we will bring this medicine back home in the name of *ujamaa?*"

Axel turned his head angrily. Not for *ujamaa*, he thought. For Kiti and Mumbai and the others. He was not going through with all of this as a political act but as an act of mercy. He was about to say just that when Despina's eyes caught his in the mirror: She looked

excited, eager. She pursed her lips, a half-kiss, and Axel smiled
back at her. He did not say anything.

They parked the Land-Rover on a side street two blocks from
the hospital. They circled the building on foot and found an entrance in the back where deliveries were brought in. The door was
open. They peered in at a long, dimly lit corridor. The pharmacy
was just beyond the first right turn, out of sight. Axel checked his
watch. Almost nine. It would most likely be closing soon.

"I'll meet you right here," Axel whispered.

Despina squeezed his hand and Ngoso clapped him lightly on
the back. Axel nodded and was off. He walked to the front and
entered the hospital through the same door he had come in the
day before. By some odd impulse he had removed his glasses—
almost as if he thought he could be seen less clearly without them
—and he saluted the sister at the reception table with them as he
passed by. She nodded back indifferently. There was only one
more person between him and Becker's office, a white sister sitting on a chair at the entrance to the wards. She was bent over a
book in her lap, undoubtedly the Bible. Axel walked as purpo-
sively as he could. She lifted her head when he was right in front of
her.

"Good evening," she said. "May I help you?"

Axel was trembling. He was still in enough shadow that he was
sure she could not make out his face very well. He could turn
around and be out of here in a minute, even run if he had to. He
just stood there.

"Good evening," he said. "I've come to pick up something for
Dr. Becker."

The sister rose and started toward him. She wore rimless spectacles and had a growth of some sort on her cheek.

"But I'm sure Dr. Becker left several hours ago."

"He did. That's why he sent me." Axel had no idea what he was
saying; the words were coming automatically. He squinted at the
sister in the dark hallway.

"Let me get the light in his office for you," she said.

"Please don't bother." Axel smiled as he continued by her and
walked directly into Becker's office. He pulled on the light. The
pad of prescription blanks was on the corner of Becker's desk, just
where he had seen it yesterday. Axel tore off several sheets, started
to leave, then walked back to the desk. Might as well take care of

everything here. He took a pen from the top drawer of Becker's desk and wrote out a prescription for Flagyl and signed it with Becker's initials. Then he thought a moment and wrote out a second prescription for codeine. He turned off the light and walked out into the hallway.

"Find what you wanted?" the sister asked as he walked by.

"Yes, thank you. Good night now."

When Axel walked out the front door, he found he was grinning. By God, he'd done it.

Ngoso was standing at the service door alone.

"Where's Despina?"

"I don't know. She said she'd be right back. She left right after you did." Ngoso's eyes were darting nervously. He'd seemed the most apprehensive of the three ever since they got out of the car. Axel touched his arm.

"Everything's going fine," he told him. "I'd better take a look at that pharmacy now."

"I'll come with you."

Ngoso followed Axel through the door and stayed behind him for the length of the hallway. At the corner Axel craned his head around the wall. The door to the pharmacy was open, the light on. He wondered where Despina had gone. The plan was for her to accompany Ngoso with the prescriptions but to stay as much in the background as possible so that she could not be described later. It was easier to remain anonymous in this city if you had a black face. If asked, Despina was to say that she was a lay teacher at Moshi in a mountain mission. Suddenly lights began going off at the end of the hallway. The pharmacy was closing.

"You'll have to go without her," Axel whispered, thrusting the prescriptions into Ngoso's hand.

Ngoso closed his hand around the prescriptions but did not move.

"It's now or never," Axel said.

Ngoso half-ran toward the pharmacy.

"Hey, man. I've got a prescription for you." Ngoso was affecting some kind of Dar slang.

"Well, you're too late for tonight, boy. We're all locked up." The pharmacist's assistant had a condescending voice.

"I've come all the way from Moshi, man," Ngoso said.

"Fine, then you're lucky to spend the night in Dar."

Axel heard a door close, a lock turn.

"My boss, he's waiting for me," Ngoso pleaded. "We've got sickness up in Moshi."

A pause. Axel tried not to breathe. If Ngoso couldn't convince him on his own, Axel would have to step in, though the pharmacist's assistant would surely remember his face.

"Well, you tell your bossman to come by tomorrow morning too. We open at six."

Axel took one step to the corner. But at that moment someone rushed up behind him and flew by his side—a white sister, her habit and veil fluttering behind her like bat wings. She moved soundlessly, an apparition, but when she spoke Axel knew her voice.

"Boy," she said sharply to Ngoso. "What's happening here? We're waiting for you."

It was Despina!

Axel held down a yelp of sheer wonder.

"I—I—" Ngoso's stammer was genuine.

Axel stepped around the corner to see Despina imperiously fling out her hand and grab the prescriptions from Ngoso.

"I'm sorry, sister," the pharmacist's assistant was saying as he reopened the door. "I'd just locked up and—"

"Just hurry now, please."

They said not one word until the box of medicine was wedged behind the front seat of the Land-Rover and they were sailing down Kivukoni Avenue, Despina between them, her veils flapping in the breeze. Then all three hooted and cheered and slugged each other's arms and told each other how absolutely marvelous they were. Despina insisted on hearing every detail of how Axel stole the prescriptions before she would divulge her own wonderful story of searching the hospital laundry for a habit—it was figuring out how to put the thing on which had taken the most time. They roared and went through it all again, both men gazing at Despina with untrammeled awe when they came to the part when she sailed down the corridor in full regalia, Sister Despina the Miraculous. At the edge of the city Despina pulled off her veil and flung it out the window, then shimmied out of the habit and tossed it out too. She pulled the SERA beret from Ngoso's head—he'd put it on the moment they got to the car—and put it on her own head at a rakish angle. Then she stretched her arms across both men's shoulders and shouted in her strong, lovely voice, "I love you! I love you both!"

Fatigue had hit all three of them by the time they turned off the Morogoro road. It was past midnight. It seemed incredible that this was the same day that Ludi had died in Axel's arms. Axel gripped the steering wheel tightly as the car slipped from rut to track in the clay road. Despina's head bounced against his shoulder, her eyes closed. Ngoso's head rested on her shoulder.

Axel was the first to see the mission jeep parked at the edge of the village. Jesus God, Becker had come to Udo after all! He'd beaten them with the medicine. It had all been in vain. All in vain.

Axel brought the car to a gradual halt, not wanting to wake the others, dreading the moment when they would see the jeep too. But Despina snapped open her eyes and saw it immediately. She closed her eyes again for a moment, then sighed and jostled Ngoso awake. It was a few seconds before he comprehended what had happened, but when he did he made an awful sound in the back of his throat.

"At least the children are taken care of," Axel said.

Abruptly Ngoso lifted the beret from Despina's head and put it on his own. He brushed his clothing, straightened his shirt. Then he reached down behind the seat and lifted the box of medicine onto his shoulders.

Axel looked at Despina. For sure, she also knew that they could hide that box now, bury it somewhere until Becker was gone, and no one would ever have to know what they had done this evening. Ngoso had already started toward the path alone. Axel stared at him, paralyzed. And suddenly Despina was on her feet too, following Ngoso. Without thinking, Axel jumped out of the car after her. All three marched toward the village, soldiers of the Social and Economic Revolutionary Army.

They were all there, their oil lamps flaring in front of the infirmary. Dr. Becker was standing with Nagomway in the doorway. Bouchard was seated on the cot, smoking a cigarette. When Ngoso set the box of medicine down at his grandfather's feet, old Nagomway just shook his head with terrible sadness and shame.

Axel and Despina rode back with Bouchard to Dar the next morning. Their trunks were in the back. They had not said goodbye to anyone. In two days they were officially terminated from the Peace Corps. And at the end of the week Rick Bouchard

accompanied them to the airport to personally see to it that they
boarded the plane for New York. Bouchard barely spoke to them
until they lined up at the gate and then he said, "I just don't
understand. You were the first, the chosen. You had a chance to be
part of history, to make something really wonderful happen here,
and you just threw it all away for nothing."

Despina smiled at him as she passed through the gate.

"Bullshit," she said.

Axel walked behind her.

9

DAVID GLIDED down the Mississippi highway, his elbow hanging out the window like a teenager's. On the radio a nasal-voiced
woman twanged that she would take back her man even though
he was lazy and cruel and drank too much. It was three in the
morning, but to David it felt like three in the afternoon. There was
a silkiness about a Southern night that made him feel inordinately
free. Even the irony in this was exhilarating.

In the backseat, Lincoln Ames pulled his knees up to his chest.
Stripped of his seersucker suit, Oxford shirt, and bow tie, the older
man had the look of an underfed prisoner. In fact, David had not
seen him eat a complete meal since they had arrived in Jackson,
and he seemed to sleep best, as now, in cars and planes. Anywhere
else he preferred to talk. And David listened. In the week they had
been down here, he was sure he had learned more about how a
lawyer actually got things done than in nearly two years of Harvard Law School.

The headlights picked up a billboard that read "Impeach Earl
Warren" and David reflexively slowed the car to fifty, reminded of
the enemy. Reg Harris, another volunteer lawyer for the Student
Nonviolent Coordinating Committee, had been detained for five
hours on a speeding charge just yesterday. Not that it really mattered how fast you went. Every cop from here to The Delta

seemed to know their automobiles the moment someone from SNCC rented one, and there was a wry creativity in the charges they stopped you for; David could easily spend the night in jail for transporting a half-naked man across the county line.

When Lincoln had asked David to accompany him to Mississippi during spring recess, David had known this was a rare opportunity. Not only would he be in a place where fundamental laws were being tested, but he would be there at the side of the foremost practicing expert of civil liberties law. His only hesitation had been Patricia. They had been talking about spring vacation ever since Christmas, when he had spent every day in the law library preparing for examinations. This time he had promised that they would enjoy their first real family vacation since the baby had been born. In fact, he had very much been looking forward to that himself. But how could he possibly pass up an opportunity to go to Jackson with Lincoln Ames?

"Why don't we all go?" Pat had said cheerily.

"I don't think that can be done."

"Why not? We'll stay out of your way. We could find a nice hotel and combine things. You know, work and play."

"A white hotel or a Negro hotel?"

Pat sighed deeply. "Then you go alone, David. You'll just mope if you don't." She had wrapped her arms around him and snuggled her head against his chest. "But you can tell Lincoln Ames that I'm never going to speak to him again."

A pair of headlights appeared in David's rearview mirror. He pulled over to the right lane, but the car stuck behind him. David slowed to thirty.

"Have we got company?" Lincoln sat up and immediately began to pull on his shirt.

"I think so." David slowed to twenty. The car was just ten feet in back of them. "Should I roll up my window?"

"I don't think that will help much." Lincoln was fitting his tie into his collar. He might have been preparing for court.

Suddenly the car pulled up directly beside them and a man no older than David leaned his head out the window.

"Fucking nigger-loving faggots!" he screamed, and screeched ahead of them.

"Thank you," Lincoln called after him. "Thank you very much indeed."

A fuzzy dawn the color of peaches rose behind them as they entered Jefferson County. A sign announced "Red Lick—Cabbage Capital of the World," and Lincoln traced his finger along the map.

"Ah, there is a logical order to things down here," he said. "Next town is Oldenburg, natural gas capital of the world."

It was almost eight when they reached McNair, where seven SNCC workers had been jailed the night before. David searched for the courthouse while Lincoln reviewed the notes he had taken over the phone in Jackson. A group of kids from a freedom house— three girls and four boys, all white—had walked into town for an ice cream late in the afternoon and there they had run into two Negro volunteers for the registration drive. One of the SNCC people had asked if the Negro boys wanted ice-cream cones too, and then two white girls had gone into the shop. They were refused service. One of the girls took it up with the store manager and, when refused again, climbed up on the counter and lay across it like a bed. She was arrested for destruction of private property and disorderly conduct, the others for blocking the sidewalk. It differed from other sit-in cases Lincoln had represented only in the charges against the one girl.

"Should make it interesting," David said, pulling into the courthouse parking lot.

"It should make it sticky, you mean," Lincoln said. "Lying on a counter could get you arrested anywhere. She's fortunate that's all that happened to her."

David followed Lincoln into the courthouse and the two men shaved in a basement lavatory. By the time they came back upstairs, the seven prisoners were already standing in a line outside the courtroom. David recognized the SNCC look immediately: The boys wore Levi's and work shirts, pens clipped to their shirt pockets; the girls wore shapeless smock dresses of the sort David's mother used to wear around the house; and all wore the earnest expressions of people who, at heart, could not believe that anyone really meant them harm. There was one exception, and David found her insolent eyes and ironic mouth refreshing. He had no doubts that she was the young woman who had sprawled across the ice-cream shop counter.

They had barely taken the prisoners' names down on the depositions when the sheriff waved them into the courtroom. David shot a glance at Lincoln—they were used to this tactic. Either they could go before the judge unprepared or they could motion for a delay that might drag on for days. Lincoln shrugged and led them in. The judge, a balding, sallow-faced man, was sipping coffee from a paper cup when Lincoln strode up to the bench, the picture of Yankee refinement in bow tie and fluttering seersucker stripes. He greeted the magistrate as if the honor of meeting him were the sole reason for his trip down here. David was constantly amazed at how effectively Lincoln used his blend of condescension and flattery in these county courthouses. After a short, inaudible exchange, the judge rapped his gavel and announced that the six charged with obstructing the sidewalk were free without bail pending a further investigation. That was quick enough. David wondered what kind of deal Lincoln had struck this time. The six were exchanging dazed smiles when the judge ordered the seventh prisoner to rise. From where David sat he had a three-quarter view of this young woman. She was darker than the others—Spanish or Italian, he thought—and although she wore the same straight-seamed sleeveless cotton dress as the other girls, hers tucked and clung in a way that showed the full sweep of her hips and the plum roundness of her breasts. The judge motioned her toward him.

"Young lady," he drawled, "your attorney has persuaded me to overlook the charge of destruction of property that has been made against you, but you also have been charged with disorderly and unbecoming conduct in a public place. Now, I don't know where you come from, but here in McNair we consider that a serious offense, especially for a female-gendered person."

The girl smiled. Raising her hand to brush a drop of sweat from her forehead, she revealed a thick bush of hair under her arm. The judged gaped at it incredulously.

"We've got laws here against inciting and provoking in public establishments," the judge went on, obviously agitated. "Laws that were written to prohibit just your kind of behavior from taking place in a Christian community."

"Do you mean from buying ice-cream cones?"

The judge's face flushed with anger. Lincoln immediately grasped the girl's arm and looked up at the judge.

"Your honor," he said calmly, "I haven't had the time to brief my client on the nature of our plea. Now if you could just give us—"

The girl abruptly yanked her arm from Lincoln's hand and turned her face toward him. Her dark eyes burned.

"Don't horse-trade with me, Charlie," she sneered.

The judge rapped his gavel. He pointed a finger at her. "The prisoner will be held until such time that she can be released into the custody of her next of kin. Return her to her cell, Sheriff."

David clenched his jaw. The judge knew full well that none of these kids' parents were within a thousand miles of here. The sheriff already had placed his hand on the girl's arm when there was a sudden commotion in the back of the courtroom.

"I . . . I am Miss Delahanty's next of kin."

The judge again rapped his gavel and David turned to see a tall, deeply tanned young man pace down the aisle toward him. He walked by David with only the slightest nod of acknowledgment. It was Axel Stenhorn.

"And what would your relationship to the prisoner be, boy?" the judge was saying.

"I am her husband."

It was over an hour before David finally got to talk with Axel. The judge had insisted on proof of his marriage and Axel had removed a wad of paper from his wallet, meticulously unfolded it, and held up his marriage certificate by the corners like a pillow-case on a clothesline. The judge had wagged his head, more dumbfounded than angry, and when he dismissed them he leaned forward and said to Axel in an almost fatherly tone, "Now you all be careful, son."

No one had said a word as they walked up the aisle and out the doors of the courtroom, Axel's hand placed lightly on the back of this beautiful and magnificently arrogant young woman who was his wife. They had been nowhere in sight when David, Lincoln and the rest of the SNCC people left the courthouse several minutes later. Lincoln was in a wonderfully expansive mood, as if he too had just been released after a night in jail, and he insisted on splurging on breakfast for them all.

"Just think of all the bail money we saved," he laughed.

They ate at "Mama's," a colored grocery with a long, oilcloth-covered table in the rear, where the owner served up a feast of sausages, eggs, grits and corn bread, along with mugs of chicory-spiced coffee. They jabbered about the incident at the ice-cream store and about their night in jail—it was the first time for all of them—and then at last David got them to talk about Axel Stenhorn and Despina Delahanty. It turned out that none of them had known that the two were married.

"I'm not really surprised though," one of the girls said. "I mean, Despina is always surprising."

Apparently Axel had other secrets too—none of his colleagues knew that he had gone to Harvard—but it was clear he was well respected, even if he was a bit aloof. His and Despina's association with some revolutionary movement in Africa was a matter of considerable status with the SNCC leadership, and they were frequently asked for their opinions at policy meetings. In general, one of the boys said, they sided with the faction that favored demonstrations over legal maneuvering. David listened to all of this with utter amazement. He kept remembering the time he had tutored Axel in the fundamentals of the Democratic Party over chipped beef in the Dunster House dining hall.

Axel was sitting alone on the freedom house stoop when David arrived. He stood, smiled and extended his hand, which David took with much relief—he had half-expected Axel to ignore him completely.

"Funny place to meet, huh?" Axel said.

"I'm more surprised than you are."

Axel lifted off his glasses and rubbed them against his sleeve. He seemed very much older than the last time David had seen him.

"By the way, congratulations," David said.

"What for?"

"Your marriage."

"Oh." Axel cast an embarrassed glance back at the house. "It's just a formality."

"A convenient one today," David said, smiling.

Axel stepped out to the road. "Want a tour of my neighborhood?"

"Sure."

David fell in beside Axel and the two walked in silence for a few minutes. They were the only whites on this side of McNair, but everyone waved or called out to Axel as they passed along the dusty, unpaved road.

"Well, where do we begin?" David said finally. "How was the Peace Corps?"

"It got me to Africa," Axel answered. He gave David an ironic smile. "But I can't say I'd recommend it. It's a funny name, Peace Corps, a dead giveaway, really. Sounds more like a branch of the Army than the Green Berets does. Now *that* sounds like some kinds of extension of the 4-H club."

David laughed. He waited for Axel to go on.

"Despina saw through it all right away, before we even left. All those psychological tests and interviews they put you through. It's really very *Nineteen Eighty-four* when you think about it."

David wanted to ask why Despina had joined the Peace Corps if she had seen through it, but he decided against it. "I take it you didn't stay in for the full two years," he said.

"No." Axel saluted an old Negro who leaned on a cane. "Going to get hotter, Rufus," he called to him.

David looked at Axel's feet, tried to match his stride. He could not catch the rhythm of this conversation. Axel seemed to be deliberately choosing what he would reveal about himself and what he would not as if anything could be held against him.

"How about you?" Axel said abruptly. "How's everything been with you these past few years?"

"The usual Cambridge grind," David said. Then he quickly added, "Except for the baby, of course. We had a little boy, Joshua Beardsley Debilio."

Saying his son's name out loud embarrassed him, and David followed it with a laugh.

"Hey, that's wonderful!" Axel grinned at him. He seemed genuinely pleased. "Give my congratulations to Pat." He fell quiet for a moment, then said, "My sister had a baby boy too. Just a few days after I got back to the States. He was 'conceived out of wedlock,' as they say, but my parents prevailed and Annalena married the father a couple of months before she gave birth. She's back in Akron now."

"Have you seen him? Your nephew, I mean." He really wanted to know if Axel had seen his parents.

"No."

They had made a complete circuit of the little neighborhood and now were ambling back toward the freedom house. David could see a few people standing on the porch. He wanted to slow down, to take another turn, to keep Axel to himself for just a few more minutes. His feeling of incompleteness came not merely from the questions left unasked and unanswered. He wanted something from Axel, some sort of recognition that the paths they had taken were not really so divergent, that they were both working for the same political ends in equally valid ways. Damn it, there was a common bond between them. He saw Despina looking toward them.

"Leary's making quite a commotion up in Cambridge these days," David blurted out.

"Leary?"

"Tim Leary. You know, the night in Newton."

Axel did not break his stride. "I'd almost forgotten about that," he said.

When they reached the house, Axel introduced David to Despina. They shook hands formally. She did not look into David's eyes. A moment later Lincoln came out and said it was time they started back for Jackson. David clapped Axel on the shoulder.

"Let's stay in touch," he said.

Axel nodded.

Just before they drove off, Despina leaned down and looked in the car window at David.

"Hope you enjoy the rest of your vacation," she said.

As soon as they got back to Jackson, David placed a call to the Beardsleys' house in Vermont, where Pat was staying with the baby. He was dying to tell her about Axel and the exotic woman he had married. His mother-in-law answered the phone. She said that Pat had left the baby with her and had gone down to Cambridge on her own for a couple of days. David called their apartment every half hour until midnight, but there was no answer. Finally he could not stay awake any longer. He dreamt that they were all back in college again.

10

Halfway through *Breathless* Jerry realized that Jean-Paul
Belmondo was definitely not going to dance.

"No dancing," he whispered in the dark. "You lied."

"But he danced last time I saw this flick. Right up the old
Champs-Élysées."

Equal proportions of giggles and "shhhs" all around the Brattle
Theatre. Jerry edged to the aisle, walked bent as a beggar to the
rear. Too depressing, all this black-and-white *nouveau angst.*

"Down in front."

Jerry turned to see Gabby hunker down and do a *kazatzki* up
the aisle after him. She was wearing her elf disguise again, tights
and tunic, the peaked felt cap with a purple plume they had
bought at Revere Beach. Peter Pan from Petrograd. On the stairs
she said, "Well, you could tell he *wanted* to dance."

They pushed through the door of the Casablanca Bar, dark as
the theater. Gayer movie down here, 3-D in the Casa B.

"Ah, the beautiful dreamers." A hand touched Jerry's shoulder
—Ralph van Hubbel, chocolate heir cum poet, a high-caloric
Corso. "I thought you Leary people didn't drink."

"True." Jerry was already searching for an escape route. "It
turns your brain to aspic, don't ya know."

"Umm, yummy." Van Hubbel gestured to his table in the corner, a ring of beatniks and clubbies and fiery-eyed Radcliffe girls
showing off their porcelain collarbones. Cambridge pretending to
be Paris.

"Just came down for a wee pee," Jerry said, shaking himself free
from Van Hubbel's clasp. "Mustn't keep Jean-Paul waiting."

Jerry started to make an about-face when he saw a hand fluttering at him from the table. He squinted through the smoke. It
was Pat Beardsley. Pat Beardsley Debilio. He waved back and
started toward her, Gabby tugging at his back pocket.

Pat rose with a tinkling princess giggle, offered him one cheek at a time, then shrugged and pursed her lips, dark as velvet. "My God, Jerry, how long has it been? A year at least."

She told everyone on the banquette to "squonch" down and patted the cushion beside her. As Jerry sat, Gabby sidestepped to Van Hubbel's chair and perched next to him on the edge, cheek-to-cheek.

"Oh, this is—" Jerry began the introduction, but Gabby cut him off.

"The Marchesa di Stranzoni," she said, doffing her cap.

Pat had wrapped both hands around Jerry's slender bicep, looking up at him with pale blue eyes.

"This is my former roommate-in-law," she announced. Her voice had the earnest rhythm of someone talking in her sleep. She had obviously been drinking all evening.

"Where's Dave?"

"In Miss-iss-ip-pi." She pronounced one syllable at a time, as if sounding it out for a spelling bee. "You know, for civil rights stuff."

"Sibyl Rites?" Van Hubbel bellowed. "Is David a mystic too?"

A sweaty, bearded man cackled from the corner and Van Hubbel bowed to him. Pat was gesturing to the girl with straight blond hair on her right.

"Melissa has been pampering me," Pat said. "Mamma's night out. I'm finally twenty-one, you know. It took eons."

Jerry grinned at Melissa. She was one of Pat's prep school friends, now at the Museum School in Boston. At David and Pat's wedding he had danced with her most of the night, locking his pelvis with hers through tuxedo and chiffon. She now stuck her tongue out at him and winked.

"You don't really take LSD once a week, do you?" she said.

Jerry kept grinning, winked back without a word.

"Oh, do tell us all about it," Van Hubbel said, leaning across the table. "Do you really have technicolor visions of heaven and hell and Newark, New Jersey?"

From the corner of his eye Jerry saw Gabby wince.

"You only see what you're capable of seeing," Jerry said. He cocked his head toward Van Hubbel. *"You* might see Newark, Ralph."

A lovely laugh around the table for this. Van Hubbel mimed drawing a knife from his heart. Pat and Melissa swung their similar heart-shaped faces closer to Jerry, with Pat still hanging on his arm.

"Aren't you afraid at all, Jer? You know that you'll try it one too many times, like Russian roulette? I heard you can go into a trance or lose your mind."

"Only if you're lucky," Gabby piped. When Jerry smiled at her, she mouthed "Let's go." He turned his head back to Pat and Melissa.

"Look, the first thing you realize when you take acid is there's absolutely nothing to be afraid of," Jerry said, suddenly feeling zippier than he had in days. "You clear out all that garbage at Level One. Carry out all the old witches and goblins and leave them on the curb. The fear that you're going to pee in your pants. Fear you're going to lose control, lose track of who you are, where you come from. Panic because you can't remember your last thought. Terror because you've finally realized that your mind has a mind of its own."

Not a peep at the table. Jerry felt like the words were coming out of his mouth in calligraphy ready for the engraver.

"You get all those witches in your brain lined up," he went on, "and then—flippity-flop—they start doing cartwheels and yelling 'Halloween!' And the incredible joke turns out to be that everything you've ever feared is exactly the very best thing that could ever happen to you. Losing control is the same as freedom. Losing track of who you are is the only way you'll ever do something new. You look again and all those witches are clowns dancing the cosmic polka!"

Pat and Melissa cheered like children at a circus.

"But don't leave us there, dear boy," Van Hubbel crooned. "You must tell us about levels Two and Three and Four and Five."

"Level Two is paradise," Jerry said matter-of-factly. "And Level Three is that paradise's paradise. And on and on. And that is why, yes, I do take LSD once every week."

"Whoopee!" Melissa cheered.

Jerry knew right then, of course, that Melissa and Pat were going to take acid with him that night. Only a few minutes ago these two girls were terrified of LSD and now they were dying to take it. Presto-chango: Jerry Halligan, magician.

The telephone was ringing as they scrambled into Pat's apartment.

"Don't answer it," Melissa said. "You'll break the spell."

"What if it's David?" Pat looked around the room as if trying to remember where the phone was and the ringing stopped.

Jerry pulled his leather marble bag from his pocket, emptied it on the kitchen table. Coins and matches, a wad of foil. He unwrapped the cube of sugar, held it between thumb and forefinger for all to see. No sleight of hand here. A simple cube of sugar, my friends. Paradise in a grain of sucrose. Gabby prowled the cabinets, produced a goblet quick as a burglar, filled it with water, and flourished it in front of Jerry, who dropped in the cube. For a moment all four stared at it. The cube sent up bubbles like a deep-sea diver.

"I feel funny already," Pat whispered.

Jerry trilled the back of her hand with his fingers, poked at the cube with a fork and gave it a swirl.

"We aren't going to do it in here, are we?" Melissa asked, shaking back her hair and squinting at the fluorescent light.

Gabby patted her head as she flew by, Danish tapers in hand, Pat's Sunday-dinner best.

"Making an altar in the living room," she said. Set and setting, Tim always said. No magic without the props.

They filed into the living room, now a kid's rainy-day fantasy, a bazaar of soft pillows on the carpet, Indian bedspreads floating on floor lamps, a cluster of candles. Jerry gave Gabby a "perfect" sign, the instant set designer. She picked a stick of incense from the band of her cap, held it in the candle, then slipped it back in her cap. She flipped through Pat and David's records.

"Where's your Dylan?" she said.

Pat shrugged, flushing. "We never have time for music anymore."

"Put on some Bach," Jerry said, remembering David's collection. He handed the goblet to Melissa as if he were passing 7-Up to a tennis partner. Keep it casual.

"How much do I take?" she giggled.

"One swallow should do the trick for now," Jerry smiled. "You can always come back for seconds."

Melissa perched her pretty lips on the goblet's rim, hesitated, then took a tiny guppy gulp. She smiled, gulped again, held it out to Pat.

"Oh God, I keep thinking I shouldn't be doing this," Pat said, holding the glass to the light like a wine taster. She drew in her breath, closed her eyes and took a deep swallow. Opening her eyes, she said, "When does it start?"

"If ya gotta ask questions," Gabby said in mock jazz dialect, "it ain't started yet."

Now Gabby swished down the liquid and passed it to Jerry. He grinned, tipped the glass in his mouth, swirled the sweet water like mouthwash, and let most of it return to the goblet. Just a tad tonight. The guide works from memory.

Gabby hit the lights, dropped the needle on a Bach partita, and set her cap with the burning joss stick onto the spindle of a ladder-back chair. Then she crawled in a circle, removing everyone's shoes, and lay back on a pillow, her feet at the center of the rug with the others'.

"We're a windmill," she said.

Jerry smiled, touched Pat's toe with his.

"Just remember," he said softly, "all the witches are clowns."

Quiet hour as the sweetness descends. Bach's intricacies become simple, patterns on the windowpane. The ball of light slips down the spine, chugging by *chakras* like an express train, the history of Hinduism compressed to a minute. Breathing is a lost art rediscovered. Your heartbeat is your lover. There is no doubt: This is it.

Later Gabby rises in slow motion, raises her hand like a magic wand and lets it settle on the record rack. Without looking at the cover, she removes a disk and settles it on the turntable. And suddenly Jerry and Pat are laughing so hard their bodies jiggle on the floor like epileptics. It is Sinatra singing "Come Fly with Me," the household's Hoboken heritage. Fly, indeed. Melissa is dancing in the foyer with Gabby, Pierrot and Pierrette, now doing *tableaux vivants* in front of the mirror: "Love Spurned," "Jealous Rage," "Mercy."

The whine sounded like a violin at first, a Sinatra serenade. Only when Jerry propped himself up on his elbows and saw that Pat was gone did he recognize her cry. He followed it down the hall and stopped at a door. Pat was kneeling on the floor, her face pressed against the bars of the crib, tears splashing onto the sheet.

"My baby," she whimpered.

Tiptoeing up behind her, Jerry looked down and sucked in his breath. The crib was bare.

"He's with Thérèse," Melissa said from the door.

"Baby," Pat bawled. "Eency, tiny baby."

"Let it go. Whatever it is, let go," Jerry whispered, kneeling down beside her, draping his arms around her narrow shoulders, her back against his chest, shuddering, whimpering. "Poor baby," he crooned. "Poor little baby Patricia."

Shrinking in his arms, now turning, eyes closed, her head in the crook of his arm, she snuggled against his breast, her breath like hiccups. Jerry felt her drool soak through his shirt.

"Ummm, baby." Melissa got down on her knees too and faced him, one arm on Jerry's neck, the other under Pat's knees. A breast pressed against Jerry's ribs, nipple hard as rubber. "Baby needs her mommy."

Behind them the good pixie Gabby twirled in, swept a hand down Melissa's back and her dress parted. Another touch and her brassiere strap popped. It fell. Her breasts glistened, beautiful fruit, and now she cupped one to Patricia's mouth, "Ohh."

Pat closed her lips around Melissa's nipple, sucked so hard the areola disappeared inside her mouth, tears gone, gurgling. Her eyes fluttered, then dropped. Gabby was singing "Rockabye" in a minor key, came around and slithered her hands beneath Pat's bottom, "one, two, three," and they lifted her, put baby to bed.

Only then Jerry saw that Gabby was naked too, slim as a boy. Melissa kicked her dress from her ankles, slid down her slip, then her panties, her pubes covered with corn silk. They danced around him now, "Ring Around the Rosey." His shirt, his pants came off in their hands, flung over a Pooh Bear in the corner, and all three tumbled to the floor, rolled on the fuzzy-wuzzy nursery rug. Playmates.

Jerry took Melissa's nipple into his mouth, licked the wetness that Pat had left there, and now felt Gabby's mouth closed around his penis, her tongue fine as a paintbrush tracing the tip. He slid one hand to Melissa's thigh, looped the other under Gabby's ass. Dampness everywhere, hands, mouth, prick, slipping, sliding. Such sweetness. His fingers crawled inside them both, twirled, frosting from the side of the bowl. They rolled again, scrambled, rearranged like magnetic toys, and now Jerry was on his back, Melissa straddling his hips, Gabby over his mouth, and up and down they went, seesaw, Margery Daw.

Suddenly, through a peephole in the flesh, Jerry saw two hands wrapped around the crib bars, a nub of a nose poking out, Pat's eyes wide and glistening as she gazed back, all wonder and joy. And smiling at her, Jerry felt the trigger trip inside his groin and Melissa gasp and Gabby shudder.

Diggitty-diggitty, everyone happy.

At dawn Jerry led Gabby by the hand through the desolate streets of Cambridge, the first scents of spring floating on the cool air. As they crossed Massachusetts Avenue, a Harvard boy appeared pulling stacks of *Crimsons* into the Yard in a red wagon. Jerry twisted his neck, read the banner headline upside down:

"DR. LEARY DISMISSED BY UNIVERSITY."

Jerry grinned. "Graduation day," he murmured.

TWO

1964–1965

11

GREG decided to come to David and Pat's Christmas Eve party wearing sunglasses, carrying a tin cup, and with a sign around his neck that said "Failed Playwright." That way he could skip answering the usual round of party questions.

Better yet, maybe he'd skip the whole party altogether.

It was not that Greg truly thought of himself as a failure. After all, twenty-five was too young to be a failure of any real stature. But the prospect of standing around in a room full of eggnog and good cheer, constantly being reminded that two of his old Harvard buddies—David and Jerry—had already had their pictures in New York papers, did not seem like the right spiritual setup for a merry Christmas. David's picture had been in the *Times*, for crissake, and he'd only been in New York for six months.

Greg had been in New York for well over three years now and all he had managed to do was write 4,212 stunts.

Stunts. They invaded the nervous system, jangled the brain. The world was a vision of stunts: sex, murder, taking a shower—all stunts. Greg wrote thirty a day and he wrote nothing else.

STUNT: Push open the screen door. See if you can toss five beanbags through it before it closes. Two tries.
STUNT: The rim of this tennis racket is lined with pins. Using it, try to hit a balloon through the hoop without breaking it. Three tries.

"I'm stunted," he would say at the end of the day, walking to the elevator on his knees.

In fact, Greg loved his job every moment he was at Bobby Burger Productions, loved his wood-paneled office overflowing with Ping-Pong balls, goldfish bowls, wooden barrels, darts, Joe Palooka Sock'em dolls, rackets and paddles of all sizes, balloons and balls of all shapes. He loved his gofer, who would run out to Woolworth's or Herman's Sporting Goods at Greg's every inspiration. He loved the prop girl who wore no bra. He loved the fact that everyone in the office, from Bobby Burger himself on down, said that Greg Gregorian was the best all-around natural stunt writer since the legendary Bob Howard of "Beat the Clock." But the moment he would emerge on Fifth Avenue and cross the street for his bus home, Greg's stomach would knot into an anxious ball. "It's a stunt," he would think, as the light turned amber. "See if you can make it to the corner before the light turns red." And hanging on to a strap in the bus and reading over his neighbor's shoulder that a Buddhist monk in South Vietnam had doused himself with gasoline and set himself on fire, Greg would taste bile in his mouth. "It's a stunt," he would think.

Greg left his apartment on Christmas Eve, still undecided about going to David's party. Wisps of snow swirled like comet tails under the streetlamps, vanishing before they reached the sidewalk. Greg turned up the collar of his corduroy jacket and knotted his muffler. David had said that, with any luck, four of the original five would show up at the party—only Todd would be missing, ensconced in his Stanford room writing his thesis on existential ontology. Crossing Eighth Street, Greg headed for Washington Square. Todd was the only one he would really like to see tonight. He could think of nothing better than sitting with his old roommate at the back table of some cafeteria discussing Camus and banana peels through to Christmas morning.

A trio of college girls passed under the Washington Square Arch ahead of him. The one in the center wore her hair held back in a comb that peeped under her kerchief. "The Gift of the Magi," Greg thought. Three queens from the Orient. He followed behind them, abandoned to miracles.

They led him to the Village Vanguard, where he slouched undetected over to the table next to theirs, sank into a sawed-off chair, smacking his knees against the table—a stunt there somewhere. A heavyset boy with bangs was tuning his guitar on the spot-lit stool. He fixed his doleful eyes on the back wall and said, in the glottal cadences of Brooklyn, that he was dedicating his last song to the memory of John Kennedy. Seconds later he was twanging like a Texan the latest Dylan gospel, "The Times They Are A-Changin'," a truly depressing song if Greg had ever heard one. He stared at the girl with the comb in her hair. Her profile made him think of the girl on the Vermont Maid maple syrup bottle. He imagined her in a snowbound cabin ladling syrup onto his stack of flapjacks. She wore a bodice. The comb dangled at her shoulders. He would love her forever.

A new singer had emerged from the shadows, his cheeks a

patchwork of stubble, hyperthyroid eyes, ears like radar receivers. His name was Rob Orbe and he strummed for a while, saying that he had written a new song last week and that other than his cat, Spot, the assembled music lovers would be the first to hear it. "It's called 'The Ballad of Cal Monroe,' " he said.

"Who's Cal Monroe?" one of the girls whispered. Greg felt his heart jump. The gift of the magi: The only newspaper article he'd read in a month was about Cal Monroe and the only reason Greg had read it was because David Debilio's picture had been at the top of the column.

"It's that incitement to riot case," he whispered in the dark. "You know, can poetry be a lethal weapon? Actually, an old Harvard friend of mine was Cal's attorney." Greg slipped soundlessly to the fourth seat at the trio's table. "The funny coincidence is," he went on as Orbe vamped his introduction, "I'm supposed to meet them all tonight for a little Christmas Eve get together."

O joy! O Yuletide gladness!

Greg introduced the girls at David's door as the Sumac Sisters, a singing group he was grooming for stardom.

"Actually, they're triplets," he said to David, wagging his eyebrows as the girls giggled. "And they insist on doing absolutely everything together. I couldn't bring only one."

"We're really just roommates," the girl with the comb said, shaking David's hand. "At NYU."

"Don't worry," David said. "Greg's friends haven't believed anything he's said in years." He clapped Greg around the shoulders. "You don't change, do you, pal?"

Greg opened his eyes wide in mock innocence. "Are you supposed to?"

David led them all to the living room, where a dozen partyers turned their faces with the studied casualness of people expecting a celebrity.

"It's only the garbage man," Greg said to the room at large. "Just dropped by for my Christmas envelope."

"Oh, Greg," Pat piped, and everyone laughed. She came over and planted a kiss on each of his cheeks, something she had never done in Cambridge. She was wearing a bulky turtleneck sweater, a short plaid kilt held together with an oversized safety pin, and knee-length socks; in all, she looked more like a schoolgirl than before she'd been married. Her hand was resting on the arm of a bony-faced, professional-looking man.

"Greg is from David's old Leary group," she said to him. "Now he's a television writer. This is Lincoln Ames, David's boss."

"David's colleague," Ames amended, taking Greg's hand. "Might I have seen anything you've written, Greg?"

"I sincerely hope not."

At the mention that Greg was a television writer, Julie, the girl with the comb, laced her fingers around Greg's arm. Her roommates stood flat-footed behind her like ducklings. David handed them each a cup of eggnog and put his arm across Pat's shoulder. There was something endearingly paternal about the gesture, the pair standing happily in front of their Christmas tree. The two years David had on Greg showed more now than they had in college, not just in the bulk which had accrued to his neck and shoulders but in the easy, unthreatened way he carried himself. He looked alarmingly like an adult.

"You're the first," David was saying. "I imagine Jerry will be fashionably late."

"Aren't you dying to see Axel?" Pat smiled mischievously. "Not to mention the remarkable Mrs. Stenhorn. Apparently she made quite an impression on David and Lincoln." She jabbed David in the arm. "I don't know why I had to badger you to call them."

"He's just hard to reach," David said.

Greg had heard that Axel and his wife were now living in New York in a large West Side apartment, along with a group of other "movement" people.

"He wasn't going to come," Pat was saying. "Not until he heard that Cal—you know, Cal Monroe—was coming tonight. Then he wanted to know if he could bring some of his 'brothers' and 'sisters' along too. Can you imagine Axel Stenhorn talking like that?"

"The times they are a-changin'," Greg said.

A small, curly-haired boy had appeared directly in front of him. His complexion and hair were dark like David's, but the pale eyes and snub nose clearly came from the Beardsley side of the family. Greg stooped down.

"By George, I think I've just made a remarkable genetic discovery," Greg said. "If you mate an Italian with a WASP you get an Armenian. This boy looks exactly like my cousin Yaggie."

"What did you bring for the tree?" The boy stared at Greg without a trace of a smile.

Greg blinked back, feeling strangely intimidated, then stood up straight. He put an arm around Julie's wrist. "Why, I brought this angel," he said.

"Too big," the boy said, and everyone laughed. A Negro woman in a starched white uniform arrived from the kitchen and led the boy away.

"Thank you, Thérèse," Pat called. "Remember, Josh, visions of sugarplums."

The doorbell rang and David excused himself. Greg guided Julie to the eggnog bowl and refilled both their glasses.

"What nice people," she said.

Greg nodded, looking around the room at the other guests, most of them lawyers, he guessed. Suddenly all of them turned their heads toward the door.

Axel Stenhorn was standing next to the most dramatic-looking woman Greg had seen in years. Doe eyes, jet black hair cut short as a man's, a body out of an Italian movie. Both she and Axel were wearing outsized army-surplus jackets with some kind of insignia buttons pinned to the collars. On Axel, gaunter than ever, the effect was of a recently released prisoner of war. But on his woman the costume made Greg imagine a musical version of *Beau Geste.* Greg strode up to them.

"Hello, Axe. God, it's been a while."

"Hello, Gregory." Axel grasped him by the wrist, as if he were handcuffing him; only when he was released did Greg realize that it was one of the new comradely handshakes. Greg shrugged, grinning at the woman.

"I'm Greg Gregorian."

"Despina," she said. She looked deeply into his eyes for an instant, then quickly surveyed the room behind him. "I should have guessed they'd have a Christmas tree."

"They have a little boy," Greg said.

Despina made a circling gesture with her hand that took in the entire handsomely furnished apartment. "Do you suppose they tell him that Santa gave them all of this for being good?"

Greg laughed. "It's not fair, is it?" he said, feeling only moderately disloyal. "I mean, it's the starving playwright who's supposed

to marry the girl with the trust fund, not the up-and-coming lawyer, right?"

"You aren't starving," Axel said flatly.

Despina abruptly started across the room. Only then did Greg
notice that there were three others in their group: a Negro boy of
no more than eighteen and two Semitic-looking girls, both with
acne. All three wore sweatshirts and dungarees. The troops.

"Well." Greg scratched industriously at his ear. "I certainly hear
you've packed a lot in since we left dear old 'Hahvahd.' "

"There's a lot to do," Axel answered.

Greg studied Axel's eyes behind his oval, clear-framed glasses,
trying to determine whether it was purposefulness or disappointment he saw there. At that moment he wished he could make Axel
laugh, shake loose one of those impetuous eruptions that used to
infect them all around the dinner table in Dunster House.

"You'll never guess what I ended up doing for a living, Axe," he
said, crinkling up his eyes. "I write stunts."

"Stunts?"

"Yes, you know, like 'Beat the Clock,' except my show's called
'Time Bomb.' I sit behind a mahogany desk all day dreaming up
new ways for Mrs. Farkus from Dubuque to get balloons into a
garbage can before the 'bomb' goes off and she forfeits her chance
to win a brand new Kelvinator refrigerator. I find my Harvard
background in post-Kantian idealism helps immeasurably."

Axel had wrinkled his forehead in a look of disdain; there was
definitely no laugh on the way.

"It's just to keep me afloat, of course," Greg went on quickly,
wishing to hell he had never brought the subject up. "You know, so
I can work on my plays free of financial pressure. That way I won't
be tempted to write some trashy commercial thing just to—"

"Isn't it all the same, Greg?" Axel said.

Just then Julie slipped up beside Greg and he latched onto her
waist like a man falling.

"Say, speaking of career plans, Axel," Greg said, deliberately
raising his voice, "what ever happened to your plan to go to medical school?"

Axel's eyes fastened on Greg's and the color rose in his cheeks.
He seemed about to say something when the boy behind him
tugged at his sleeve. Coming down the hall arm in arm with David

was Cal Monroe, the two of them looking much as they had on page sixteen of the previous Tuesday's New York *Times*.

"My man," the tall Negro was saying as he breezed into the living room. Every head turned to look at him. He had a broad, muscular face with glinting, confident eyes. He looked powerful and he looked thoroughly sexual. He clapped the young Negro boy on the back, peered for an instant at the button on Axel's lapel, then took in the room in a single, sweeping glance. "Hey, Merry Christmas one and all."

Before David and Monroe could reach the eggnog bowl, the entire party closed in around them like the defensive line after the man with the ball. Beside Greg and Julie, only two young lawyers lingered outside the circle. Greg guessed that neither of them had yet had his picture in the *Times*.

"How about a refill while the coast is clear?" Greg said. He planted a kiss on Julie's cheek as if they had been married for years.

"God, this is all so fantastic," she said. "And I thought I was just going out for a little drink with my friends."

Sucking down his third cup of the sticky-sweet eggnog, Greg looked again at Julie's profile, her soft, downy pink cheeks, the comb at the back of her head, but he could not quite recapture the vision of being snowbound in Vermont with her. He peered at the group surrounding Cal Monroe.

"So, my man here has this ofay pig on the stand," Monroe was saying, rapping David on the shoulder with his knuckles. "And he says to him, 'Officer Pig, suh, I would like to pursue your distinction between a legitimate poetry reading and foul, inflammatory rabble-rousing!"

He paused and everyone laughed. It struck Greg that there was more than a hint of parody in Monroe's delivery when he quoted David, but it obviously didn't offend David. Monroe extended his long-fingered hands in front of him, waiting for the laughter to end. He had been arrested in Bryant Park for springing onto a park bench and declaiming a poem to the secretaries and students who were eating sandwiches out of paper bags. The poem was entitled "White Meat on Black Bread," and when he came to the stanza that went "Going to stop begging on fuckin' Whitey's street. Going to spread my bread with his pure white meat," two park patrolmen had pulled him off the bench, wrestled him to the ground and handcuffed him. He had been charged with public profanity and inciting a riot.

"So then Davey points a finger in this fat man's face," Monroe went on, "And he says, 'Now, if Mr. Monroe had been reciting a Shakespeare sonnet for the people's edification, would you have had cause to stop him?' And the pig shakes his wobbly cheeks and says, 'No, sir. But that was no Shakespeare this man was reciting.'" And Davey says, 'How about if he was reading from the great American poet Robert Frost?' And the pig says, 'No. That'd been okay.' And Davey says, 'Good. I can see you are a man with a fine ear for poetry.' "

There was another burst of laughter, this time led by a high-pitched, musical voice that Greg was surprised to see belonged to Despina. At that moment she looked more like a gamin than a revolutionary.

"And so now my man pushes his fine Roman nose right in the pig's face and says, 'Tell me, Officer Rutledge, sir, would you have had any objection to my client reading from the works of that famous American e.e. cummings?' And the officer scratched his head and looked over at the judge, and finally he says, 'No, no objection to that.' And so Davey whips out his book and starts reading,

> 'i sing of Olaf glad and big
> whose warmest heart recoiled at war:
> a conscientious object-or.' "

Monroe continued, declaiming line after line of the poem with spellbinding intensity, but as he approached the end of the first stanza he faltered. Barely missing a beat, he thumped David's shoulders and said, "You take it, man. It was your moment, your show."

"Just a second. I've got the book right over there."

David took one step toward the bookshelf when, abruptly, a trembling voice rose from the group, continuing from where Monroe had left off:

> "Olaf (being to all intents
> a corpse and wanting any rag
> upon what God unto him gave)

responds, without getting annoyed
'I will not kiss your f.ing flag.' "

The voice was Axel Stenhorn's. For a moment no one spoke. Then Monroe reached out and clapped Axel on the back and said, "Bravo, my man. I can see you have a fine ear for poetry."

This time the laughter was so loud that only Greg, at the edge of the circle, heard the doorbell ringing. He slipped down the hallway and opened the door.

"Gregorio!"

Jerry Halligan wrapped both arms around Greg, nearly lifting him off his feet, then held him at arm's length and beamed at him with his crystal blue eyes.

"You look beautiful, my friend," he said. "Hasn't anyone informed your cells about aging? Or do you hibernate in a freezer somewhere, waiting for your divine historical moment to thaw?"

"Well, if you must know the truth, I've got a portrait stashed away in my attic that looks like pure hell."

Both men laughed uproariously. What a pleasure to see the incredible Jerry Halligan again. Jerry stepped inside and, with a bow and a flourish, ushered in a line of young women who appeared to be in costume for a trapeze act. Everyone was traveling with an entourage tonight. Four, Greg counted. One more than he'd brought.

"Ladies," Jerry said. "Meet Gregorio the Great, the clown prince of television. A genius, the real McCoy."

A wide, giddy grin stretched Greg's face as Jerry's four ladies reeled around them like mute Graces.

"How'd you know I worked for T.V.?"

"I tapped your brain waves," Jerry laughed. "I've got a friend who's an operator on the cosmic switchboard." He leaned his head toward Greg's and said confidentially, "We really must talk about television, Gregor. Tim says it's a fantastic shortcut, could save us decades. And it's good to have a member of the family on the inside learning the game." He winked. "Tim sends you his love, by the way."

Greg had not stopped smiling. He hadn't the foggiest idea what Jerry was talking about and he was positive that Timothy Leary would not remember him if he were standing in front of him right now, but there was no denying the fact that just being with Jerry

Halligan for two minutes had made him feel inordinately happy.
For the first time that evening he was glad he had come to David's
party.

Jerry stood at the edge of the living room, surveying the party,
unseen, before he entered. He was more attractive than ever, all
the softness of puberty erased, his face leaner, more angular. He
wore his sandy blond hair pageboy length and held it back from his
face with a beaded headband. Both he and Leary had been wearing headbands in the *Village Voice* photo of them lounging on a
terrace somewhere in Mexico, summer headquarters for Leary's
International Foundation for Internal Freedom. Jerry had been
identified as the foundation's director of communications, whatever that might be.

"Axel!"

Jerry swooped toward Axel with his arms spread wide and enveloped him in a bear hug that almost knocked him off his feet. A
flinch shot through Axel's face—he looked like a man under attack
—and Greg cringed, afraid something awful was about to happen.

"Brother Axel." Jerry patted Axel's back. "God, I've missed you,
friend."

The party had opened into a half-circle around them and, standing in the hallway, only Greg could see Axel's face as it suddenly
softened. A moment later Jerry released him, turned to David and
hugged him too, rocking back and forth, saying nothing. Greg
watched Axel slip away to the window, his thin shoulders hunched
forward.

"Who is *that?*" Julie had sidled up to Greg and was staring at
Jerry in utter awe.

"I don't know," Greg murmured. "But he left this silver bullet."

David was now introducing Jerry to Lincoln Ames and Cal
Monroe. Greg noticed that Jerry went easily from a conventional
handshake with Ames to the tricky wrist thing with Monroe; Leary
could certainly find no better director of communications than
Jerry Halligan. Someone dropped a Nat King Cole album onto the
turntable and the four girls from Jerry's entourage joined hands
and danced around the Christmas tree to "The Bells of St. Mary's."
The tallest of them, an aristocratic-looking blonde named Melissa,
reached out and grabbed Pat by the hand, bringing her into the
circle. Pat blushed. She looked like a little girl abducted by elves.

Greg wandered alone to the eggnog table, feeling rather

Christmasy. He raised his cup in a toast to David. "Merry Christmas," he said.

"To you too, Greg." David turned his head. "Well, hail, hail, the gang's all here."

Jerry was leading Axel by the arm toward them.

"I didn't know where you were," Jerry was saying. "I guess I assumed you were still in Africa. But the second I heard the man say, 'The President has been shot,' I thought of you. Tried to make mental contact with you. I kept seeing that picture of you and Kennedy shaking hands with that mysterious blurry specter between you. Did you ever notice that, Axe? It was like that part of the photo was half developed." Jerry picked a cherry off the fruitcake. "It was like a photographic premonition."

Axel shrugged. "Actually, I was in Mississippi," he said.

"Todd called me in the middle of the night," Greg said. "He said he'd been trying to get through for hours. Remember how all the lines were jammed, everyone checking in with everybody, as if they half-expected you'd been shot too? And you know the first thing Todd said? He said, 'Huxley is dead.' Aldous Huxley had died on that same day, but that fact was lost in all the other news, of course."

Jerry looked intently into Greg's eyes. "Todd knows," he said with a kind of "Twilight Zone" tremor in his voice.

Greg could not stifle his giggle. He'd have to remember to tell Todd that he *knew*. He was sure he'd be much relieved.

"The thing that gets to me," David said seriously, "is the way everything just keeps going. I mean, I've gotten thoroughly used to Johnson and Lady Bird and all of them. I cried for three days and then everything just kept on going."

"Yes, I know," Axel said softly. For the first time that evening it sounded like his own voice.

Greg raised his cup. "To keeping on going," he said.

"God, I wish I had a flash camera," David said. "This moment should be preserved."

Almost as soon as he said that, the shortest of Jerry's young ladies twirled away from the others, her opera cape flaring, and she began to pantomime setting up a box portrait camera in front of them. She was an exquisite mime, with a precise, Chaplinesque style. She stooped and flipped her cape over her head, pretending to examine the four young men through the lens. She motioned to

Greg and Dave to stand shoulder to shoulder, then to Jerry and Axel to drop to one knee. With surprisingly little hesitation Axel obeyed.

"You're a wonder, Gabby," Jerry said.

She raised one hand, signaling for them to hold still, then held out the other, waiting to snap the shutter. It was just at that moment that Axel jumped up.

"Where are you going?" Axel's voice cracked.

Greg looked over at the hallway door. Cal Monroe was passing through it, his hand squarely on Despina Stenhorn's back. Neither of them turned, and a second later the apartment door opened and closed. Jerry was immediately on his feet behind Axel, gripping him firmly by both shoulders.

"Let it happen. Let it happen," he repeated soothingly in Axel's ear. "It's not happening to you, my friend. Not to *you.*"

Axel pulled himself away.

"What are you talking about?" he said sharply. "The only reason we came here was to make contact with Monroe."

Someone merciful turned over the Nat King Cole record and dropped the needle on "O Little Town of Bethlehem." Greg searched the room to make sure Julie was still there. He saw Axel already leading his three young cohorts toward the door. Obviously he was not planning to say good-bye to anyone.

"I wish I could take him back to Millbrook with us," Jerry said as the door closed. "He's got a lot of bad karma to get through."

Greg could not help thinking of Axel's performance that night in Newton. He was pretty sure that Leary's colony in Millbrook was not where Axel belonged.

"This has been truly fantastic, everyone," Jerry was saying. "But Tim's waiting for me uptown."

The party was over.

In the elevator Greg and Jerry smiled at one another from the corners, seven women between them, and on the street they embraced again. Jerry had said a last farewell, when he abruptly called to Greg to wait. He dug into his pockets.

"I almost forgot," he said, handing two tiny gift-wrapped squares to Greg. "I brought everyone Christmas presents. You take Todd's."

Greg knew from the touch that they were magic sugar cubes.

"Merry Christmas," Jerry said.

12

TODD BREWSTER hung up the phone and immediately started chuckling all over again. No one made him laugh the way Greg did —certainly not Søren Kierkegaard or Jean-Paul Sartre. God, he wished he had been at that party tonight instead of spending Christmas Eve rereading "Fear and Trembling." But, then again, maybe hearing Greg's inimitable version of the party was better than actually being there.

Sure. And maybe studying philosophy was better than actually living.

Todd picked his watch off his desk. Almost midnight. He sat on the edge of his bed and kicked off his shoes, then slid out of his pants—his "Kansas gabardines," as Greg used to call them, "convenient for traveling because they double as a mirror." He grinned. Jesus, he missed having Greg around. In college he'd been his anchor, his reality principle. "The trouble with Harvard," Greg was always saying, "is that it makes you think your life is something you can figure out before it happens."

At his closet Todd removed his pajamas—extra-extra longs sent by his mother from Tall Tim's in Emporia—and pulled them on. Is that what he was doing in graduate school—trying to figure out his life? No, not in the sense Greg meant. He didn't look to Hegel for career counseling or to Kierkegaard for tips on his social life. What he did with his life—the details of what and where—did not really matter if they weren't connected to some larger meaning. But what made him think he would find that larger meaning reading books in a too small room in Palo Alto, California?

Todd lay on top of his bedcovers and stared absently at the overhead light. Twice before, lying here like this, he had had flashes vivid as dreams of that night in Newton, the extraordinary sensation he had felt just behind his eyes. The sensation had seized him very late into that night, after he had left the others in Dr.

Leary's living room and wandered into the kitchen. For no reason he could remember he had opened a cabinet door and gazed inside at the box of pearled barley, the container of Morton's salt, the vanilla extract, the Parmesan cheese, and then, like a flash of light from inside his skull, the feeling had come and, seconds later, the tears had burst from his eyes and rolled down his cheeks. God knows how long it would have gone on or how the feeling would have changed if Axel's scream had not snapped Todd out of it. Later, over breakfast, Jerry had asked him about his experience and Todd had told him about the episode in the kitchen. He had said, "It just suddenly dawned on me that everything—salt, cheese, head, heart—were just exactly what they were, nothing more, nothing less. And that realization was such a fantastic relief. It made me feel holy." Jerry had taken it all down on his pad, nodding sagely—he had done a great deal of sage nodding that morning—as if it all made perfect sense to him. But other than those two flashes Todd had had since, the meaning of the experience completely escaped him.

He switched off the light and got under the covers. "Todd *knows*," Jerry had told Greg at the Christmas party. Todd smiled in the dark. He imagined the two gift-wrapped doses of LSD sitting in Greg's refrigerator in New York. Greg had promised to save them until they got together. Visions of sugar cubes.

13

WHEN DAVID and Pat finally slipped into bed that Christmas Eve, Pat rested her perfect oval head on David's shoulder and said, "We're so lucky. Everyone else seems to be at such loose ends. I feel like we're everybody's parents."

David kissed the top of her head contentedly. He had never imagined that life could be as good as it had been since they moved to New York. Certainly there had never been a better time to be practicing civil liberties law, nor a better lawyer to be practicing it with than Lincoln Ames. And if movement lawyering paid considerably less than the jobs he had been offered on Wall Street, the monthly checks they received from his father-in-law's Boston bank more than compensated for the difference. The whole family reveled in their spacious Bleeker Street apartment after their cramped Cambridge quarters. Pat was pleased to be back in school again; she had settled on a fine arts major, thinking that she might eventually go into gallery work. She certainly was not going to make a full-time career of mothering; none of the Beardsley women did. And after a shy start, Joshua was blooming at the Bank Street School progressive nursery. Even Thérèse, on what Pat called "lend-lease" from her parents, seemed to find life in Greenwich Village a cheerful improvement over staid Boston. In the late evenings, working at opposite ends of the dining room table—David preparing briefs, Pat studying color reproductions of Renaissance and Flemish paintings—David would raise his head, smiling, and say, "Are you absolutely sure we deserve this?"

"No one deserves it more," Pat would answer, blowing him a kiss.

In the spring that followed, David was called away more and more frequently to bail out demonstrators who had chained themselves to construction sites or lain down on expressways. The dingy labyrinths of the "Tombs," where the demonstrators usually were jailed while awaiting bail, became a familiar haunt, like some subterranean café where he could always count on running into other young movement lawyers or their counterparts from the district attorney's office. More often than not, the name of the prisoner who called him there was unknown to David, some sullen-faced kid with stringy hair who only became animated when he recounted his tale of police brutality. David never doubted these kids' sincerity—and certainly not their cause—but there was a smug masochism in many that irritated him; their "passive resistance" seemed like a natural outgrowth of inert, coddled childhoods. When he asked them where they had gotten his name, they invariably responded without enthusiasm, "You're on the list." They meant the mimeographed register of movement lawyers which circulated at rallies and demonstrations. David Debilio was at the top of that list.

When a cadre of radical CORE people lay across the Triboro Bridge between barricades of overflowing garbage cans, David set off for the "Tombs" even before the arrests were made. An hour later they were herded in, screaming "Pig!" to everyone in sight and giving off the collective odor of day-old garbage. It was a long evening of bargaining. The D.A.'s office had obviously been instructed to get tough on this one: Snarling commuter traffic on a bridge was far more unpopular than chaining bodies to cement mixers. David finally left at nine, taking a cab to Sheridan Square, then walking on to Bleeker. It was cool, a New York night without a hint of any season. He was hungry and tired and glad to be going home.

At first he did not recognize the spicy, acrid smell that floated up the hallway toward him as he let himself in the apartment. He followed it past the living room to the kitchen, where Pat, her friend Melissa, and a pock-faced boy were eating English muffins spread with peanut butter. A hand-rolled cigarette the size of a small cigar smoldered in the ashtray—the origin of the smell. David clenched his teeth.

"Hooray, you're home." Pat smiled happily up at him, not moving from her chair. "I was afraid something horrible had happened to you."

"Like what?" David walked to the window and quickly surveyed the brownstone behind theirs before pulling the curtain shut.

"Oh, I don't know." Pat grinned at Melissa. "You know, like somebody locked you up by mistake, way back in some cell that nobody ever goes to."

The boy giggled. "Yeh, and like ten years later somebody finds you and you've been living on rats and cockroaches and you can't even remember your name and all you keep saying is, 'I'm innocent. I swear, I wasn't even in the country at the time.' "

Both young women laughed uproariously, smacking the kitchen table with their open palms.

"Where's Josh?" David stood in front of the refrigerator. He still had not removed his jacket.

"Sleeping. Thérèse put him to bed ages ago."

"And where's Thérèse?"

"I don't know. Watching 'I Spy,' probably." Pat tilted her head, folding her hands under her chin like an angel. "Hey, honey. It's just me, remember?"

David opened the refrigerator door and started to reach for a beer but desisted, thinking it might be inappropriate for what he had to say. He removed a slab of meat loaf, ketchup, and a Coke and sat down at the table. He took a few bites, then managed a smile at Melissa.

"That feels better," he said. "The beast was ravenous."

Melissa smiled back, focusing somewhere above his eyebrows. She had grown progressively thinner since she had dropped out of art school in Boston and come to New York. The hollows beneath her high cheekbones bordered on the ghastly, although Pat once said that everyone thought she was a fashion model.

"Look, Melissa, I know this is going to sound like I'm some kind of old fart or something. And I'm sure Pat was too embarrassed to mention it. But the fact remains, I'm in a somewhat touchy position with the work I do. And there are certain risks I can't take, much as I'd like to."

"Hey, that's cool," Melissa said. She took the Coke bottle from his hand and drank.

David shrugged gratefully. "If I couldn't name half a dozen people in the D.A.'s office who would like nothing better than making a bust in David Debilio's apartment, I'd be smoking marijuana every night myself."

Melissa patted David's arm and stood. "No you wouldn't, David," she said.

The boy picked the cigarette out of the ashtray, pinched the end, and fitted it into a pack of Newports. Standing, he was half a head shorter than Melissa.

"Listen, I didn't mean you weren't welcome to stay," David said.

"You're really too too kind," the boy replied in a mock British accent. Pat and Melissa followed the boy down the hallway, giggling all the way.

David took a couple more bites of meat loaf, but he was no longer hungry. He listened for a moment as Pat and her friends whispered at the door, then wandered to the bedroom feeling much guiltier than he wanted to. He stripped down to his shorts, turned on the news, and lay back on the bed.

The Triboro Bridge incident had not made the national news,

but it was the lead item on the local edition. David bolstered himself up on his elbows. By God, there was Despina Stenhorn being interviewed by Gabe Pressman.

"We aren't trying to punish anyone," she was saying very pleasantly. Her hair was longer and wavier than it had been at Christmas. She looked like an actress promoting some product. "It's simply that people do not pay any attention to injustice unless you do something like this that makes them stop and think."

David had barely noticed that Pat had returned, passing in front of the bed on her way to the closet. She snuggled up to him, her breasts pressing against his ribs. "Hi," she said. "Waiting for me?"

David could still smell the odor of marijuana on her breath. She smelled like ashes. The urge to apologize had long since passed. The local news moved on to a meat-packers' scandal. He switched the television off, then the light.

"I have to be in court at nine," he said.

His first reaction when he felt her lips on his belly was to gently push her head away, as if she were a rascally puppy lapping at him, but she swung back over him, her hair sweeping against his ribs.

"Relax, honey," she whispered.

"I *was* relaxing," he said, forcing a little laugh. "In fact I was so relaxed I was almost asleep."

"Come on. I promise this won't hurt."

Her head lowered. He felt her tongue circle the rim of his navel, then dip inside. It felt strangely electric, as if he were being probed by light. David closed his eyes. Pat was crawling to the foot of the bed, her tongue slithering down the line of hair that led to his groin. He felt her nipples brush the tops of his thighs. His penis pulsed, began to rise. Pat's fingers slid under the waistband of his undershorts, now tugged at them. She tapped his buttocks, a signal to lift so she could pull off his shorts. It was just enough to make him aware of the question he had been holding back.

"Are you still high, Pat?"

"I don't know. Maybe a little. Why?"

"Well, this *is* kind of a new procedure for us, wouldn't you say?"

"It could be," Pat laughed softly, "if you'd only shut up."

She tugged again at his shorts and this time David arched his back and pulled them off himself. There was still something in him that protested, that felt this was not purely Pat who was making love to him, but as her mouth slipped over his penis, her tongue flicking the tip, the idea no longer bothered him.

What did bother David those next few weeks was the way Pat would laugh like a giddy teenager at the slightest provocation—a man in the street with odd-shaped ears, a puerile joke in a television ad. One evening, when she met him at his office for dinner, she burst into one of her laughing fits while David was still on the phone.

"What was so funny?" David asked the moment he hung up.

"Oh, just the way you scrunched up your face like you were getting shock therapy or something. You always make that face when you're talking to another attorney." Pat started to laugh again, a breathless gurgle that brought color to her cheeks.

David sat down heavily on the corner of his desk and sighed. "Tell me something, Pat," he said quietly. "Have you by any chance been smoking marijuana today?"

A slow, Cheshire cat grin spread across Pat's face. "Can't you tell, David?" She did a little pirouette in front of him, her miniskirt flaring just enough to reveal the scoops of her panties. "Do I seem like a person who's been smoking marijuana?"

"Just answer my question, okay?"

"So you can't tell!" Pat laughed gaily as she walked to the window and looked down on Madison Avenue. "You know your problem, David? Stuck up here, you don't really know what's happening, do you?" She turned back and looked at him seriously. "Do you know what Leary said on the radio? He said twenty years from now all the world's leaders will be higher than kites."

It was only a few weeks later that Pat announced at breakfast that she had decided to drop out of NYU.

"It just all seems so irrelevant," she said. "Tintoretto and Botticelli. It's just all so orderly and cramped."

"But what are you going to do, Pat?"

"I don't know. I got the New School catalog yesterday. There are about a zillion courses there I could really connect with."

She did not register at the New School, however, and after reminding her about it a few times David let it drop.

"Just let her be," was Lincoln's advice. "Patricia missed so much of simply being young and irresponsible, getting married when she did. She was always planning that trek through Europe, you know, and now she's got you and Joshua. But if she's anything like her mother, she won't be idle for long."

It was hard to say whether Pat was idle or not. She frequently breezed home in the evening minutes after David, one day sporting a new pair of white patent leather boots, the next day with her hair freshly clipped short like Peter Pan. She would say that she had been doing galleries all day, or that she had spent the entire afternoon in the Figaro Café talking with some people who had just come back from Afghanistan. Always she seemed breathless and, undeniably, always she seemed quite happy.

The fact was, David's mind was entirely occupied with the *Tribune* case these days anyhow. He had been intoxicated with it from the moment Lincoln outlined it to him. The previous summer the *Tribune* had run an editorial calling the police force of Athens, Georgia, "brutal bigots" for the way they had knocked heads at a civil rights demonstration. The Athens commissioner of police had retaliated with a suit for a million dollars in damages to his "good name," and when the case was tried before an all-white Athens jury, he was awarded every penny of it. The *Tribune* had appealed the decision through every Georgia court, without success, spending well over a million in legal expenses already, but they were determined to carry their challenge to the Supreme Court.

"My God, it's so pure, so fundamental," David said, slapping his fist against his palm as he paced around Lincoln's desk. "If any paper can be blackmailed into holding back their editorial opinions on something like this, we can just toss the First Amendment right out the window. End of freedom of the press. Forget it."

"Every case is fundamental," Lincoln said with a half-smile. "And I personally have seen the First Amendment tossed out the window a good hundred times over the past thirty years."

From the start David and Lincoln knew they would have to challenge the right of any public official to sue a responsible newspaper for libel; they would have to prove that public officials were a category apart from the rest of the population. David devoted every waking hour to preparing their brief. When he was not holed up in the Columbia Law School library reading libel cases back to Blackstone, he was picking every law professor and social thinker's brain from Cambridge to Atlanta. In Atlanta David met with his old client, Cal Monroe, now a prominent member of the

new SNCC hierarchy. Cal seemed both angrier and more frightened these days. He did not want to be seen with David in a
"colored" restaurant, so they had sandwiches across Monroe's
desk.

"Can you imagine a black man winning a libel suit against some
whitey newspaperman because the paper called him a lazy nig-
ger?" Monroe flashed his well-photographed haughty grin. "A
white jury would laugh him out of court. To use the word 'lazy' to
describe a black man is a redundancy for them. Just like the words
'bigot,' 'brutal' and 'asshole' seem to connect themselves kind of
naturally to the word 'whitey' the way we see it."

David laughed. "If you don't mind, I don't think I'll quote you
on that in the Supreme Court."

As he was about to leave, David asked Monroe if he had had any
contact with Axel or Despina since the Christmas party. Monroe
raised both hands and rolled his eyes, parodying a small boy who
has been caught stealing.

"I swear, officer, dat woman done tol' me she had a black
mamma and I done believed her. I wouldn't a touched her if I
done known she was white."

"I meant, do you know what happened to them after SNCC
decided to exclude whites?" David said sharply. He did not feel
like being part of Monroe's little man-to-man joke.

Monroe shot David a look of pure contempt. He had obviously
taken David's reaction to mean that David was just another white
man who could not stomach the idea of a black man messing
around with white women.

"Yes, I know what happened to them," Monroe said with undis-
guised relish. "They were right up in the front row at that historic
meeting. And once Miss Despina got the message, she started
bawling so hard that her hubby practically had to carry her out of
the hall."

"That's too bad," David said, looking Monroe straight in the eye.
"They gave you two good years of their lives."

On the flight home David found himself thinking about something other than the *Tribune* case for the first time in weeks. He
kept picturing Despina Stenhorn's face as it must have looked
when she burst into tears. Poor woman. Poor, beautiful woman.

David and Lincoln took an afternoon train down to Washington,
D.C., the day before the case was to be heard. They stayed in a

large suite at the Dupont Plaza Hotel and ate a steak dinner in their room. "The night before the fight," Lincoln called it. Late in the evening the older man ordered up a bottle of champagne. He toasted David. "I think you ought to know, David, that the most telling arguments in our brief came out of your work."

"Thank you."

They clinked glasses and drank. They finished the entire bottle before they retired.

The hearing began promptly at ten the next morning. Walking up the steps of the Supreme Court building at Lincoln Ames's side, David saw a group of young men and women with longish hair peering up at them from the sidewalk—law students on a holiday, he guessed. He imagined how he and Lincoln must look to them— the tall, bushy-browed patrician and his muscular, dark colleague striding toward the portals of the highest court in the land. One of the young men raised his hand, extending two fingers in a victory sign, and David nodded back before following Lincoln through the doors.

The next two hours moved by with the erratic distortion of a hallucination: Single questions hung in the air for what seemed like days; the clock on the balcony wall spun like a windmill. The courtroom was packed, the gallery a Who's Who of civil liberties lawyers. The nine justices in their black robes, sitting in a row on the high bench, looked surreal, elongated figures from an El Greco vision; but from the moment Judge Warren called the session to order in his earthy, California voice, a sense of fundamental reality prevailed. This was the world of civilized men. Here the power of thought and word were all. It was the very essence of why David had chosen to devote himself to law.

One at a time, the lawyers made their presentations, summarizing their briefs, narrowing the issues to the moral fundaments of either/or. Lincoln rose and spoke fluently for twenty of their allotted thirty minutes. He made sweeping gestures with his arms to emphasize each point, like a New England minister delivering a sermon. Finally it was David's turn to speak. He stood, drew in his breath and opened his mouth. For one nightmarish moment no words came, but once the first word was out, the others followed easily and it seemed that before he drew his breath again his ten minutes had passed. Justice Harlan signaled him to remain standing.

"Tell me, Mr. Debilio," the judge said, "are you not worried at all by the good man whose good name is impugned by an unrestrained press? Is he to have no redress at all?"

"If that good man has chosen a life of public service, of existing daily in the public eye, he can keep his good name by his actions," David answered, looking directly into the judge's eyes. "But if he keeps his good name by intimidating the press, his actions will be accountable to no one."

"Thank you, Mr. Debilio." There was the slightest hint of a smile on the older man's face. "We are pleased to welcome you to the court."

The session ended exactly at noon. There was a long luncheon given by the Civil Liberties Union back at the hotel, but David could barely eat or speak. On the train, when he took off his jacket for the first time since the hearing, he saw that his shirt was streaked with gray stains; he had sweated all the way through his suit.

"And now the hard part begins," Lincoln said, settling back for a nap. "Now we wait for the decision."

David let himself into his apartment at a few minutes past ten. The lights were out, so he dropped his overnight bag in the hallway and tiptoed to the bedroom. The bed was made, empty. He wandered through the apartment turning on lights as he went, growing more and more uneasy. He was about to open the door to Joshua's room when Thérèse stepped out of hers. She was tying the sash of her robe. Her hair was covered with a net.

"You'll wake him," she said softly. "He wakes up so easy, that boy."

"Really?"

The black woman nodded.

"Where's Pat?" David said.

"They all went out this afternoon." Thérèse lowered her eyes. "She didn't say when she'd be coming back."

"Who went out? Who was she with?"

Thérèse put a finger to her lips, signaling for David to lower his voice. "I don't know those people, Mr. Debilio," she said quietly. "They're always different."

David felt his face blanch. He was suddenly aware of how tired he felt. A cold shiver shrugged his shoulders.

"I'll make you a cup of tea," Thérèse was saying.

David followed her numbly into the kitchen and sat down. He watched her methodically go through the steps of making a pot of tea. For one peaceful moment the thin black woman reminded him of his mother in her kitchen in Hoboken; like his mother, Thérèse sighed as she set his cup in front of him. David motioned for her to sit across from him. Thérèse sat down tentatively on the edge of her chair.

"How's Josh been?" David said.

"He's fine. He's a smart boy."

David nodded, then sipped his tea. Neither of them spoke.

"I talked with Mrs. Debilio's folks," Thérèse said at last. "They said it would be all right if I went back to them. Course, I won't go until you find someone else to care for Joshua."

David stared at her. "What are you talking about?"

"I'd like to go back to Boston, Mr. Debilio."

"Whatever for?"

Thérèse looked down at her hands. "I'm just more comfortable with the way they live," she said quietly.

David abruptly stood, his legs smacking against the table, spilling his tea.

"You have no idea how we live," he said loudly, his heart thudding in his chest. "Don't *you* judge us. Not you!"

He strode into his bedroom and fell onto the bed. His whole body was shaking. He slept in his clothes.

The *Tribune* decision came four weeks later, first in a telegram from the chief deputy of the Supreme Court, the next day in a letter that contained the opinion written by the chief justice. They had won, and the decision was unanimous. For the second time since he had arrived in New York David Debilio's picture appeared in the *Times.*

14

"ORBE," the young man on the telephone shouted, "as in eyeball. Actually, you've laid eyes on me, but that momentous occasion has probably slipped your mind. But I know all about you. I was on to you back when you defended Cal Monroe. Fantastic defense. Real school yard dago trickery. Did I say dago? I meant Day-Glo. I wrote a song about it, 'The Ballad of Cal Monroe—' "

"What can I do for you, Mr. Orbe?" David had to raise his voice to cut him off. The boy had been going at full tilt for close to a minute; he spoke without the slightest regard for vocal punctuation.

"I want you to be my lawyer."

"I understand that, but what for?"

"I'm going to be busted tonight at the Village Gate for putting naughty words to music."

David committed himself to attending Orbe's performance, nothing more, and he only agreed to do that to make Pat happy. She had called from a pay phone in some café, all aflutter with how fabulous this friend of Melissa's was, how "in," and how he personally was pushing freedom of speech to its absolute limits. If nothing else, David was gratified to see that Pat was still in touch with what he did for a living—she even said something about "expanding the First Amendment"—but he had serious doubts that Melissa's putative folksinger would push anything but his lungs to their absolute limits.

The line to the Village Gate that evening stretched halfway down the block, a mix of college kids in tweeds and sweaters and long-haired boys and girls in muslin and feathers. David was sure he was the oldest one there. He guided Pat past them toward the entrance.

"David!" A hand reached out from the line and grabbed his sleeve.

"Greg Gregorian! Hello!"

"Ah, and the Golden Patrice." Greg kissed Pat's cheek. He then reached back into the line and, as if at random, pulled a young woman out by the hand. She had straight brown hair parted in the middle and round, downy cheeks; she was certainly no more than eighteen. Greg had to be at least twenty-six by now. "This is Ellen," he said.

"Eileen," the girl corrected, smiling pleasantly.

"And this—" Greg cupped his hands around his mouth and produced a credible-sounding trumpet flourish—"is David 'Supreme Court' Debilio, pride of the class of '61."

David shrugged uncomfortably. "What have you been up to, Greg?"

"Thought you'd never ask. Actually, somebody's finally doing a play of mine. It's only the Caffè Cino—not exactly the Winter Garden—but it's better than nothing, right?"

"That's terrific. When does it open?" David saw that the line had begun to move. "Listen, we're got to get going—they're holding seats for us. Give us a call, okay?"

Greg nodded, looking somewhat hurt, but then his face brightened and he again grasped David's sleeve. "So, they *are* going to bust Orbe tonight, eh, pal?"

"You got me. I'm just a music lover." David gave his old friend a wink and led Pat to the door.

When Orbe skittered onstage, David immediately remembered seeing him at his kitchen table, although the boy looked even more diminutive and pockmarked than he recalled. Orbe wore tapered, shiny black trousers held up by suspenders strapped across his bare chest, and he had fuzzy, child's slippers on his tiny feet. He hopped up onto the spotlit stool, shot off a machine-gun riff on his guitar, and then stopped short, grinning as the audience burst into wild cheers. The times certainly seemed to be producing peculiar-looking heroes. Orbe leaned down to the microphone.

"I'd like to dedicate my first song to Rocco and Billy and Mickey and Acky—" he swept his eyes around the room, smirking "—and all the rest of the guys on Flatbush Avenue who made my childhood into such a fucking nightmare."

He vamped a slow introduction in a minor key to bursts of laughter. Pat touched David's hand.

"This one's terrific," she whispered. Orbe crooned:

> "Turkey on the table, smells so sweet,
> Tongue in a sweat for the taste of meat,
> One breast for poppa, the other for Sal,
> Drumsticks for momma, wings go to Al,
> Now when you all finish slide
>   them bones down to Rob,
> Boy, give that marrow a good suck job.
> Sloppy seconds, yeh,
> Sloppy seconds—"

At the chorus the audience yelped and cheered. David stifled a sigh. He felt even older than he had outside. Orbe's joke was infantile, obvious; his tune stale, more like a T.V. jingle than a folksong. And if these locker room double entendres were typical, the only way he was going to get arrested tonight would be on a charge of self-pity. David looked over at Pat: Her face was flushed and she was slapping her thigh rhythmically to Orbe's song. This time David could not hold back his sigh.

In the second verse, Orbe predictably, cast himself as the poor slob who only got the girl after every other guy had slept with her.

> "Sloppy seconds, yeh,
> Sloppy seconds."

Orbe slipped up a third, slowed his tempo by half. The audience fell silent.

> "Sweet Jack made me promises, promises to keep,
> Food on the table, warm place to sleep,
> Nobody's nigger, somebody's man
> Leftovers over in the garbage can,
> Shot out his brains on a warm Dallas day
> We're off to a barbecue with LBJ.
> Sloppy seconds, yeh,
> Sloppy seconds,
> Sloppy seconds all over again."

Orbe hit a grating chord and held his guitar up to the micro-phone. As it faded, no one spoke or applauded. In spite of himself, David felt a shiver cross his shoulders.

"Fuckers!" Orbe shouted.

Suddenly everyone was cheering, stamping feet, screaming for more. Orbe snickered into the microphone, "Well, well, what a lovely bunch of sentimental shitheads we got here tonight."

David had to laugh. The audience was thriving on Orbe's con-tempt for them. He introduced his next song by reading a crum-pled clipping from "that surreal rag, the New York *Times*." The story described a bill introduced in the Tennessee legislature re-quiring all executions to be televised so that they could truly serve their purpose as a deterrent. The bill had been defeated, having been called "obscene" by its detractors, but it had provided Orbe with a new song which he called "Dead and in Color." It was a talking blues, told from the point of view of a Hollywood television director who is running the "dress rehearsal" of an execution. At the end the director admonishes the prisoner for mumbling his "last words":

> "I'm talking a forty-eight Nielsen in the middle
>   of prime,
>   Fifty million viewers giving you their time,
>   And nobody likes a mumbler, man, mumbling's a
>   crime."

It was as biting a piece of Swiftian satire as David had heard in a long time, and he enthusiastically joined in the applause, but by now he was pretty sure that Rob Orbe's peculiar genius included inventing the story of his imminent "bust" just to have people in to listen to him. Orbe abruptly leaned over to the microphone and squinted down the front row directly at David.

"Got me a hot shit civil liberties lawyer here tonight," he bel-lowed. "What do you say, Debilio—have I given them enough of the socially redeeming bullshit? Can I have some fun now?"

David felt the blood shoot to his face. His instinct was to leave immediately. He grabbed Pat's hand and started to rise when Orbe again leaned toward the mike.

"This one's it," he said in a stage whisper. "I'm going to need you, man."

Pat tugged David's arm and he reluctantly settled back in his seat as Orbe strummed the introduction to a Western-sounding ballad.

"You meet a better class of people when you whack off," he yodeled. "A regular 'Who's Who' yanking on your tool."

There were hoots and cheers all around the room.

> "Got Lollobrigida in the shower stalls,
> Muriel Humphrey grabbing my balls,
> A finger sliding straight up Lynda Bird's ass
> (Funny, don't feel like class)
> Got Jayne Mansfield sitting on my face,
> And, why, look who's here, it's Princess Grace—"

David saw a figure flashing by. In a matter of seconds it was all over: One plainclothesman had pulled the plug on the microphone, the other had bounded onto the stage and was pushing his badge, straight-arm, into Orbe's face.

"You're under arrest for violation of Penal Code 808, lewd and obscene conduct in a public place."

For an instant everyone in the audience froze, stunned. Then a voice in the back shouted "Pig!" and immediately everyone was on his feet, waving his arms, chanting "Pig! Pig! Pig!"

The second detective leapt on the stage. He put a bullhorn to his mouth.

"Down!" he shouted. "Down in your seats! We're checking I.D.'s before anyone leaves here."

David turned around. There were uniformed policemen at each exit. He grabbed Pat's hand and strode to the stage.

"I'm David Debilio," he said, "Mr. Orbe's attorney."

The detective scowled, gesturing for him to follow them backstage. Behind them the crowd was quieting, frightened. Someone dropped "Like a Rolling Stone," onto the P.A. system. The cop led them to Orbe's dressing room and closed the door.

"Your client has two minutes to get into something decent," he said.

Orbe snapped his suspenders on his bare chest and shot back a jittery grin. "Got any pasties?"

David saw the second detective, a flat-faced man, reach into his coat pocket and heard the unmistakable jingle of handcuffs. He stepped in front of Orbe.

"Listen, I'd advise you not to say anything that could be held against you. The sooner they take you in, the sooner I can get you out."

Orbe hopped behind the bamboo screen in the corner, then peered over the top, batting his eyelashes. "You big boys just make yourselves at home, you all hear?"

Pat let out a tiny giggle and again the flat-faced detective put a hand into his pocket.

"May I see your warrant, please?" David snapped.

With a faint smirk the detective reached inside his jacket and removed a typewritten document. David quickly flipped through it. This was not the first of Orbe's performances the vice squad had attended; they had quotes from his songs for the entire week, including parenthetic explications of such phrases as "yanking on your tool" and "sitting on my face." David handed the warrant to Pat. "My secretary," he said to the detective.

"Your client has ten seconds," the detective answered.

David looked up. Orbe's face still hung over the screen like Kilroy's, but his eyelids now drooped and his pocked cheeks were flushed a bright pink. At that moment he shut his eyes completely and made a soft, almost feminine-sounding moan. He grinned blissfully.

"Let's go!" the flat-faced detective barked.

Orbe stepped out from behind the screen, still grinning. He was zipping up his fly. He had on exactly what he had worn onstage.

"Ready," he said cheerily.

Melissa, thin as death, suddenly appeared from behind the screen, pressing a wad of tissues against her lips. There was no doubt what she had been doing back there.

"Jesus Christ!" The detective pulled out the handcuffs, snapped them on Orbe's wrist, and pulled him like a dog to the door.

A picture of Orbe, bare-chested and manacled, made the front page of the *Daily News.* Pat bought half a dozen copies at the all-night newsstand in front of the courthouse as they finally left for home.

"He looks so ridiculous," she squealed in the back of the cab. "Like some hillbilly chicken poacher."

"They don't set that kind of bail for chicken poachers."

Pat leaned her head against David's shoulder. "Jesus, you were impressive in there," she said. "Everybody in New York seems to know you. And they're all afraid of big bad David Debilio." She pressed her lips against his neck and sucked so noisily that David automatically glanced up to see if the driver was watching them.

That night they made strong, joyful love until dawn. It reminded David of those miraculous afternoons in Dunster House. It had been a long time.

Lincoln Ames was less than enthusiastic about the Orbe case. Since the *Tribune* decision the office had been flooded with free-speech challenges, and after conferring with their ACLU colleagues, they had decided to take on only those cases which could expand the concept of "socially redeeming value."

"Your friend Orbe is a little deficient in that area," Lincoln said. "With this court we've got a chance to redefine the First Amendment in ways we never dreamt of. I don't feel like blowing all that fighting for the right of some little twerp to fantasize out loud about Lynda Bird's bottom."

"Lincoln, this guy's loaded with socially redeeming value."

"Not with the press he's been getting." The older man lit his pipe. "Do what you think is best, David. I'm just telling you where I stand."

David was halfway out of Lincoln's office when Lincoln called to him. "Listen, there's one other thing, David. I happened to overhear a little scuttlebutt at the ACLU office that I thought I ought to pass on to you, friend-to-friend. It seems some of your learned colleagues think you have a predilection for clients who get their pictures in the paper."

David felt his face coloring. "In the words of Rob Orbe," he said, "fuck 'em."

He was immensely relieved to hear Lincoln burst out laughing.

After dinner that evening—they had been eating later and later since Thérèse returned to Boston—Pat announced that she had a surprise. She disappeared for a moment and returned to the dining room with two cameras slung around her neck.

"Voilà, Patricia Debilio, photographer. What do you think?"

"It looks dumb, Mom," Josh said. He slipped off his chair and headed for the television set.

"It's what I've always wanted to do," Pat went on, her cheeks coloring. "You know, something artistic, but like involved too. I'm going to take courses at the School of Visual Arts. And if it's okay, I thought we could turn the guest room into a darkroom. So?"

David walked straight up to her and took her face in both his hands. "I think it's terrific." He kissed her. "I think *you're* terrific."

It was just as Lincoln had said: The Beardsley women did not stay idle for long.

For two weeks David did not hear a word from Rob Orbe; he only read about him in the papers. David's secretary tried to call Orbe at his apartment—phone disconnected—and at the Village Gate—barred from the premises. Finally, though the hearing date still had not been set, David sent him a registered letter telling him to contact the office. Orbe called David at his home at nine-thirty on a Thursday night.

"Debilio? This is Orbe. Listen, I'm giving an exclusive interview to the *Voice.* Very heady. This guy keeps quoting Henry Miller and Thomas Jefferson. Tricky. I think I should have my attorney present, don't you?"

"Yes, I do."

Orbe was at the door in less than five minutes. Besides the *Village Voice* interviewer, a tall, effete-looking fellow who sported a Vandyke, he had Melissa with him. Orbe shook David's hand, pecked Pat on the cheek, and then headed directly for the kitchen. By the time they all followed him there, Orbe had the refrigerator door open and was sliding chunks of cheese and pea-nut butter and jelly jars onto the kitchen table. David was the last to sit down.

"Where was I?" Orbe scooped a glob of peanut butter from the jar with his forefinger and stuffed it in his mouth. "Oh yes, you see, I've got it on good account that Miss Lynda Bird is flattered as hell that anybody has even mentioned her ass. She's immensely proud of it, you know. Maybe we should call her as a character witness. Better yet, maybe she'll let us use her ass as Exhibit A!"

The reporter scribbled away in his pad. David smiled.

"If your editor prints that," he said, *"his* lawyer is giving him lousy advice."

The reporter laughed. He looked at David. "Are you really going to argue that this"—he pointed his pen at Orbe—"has got socially redeeming value?"

"I certainly am. He's as much a social critic as the editorial writers of the *Times.* Probably better."

"Bullshit, Debilio!" Orbe broke off a piece of cheese and stuffed it in Melissa's mouth. "Let Norman Cousins be a social critic. I've got a divine purpose. Yeh! I am the tool of God!" He cackled and Melissa laughed too, a dry, rasping laugh. Orbe stood, raising both arms in the air like an evangelist. "Let me tell you about socially redeeming value. I speak the truth about cocks and cunts. And the truth shall set you free!"

"We're saying more or less the same thing," David said, smiling.

The man from the *Voice* laughed politely, then went on to question Orbe about his future plans. In a surprisingly lucid manner the boy explained that he was suspending all live performances until his trial was over, and that in the meantime he was negotiating a record contract with Atlantic. He turned to David. "I told them to call you, man," he said.

"I don't negotiate record contracts," David said. "Get yourself an agent for that."

"Come on, Debilio. You went to Harvard, didn't you?"

David was about to protest again when he heard a click behind him. He turned. Pat was crouched at the end of the table with her new camera up to her eye. She blushed.

"Don't pay any attention to me, everybody," she said. "Just practicing."

"Well, let me know if any of them come out," the *Voice* reporter said. He turned again to Orbe. "One last question. I heard you've been getting hassled by a lot of people lately. Barred from the Gate, thrown out of your apartment—"

"Hey, they'd bar Jesus from the Gate if they thought they'd lose their liquor license."

"Where can you be reached now?" David asked.

"Who knows? I'm just crashing here and there. It's a drag, really."

"Why don't you stay here?" Pat said.

"Hey, thanks," Melissa said.

It happened so quickly, so naturally, that it took a moment to register with David. He cleared his throat.

"Sure, you can stay for a couple days," he said, managing a smile.

The *Voice* reporter rose from the table, chortling. "Any longer than that," he said, "and he might socially redeem your whole family."

Orbe was still there at the end of the week.

"It's just like Duncan and Margot's," Pat said several times. "You know, people in the house all the time, like a big family."

It did not seem like a family to David. And Orbe and Melissa certainly did not remind him of the houseguests at the Beardsleys' Vermont cottage, who played chamber music in the afternoon and talked philosophy late into the summer nights. Orbe rambled—he did not talk—and when one track of free association came to a dead end, he beat his way to another with a drumroll of obscenities, while Melissa, glaze-eyed and grim, sat silently by the wall. What was remarkable was how much Pat and Joshua seemed to take to this pair. Pat was in a perpetual flush from laughing at Orbe's monologues and Joshua, with the mysterious sympathies of his child heart, fastened himself to Melissa's side like a siamese twin.

At the office David contacted poets, professors, and columnists by the dozen, soliciting their testimony as to Robert E. Orbe's "social significance." As well, discovering that it was simply easier to deal with the lawyers from Atlantic Records himself than to find Orbe an agent, David negotiated Orbe's recording contract, getting him a five-thousand-dollar advance on his album. By the end of the week David figured he had done more than enough for Robert Orbe. He brought the check home and handed it to the singer after dinner.

"You won't have any trouble getting your own place now," David said pleasantly.

"Shit, Debilio, are you trying to get rid of me?"

"It seems like the right time for you to get settled," David replied.

Orbe suddenly grabbed Joshua off his chair and popped him onto his knee like a ventriloquist's dummy. "Golly gee, Poppa," Orbe squeaked, barely moving his lips. "Uncle Robbie promised to teach me how to play the guitar. Don't throw the fucker out now."

Joshua giggled and Pat and Melissa laughed softly. They were all looking at David. He scratched at his jaw. "Look, believe it or not, I've actually enjoyed having you here," he said. "In a way, it feels a little like being back in college—"

"Yeh, feels a lot like Harvard to me too, old bean," Orbe said, grinning like an idiot.

"But we have to start getting to work on your defense, Rob,"

David continued, "and I know I could do a better job for you if we maintained a little personal distance between our lives."

"Fuck, Debilio, you'd do a better job for me if you loved my ass! It ought to be a fucking requirement—every lawyer's got to live with his client for a month. An act of faith, dig? Like if you're defending some mass murderer, you'd have to take him home, leave him alone in the house with your wife and kid. Then when you stroll into the courtroom everybody knows you really believe in this guy." Orbe cackled, then stopped and rolled his eyes like a ghoul. "Either that or you walk into the courtroom a fucking widower."

He cackled again and they all laughed, David included.

"I'll pass your suggestion on to the bar association," David said. "In the meantime, I think I'd do best to follow precedent."

"Bullshit, David. You're just afraid of Rob." It was the first time Melissa had spoken all evening. Her hooded eyes fastened on David's. "You're afraid he'll make you lose all your precious control."

David's face froze in a polite, moronic smile. He could feel muscles tightening all over his body. "That's a little silly, Melissa," he said.

"Fuck it is, Debilio," Orbe said cheerfully, "but all that control is what makes you such a crackerjack lawyer, isn't it?" Orbe stood and flourished his five-thousand-dollar check in front of David. "Look, man, if it's a question of paying my own way, I don't want to sponge or anything."

"For Christ's sake, put that away, would you?" David's face had grown warm. He felt drops of sweat forming along his hairline. He drew in his breath. "Look, there's really a very mundane reason for all this that I haven't even mentioned," he said, trying to sound every bit as cheerful as Orbe, "and that's Pat's photography. We're setting up a little darkroom for her in the guest room, so we'll be needing—"

"Oh God, David! Please!" Pat's face flushed a deep red. She was about to say more when she abruptly stood and marched to their bedroom, slamming the door. Joshua immediately burst out crying. Before David could respond, Orbe was on his feet with the boy in his arms, Melissa beside him.

"Hey, man, if it's going to be a hassle, forget it, okay? We'll split in the morning." Orbe closed the guest room door behind him.

David was alone. His forehead was dripping with perspiration and his heart was racing. This was preposterous, all totally preposterous. How in the name of God had he allowed any of this to happen? He did not move for a full minute. Then he walked into the bedroom. Pat was sitting cross-legged on the bedspread. Her eyes were red.

"It's all got to be one way, doesn't it, David?" she murmured, not looking at him. "All your way. I was really trying, you know. The photography and everything. But that doesn't mean a thing to you, does it?"

David looked down at her from just inside the door. He did not answer.

"I don't know what it was like in Hoboken," Pat went on, "but in Duncan and Margot's house anybody was welcome who needed a place to sleep. It didn't matter who they were or what their background was." She began to weep, tears silently slipping down the sides of her nose. "Duncan said it was the first rule of having your own home."

David walked slowly to the bed and sat on the edge. "Look, let's talk about it, okay? Nothing's been done that can't be undone."

He reached out his hand and touched Pat's shoulder and she immediately began crying in earnest. She pushed her face against his chest. He closed his eyes, wrapping his arms around her.

"It just all seemed so perfect," Pat sobbed, "like we had finally found something we could all do together."

David stroked her hair.

"I mean you defending Orbe," Pat went on, "and me his official photographer."

David's eyes opened. His mouth felt dry.

"You know, like Orbe said I could do his album cover," Pat said breathlessly, "and I'm doing this whole spread for *RAT* on, you know, just him hanging out at our house."

David's head was spinning. He needed to take a breath, but it felt like there was no air left in the apartment. It had all been sucked out by Rob Orbe.

He was there when David came home from the office the following evening. David had never really doubted that he would be. David heard the twang of his guitar as he fitted the key in the door, the nasal whine of his voice as he entered the hallway.

"Yes, He's Jesus come to save you
From the fuckin' ruling class.
Love, O love your lawyer,
Love his bleeding liberal ass."

David stood in the archway to the living room. The guest room mattress sat in the middle of the living room floor like a soft stage, with Orbe perched on top of it. He wore striped doorman's trousers; his chicken-ribbed chest was bare. He grinned at David.

"A little valentine for you, Debilio. I wrote it this afternoon." He mouthed a big kiss to David and laughed.

From the corner Joshua echoed Orbe's laugh. The boy, too, was shirtless. He strummed on the ukulele Orbe had bought him. Beside Josh was Melissa, wearing blue dancer's tights so sheer that the outlines of her areolae showed through like coat buttons. Her eyes were closed. Pat sat directly in front of Orbe. She leaned back her head and looked up at David.

"You look funny upside down," she said.

David stared at her for a second, then looked back at Orbe. "Your grand jury hearing's been set for two weeks from today," he said flatly, as if dictating a letter. "I understand the state is bringing in half a dozen psychiatrists who'll claim your little ditties promote dangerous and deviant behavior."

"Hey, I'm trying my best," Orbe chimed.

David pulled a beer from the refrigerator and took it into the bedroom with him. He turned on the radio to drown out Orbe's insidious drone, then opened his briefcase and took out the envelope the ACLU had sent over that afternoon. It was the brief for the *Fanny Hill* case that was now being deliberated in the New York State Court of Appeals. David leafed through it. The ACLU lawyers hit basically the same points he planned to: the artistic merits of the work; its educational value; the inability of social scientists to establish a positive correlation between obscene language and antisocial behavior. No surprises.

"Hi." Pat had poked her pixie head inside the bedroom door. As she stepped in, she looked like a high school majorette, her camera straps crisscrossing her chest and pressing triangles of T-shirt against her small breasts. "We're going out for pizza. Want some?"

David took a long swallow of beer. He peered at her for a

moment before he spoke. "What exactly is it that you do all day, Patricia?" he said quietly.

Pat tilted her head to one side. She said nothing.

"I mean besides providing a live-in audience for our friend Orbe." David leaned forward. "Do you all smoke pot and giggle and have brilliant thoughts that nobody can remember two minutes later? And then you take a few pictures and decide they're so wonderful that you're going to go out and reward yourself with a pizza pie? Is that it, Pat? Is that really what you want to be doing with your life? Is that what we want to teach Josh that life is all about?"

Pat stared back at him, her face drawn tight like a serious child's, and then she began to walk slowly toward him. She dropped to her knees at the side of the bed and looked up at him plaintively.

"Poor David," she said softly, "you never really did have a family, did you? And now that you have one of your own, you don't know what to do with us. You never have any fun, do you? It's all those words; all day long, all those words. They just drive the fun right out of you."

David closed his eyes. It was true: There was no pleasure left inside him. But it was not words which had driven pleasure out. It was the threat that every other man in the world was freer and looser than he was. David did not open his eyes until Pat was gone.

Late that night David was awakened by the smack and thump of colliding flesh coming through the wall from the guest room. His eyes flashed open in the dark and reflexively he reached out beside him. Pat laughed.

"Hard to sleep, isn't it?" she whispered.

She licked the back of his neck, then stabbed her tongue inside his ear. It felt unpleasant, like a tropical animal loose on the pillow. David held still.

"Just relax," Pat whispered. "Like pretend you're still dreaming."

Her hand burrowed under his pajama top, flopped around his belly like a fish, then dove beneath his waistband and scooped his testicles. From behind the wall the grunts grew louder, hoarse, raw. David felt his penis shrink as if he had plunged into ice water. Pat giggled. "Hey, come on, Debilio."

David bolted straight up, his heart thudding in his chest.

"Anybody can *fuck!* Don't you know that, Patricia? Dogs in the street can *fuck,* for Christ's sake!"

For the rest of that week David worked late every evening, taking his dinner alone at Horn & Hardart's, stopping for a beer or two at the Lion's Head on his way home. He counted off the days to Orbe's hearing like a prisoner coming to the end of his sentence. He slept on the edge of his mattress. On Friday afternoon Lincoln dropped a telegram on David's desk. It was the *Fanny Hill* decision; the state had ruled unequivocally that obscene language was protected under the First Amendment. At six o'clock Max Goldblum from the district attorney's office called: In light of the *Fanny Hill* rendering, charges against Robert Orbe, folksinger, were herewith dropped.

"Thanks for calling, Max," David said.

"Didn't want you working all weekend," Goldblum said. "Between you and me, I never thought we had much of a case anyway. I felt like we were prosecuting some little kid for saying 'Kakadoodie' in front of his mother."

David laughed. "Between you and me," he said, "Orbe is a first-class shmuck."

David had scotch at the Lion's Head that evening. It was over. He would give Orbe a day to get out of the apartment. He was not going to argue with him or Pat or anyone else. The case was closed.

The apartment was dark when David let himself in. It smelled of sweat and spilled wine. There were pillows strewn on the living room floor, snuffed-out candles, an open bottle of wine—Rob Orbe's perpetual party.

"Pat? Josh?"

No answer. No note on the kitchen blackboard. David sat down at the kitchen table with an unopened bottle of beer. Streaks of peanut butter covered the tabletop like finger paint. Suddenly he stood, pulled off his jacket and rolled up his sleeves. He yanked a broom and a mop and pail from the closet, a sponge from the sink. He strode to the guest room door and kicked it open, snapping on the light with his elbow. The room stank of clothes and ashes. David marched to the far wall and threw open the window. A sleeping bag sagged, half-opened, against the radiator. He started at the far end, sweeping all the debris toward the sleeping bag: the underwear, the song sheets, the cigarette stubs, the books and paper cups, Orbe's fuzzy slippers. David was leaning over, stuffing it all into the sleeping bag, when he saw black-and-white proof sheets sticking out from the pages of a magazine, lines of photographs too small and dim to make out. It was the work, no doubt, of Orbe's official photographer, Patricia Debilio. David pulled the sheets out and held them under the light.

In the first shot Orbe, his eyes crossed and his tongue hanging out, sat on the mattress in the living room, strumming the wrong end of his guitar. Goldblum was right: Orbe was closer to Howdy Doody than Lenny Bruce. David skimmed the first row, then the next. At the end of the third row his eye stopped. The last frame pictured Orbe, stark naked, lying on his back on the sofa with a pen in one hand and a sheet of music in the other. His skinny, uncircumcised penis curled like a worm on his thigh. He grinned at the camera. In the next shot Orbe's cock arched between his legs like the nozzle of a hose. In the next Melissa, wearing a dress and large spectacles, sat beside him with a pen and pad in hand, like a cartoon secretary, staring at his cock as if she could not quite tell what it was. In the next picture it was in her mouth. David's hand trembled, but he continued to look methodically from picture to picture: Orbe strumming his guitar and singing while Melissa sucked him; Orbe jotting on a music sheet that rested on Melissa's back while he fucked her from behind; Orbe and Melissa, side by side, blowing kisses to the camera. To Pat.

When the lock clicked and the apartment door swung open, David was still standing in the center of the room holding Pat's photos in both his hands, perspiration dripping from his face onto them. He listened, not moving, as the sound of steps moved down the hallway toward him. Melissa, hands on her hips, appeared at the door to the guest room. She was alone.

"Ah, the cleanup committee," she said with the faintest of smiles. "Making room for your next client?"

David stared at her. His heart yammered in his chest. He said nothing.

"Orbe and Pat are out celebrating," Melissa went on. She unbuttoned her coat and let it fall on the floor. She wore a dancer's scoop-necked top and a miniskirt. "It looks like an all-nighter. They dropped Joshy at the sitter's."

David looked down again at the photos: Orbe holding onto his erect cock like a microphone, Melissa laughing. David dropped the sheets onto the rest of the garbage at his feet.

"Take what's yours, Melissa," he said. "You don't live here anymore."

Melissa laughed. "No fun winning the way you did, is it, David? No big day in court. No moment of truth. Orbe already wrote a song about it: 'I Rode My Way to Freedom on Fanny Hill's Tail.' "

She laughed again, then coughed. She reached into the waistband of her skirt and pulled out a half-smoked joint. She stuck it in her mouth.

"Just go," David said, his voice trembling.

Melissa turned, walked to the kitchen and lit her cigarette on the stove. She inhaled deeply and held the smoke down. Then she turned back and strode directly into the guest room. She stood in front of David.

"It wasn't my idea to stay here, you know," she said. "To tell you the truth, it gives me the shits, like living with my parents or something. But Orbe has this whole thing about you, David, this whole little brother–big brother number. He really thought he'd get to you if he stayed here long enough. He actually believed all that crap about wanting you to love his ass before the two of you walked into the courtroom together." Melissa laid her palm on David's chest. "That's the main reason he wanted to fuck Pat, you know. Just to get a piece of David Debilio."

David held himself so tight he trembled. Melissa's hand burned on his chest.

"You know, sometimes Orbe actually begged me to fuck you just to make the circle complete. Just to make it one big happy family."

"Shut up! Shut your fucking mouth!"

David grabbed her by both shoulders, his fingers digging into her skin. He shoved her backward toward the door. His whole body seethed.

"What the fuck are you afraid of, Debilio?"

She was against the wall, her long legs splayed, her little skirt hiked above her hips, and when David tore open his pants and drove himself inside her, he spewed one obscenity after another into her ear.

In the middle of that night David lifted the ringing phone from the kitchen wall.

"I have a collect call for David Debilio from a Mr. Halligan in Laredo, Texas," the operator drawled.

"I'll take it."

"David, how are you?" Jerry said. "Listen, when can you get here, pal? We need you. Would you believe it—some idiot has actually arrested Timothy Leary for having a few crumbs of pot in his car."

David was on a plane before Pat ever came home.

15

A WILLOWY brunette was collecting money for the "Leary Defense Fund" at the door to the Caffè Cino on the night Greg Gregorian's play opened there. A lucky sign, for sure. Greg dropped a half-dollar into her goldfish bowl and winked.

"Good defenses make good de-neighbors," he said, but the girl only looked back at him blankly and mumbled, "Thanks." A bad sign, that. All told, the good signs and bad signs of the past week came out about equal: His play was going to have to make it on its own.

Greg wandered over to the side of the stage and scanned the audience. He had had postcards printed up—a caricature of himself with a pistol at his head on one side, the time and place of his "world premiere" on the other—and mailed them to everyone he knew. Bernie Jacoby, his agent, was there in the front row, alongside Bobby Burger, his employer at "Time Bomb." They both somehow looked more like dutiful parents than like people who were preparing themselves for a stunning breakthrough in the history of drama. Betty Ehrmann, the prop girl from "Time Bomb," sat a few seats behind them—without a date, it appeared. She, at least, looked eager. On slow days at the T.V. studio he would occasionally slip obscene stunt cards into her clipboard and she would giggle and slap his hand. In the back, half in shadow and looking tragic, was Eileen, the girl he had stopped calling a couple of weeks ago. She was Dr. Nussbaum's dental assistant and Greg had fallen helplessly in love with her, with his mouth open and riddled with Novocain; without Novocain, however, his feelings for her had quickly dulled. Eileen was the only other person he knew in the audience.

But whom had he expected, really? Certainly not his Cedar Bar crowd—heaven forbid they should miss one night of their perpetual argument. And his classmates in his improvisation lab had excused themselves one by one, too jealous to witness his success. But not even his true friends, his Harvard friends, had shown up. He had not expected Axel, of course—Off-Off-Broadway theater was not quite his thing—and Jerry, he'd heard, was in Mexico someplace being transcendent; Greg had searched for his name in the accounts of Leary's border arrest. But Greg had expected David, at least David and Pat. Hell, they only lived a few blocks away. Todd, God love him, had made plans to fly out from San Francisco just for the night, but at the last minute he had to call it off because his wife was in labor. Greg shook his head yet one more time in utter incredulity; in the space of just a year Todd had managed to drop out of graduate school, find a job as a hospital orderly, get married and—any minute now—have a child. According to Todd, he had decided it was time to "condense" his life. "Being so big, I've always had trouble getting things off the ground before," he had written Greg. And this was the guy Greg was always accusing of being totally incapable of action. The lights dimmed and Gregory slunk along the wall to the rear as Joe Cino mounted the stage with his loopy grin and announced that it was magic time.

An alarm clock was ringing onstage as the lights came up on a middle-aged couple slowly clambering out of an old double bed. They stretched and yawned, the woman unpinned her hair net, the man pulled on his robe, and then they turned and looked at one another with expressions of utter bewilderment.

"Excuse me," the man said, "but haven't we met before?"

Several people in the audience tittered.

The play was called "You're Fine, Who Am I?" and the entire idea for it had come to Greg one morning while he was making love in his oak bed to a young woman while trying desperately to remember where he had met her. In the play a whole town wakes up with mass amnesia, and during the course of the first act it becomes clear that all of them are infinitely happier than they have ever been before. But at the first-act curtain the town intel-

lectual—Greg had had Todd in mind when he created the character—admonishes them all that they have to find out exactly who
they are—or were—so they can fulfill their destinies.

Greg scooted for the door the moment he heard the first-act
applause begin, but before he could get outside he heard one
collegiate-looking kid moan to his date, "I heard he writes for
television. It figures."

Shithead! Probably studying drama at NYU and doesn't know
Gogol from go-go. Greg loped along Cornelia Street, cursing. At
the corner he turned and skipped into the White Rose, sidled up to
the bar and ordered a bourbon. He glanced at the clock behind the
bar: five minutes to the second-act curtain. He poured the drink
down his throat and gazed the length of the bar. Remarkable!
Here he was on the very threshold of his new life as a playwright,
the culmination of what he called his "prelude to greatness" period, and everyone at the White Rose was totally wrapped up in
the Knicks game. It gave one a little perspective. He waved a
dollar bill at the bartender.

"Gotta get back to the Cino," Greg told him with a little shrug.
"They're doing one of my plays tonight."

"No kidding," the bartender said, smiling. "I had a play there
myself last year. Joe does a nice job."

They were halfway into the second act by the time Greg returned. All the characters but one had reconstructed his identity
and had become terribly despondent in the process; the only pleasure left to any of them was in badgering the one remaining
amnesiac—a blissful fellow—into doing the same. Greg surveyed
the audience from the rear: Not a single person had left during the
intermission. An excellent sign. And here is where the play's true
brilliance shone, the epistemological ironies, the zen flip-flops, the
philosophical wit.

"But I don't have to know who I *was* to know who I am now,"
the character was protesting. "At this moment I am the song of
that bird, this itch on my shoulder blade, this wonderful lust I feel
for every marvelously unfamiliar woman I meet."

Someone on the side yawned audibly and several people around
him giggled. It was the biggest laugh Greg had heard since he'd
returned. He stumbled back out the door. Oh, Jesus! He had rehearsed this evening in his head a hundred times, imagined his
play bombing at least as often as he'd imagined it a hit, fantasized

reviews of it by the dozen—from "Existential Sitcom Worth For-
getting" in the *Voice* to "An American Becket Debuts" in the
Times—but what he had never imagined was that it would be
neither hit nor flop but, good Christ, *mediocre!* "Derivative but
Diverting Little Play Opens in Village." "Nice Play, Excellent
Coffee at the Cino."

Greg turned up his collar as he swung around the block into the
wind. By the time he had come full circle and put his face to the
window of the Caffè Cino, the play was over, the audience gone.
Except one. Sipping a cup of coffee alone at a table was Betty
Ehrmann, the prop girl from "Time Bomb." Greg opened the
door and strode directly up to her.

"How'd you like to make love to the king of stunts?" he said.

16

"ON SECOND thought, Debilio, I think we'd just be fudging if we
went the cruel and unusual punishment route, don't you?"

David gazed up at the meringue-swirled ceiling of the Bolero
Motel in Laredo, Texas, a slow smile spreading his lips. He
propped himself up on one elbow and looked down at Amanda
Farber, the defense attorney of record in *The People* v. *Timothy
Leary*. Her breasts, large as Spanish melons, sat proudly exposed
just above the sheet.

"Are you in the habit of discussing your cases like this, Miss
Farber?"

The dark-eyed woman smiled back. "Only when I get lucky."
She inched closer, one breast lolling in the crook of his arm. "I like
to take advice lying down."

David laughed softly. Doubtlessly Amanda Farber had used that
line with other colleagues—other visiting liberal lawyers—and
God knows who else, but that did not really matter at all. Since
returning from the U.S. Commissioner's Office together that afternoon, the two of them had made love three times, playfully, volup-

tuously, each time more deliciously satisfying than the last, and the overwhelming relief David felt was better than love. He felt cleansed.

"You haven't answered my question," the woman said, nudging him.

"I think you're right. Nobody's going to buy cruel and unusual punishment. Not with Leary. He's taking on the proportions of the Antichrist these days. But there's something screwy about your law down here that gets you for failing to pay import tax for bringing marijuana over the border. If you did pay it, it'd be self-incrimination. It's really a constitutional question."

Amanda leaned over and kissed David's shoulder. "Oh my. I'm glad they sent me you instead of some skinny Jewish boy with a mustache and a work shirt."

There was a hint of Southernness in her "Oh my," although she was a New Yorker and Jewish herself, transplanted by choice when nobody else wanted to start up an ACLU office along the Rio Grande. She had gone to City College, where she was a founding member of its SANE chapter, and from there she had surprised everyone by getting into Cornell Law School, where she graduated near the top of her class. She had once codefended a SNCC worker with Lincoln Ames. She was single. That was all David knew about her.

"Nobody sent me," David said. "I came down as a personal favor to Jerry Halligan. We're old friends, sort of. We roomed together at Harvard a million years ago."

"So he told me," Amanda said. "You must have been strange bedfellows even then. Or was he a straight arrow before he started adding chemicals to his brain?"

"Jerry always had potential," David said, and she laughed. He wondered just how well she had gotten to know Jerry Halligan before he had taken off for New York to coordinate Leary's defense fund.

"I heard you tripped the light fantastic too, back at Harvard, when they were still calling it seminars."

David let himself back down on the pillow and gazed again at the swirling ceiling. "Yup," he said.

Like the other end of a seesaw, Amanda propped herself up on her elbow. "Feel free to give more than one-word answers." She reached under the sheet and pinched his thigh. "Come on,

Debilio, I'm one of those people who's been dying to take LSD for years, but somehow I can never keep my nerve up long enough to do it. It's my new virginity."

David gazed up into Amanda's dark, ironic eyes. In five years he had never told Pat the truth about the night in Newton, although, God knows, she had pestered him enough about it.

"Well, if you must know the truth, it scared the living shit out of me. I felt like the world was flat as a chessboard and I was hanging off the edge by my fingernails. That's all. I hung on for ten hours. For weeks I had muscle aches and headaches and a sore neck. The morning after Jerry informed me that I had resisted the experience."

The girl laughed again, a free, throaty laugh, and then she covered his matted chest with wet little kisses.

"You're a love," she said. She rested her chin on his chest, and they were both quiet for a moment. "The funny thing is, your friend Halligan is on the way out," she said finally. "At least that's the scuttlebutt in the Leary circus. They say he's a regular junior executive, always putting out memos for taking over the world. A whole bunch of long-haired kids who aren't even twenty have edged him out. Even his girl has dropped him."

"You're kidding me."

"No. They all say he *thinks* too much. I guess you can take the boy out of Harvard, but you can't—"

The laughter that erupted from David's throat shook him so hard that Amanda's head literally bounced off his chest. He fumbled like a drunkard to sit up, but the fit of laughter kept throttling him back to the bed, his stomach heaving, tears dripping from his eyes. "Oh, no," he kept gasping. "Poor old Jerry."

In the morning, after making love one more time, they ate breakfast in the motel and Amanda drove David to the airport.

"Let's keep in touch," he said.

"Sure." She kissed him on the cheek. "And say hello to Lincoln Ames for me."

Something in the way she said it made David stop and study her eyes. He felt a pang of fear and an all-too-familiar raw pain. He could not stop himself. "Did you sleep with Lincoln?"

She looked down with disappointment, not shame. "Come on, David, we're all beyond that, aren't we?"

David held himself very still and then he smiled. "Maybe," he said, touching her hair. "Just barely."

17

COMING HOME from the night shift at the hospital, Todd made a stop at Smitty's for two coffees and donuts to go and a fresh-smelling copy of the morning's *Examiner*. He drove on three blocks to Filbert Street and, just as he turned, saw his neighbor, Dick Rinzler, take off for work in his Volkswagen, leaving a parking space for Todd in front of his house. It worked out that way four days out of five, a perfect unspoken arrangement, the kind that made the world go round.

Todd took the steps two at a time to the top floor and opened the door. May sat in a straw fanback chair by the window, her nightgown lowered like an apron at her waist, an infant at each breast.

"Hi, Poppa," she said.

Todd let himself down to his knees and, still a giant, stooped to kiss the tops of the children's heads. Then he lifted his face to his wife's and kissed her, touching the back of her head lightly with both his hands, his arms a tent top above the twins.

"How'd the night go?" he asked.

"Spectacular," May said, smiling. "They slept four hours in a row. Times two, that's eight hours."

Todd laughed and kissed his wife again before opening the paper sack and setting the coffees and donuts on the glass-topped coffee table. "Want a bite now?"

"Please."

Todd held a donut to May's mouth and she took off half of it in a single bite. She was a big woman with a big jaw, horsey some would probably say, magnificent in his eyes. Her father, long dead, was a Finn and her mother was a Swede—Viking stock, a giant like himself. He had fallen in love with her in a matter of days after meeting her on the ward at General, where she was a nurse and he an orderly-in-training. She had thought he was foolish to be working there, with all the education he had, and he had thought she was infinitely wiser than he. Todd cherished her calm, her innate tolerance and love. It seemed to him that she lived in the immanent world with the grace of a deer in the wild. She had wisdom, he thought, that was beyond any philosophy. She was the first woman he had ever slept with, and when, only months later, she announced that she was pregnant, he was thrilled. He sat across from her, flattening the newspaper on his lap.

"All right, kiddies, Poppa's going to read the news. Listen carefully. I'm going to ask questions later." He scanned the front page. "Well, the Christmas truce has held yet another day; that's good news. If this works, I think we should all give Christianity another chance. What do you say, Skeezix?" He reached out and took the infant swaddled in pink from May. He held her straight-arm in front of him. "Or do you think it's McNamara who deserves all the credit?"

He gently patted his daughter's back while May burped their son across from him.

"Hey, did you see this, kids? They're having a hippie festival in the park in a couple of weeks, a meeting of heads, so to speak. Maybe we should take a look, huh?" His daughter belched in his ear. "Brava! Brava! She's talented, I'm telling you."

Suddenly Todd's eye fastened on a headline at the bottom of the page. "Jesus Christ, they want to put old Tim Leary away for ten years. Can you imagine that?" He cupped his hand around the infant girl's head. "But don't worry," he whispered. "Nobody can lock up the zeitgeist."

THREE

1967–1970

18

"WE MUST achieve freedom of the nervous system before we try anything else. You have to be out of your mind to pray."

Scattered "Wows" like hallelujahs at a revival meeting. Tim was really working them now. Half a dozen search and seizures in the past year, sentences pending in two states and he was still the mastermind. Still a movie star. Jerry Halligan stood behind the last row in the Village Theater, peering at Timothy Leary like an understudy.

"The mind of the middle class is being blown. The most conservative estimates are that several million Americans are taking LSD. Turning on correctly means to understand the many levels that are brought into focus: It takes years of discipline, training and discipleship."

Jerry smiled, sure he'd caught Tim's eye over the heads of the novitiates. It had been a year since Texas, since Jerry had hitchhiked back East to New York on his own. But the vibes were still the same. Tim and he were still on the same wavelength.

"Aldous Huxley warned us that the powers released by LSD would have to be socialized in a new form," Tim was saying, his voice subtly raised just above the background track of the Beach Boys. "We have formed a religious group. The temple of our religion is the human body. Our shrines are in the home. The congregation is a small group of family and friends—an underground brotherhood. A spiritual renaissance is inevitable and long overdue."

Outside there had been a bad moment at the box office, a mixup. Nobody had gotten Jerry's message. Nobody had left a ticket for him. Ridiculous, really—Jerry Halligan paying three bucks to see Timothy Leary. Couldn't the lady in the box office tell? I mean, couldn't she just tell by looking at Jerry that he was one of *them?*

"To drop out is the oldest message that spiritual teachers have passed on," Leary continued. "You can win only by giving up. The act of dropping out is done tenderly. You hardly notice. Then one day, down at the office, they say, 'What happened to him?' "

Tim waited for the laugh, then strolled toward the footlights, holding his microphone aloft like a scepter. A young woman suddenly dashed to the stage and laid a rose at his feet. Jesus, beautiful. Tim smiled a benediction. Jerry studied the smile, the cast of his eyes, the flutter of his Nehru pajamas.

"You must give up all mental life as you know it," Leary intoned.

A hand touched Jerry's shoulder and he turned slowly, sure it would be Gabby, sure she'd been looking everywhere for him since she'd come to New York. But it wasn't Gabby, it was Burt, the kid whose pad he'd been crashing down on Avenue B.

"Let's split," Burt whispered. "We gotta be on the street before these kids are out there. Like we gotta set up shop."

Jerry spun away, gazed back up at Tim.

"Death of the mind," he was saying, "that is the goal you must have. Death of the mind. Nothing less will do."

A hush. No one moved. All eyes on Tim. Waiting. Waiting for the secret.

"Hey man, come on," Burt whispered in Jerry's ear. "Do you want to unload your acid or don't you?"

19

AXEL SAT cross-legged on the bare floor, his back against the wall, watching the seven o'clock news. Like yesterday and the day before, the long segment after the first commercial featured army medics leaping from helicopters and scurrying, bent over like kangaroos, to gather up wounded soldiers and bleeding children. With its lush greens and brilliant reds, Vietnam always reminded him of Africa. Axel clicked his stopwatch as the segment ended, replaced by a cat food ad; then he marked its length on his clipboard. Axel's assignment for the last two months was to monitor T.V. programing, analyze it and, ultimately, draw up a manifesto that demonstrated how the movement could manipulate it. Unexpectedly, it had turned out to be an assignment that he could take some satisfaction in. Not the least of its pleasures was sitting alone in the dark.

"Who's winning?" Angie leaned against the doorjamb in a seemingly casual pose, but Axel noticed that she kept all of her body outside the T.V. room in strict observation of Despina's "no entry" rule. The color T.V. set had cost the group over four hundred dollars—more than all seven of them spent on food in a year—and it was not about to be used for their bourgeois pleasure or stupefaction.

"The guys in the white hats," Axel answered. He looked back at the screen in time to see the beginning of yet another follow-up story on the March on the Pentagon. Over for a week, it was still news. Axel pressed his glasses against the bridge of his nose.

The group had voted that he stay behind during the march to analyze its coverage: Whose speeches did they feature? Which demonstrations were most convincing? He had barely protested. The idea of having the apartment entirely to himself was more appealing than he dared admit to any of them, certainly Despina. Solitude, too, was a bourgeois pleasure. He had sat alone in the room for twelve straight hours switching from channel to channel, charting every shot. Coverage was better than any of them had predicted. After the first day Axel's main conclusion was inescapable: The most telling moments on the screen were the simplest ones: a child riding on her father's shoulders; an old woman resting on her cane, with one hand raised in the peace sign. More than the rhetoric, more than the mock coffins or effigy burnings, these were the images that could turn Americans against the war, if any could, and, fortunately, these were the images that the cameramen and news directors instinctively picked up. But Axel knew he would have to keep his conclusion to himself: It left nothing for their group to do. It undermined Despina's last reason for its existence.

At ten o'clock on the Saturday night of the march, Axel had abandoned his post and had walked out onto upper Broadway, tonight teeming with blacks and Puerto Ricans proudly laying claim to the turf while their white neighbors were down in Washington protesting the war in Southeast Asia. A few of the older blacks nodded to Axel as he strode by. He and Despina and Angie and Cord had lived on this street since they had come back from Mississippi and set up the neighborhood headquarters for SNCC three years ago. They had been a brilliant team then, Despina and he, recruiting, organizing, holding forth day and night in the apartment's living room with an ever-changing circle of Columbia students, street kids and black mammas. "Beauty and the Beast" was what Morley, from SNCC Central Headquarters, used to call them. Axel hunched his shoulders as he crossed Ninety-sixth Street against the light. Just the thought of Morley still made him feel shaky.

Morley was the first man Despina had gone off with down in Mississippi. When she had come home two nights later, Axel did not say a word about it, but nonetheless Despina had insisted on repeating her dictum that their marriage was a political alliance, no more, no less. Axel had not flinched. His only question then, as always, had been whether or not that meant they would stay together, and her answer, as always, had been a shrug. But they did stay together, slept in the same bed in McNair and New York. And when Axel least expected it, Despina would reach for him under the covers and his flesh would burn.

A year after they had established themselves in New York, the SNCC purge had come; all whites were expelled. It was a rejection Axel had predicted, and he was neither stunned nor pained, but Despina suffered deeply. Humiliated, she had clung to Axel. He remained with her in their bedroom for days, nursing her, feeding her, while beyond the door they could hear Cord and Mott packing the files, posters and pamphlets into cardboard boxes and lugging them out into the hall to be picked up by workers for the new leadership. Mott had gone with them; of the original blacks that had lived there, only Cord, a homosexual boy who had followed them from McNair, remained. For Axel those days alone in the bedroom with Despina had been extraordinarily beautiful. She had responded to him with a tenderness he had not felt since Udo, and it had purged the pain of his own humiliations. She wanted to make love every morning as soon as she awakened and every night before she could fall asleep. On the day she was ready to come out of the bedroom and begin again, Despina pulled Axel's head against her bosom and whispered, "You would never leave, would you, Axel?"

Oh God, no! Never, never.

But in the months that followed, Despina's despair hardened into something that Axel did not know how to live with. One evening not long after emerging from the bedroom, Despina called a meeting of the four who still lived in the apartment. She declared that it had been weak and ridiculous of them to depend on SNCC all this time for their identity. They were floundering, and they needed to organize. She opened the floor to nominations for officers, and when Angie and Cord gaped at her like students who had wandered into the wrong classroom, she nominated herself for chairman. She won, unopposed. A few days later she harangued them for two hours straight about how lax they had become, how flabby and purposeless. That is when the assignments began. Angie and Cord were sent out to recruit—to "fill in the ranks," as Despina put it—while Axel's assignment was to study movement trends in search of gaps their cadre could fill. At times, poring over piles of underground newspapers and movement memoranda, Axel felt his assignment was like finding them all a job with career potential.

It was in a report from Tanzania in the underground newspaper *Black Angel* that Axel came across a picture of Ngoso. Yes, by God, *their* Ngoso from Udo—the shame of Chief Nagomway, now President Nyerere's Minister of Cultural Affairs. Axel laughed out loud with sheer pleasure. He had not heard anything about their African friend in nearly five years, although he had wondered about him frequently as he followed SERA's rise to power in Tanzania. Seeing Ngoso's name, Axel thought again of those two miraculous days they had spent in Luhira, the honest magic of the "woolly trinity." It had been then that Axel first began to believe that people could build a new life from the ground up. When Despina came home that evening, Axel immediately showed her the article in *Black Angel* and stood behind her, smiling, while she read it.

"Well, he's done well for himself. I'm not surprised," Despina said when she'd finished.

"It made me think of Luhira," Axel said. "Sometimes I feel like we've lost touch with that, you know?"

"If you think it's relevant, stick it in your report." Despina studied the photo a moment longer, a half-smile on her lips. "He's still a sexy-looking buck, isn't he?"

Axel pressed his hand against the wall, his mouth suddenly dry, his head spinning.

His thirty-page report on the state of the movement, mimeographed and distributed to their now expanded group of seven, concluded that the movement needed to find new ways to gain the media's attention if it was going to survive, and that no one, save the Yippies, even began to understand how the mainstream media operated. The report made no mention of the spirit of Luhira.

"I think you're having too goddamned good a time in there." Despina stood in the doorway of the T.V. room, her legs spread wide, her hands on her hips. "We've been back from Washington for a week and you haven't produced shit."

"I'm working on it," Axel answered, waving his clipboard.

Despina had been in a state of relentless anger since returning from Washington. She kept ranting that they were running out of time, that everyone else was already making plans for the conventions in Miami and Chicago next summer. "We're nobody!" she screamed. "People in Washington didn't even know we existed anymore." If Axel tried to calm her, she accused him of being soft, spineless. She was right about one thing: They were running out of time. But Axel still did not have anything to report, at least nothing that she would want to hear.

"By the way, how did this get here?" Despina sailed an envelope into the room and it dropped beside him. "Somebody's got your address."

Axel did not look down at the envelope until she was gone. It was a long, chatty letter from his sister Annalena, the only person he had entrusted with his address. He read it slowly, trying to conjure up mental pictures of his nephews. Near the end of the letter she wrote that she was trying to convince her husband Les to let them go to Washington for the march. Axel smiled in the flickering light, wondering if she had made it—Annalena, with her bright, midwestern face, corn-colored hair and her two young sons, a perfect image for the network cameramen.

"One last thing," Annalena added at the bottom. "Father asked me to send the enclosed mail to you. I hope to God it's not what I think it is. Good luck and good love, Sis."

Axel looked again in Annalena's envelope: There was another envelope folded inside it. It was from the United States Government and it informed Axel Ericson Stenhorn to report to the Akron Armory on the third of December for his induction into the United States Army.

Axel did not leave the T.V. room for supper that night. He sat cross-legged against the wall while one program after another appeared on the screen. In some way that he could not begin to understand, he felt exhilarated. Late that evening, half-asleep, Axel saw Greg Gregorian's name roll by at the end of a program, and for an instant it seemed like an omen.

20

GREG STOOD on the corner of Fifty-fifth Street and Sixth Avenue playing a game of "Shotgun Wedding" while he waited for Axel to make his appearance. Only three minutes to go and Greg still hadn't picked out a wife from the women parading by on the avenue. It was a tricky business: If he failed to make a choice in the allotted time, he had to marry the last woman he saw. Yesterday on the bus home he'd played it too close and ended up living out his days in Scarsdale with a thin-lipped clubwoman twice his age. Greg squinted at the crowd crossing the street toward him. Ah, fantastic—a beauty worth waiting for! Chinese or Japanese, her jet black hair swung behind her like a silk curtain, her miniskirt mere inches below, exposing lemony thighs. She passed in front of Greg, giving him a hint of a smile, and just as he was about to commit himself to her for all eternity, his eye caught on the book she pressed against her bosom: *The Prophet* by Kahlil Gibran. Oh, no! One month, two at best, and he'd be flinging it at her, accusing her of trading in five thousand years of oriental wisdom for bubble gum philosophy. Another perfect marriage shot to hell.

Greg had invented "Shotgun Wedding"—one of his series of "stunts to live by"—a couple of days after Betty Ehrmann left his bed and board. Betty had gone at his request, of course, but nonetheless the game was meant as a consolation, a reminder of life's infinite arbitrariness. God knows, he had wanted to love Betty purely and contentedly forever after. She was absolutely wonderful. And she did *believe* in him—Jesus, how she believed in him. She had told him every morning how brilliant he was, and in the evenings after dinner she had prepared his desk with fresh sheets of paper as if it were a wedding bed. With Betty gone, Greg hadn't touched his plays in months.

Greg clapped a hand over his heart—Lord what a marvelous-looking woman! Reflexively he checked his watch: one minute left. He looked again at the exotic, raven-haired woman with luminous skin who was striding across Sixth Avenue directly toward him. Yes, yes! I do! I do! For a split second Greg's eye shifted to the bearded, Amish-looking man at the woman's side. Good Christ, it was Axel. Greg's face colored. "I barely recognized you," he said, smiling at Axel and Despina.

"I let my hair grow," Despina answered. Her eyes glowed.

Greg shook Axel's hand—no fancy grips this year, just a quick, formal pump. "How've you been, Axe?"

"Okay. You, Greg?"

"Up and down."

Greg looked into Axel's face. He looked calmer than when he last saw him at David's party a few years ago, but his eyes, now framed behind rimless, Lennon spectacles, looked worn, strained in the bright sun. Greg noticed a single silver hair in Axel's beard. Jesus, you couldn't even pretend to be just kids anymore.

"Well, why don't we get started. We're shooting a stunt up at Bergdorf Goodman's you might want to see." Greg gestured with his head and led them across the street. He really had little idea of what Axel was looking for. A few days ago he had called out of the blue, saying he'd seen Greg's name on the "April Fools" credits and wondered if they could get together. He had said he was doing a survey of some sort on T.V. techniques and that "April Fools" was particularly relevant to his study. That was about all he had volunteered.

"I take it you two are still involved in, uh, political stuff," Greg said, trying to sound casual.

Despina laughed. "Oh, yes, political stuff."

As they approached Bergdorf's, Greg told them to follow him and not to talk to anyone until they were hidden. He led them to the back of the store, into a stockroom, then around to where a black curtain hung across the tops of two shelves. He pulled the curtain aside. In a space no larger than a utility closet were two sound men at a spinet-sized console and a cameraman and his assistant, both dressed in black. They all smiled briefly at Greg and Axel before gazing at Despina.

"Old friends," Greg whispered. "Anyone mind if they poke around?"

"No problem at all." Sam, the cameraman, reached for Despina's hand and gently tugged her toward the wall where his camera was poised behind a plate of glass. "One-way mirror," he said, pointing. "They can't see us, but we can see them. Here, look through the eyepiece."

Greg quickly glanced at Axel, who hung back against a shelf of ladies' slippers. Undoubtedly he was inured to the special attention his wife received. Greg stepped over to his old friend.

"We're set up for a simple stunt," he told him. "One of the saleswomen is a plant, an actress working for us. None of the customers know that, of course. The plant's assignment is to try to convince a customer that a pair of lady's mountain-climbing boots are the latest high-fashion trend in formal wear."

Axel nodded. Despina had just taken her eye from the camera. Her face was flushed. The head sound man raised his index finger. "Pamela's got a live one," he whispered.

Sam immediately put his eye to the camera, pressed it on. On the console the tapes began to roll. The assistant sound man handed out extra headphones.

". . . a little pre-theater party," a woman's voice was saying. "I'm wearing my blue chiffon, but I'm just completely bored with pumps, do you know what I mean?"

Greg squinted through the one-way mirror. The customer had streaked, bouffant-style hair and an affected way of speaking—a perfect subject for the stunt. Pamela, the plant, was working her with all the finesse of an expert con man, first showing her a pair of Italian stiletto-heeled shoes, then silk pumps, all the while saying that the customer seemed like a trendsetter, not a follower. Finally Pamela leaned forward and, *sotto voce,* asked the customer if she'd heard about the new look that was just catching on in Paris, "the *montagne* look." With that she swept open the box of mountain-climbing boots.

Sam zoomed in for a close-up of the customer. She raised her eyebrows. "Of course I've heard about it," she said, gingerly fingering the coarse-grained boots, "but I guess I imagined something more, you know, delicate. I don't really think I'm young enough to carry it off, do you?"

Fantastic! Greg checked around their hidden control room. Everyone was smiling, even Despina.

"But they were made for you," Pamela crooned. "Try them on. You'll see what I mean."

The customer hesitated, then shrugged girlishly and extended her foot for Pamela to put the boots on her. She stood and took two tentative steps. "Oh God, I suppose I would be noticed, wouldn't I?"

A few seconds later Pamela did the "reveal" and the subject stared deliriously into the hidden camera. "Oh no! You mean I'm actually on television?"

It was a perfect take, the best they'd had in two days, and after a few more minutes Greg led Axel and Despina out through the store.

"What's really remarkable," Despina was saying, "is how eager that ridiculous woman was to give you permission to use the film after she'd made such an asshole of herself."

"It's not really so hard to understand," Greg said, smiling at her. "Everyone wants to get into show business." He held her eye for just a second before pushing through the door.

As the three walked toward Central Park, Axel quizzed Greg about the program: how much it cost to produce; how many millions watched it each week. Suddenly Despina came to a halt.

"Thirty million people?" She thrust a finger in front of Gregory's face. "Do you know what I could do if I had thirty million people's attention for just five minutes?"

Greg shrugged. "Not really. What would you do?"

Despina stared back at Greg. She looked perplexed, then angry.

"We've got to find ways to morally reeducate this country," Axel cut in quickly, "and we've got to do it before too many people get killed."

"We're running out of time," Despina said, picking up the beat. "We've got to get people's attention now. That's why we need television." She put one foot up on a bench. "Ideally we'd commandeer a station and do our own broadcasts."

Greg stared at the ground, trying desperately to suppress a smile. His problem, Betty always told him, was that he had no idea what it was like to be truly committed to anything.

"We want to make something happen that will capture television's attention," Despina was saying, "something that will reach people at their own level and force them to think."

Greg looked up at her. "How about a stunt?" he said.

Greg had no particular idea in mind when he made that remark, but something in it excited him, and he knew the next step would be for them to meet with his friend, Russell Burns, a unit producer at CBS local news.

From the moment they walked into his office, Russell's total attention was focused on Despina. Greg attempted to interrupt, to bring Axel into the conversation, but Russell was off and away with his "star system" theory of T.V. news, a riff of hip cynicism that Greg had heard him use with women a hundred times before.

"Let's say we've got two murders, one uptown and one downtown," Russell was saying, leaning back in his chair. "You know what the first thing we want to know is? Which has the best-looking corpse? The youngest corpse, the best-dressed corpse, the sexiest corpse. The corpse is the star of the segment, dig?"

Despina looked back at Russell impassively, apparently unimpressed. Thank God for that. Greg was already feeling guilty about bringing her here.

"Do you decide what stories you're going to cover?" Despina asked.

"More or less."

Despina stood with her face inches away from Russell's. Suddenly she gave him a dazzling smile. "I'd like to watch you work for a couple of days, if you don't mind."

Russell grinned. "Don't mind at all."

Greg could barely look at Axel as the two of them walked out to the hall and waited for the elevator. On the street Axel said that he did not have time to have lunch with Greg.

"I'm really going to come up with a terrific idea for you," Greg promised, trying to hold him a few minutes longer, but Axel was already backing away, turning, waving, disappearing into the crowd on Sixth Avenue.

That evening, as Greg looked out his bus window at Macy's, he kept his promise.

21

ALL GREG had was ideas. They sprang into his brain unannounced, like extraterrestrial visitors while he waited in bank
queues, sat in barber chairs, stood at urinals. Willy-nilly he received ideas for plays, lines of dialogue for movies he had not
begun to write, stunts, songs, toys. He jotted them down on the
three-by-five cards he always carried in his breast pocket, cards
which he piled on his desk until they toppled over, then bound
with rubber bands and dropped into a drawer. Often ideas saved
him, as if dispensed by a guardian angel. At his Harvard interview
ten years ago, after suggesting that a young man of Greg's abilities
might be better suited to one of the state universities in California,
the dean of admissions had concluded by asking Greg what he
would expect to gain from the "Harvard experience." Suddenly
inspired, Greg had sprung to his feet and quickly sketched a series
of figures on the dean's memo pad—a parody of Cro-Magnon man
evolving to Homo sapiens which showed a scruffy-looking Greg
Gregorian evolving into the quintessential Harvard man. Brilliant!
The inspiration had gotten him into Harvard.

Sometimes Greg's ideas gave the impression of great intelligence, but they were not the same article and he knew it. Living
for four years with Todd Brewster, Greg had witnessed the ab-
stract leaps and deductive thrusts of a truly brilliant mind. Often
as not, when they discussed philosophy Greg could barely follow
him. Even David's plodding logic eventually left Greg behind, but
Greg's ideas kept coming, got him through college, got him by.

Over the past few years Greg had begun to spot his ideas crop-
ping up here and there: The hit Off-Broadway play *MacBird!* was
an idea of his—he even still had the "card" on it; John Lennon's
announcement that the Beatles were more popular than Jesus
Christ came only weeks after Greg had sketched a cartoon of the
four at the Last Supper; Greg had been joking about topless bath-

ing suits for years before Rudi Gernreich created his scandal on the California beaches.

"Somebody's stealing my ideas!" Greg would rant late at night, half-believing it. "Somebody's picking my brain to pieces."

That had been near the end of Betty's tenure in the apartment.

"Nobody's stealing your ideas," she would answer as he paced around her, "but a hell of a lot of people out there are doing more than just writing their ideas down on little cards."

An hour before Axel's "event" at Macy's was to begin, Greg left his apartment and started uptown on Fifth Avenue. It was a cool Saturday, the first in December. Axel had chosen the date himself —the third of December; in fact, he'd been surprisingly adamant about it when Greg suggested that the event might be more effective closer to Christmas. But he had accepted every other detail of the idea totally uncritically when Greg called him with it late that same day they had gone to CBS News together.

"Why don't I come up to your place and run it through for Despina and the others," Greg had said on the phone. After years of working in television, blank acceptance made him nervous. "I could answer any questions that might come up. There are probably some angles I haven't thought of."

"That won't be necessary."

Greg hesitated. "You know, Axe, I think this is one of the best ideas I've ever had. I could hold on while you got Despina's reaction."

"I'll have to call you about that later," Axel had answered evenly, and it was only then that Greg finally realized that Despina was still not home, that long after the CBS Six O'Clock News office had closed for the day she still remained in the company of Russell Burns. Greg had wanted to apologize to Axel but, of course, there was nothing to say.

A week later Axel had called Greg at his office to tell him that everything was set for the third.

"Isn't there anything I can do?" Greg asked. He felt excluded, the playwright barred from rehearsals.

"No. But thanks, Greg. I do appreciate everything you've done."

There was something oddly formal in the way Axel had said that, reminding Greg of the way Axel used to shake hands when they met for dinner back at Harvard. It had struck Greg then that his awkward handshake was the only way Axel dared to touch his friends. Strange, brave Axel. What was he putting himself through all this for? Why, in God's name, hadn't he just gone to medical school?

At Thirty-third Street Greg saw the CBS News van cutting across traffic, a cop waving it into a no-parking zone—professional courtesy. Greg jogged up just as Russell Burns stepped down from the van. Russell wore his rust-colored hair long, his sideburns a wedge halfway down his jaw—the new amalgam of hippie and uptown styles.

"Merry Christmas, Gregorian," Russell said, smiling. He pulled a press pass from his pocket and handed it to Greg. "Wear it proudly, old boy. It gets you free candy wherever you go."

With a cameraman and a sound man trailing behind them, Russell and Greg strode into Macy's, the crowds of shoppers parting in front of them. You could stroll unharmed through Hades with a press pass. A ruddy-faced man in a blazer walked up to them, his hand extended. "Bob Murphy, public relations," he said much too loudly. "I'm your slave for the day."

Russell clapped him on the back. "Just what I always wanted."

On the escalator Russell said into Greg's ear, "Officially we're here doing a story on this year's Christmas toys. We should get the red carpet right up until the shit hits the fan."

The head buyer of the toy department, a gnomelike fellow with a sprig of plastic mistletoe in his lapel, met them on the third floor and immediately launched into a rundown of the season's hot items. He pulled a string bag from his pocket.

"This here's our biggie." He winked and then opened the bag. A burst of mechanical laughter issued from it. He guffawed. "It's called 'Bag Full of Laughs.' $3.95. Want me to do that again for the camera?"

Greg excused himself, eager to find a good vantage point before the event began. The fact was, no matter what Axel and Despina and their "cadre" expected to accomplish this afternoon in the name of world peace, Greg thought of the event as pure, ultimate theater: the stunt as world news; the stunt made sublime. "A Bag Full of Laughs," by Greg Gregorian. He had wandered past the holiday display of model trains—"A Whistle-Stop Tour of Candyland"—when he saw his first Santa. It was Despina.

Even swathed in red flannel and white fur, padded with pillows, and half-masked with a silky white beard, she was unmistakable. The magnificent curve of her cheekbone was visible just above the beard, the ice-blue glow of her eyes shone beneath the fuzzy rim of the stocking cap. Wrapped in burlap, her beauty would still burn through. Greg watched her move down the aisle. Maybe he and Axel were not so different after all. God knows, if Axel had become a doctor in Akron, Ohio, he never would have met that woman, never even met the likes of her, let alone married her. She was now handing out candy canes from her sack.

Greg glimpsed Russell with his peripheral vision. He had set up the camera on a little balcony that jutted from the wall behind the train display. He motioned Greg toward a door just below him. Walking over to it, Greg passed within a foot of Despina.

"And what do you want for Christmas?" she was saying to a little boy. She glanced in Greg's eyes for an instant without even a flicker of recognition, the consummate actress.

From the balcony Greg could take in the entire floor, from the elevators to the Christmas tree surrounded by shiny, life-sized elves.

"Max is roving with a mike," Russell said. "I've got him on two-way if we want to move him someplace. Right now he's trying to shake that asshole from P.R." He squinted. "Oh Jesus, here we go, Greg. Santa Claus number two just stepped off the elevator. Number three's on the escalator. Four and five are right below us."

Greg looked down. Two more Santas were just exiting from the other elevator. That brought the count to seven, the whole group. Greg checked his watch: exactly twelve-fifteen, curtain time. Revolutionaries were clearly more punctual than actors. Greg rubbed his hands, grinning. This was really happening and it was infinitely more exciting than his play at the Cino had ever been.

"Which one's your friend?" Russell asked.

Greg scanned the floor. There was one Santa in every other aisle. The farthest, just in front of the elevators, had a brown face. He was handing out his candy canes two at a time—a little too frenetically, Greg thought. Two aisles up was a diminutive Santa— probably one of the girls, Greg guessed. In front of the tree, flanked by plastic elves, was the tallest Santa, Axel. He was still wearing his rimless glasses, giving him a distinctive Kris Kringle

look. The Santa-Despina was two aisles away, facing him. Greg
pointed Axel out.

"Just another little elf, isn't he?" Russell said.

Greg nodded, not taking his eyes away from the scene below.
He didn't really like Russell Burns, he decided.

"Okay, Ted, pan in from the elevator, picking them up one at a
time." Russell spoke quickly to the cameraman while pulling on
his headphones and adjusting the radio mike. "Max," he said into
the mike, "why don't you sashay up toward aisle six and kind of
float inconspicuously around the blue-eyed Santa, right?"

Despina was to be the star, of course.

Greg checked his watch: twelve-twenty. No one seemed dis-
turbed by the superabundance of Santas yet. He focused on Axel,
who was now moving toward a counter piled high with fuzzy
penguin dolls wearing bow ties. A gang of little children followed
behind him, their mothers clutching at their coat sleeves. Axel
reached for one of the penguins and held him high, manipulating
him like a puppet. Then he swooped down, dropping the doll into
the hands of a little girl in front of him.

"Aisle eight!" Greg blurted. "It's happening!"

Greg gaped, grinning, as one by one, Axel picked the penguins
from the counter and dropped them into the outstretched hands
of the youngsters surrounding him. Axel was smiling, almost dancing, as the circle of children around him grew. Now mothers were
also stretching out their hands, grabbing two, three penguins at a
time. The counter was nearly bare. The din of the crowd rose to a
roar.

"Oh, shit! I wish I had three cameras!" Russell cried.

In front of the elevator the brown Santa was dashing up and
down the aisle grabbing plastic dump trucks and fire engines from
the display racks and practically flinging them into the shoppers'
arms. The smallest Santa, two aisles away, was gaily bouncing
teddy bears in the air like a juggler before kissing them and ceremoniously presenting them to her entourage of children. And in
the center of the floor, resting on one knee, Despina was handing
out boxes of Monopoly to an orderly line of children. Greg could
see Max, the sound man, to her right and Murphy, Macy's public
relations man, just behind him. Russell handed Greg a pair of
earphones.

"And have you been a good boy this year?" Despina's voice

crackled in Greg's ear. With the earphones on, Greg could suddenly see the scene below as it would look tonight on the Six O'Clock News—flattened, framed, distanced. He let out his breath, just now aware that he had been holding it. All danger gone; this was television.

"I don't understand . . . I don't think this is right. Not our people. We don't give away Monopoly sets." It was Murphy, the P.R. man. "May I see your identification? . . . Just a minute. Jesus, your people aren't still filming, are they?"

Max pointed. Murphy stared up at the camera and wildly waved both arms, signaling Russell to stop the cameras. Russell smiled back.

"I demand to see your identification!" Murphy yelled at Despina. Two shoppers pushed him to one side.

Greg quickly surveyed the rest of the floor. Act Three had just begun. At almost the same instant all the sales people abruptly caught on: They were being robbed. Greg spotted two saleswomen on phones; a third was barking over the P.A. system:

"Your attention please. These Santas are . . . are imposters . . . They are not associated with Macy's. Do not accept gifts from them. All merchandise must be paid for at the cashiers. I repeat: These Santas are not real."

Greg could not have scripted it better himself.

Russell pointed down. Three uniformed security men were approaching, nightsticks in hand. Suddenly the Santas leapt onto countertops, the model train table and the platform surrounding the tree. In unison they pulled their banners from their sacks and unfurled them:

Eighty-seven Children Died in Vietnam Last Week.
Merry Christmas!

Santa Lives! Give the Gift of Peace!

No Presents in Vietnam This Year—Just Napalm!

Greg began counting down in his head—ten, nine, eight. Timing was everything now. They had to hold their banners aloft just long enough for the camera to read them. Then they would drop them, yank off their Santa costumes, and meld into the crowd before they were apprehended. The security men were advancing, splitting up, pushing through the crowds of shoppers.

"Jesus! Can't you stop those cameras?" It was Murphy over Greg's headphones. Greg spotted him waving his arms, swimming like a turtle toward the oncoming security man. He stopped and looked up at the balcony. He grinned idiotically, then grabbed at one security man's nightstick, terrified that it would be seen by the camera. It was a P.R. man's nightmare. Unknowingly he was giving the Santas a few extra critical seconds.

The banners suddenly dropped. Three of the Santas had already pulled off their beards and costumes and had jumped back into the aisles, now just so many anonymous Christmas shoppers. Greg saw Despina as her disguise dropped to her feet—she had designed the breakaway costumes herself. For one magnificent moment she remained poised on the model train table, smiling beautifully up at the camera, both hands raised in the peace sign; then she donned a pair of harlequin sunglasses and leapt down into the mob, erased.

Two of the security men had grabbed a bearded teenager in a red-checked jacket just below the balcony. Greg leaned forward, squinting. The boy was not a member of Axel's group, no Santa. By God, the group had pulled it off. Not one of them had been caught.

"Holy shit! Ted, the tree! Pick up the tree!" Russell was shouting at the cameraman over the roar.

Greg stared, stupefied. One Santa remained in full costume among the plastic elves surrounding the Christmas tree. It was Axel and he still held his banner aloft in both hands:

Santa Carries Presents, Not Guns

A single security guard was moving toward him and this time the shoppers let him pass freely. Everyone was staring at Axel. It had suddenly become much quieter. There was no way Axel could get away now. Clearly he was not even going to attempt to. The security guard slipped his nightstick into his belt as he approached the platform where Axel stood.

What happened next came so fast that Greg could not really sort out the sequence until six-fifteen that night, when he saw it all in close-up on the local news. Axel dropped his banner and pulled a sheet of paper from his coat. Then he unfolded the paper and held it straight-arm in front of him. It was his notice to appear before the Akron draft board that afternoon. A second later that piece of paper was ignited with a match, and a fraction of a second after that the fuzzy cuff of Axel's Santa outfit burst into flame. Axel was on fire.

The security guard bucked Axel with his shoulder, knocking him to the floor just as the tree ignited. The crowd was in a panic, screaming, running, shoving. The fire alarm clanged. A pathetic spray issued from the ceiling sprinklers. Someone threw a coat over Axel, smothering his flames. Out of nowhere five New York City policemen appeared. One sprayed the tree and elves with a fire extinguisher. Two others pulled Axel's arms behind him and handcuffed him. It was over. Curtain. Greg was trembling. There were tears in his eyes.

"Incredible!" Russell was saying. "Just fantastic!"

Greg called David from a pay phone in the basement of the store. David had to tell him to slow down several times.

"I'm sure they took him to a hospital first," David said finally. "That'll give us a couple extra hours. Do you know if his family still lives in Akron?"

"I think so. Do you really have to involve them in this?"

"No, not necessarily," David said coldly. "You wrote the script, Greg. You tell me who's supposed to come up with the bail."

22

GREG SAW her sitting on his stoop from half a block away. No one sat on stoops at this time of night; it was too cold for the old Italian supers, too early for the overflow of freaks from Trude Heller's. Her bare head shone in the blue light of the streetlamp. The fog from her breath veiled her face. She smiled when Greg started up the steps.

"Greg Gregorian?"

"Yes?"

She stood, jutting her hand out toward him. There was something oddly familiar in the gesture, but Greg was certain he had never seen her face before. A sweet face. "I'm Annalena Berglin. Stenhorn, really. Axel's sister."

Greg took her hand. The Stenhorn handshake. She had clear blue eyes set in a broad, somewhat flattened face, and she wore her gold-colored hair short.

"I've been waiting for you," she said, still smiling. "Didn't Axel tell you?"

"No. Tell me what?"

"He said he'd meet me here after they released him and he took care of a few things at home. For some reason he didn't want me coming up to his apartment. Axel and his secrets." She put her hands in her coat pockets, cocked her head to one side and laughed. "I imagine you had other plans for the evening."

"True. I was thinking of a light supper followed by an early suicide." He pulled his keys from his pocket and grinned at her. "Care to join me for the supper?"

As he held the door open, he noticed that she had a small suitcase with her. "Good God, you've come all the way from Akron, haven't you?"

"Yes, the family courier. I brought the letter from Father's bank. Axel's bail. I didn't see you in the courtroom, did I? I barely made it myself."

"No, I wasn't there." Greg led her up the stairs. "I was afraid I'd burst out singing the 'Internationale' and they'd carry me off in manacles for contempt of court."

Not quite the truth, that. After a round of sanctimonious put-downs from David down at the Tombs, where Axel was being held, Greg had headed straight for the Cedar Bar and nursed a brandy straight through the bail hearing. Axel's sister said nothing. No doubt she had been able to detect the tinniness in Greg's reply even if she was from Akron. At the fourth-floor landing he looked at her. "Did Axel tell you about my little part in this afternoon's fiasco?"

"I guessed," she said brightly as Greg led her into his apartment. With her hands in her coat pockets, she gazed around Greg's one large room. For a man whose career spanned three T.V. game shows and one Off-Off-Broadway play, Greg had managed to deco-rate his walls with enough posters and *Playbills* and framed T.V. credit rolls to make it look as if the apartment belonged to Noël Coward. Axel's sister seemed to like it, though. She looked at her watch. "Ten past, already. You don't suppose we've missed the broadcast, do you? I've already missed it once."

Greg hesitated. Just an hour ago he had seen Axel burst into flames on the local news in the Cedar Bar and he had sworn to himself that he was not going to watch it again on the world news. It was bad for his health. The worst part was that he had actually caught himself feeling jealous of his burning friend: Axel's third-act climax was infinitely better than the one Greg had thought of. Greg's third acts tended to dribble off inconclusively, his characters still uncommitted, backing offstage with a quip and a grin the way Despina and the others had disappeared into the crowd at Macy's.

"You do have a T.V., I hope?"

Greg yanked his set from behind the couch, set it on his desk and turned it on. Cronkite was just wrapping up a story about prostitution in Saigon, and it was followed by a commercial for a bank. Greg took Annalena's coat and lingered with it by the closet. Although he had been assured that Axel had only suffered first-degree burns on his hands and neck, Greg still felt a knot of guilt in the pit of his stomach. Right now it was beginning to feel like nausea.

Axel's was the last story on the program. Cronkite introduced it with a twinkle of irony in his eye, careful not to reveal the surprise. Scrupulously he explained that the CBS cameras were at Macy's to do an item on new Christmas toys. No collusion, no blame. Greg braced himself against a bookcase, watching Annalena watch. Her face was so much more animated than her brother's. She leaned forward. Her eyes sparkled. She sucked in her breath in noisy Scandinavian style as the Santas began giving away the merchandise, and when the voice on the loudspeaker announced that these Santas were not real, she let out a free, hooting laugh. A split second later she was quiet again. Greg glanced at the screen: Despina had just ripped off her beard and was holding up her hands triumphantly.

"She certainly is beautiful," Annalena said softly.

Greg nodded, but for the first time he realized what that grand moment had cost Despina: The police had all the evidence they needed to arrest her too. No wonder she had not shown her face down at the Tombs. Greg looked again at Annalena as the camera swung toward Axel. He was just igniting his draft notice. Annalena gasped and Greg averted his eyes. Oh, shit!

Suddenly Annalena was on her feet in front of the television. Axel was burning. Annalena stared, tears in her eyes. Greg tasted bile in his mouth. Then abruptly the world news was back in the studio again and Cronkite was summing up:

"Defense attorney David Debilio pleaded for a suspension of bail, claiming that Mr. Stenhorn, a Harvard graduate and a veteran of the Peace Corps, had not harmed anyone but himself. The plea was denied." The camera moved in for a close-up; Cronkite offered the merest hint of a smile. "Apparently the law does not provide a 'Santa' clause."

The gag finish, of course. Something Greg was eminently familiar with. He raced to the television set and snapped it off just as Cronkite was saying, "And that's the way it is, December 3, 1967," relegating the day to history. The apartment was unbearably quiet.

"It's brilliant, you know."

Greg turned around slowly and looked at Annalena. The expression on her face was almost beatific.

"I mean that," she went on softly. "It's a passion play. A Christmas passion play for our time."

A peculiar sound blurted from Greg's mouth, half-swoon, half-laughter. Annalena's words were positively the most wonderful ones he had heard anyone say all day. He felt so unburdened he was light-headed. "Jesus, I'm hungry," he said.

"Me too. Famished. Last time I ate was at a breakfast nook in Akron."

Greg roared. It was like a punch line to a shaggy-dog story. His laughter seemed to shake the last vestige of guilt out of him. He danced across the room, snapping his fingers and singing, "Take me back to my breakfast nook snack in Akron, Ohio." At the refrigerator he dropped to one knee and opened it. Annalena was laughing. The phone rang.

"Go away!" Greg shouted at the phone. He pulled out a box of *lamejun* meat pancakes, some stuffed grape leaves and a container of yogurt before getting to his feet and picking up the phone. It was Betty.

"It was marvelous," Betty said. Her telephone voice had always sounded like bad acting. "You know, Greggy, you really have to *use* it in something—a play, a movie. All those Santas everywhere. It was really quite fabulous."

"But it *is* a movie," Greg said in a flat voice. "You just saw it."

"Oh Greg, you know what I mean." She laughed and then was silent for a moment. Greg glanced over at Annalena. He pantomimed hanging himself, his tongue lolling on his chin. Annalena blushed and looked away. "Greg, I was hoping we could get together tonight," Betty went on in all seriousness. "Auld lang syne or something like that. I've had this funny unfinished-business feeling all day, know what I mean?"

"Sort of. Look, Betts, I've got some friends over. Why don't we talk next week, okay?"

"You're a shit, Gregorian."

Greg held the receiver in front of his face for a moment, then very quietly hung it up and did a little soft-shoe number to the stove, trying to recapture some of that lightness he'd been feeling just moments ago. He slipped four *lamejun* into the oven and turned it on.

"I'd feel awful if I thought you were missing something because of me," Annalena said. "Axel really wasn't very specific about when he'd get here. I could just leave a note on the door and meet him somewhere else."

"No!" Greg blurted, surprising himself with his vehemence. He forced a grin and pointed at the phone. "That was my mother. She always calls on Saturday nights to see if I'm married yet."

Annalena shook her head, laughing.

"Well, it certainly *felt* like my mother," Greg said. He brought the food and a bottle of wine to the table. He dropped a dollop of yogurt onto each *lamejun* pancake, rolled them into scrolls and handed one to Annalena. "Armenian soul food," he said.

They barely spoke while they ate. A few times Annalena made little humming sounds to show how much she was enjoying the food. Each time she lifted her glass she said, "Skoal." When they had finished, she brought their dishes to the sink.

"Do you and Axel see a lot of each other?" she asked.

"Counting this afternoon, I've seen him exactly three times since Harvard."

"That's three more than I have. Except for today, the last time I saw Axel was at his graduation." Annalena smiled. "He was pretty vague then too. Off on some secret mission with you and Jerry. I was all of eighteen at the time."

"Ah yes, that famous night in Newton," Greg said. Annalena had just begun to rinse the dishes, but now she turned off the water and looked inquiringly at him. So, apparently Axel had never told her what they had done in that Newton living room. Greg raised his forefinger dramatically. "That was quite a night," he said. "In fact, that was the night that the sixties officially began."

That was the way the story started; Greg had told it at least twenty times to as many young women, usually right here in his apartment. It was the best story he told. It had everything: Harvard, Leary, humor, madness. Even a moment of panic. Greg bit down on his lip. He could not tell the story tonight. It was not his to tell to Axel's sister. She looked at Greg a second longer and turned on the water again.

"You know, I recognized you right away," she said. "Axel never introduced us to any of you, so I memorized your pictures from his yearbook and made up wonderful stories about all of you. I imagined you in a place just like this. Young playwright's Village garret."

"Young *unknown* playwright."

"You're terribly famous in my house." Annalena laughed as she started back to the table. It was a lovely laugh. "My children have never heard of Arthur Miller, but just mention the name Greg Gregorian and they know exactly who you're talking about."

Her children? Greg felt his ears instantly turn red. She'd been in his apartment for over an hour and suddenly there were all these children? She was as goddamned secretive as her brother. Greg drank down his glass of wine.

"But this isn't really fair," Greg said, raising one eyebrow. "You know all about my apartment, but I don't have a clue to what your house looks like. Tell me about your breakfast nook. Is it pine-paneled? Formica-topped? Fresh daisies in a bowl every morning? And, by the way, how many of you are there at breakfast? Eight? Twenty?"

She smiled, but her face had also reddened.

"Four," Annalena said. "My husband, Lester, my two sons and myself."

"Well, I'm glad to see some people are keeping up tradition in these godless times," Greg said. "How marvelously *Akronistic.*"

Annalena looked down at the tablecloth.

"You really are clever," she said quietly, not a trace of sarcasm in her voice. "I could never keep up with you."

Greg filled both their glasses with wine. They sipped in silence for several minutes. Greg could barely look in her face. He wanted to kiss her.

"I should call home," Annalena said at last. "No one knows where I am." She walked slowly to the phone, then turned and looked again at Greg. "Can you imagine? This is the first time I've been on my own since I was eighteen years old."

Don't call! Greg wanted to scream. He silently watched her dial the operator, give a number in Akron.

"Hello, Mom? It's Annalena. How are the kids?"

Greg walked over to the radio, switched on WBAI's jazz program just loud enough to screen out Annalena's voice, then ambled on to the window and looked out. The brownstone directly across the street had a single white Christmas candle in each window. Oldtime New York. Greg felt damned peculiar. He did not feel jazzy at all.

When Annalena finally hung up, she remained standing with her back to Greg for several seconds before abruptly turning and marching up to him.

"As usual, my brother seems to be operating on his own schedule," she said quickly, her voice flat. She glanced around the room. Her overnight bag was next to the couch. She jutted out her hand. "Well, I'm glad I finally met you in the flesh, Greg. And thank you for dinner. If you don't mind, I'll call later to see if Axel—"

"Where are you going?"

"A hotel. It's late. Past nine and—"

"Stay." Greg's heart was yammering in his chest. "He'll be here any minute. I'm sure of it."

Annalena stood quite still. She turned her head and looked out the window at the street below. She was trembling.

"Sometimes it feels like I've spent most of my life waiting for Axel. Waiting to see what he'll do. Covering for him. Compensating for him." She drew in her breath. Her cheeks were flushed. She looked directly in Greg's eyes. "I don't mind living in Akron at all," she went on softly. "I love my children more than you can imagine. And . . . and it's not something I think about from one year to the next, but I might have lived in New York, at least for a

while, done something else, been someone else." Again she drew
in her breath and let it out slowly. "I was a freshman at Oberlin
when I got pregnant with Timmy. It was the same year Axel had
broken my father's heart by skipping out on medical school. There
really wasn't very much I could do."

"I love you," Greg said.

Neither of them spoke for several minutes. The phone rang.
Greg finally picked it up on the fifth ring.

"Hello?"

"Gregory? It's Axel." His voice crackled on the line. Rumbling
sounds behind him. "Is my sister there?"

"Yes." Greg waved Annalena to the phone. "Where are you,
Axe?"

"I'm afraid I only have a minute," Axel said. "Can you put
Annalena on?"

Greg handed the phone to Annalena. She held it a little away
from her ear so Greg could listen. Their cheeks were almost touching.

"Hello, Axel," Annalena said. She laughed. "You're late."

"I'm not coming," Axel said. "I can't. I'm a hundred miles away.
I had to get away."

"Why?"

"The Army. New York. Everything. It's not easy to explain."
There was a racket in the background. "My bus is leaving. Look,
I'm sorry. I really wanted to see you. More than anyone, Lena.
Next time, okay?"

"Okay, Axe."

"And listen, I owe Dad three thousand dollars for the bail. I
know that. I'll pay him back."

"I'll tell him."

"Oh, there's one other thing. Tell Greg that if Despina calls, he
doesn't have to say he heard from me." He was silent for a moment. "It doesn't really matter," he said, and hung up.

It might have been Despina who called an hour later, or it might
have been someone from Annalena's family. Greg never picked
up the phone.

They had kissed the moment Annalena put down the phone and
only minutes later they had climbed into Greg's big oak bed and
made love with the joy and urgency of people who are suddenly in

love. They ate again. They talked. They made love again, infinitely more slowly than the first time. At some hour before dawn, Greg sat up and sang every Christmas carol he knew. And in the morning, without either of them having slept, they took a taxi to La Guardia Airport, where Annalena boarded a plane for Akron, Ohio.

23

IT WAS snowing when they rolled into Erie. It swirled and smacked against the bus window like a storm inside the glass globe of a Christmas paperweight. Axel had slept fitfully since Scranton, waking every time the raw skin on his neck and chin brushed against his collar. When he slept, he dreamt that he was burning.

Despina was the fire. His flesh burned. He could not breathe.

The bus rumbled into a tunnel and the snow cleared, replaced by Axel's reflection. On the layover in Scranton he had shaved off his beard and chopped his hair. The bus driver had even asked to see his ticket stub when he came back on board.

The flames enveloped him like a pyre. His heart ignited. His heart was ashes.

The Erie terminal was just outside the tunnel. Axel swayed when he stood, helping the lady beside him with her bag. He had no luggage himself. He would have a coffee and then call Benno from here. He had his phone number memorized. Benno came highly recommended in the underground. He was an expert on making people disappear.

There was only one escape.

24

"WHERE the hell is he?"

David looked over the top of his newspaper. Despina Stenhorn was standing in the doorway to his office, one hand on her hip, her eyes blazing. Scooting down the hallway behind her was Mrs. Kimpsky, the receptionist, looking more flustered than usual.

"Mr. Debilio, this young woman—" Mrs. Kimpsky began, but David waved her away.

"It's all right," he said, standing. "Mrs. Stenhorn is a personal friend." He smiled. "What can I do for you, Despina?"

"You can find out what the hell they've done with Axel," Despina said. She strolled up to David's desk, taking in his office in a single, smirking glance. She obviously wanted there to be no doubt that under normal circumstances she wouldn't be caught dead in here.

"I don't think 'they' have done anything with your husband," David said. Lately he seemed to spend half his time disabusing his clients of one conspiracy theory or another. A lawyer could devote his entire practice to investigating these paranoid visions; today Daniel Webster would be suing the Devil. "Axel was released on three thousand dollars' bail last night at around six o'clock. I was there when they signed him out."

"But he never made it home," Despina snapped.

"Perhaps that's not where he intended to go." David fought the urge to smile. It probably did not happen frequently that Despina was stood up, certainly not by her husband. It was hard to imagine Axel sneaking off with another woman, but who could tell? Axel was the subculture's hero for a day or two. Maybe some little movement groupie had taken him home to tend his wounds. No one was immune anymore. Why should Axel be?

"Look, of course he wouldn't come directly to the apartment if he thought he was leading some pig to us. But he would have gotten a message to me—to us—by now. It's protocol."

This time David did smile. What a lovely word—protocol. It smacked of 'Robert's Rules' and the House of Commons; American revolutionaries were still in the stolid hands of the British.

"Look, Despina, there were a lot of people chasing after Axel down at the hearing. Press people. Movement people. His sister. Some people from the Draft Resisters League. As a matter of fact, I advised Axel to talk to the D.R. people. With all this publicity, I don't think his draft board would dare deny him C.O. status right now." David lit a cigarette. "Chances are Axel is in Akron this very minute making his C.O. plea. I'm sure he'll contact you soon, Despina."

"You're full of shit. Axel would never go C.O." She planted her hands on the edge of David's desk and leaned her face in front of his. "C.O. is their category, their game," she hissed. "Another part of the lawyer's game."

David sat still for several seconds. Last night, watching the episode on the world news, he had been struck by the way the camera swung away from Despina's gesture of triumph the moment Axel set himself on fire. It was probably the only time Axel had ever upstaged her. David stood.

"It's all games, Despina. Fun and games. Dressing up like Santa Claus, waving at the camera, showing your pretty face on national T.V." He didn't know why he was saying all of this. "Do you honestly believe one bomb won't fall because you played Santa in Macy's?"

Despina's face was livid.

"Fucking lawyer! Fucking Harvard lawyer! What the hell are you doing? Waiting for the war crimes trial so you can be star prosecutor?"

Their faces were only a foot away from one another. David felt his pulse throb, sweat soaking through his collar and covering his chest. No wonder Axel hadn't come home. David rubbed the back of his hand across his jaw. He pressed his intercom.

"Alice, get me Mrs. Berglin in Akron, Ohio."

Despina stared at David, not moving. The phone on his desk rang. He picked it up.

"This is David Debilio in New York," he said, looking straight at

Despina. "Have you had any contact with your brother since the bail hearing last night?"

For a moment there was no reply, then she responded, "Yes. He called me. He's run away. I don't think he intends to go into the Army or to stand trial either. None of it. I'm sorry. I should have called you, I guess."

"That's all right, Mrs. Berglin. It wasn't your responsibility. Good-bye." David replaced the receiver. He had not taken his eyes off Despina. "He's gone," he said quietly. "He's disappeared."

Despina sank into the chair on the other side of David's desk. She crossed her legs and touched a hand to her forehead in a stylish, casual-looking gesture, but David had seen the blood drain from her face and the awful look of helplessness in her eyes.

25

TODD COULD never get the job he wanted. After six months as an orderly at San Francisco General Hospital, the director of clinical services promoted him to ward supervisor. Todd protested. Being an orderly suited him just fine, he told the director. He did not want to supervise anyone. But the director only laughed. He offered to raise his salary to twelve thousand dollars a year, and when that did not change Todd's mind he threatened to fire him if he did not accept the promotion. Todd took the job. A year later, when he was promoted again, Todd knew it was a losing fight. "Brewster's Law of Upward Mobility" his wife May called it. The surest way to rise in the world was to aspire to nothing.

In the spring Todd began to have qualms of another, graver sort about the work he was doing. Half the young orderlies reporting to him were conscientious objectors fulfilling their alternate service, every one of them college educated, every one of them white.

"Who the hell is fighting the war?" he said to May one morning after working the night shift. "Not Harvard men. Not philosophy majors. No, we're all too busy getting deferments and getting radicalized while somebody else is over there getting his legs blown off."

"Nobody should be over there," May said.

"But somebody *is*," Todd said. "Fifty thousand of them. Something's wrong."

Todd could not let go of the thought. The war in Vietnam was immoral, he was sure, but it was dead wrong for him to be sitting it out in San Francisco. It was simple arithmetic: If Todd did not go, someone else did, probably some poor black kid who could not go to college if he wanted to, who had never heard of deferment or the right to conscientiously object to anything. At the beginning of the fall Todd told May that he was thinking of enlisting.

"You're crazy," she said, tears filling her eyes. "And you're cruel. Are you going to make me a widow for the sake of some convoluted moral principle?"

Todd put his arms around May, but she pushed him away. She was crying in earnest now. "What are you going to do over there, Todd? Shoot Vietcong?"

"No. I won't shoot anyone."

"Jesus Christ, you aren't even consistent!" May yelled. In the other room the twins rustled in their cribs.

Todd argued that he was consistent, that maybe the precise place for a pacifist to be was in the Army with an empty gun, that at the very least pacifism should not be a privilege. But he hated to see May cry, hated the righteous sound of his overeducated voice, hated the idea of leaving his family for even a day, let alone years.

When Greg called on Thanksgiving and told Todd about the protest Axel was going to stage at Macy's, Todd told him that he was thinking of enlisting.

"Just run through it for me slowly, would you, pal?" Greg said. "Remember, I only got into Harvard on the Armenian quota." After Todd finished his explanation, Greg said, "You know what they'll do with you in the Army, Todd? They'll make you head of the typing pool in Fort Ennui, Texas, and the same miserable black slob will still get his legs shot off in Vietnam."

"Maybe."

"Please," Greg said. Todd could hear his friend's voice break. "I couldn't stand it if anything happened to you."

Todd watched the Macy's incident on a T.V. set in a patient's room. The patient, an old man who had just had a tumor removed from his neck, laughed when Axel burst into flame. "Crazy kids," he said.

The next morning after breakfast, without a word to May, Todd walked to the post office and filled out an application for the United States Army. Two weeks later he spent an entire afternoon undergoing his preinduction mental and physical examinations. After he had dressed he was directed into a captain's office.

"Why have you chosen to enlist at this time, Mr. Brewster?" the captain asked.

"I figured my turn had come up."

"As a married man with children, you have no obligations to the military at present, you know."

"Yes, I know."

The captain looked down at a sheaf of papers on his desk. "I'm afraid you do not qualify for service," he said.

"Why is that?"

The captain smiled. "Too old, too big. It says here that your back is chancy, probably wouldn't last two weeks in basic before a disk popped. Our average recruit is eighteen and a half years old, Mr. Brewster. I think you'd serve your country better doing just what you've been doing. I'm very glad you came down here, though."

"I'd like to appeal this decision," Todd said, his voice quavering.

"Please, Mr. Brewster," the Captain said. "Don't waste valuable time for both of us."

When Todd arrived home that evening, May was putting the twins to bed. He leaned his long torso over the sides of their cribs and kissed the tops of their heads. Then he pulled May to his chest with both hands and rocked her slowly. "God love you," he said.

He never told her where he had been that afternoon, and for several weeks he managed to push the episode to the back of his mind. Then, in the middle of a rainy January night, he received a totally unexpected phone call at the hospital. He was standing behind the glass wall of a nurse's station, a clipboard in one hand, when the head nurse handed him the phone.

"Todd Brewster?"

"Yes. Who is this?"

"You'll probably recognize my voice in a minute, Todd, but please don't say my name out loud, okay? We used to have dinner together in Dunster—you, Greg, Jerry and—"

It was Axel. Todd sat down. Greg had written to him about

Axel's disappearance. "Yes, I remember very well. Where are you, friend?"

"In the neighborhood. I'd like to see you, Todd."

"Terrific. Same here. Want to meet here or at my apartment?"

"I'll just kind of show up, okay? Sorry to be so vague, but I'm sure you understand."

"Of course."

"And Todd, I have to tell you that there is some risk to having me at your place, and if—"

"You are always welcome in my home," Todd said quickly.

Todd could not sleep when he returned home in the morning. He stretched out on the couch and closed his eyes, only to jump up moments later and pace to the window and look down at the street. By evening he began to worry that somehow he had put Axel off, that he had not made his welcome strong enough. Todd and May had just finished dinner when their buzzer sounded. Todd buzzed the door open and then sprinted down the stairs. He almost collided with Axel on the first landing. Todd threw his big bear arms around him.

Axel wore a long tweed coat with the collar turned up. His skin was darker than Todd remembered it, weathered. His night watchman's cap was low on his forehead and he wore brown horn-rimmed glasses that gave him the appearance of a sales clerk.

"Have you eaten?" Todd asked as he led him upstairs.

Axel smiled. "Not lately."

May set out the Swedish meatballs and pickled red cabbage all over again, as if she and Todd had not just eaten. Todd brought out a bottle of wine. They all smiled frequently to one another while they ate, but they spoke very little. When he had finished a second helping of May's plum cake, Axel pushed his chair from the table and said, "I don't think I've had a meal like that since I lived with my parents."

May thanked him. "Would you like to peek at the children?" she asked.

The three of them tiptoed into the twins' room. Axel removed his glasses before leaning over the sides of the cribs. He stared at each of the sleeping infants for several minutes. Back in the living room, he said, "I'd like to stay here for a little while, if I could."

"As long as you want," Todd said.

Axel was asleep on the couch when Todd left for the hospital that night. Todd had not slept in a day and a half, but his mind was buzzing. After all these years of following Axel's adventures through Greg's stories, it was strange to see him in the flesh. He still seemed the same pensive, withdrawn boy he had known at Harvard. For the few hours before Axel retired, they had talked about San Francisco, hospital work, and Greg, but not a word was said about where Axel was coming from, where he lived or what he did. When Todd returned in the morning, Axel was dressed, sitting by the window with Todd's son Jan in his arms. He looked like a visiting bachelor uncle. He looked nothing at all like a criminal on the run.

"How was your night?" he asked.

"Good," Todd said, setting a bag of fresh donuts on the table. "Two cardiacs died in intensive care, four healthy babies were born in maternity. A nice ratio."

May walked in from the bedroom with Kristin in her arms. She kissed Todd and handed him their daughter. "I'll tell you what a nice ratio is," she said, smiling, "two husbands for every wife. Especially convenient with twins."

Todd laughed as he carefully lowered himself into the chair across from Axel. The two men, each with a child in his arms, smiled at one another.

"I had a little hospital of my own when I was in Africa," Axel said quietly. "It was about half the size of this room. Mostly we took care of children—scabies, conjunctivitis, ear infections, that sort of thing. I was the resident physician." He smiled, not looking up from the little boy in his arms. "In the kingdom of the blind, you know."

Todd slept all afternoon. When he got up, May said that Axel had gone out at around two. He did not return until seven. That evening Axel barely touched his dinner. May was serving coffee when he abruptly pulled a folded piece of paper from his breast pocket.

"I need a few things from your hospital," he said in a monotone, "mostly broad-spectrum antibiotics, some sulfa drugs, a few pain-killers. It's all here. If possible, I'd also like a few pads of prescription blanks." He handed the paper to Todd, glancing quickly in his eyes before looking down at his coffee cup. "It seems I've landed in another kingdom of the blind. People who are hiding from the Army or the police. People who can't risk seeing a real doctor."

May was standing just behind Todd with the coffee percolator in her hand; she seemed to be holding her breath. Todd stared at the piece of paper in Axel's hand.

"Of course," Axel went on, "if I get caught with anything, it could probably be traced back to you." He shrugged his shoulders. "That's about all there is to say about it, Todd."

Todd suddenly took the piece of paper and stuffed it in his shirt pocket. He tried to pick up his coffee cup, but his hand was trembling and his eyes had filmed over. He was not afraid of getting caught stealing supplies from the hospital. No, that risk felt like a chance, a gift.

"No problem," he said. He looked up at May and smiled.

In the morning Todd brought home two shopping bags filled with medicine and prescription blanks. To Axel's list he had added a sphygmomanometer, a stethoscope, and a set of scalpels. He had also included an envelope containing a hundred dollars. May packed it all in her old leather overnight bag. After breakfast, as Todd had guessed, Axel said that he had to be leaving. He held the children one at a time. He kissed them and then he kissed May and shook Todd's hand. Todd watched Axel from the window as he walked down the street in his long coat and navy hat, the leather bag swinging at his side. And then Todd stretched out on the sofa and slept better than he had in months.

26

"DETAILS! I want details."

"I don't know what to tell you, Greg."

"Everything. Imagine I'm writing a movie of your life. Very *vérité*. Lots of close-ups of your nostrils."

Annalena laughed into the phone. "All right, you asked for it. After brushing my teeth thoroughly with Pepsodent, I felt a little itch in my inner ear, my *right* inner ear, so I removed a Q-Tip from the medicine cabinet, plunged it in and rooted around for a little while . . . How am I doing?"

"Fantastic! For a moment there I was that Q-Tip deep inside you, firm yet fuzzy—"

"Is this an obscene phone call?"

"At these prices I certainly hope so."

She laughed again and Greg imagined the color rising in her round, open face as she stood by the wall phone in her kitchen in Akron. He had spoken with her at least once every weekday since the night Axel had disappeared. Usually she would call him collect after her husband had left for work and her eldest son Timmy was off to kindergarten. Sometimes Greg could hear the little one, Teddy, racing by on his truck. The truck was made of white plastic with green trim and had a gate which opened in the back. Details —they were all Greg had to go on.

"I can barely wait for Ashtabula," Greg said. It was the Lake Erie town where they planned to meet the following Tuesday for three hours in the middle of the day. It was close enough to Akron for Annalena to drive there, far enough away so no one would recognize her. The choices had been Willoughby, North Perry or Ashtabula. Greg had chosen Ashtabula for the rhythm of its name.

"I can't wait either," Annalena said. But Greg detected a touch of hesitancy in her voice and his stomach churned.

"What's wrong?" he said.

"I don't know. What if we're just being silly? What if you come all the way to Ashtabula and see me getting out of my car—"

"Your light blue Impala station wagon—"

"Yes, Greg, you see me and you say to yourself, 'Good Lord, what has all the fuss been about?' "

"What fuss?" Greg said in mock incredulity. "You mean the palpitations? Or that business of murmuring your name in my sleep?"

She was laughing again, thank God, that free, singing laugh of hers which she insisted only Greg tapped out of her. He himself had no doubts at all that the love he felt for her would still be there on the banks of Lake Erie. He had never been surer of any feeling. He woke up with it every morning and his days floated on it. Since the night they had spent together in his apartment, Greg's life had been propelled by a pure, right-feeling energy which, among so many things, had helped him create his first three-act play—over a hundred pages that had flowed directly onto paper the first two days after Annalena returned to Akron. That same week he had quit "April Fools" to devote full time to writing. Annalena was his muse and magician, his ballast and therapist.

The three hours in Ashtabula were more wonderful than either of them had expected, a delirium of perfect clarity. They met at the Canal Motel, where they ate lunch overlooking a snow-crusted miniature golf course.

"I've got it," Greg said. "I'll just move here, right here, and I'll run the miniature golf course in the summer and write plays in the winter and every Tuesday and Thursday you'll come up and we'll make love all afternoon."

Annalena smiled. "What about Mondays, Wednesdays and Fridays?"

"I'll lose myself in my work." Greg kissed her hand. "You know, pruning my greens, polishing my putters."

They took a long bath in their room's square tub, their feet cupping each other's waists, laughing and splashing, stretching out the time before they made love, trying desperately to ignore their deadline. The lovemaking was a dream within the dream of the afternoon. They touched one another in slow motion, held back the end until it was irresistible. Greg trembled when Annalena dressed. He cried as he watched her car disappear. He slept in their motel room that night and called her from the Cleveland airport in the morning.

"Marry me," he said.

"Oh God, don't, Greg, please . . ."

"Marry me."

In New York Greg wrote a new play in February, a third in March. His agent read them, pronounced them both extremely promising and began circulating them to his first-line producers.

"This is how it starts," he told Greg, "with plays just like these."

Greg imagined the plays opening within weeks of each other on Broadway. There was only one question: How could he bring Annalena to his premieres?

"I'd come if you wanted me to," Annalena said seriously.

"Of course, I'd want you to," Greg said. "That's what it's all about, don't you get it?"

"Tell me everything Bernie said about the plays," Annalena said.

The following Monday morning she did not call. By eleven Greg had called the telephone repair service twice to check her line.

Then he cursed himself for tying up the phone at precisely the moment Annalena was undoubtedly trying to reach him. At noon he called her, but there was no answer. There had been an accident, he was certain. Teddy had wandered into the street. Or perhaps the two of them, driving back from the grocery, had been hit by a truck running a light. Greg called Akron information, but they refused to give him a listing of hospitals. He tried Annalena's number again, but there was still no answer. By the middle of the afternoon he forced himself to go outside, eat lunch at the Bigelow and sit through *The Graduate* for a second time at the Waverly. It seemed trivial this time though. When Greg called in the evening, Annalena's husband answered the phone. He sounded much younger than Greg had imagined him.

"Ralph Zinsler here, from Mutual of Omaha," Greg said. "Does your medical insurance cover intensive care?"

It did, Lester Berglin told him, but he appreciated Zinsler's calling. In the background someone was watching "The Man from U.N.C.L.E." Jesus God, life goes on in Akron, Ohio.

Annalena called at nine the next morning.

"Was that you selling insurance last night?" she said cheerily.

"What happened to you yesterday?"

"I slept late, that's all. And then I'd promised to take Teddy downtown for a new snowsuit."

"You could have just called to tell me that," Greg said.

"I know."

Neither of them spoke for several seconds.

"What the hell is wrong, baby?" Greg moaned. "I'm dying here."

"I'm sorry. Everything's all right." She sounded to Greg like a kidnap victim with a gun at her temple.

"No, it's not," Greg said.

"Maybe just a mood. It'll pass."

"I'm coming out there right now. I'll call you when I get to the airport."

"Don't! Please don't. I love you. I have to go now."

Greg put down the receiver. He wandered around the apartment tapping things and peering at himself in the closet mirror. His eyes looked dead. He looked older than thirty. For the second day in a row he did not touch his typewriter.

Annalena called at eleven-thirty the next morning.

"I'm just on my way out," she said. "I didn't want you to worry."

"Where are you going?"

"Errands. Housewifey stuff."

"Details, baby! I need details."

Greg could hear her sigh on the other end of the line. "The details are actually what I do all day, Greg. Teddy's real. Timmy. Lester. Those are the details."

Greg closed his eyes. "Marry me, Annalena," he said softly.

"I'm pregnant, Greg," she whispered.

"Oh, Jesus!"

Annalena laughed quietly. "It's half Armenian," she said. "Ashtabula."

"Are you positive?"

"Yes."

"Jesus. How did that happen?"

"The usual way. I'd just had my period when I saw you. I didn't think anything could happen."

"Oh God, what are we going to do?"

Annalena did not answer right away. "I was hoping I wouldn't even have to tell you about it," she said at last. "I have a friend who has a friend who knows a doctor who takes care of these things here in Akron. But I found out yesterday that the doctor just closed up that side of his business. I don't know what to do, Greg."

Her voice had begun to quaver. Greg felt tears forming in his eyes.

"There . . . There must be other options besides that," he said.

"I can't have this baby while I'm married to Lester," Annalena said. "That kind of narrows down the options."

"You could always marry me," Greg blurted. The words seemed to hang in the air somewhere between New York and Akron. Greg held his breath.

"I'd have three children, Greg. And I couldn't take Timmy and Teddy far from their father."

"I could move to Ashtabula, scene of the crime." Greg laughed. "I wonder if you need a license to operate a miniature golf course."

Annalena was quiet. "I really do have to go now," she said after a moment. "We'll talk later."

"I love you," Greg said. It sounded like a plea.

"Yes. Me too."

Greg hung up and immediately paced to the window. "Not happening," he said out loud. "This is not happening."

For the rest of the day Greg had alternating fantasies: In the first he was living with Annalena and the three children in a four-room house in Ashtabula; in the second he was jumping off the roof of his apartment building. The fantasies were interchangeable: His life was over. One child was just barely imaginable, but three was an orphanage. He would trade in his typewriter for a bassinet, his books for diapers. Oh God, Annalena!

Late in the afternoon Greg called Russell Burns at his office at CBS. He asked him what he knew about abortionists.

"Ah, Gregory, the barn door. They call them 'angel makers' in France, you know. I have a few names. Some Park Avenue docs. But old Dr. Spencer in Ashland is still the best bet."

Gregory copied down Spencer's address and phone number.

"By the way, Greg, I was going to call you. Do you know what's become of our friend Despina? Her phone is disconnected and her mail comes back stamped 'addressee unknown.' Has she gone underground too?"

"You got me, Rus," Greg said.

Annalena phoned only minutes later. She was in a downtown delicatessen.

"I ate an entire corned beef sandwich," she said cheerfully. "I haven't done that since I was carrying Teddy."

Greg's stomach squirted something foul up his throat.

"I'm glad to hear you're feeling better," he said. He was afraid it sounded like an accusation.

"I do feel a million times better than I did," Annalena said. "I hated keeping this a secret from you. I told myself I was protecting you or something, but really I was just afraid of how you'd react. I don't have a good record with surprise pregnancies, you know."

The thought had occurred to Gregory too. He wondered how Lester Berglin had taken the news six years ago—he couldn't have been much more than twenty then.

"Exactly how far along are you?" Greg asked.

"You know, five weeks. It's just five weeks since we were together."

"And you've had the test and everything?"

"Yes, Greg. It's not a false alarm." Greg could tell from her tone that he had already managed to knock the good spirits out of her.

"I just needed to be sure of the particulars," Greg said. He forced a little laugh. "I'm researching our options."

"An abortionist?"

"Among other things."

Annalena said nothing for several seconds. "Do you realize that two months ago we didn't even know each other?" she said at last.

Greg closed his eyes. "I love you," he said.

The following morning Greg and Annalena chatted away on the phone for ten minutes as if nothing had changed. Just as they were about to say good-bye, Greg told her that he had made an appointment with Dr. Spencer in Ashland, Pennsylvania.

"We don't have to keep it or anything," Greg said quickly. "I just thought we ought to keep our options open."

Greg heard Annalena swallow hard before she spoke. "You don't have to come all the way out there too," she said softly.

"Yes I do," Greg whispered.

When Greg saw Annalena coming off the plane in Harrisburg, he knew that he loved her more than ever. She wore a forest green loden coat with the hood around her face, and she carried a blue half-sized suitcase of the kind college girls used to arrive with in Cambridge for a weekend. She looked no older than a college girl herself. Greg touched her arm the moment she walked through the terminal door.

"Hi." He put his arms around her, his cheek against hers.

"I've missed you," she said.

In the car Annalena told Greg how she had almost not made it to Harrisburg. Everyone thought that she was going off to visit an old college friend from Lancaster, but yesterday that friend had called, Lester had answered, and the friend had made a terrible mess of the lie she was supposed to tell. It had taken Annalena hours to smooth that one over. She told Greg the entire story in an animated, girlish manner, as if she had stolen away to be with him for a romantic tryst.

"What if I'd never made it?" she said, still smiling.

"I guess I'd have to find somebody else to take to the prom."

They both giggled. The windows of the car fogged up with the heat of their breath. As they followed the Susquehanna River north, the talk and laughter continued in an easy rhythm. They peered at the hard-edged landscape of coal country, hands clasped. Annalena rested her head on Greg's shoulder and sang a camp song about the Susquehanna. At Sunbury Greg left the river and took a country road east to Ashland.

From the moment they reached the outskirts of that small Pennsylvania Dutch town, the road abruptly changed, suddenly out of kilter with the rest of the landscape. One neon sign after another beckoned them to eat, sleep or even buy a souvenir, while the scarred black hills looming beyond the signs screamed of poverty. In the hills were the coal mines which had once made the town solvent and then, scraped clean and abandoned, had made it poor. It was this poverty, Russ had said, which made it possible for Dr. Spencer's nationally known abortion clinic to flourish here. It was the town's new industry, its unique tourist attraction, like Lourdes's miracle or Plymouth's rock, and if the county's medical examiner turned his head the other way, it was only because the survival of the living came first. The ironies did somersaults in Greg's mind.

"God bless America," he yodeled as they sped toward town, Annalena laughing softly at his side.

It was only noon when they registered at the Ashland Motor Court Inn, still three hours before their appointment. The instructions did not permit Annalena to eat all day; Greg fasted with her —he'd barely been able to eat for the past few days anyhow. Annalena set her suitcase at the foot of their bed and, without a word, walked to the bathroom and turned on the water in the tub. She had already unbuttoned her blouse when she returned to the bedroom. Greg watched her, sweet, beautiful Annalena. His heart ached. Then he too began to undress. He followed her back to the bathroom, where they sank into the tub the way they had two months ago in Ashtabula, face to face, ankles to waists. They barely spoke then, nor much later, when they folded back the sheets on the bed and lay on their sides facing one another, holding one another. They did not take their eyes from one another's faces when they made love.

The motel clerk told them they could walk to the clinic. Greg took Annalena's overnight bag in one hand, her arm in his other, and they set off down the main street of the gray-colored town, all diners and motels and drugstores. In the center of town they crossed into a village green, surprisingly picturesque, with its well-spaced ash trees and a huge war memorial in the middle. Another couple had entered the little park from the corner, their path running parallel to Greg and Annalena's. Greg could tell from the cut of their topcoats and the smartness of their gait that they were out-of-towners too, probably from New York, undoubtedly here for the same reason all visitors came to Ashland. The couple were both smiling as they gazed around. The man caught Greg's eye and gave him a conspiratorial nod. The blood drained from Greg's face. He ducked his head. Without realizing it, he had begun to cry. The tears fell onto his cheeks like the drops of an icicle. He stopped walking. He set down Annalena's bag and held her in both arms.

"Oh God, let's not do this," he sobbed. "Not this."

Annalena put her arms around his neck. "What can we do?" she whispered.

"Let's just go someplace, just go and live." Greg's heart was thundering. He put his hands on Annalena's waist and held her away from him, looking into her eyes. Suddenly a marvelous feeling rushed through him. "Why not?" he cried. "Let's just do it. Go to Paris, Rome. Disappear. Start again. You and me and the child." He danced away from her, holding up his arms like a revivalist. "We can do anything we want, did you know that? Anything we want!"

His voice soared, floated above them. Annalena's eyes closed. Neither of them moved. A minute passed. Another. A church bell struck three o'clock. Annalena opened her eyes, walked over to her suitcase, and lifted it.

Greg picked her up at the clinic in the morning and they drove directly to the airport in Harrisburg. They did not speak to each other on the phone until the following week, and then not again until the week after that. In April Greg found someone to sublet his apartment, and at the beginning of May he left for Paris alone.

27

AXEL HUNCHED in the rear of the Volkswagen bus, fingering the handles of his medical bag. It was pitch black outside. Far below them hippie campfires flickered on Pismo Beach. The bus had been parked on the shoulder of the highway outside Men's Colony West, San Luis Obispo Prison, for over three hours now and Axel's back ached.

"Want a bite, Doc?" The kid in the driver's seat held a ragged, half-eaten sub sandwich back to him.

Axel shook his head. He did not know anyone in the group who was working this operation. The long-haired kid up front could not be more than nineteen. There was a boy of ten in one of the other cars. They had sent for Axel at the safe house outside Eugene last week, driven him down in a Jeep and put him up in a first-class motel in Santa Barbara. There seemed to be no lack of money. Someone said there were thirty thousand dollars behind it, drug-dealer money, an offering to the King. But they weren't doing this for money, they said. This was a symbolic act. They were freeing the living symbol of psychedelic freedom, who had been locked up on a bum rap. Axel did not want to know about it. He never did. He just wanted to know the medical problem, not the politics, not the justifications. All he understood were medical problems now.

In the course of two years Axel had tutored himself in every branch of emergency medicine. He had acquired a medical library that filled a trunk. He had dissected two corpses stolen from a medical school morgue. By now he had removed bullets from half a dozen men, officiated at twenty births and performed twice as many abortions. Tonight he was just on call. There could be cuts or lacerations from the barbed-wire fence, maybe a broken bone from the jump, even the possibility of bullet wounds if the prison guards spotted the escapee. Axel let his bag drop to the floor of the bus. The radio up front crackled.

"It's happening," a voice said.

The kid turned on the ignition and slipped the vehicle in gear. Ahead of them a Beetle pulled onto the road, its lights still off. Again the radio crackled. "Number Three's making the pickup."

Axel pressed his face against the glass, searching in the darkness.

"There he is," the driver hissed. "Doesn't look like he needs you, Doc."

Axel swung his head around to the rear window. The long, familiar face was gliding by like a ghost in a delirium. Axel held his breath. His head reeled. Timothy Leary was smiling.

FOUR

1972–1974

28

"HERE'S what we're offering," Capinagro began with a poorly concealed simper. One of the new breed of knife-twisters, John Capinagro was an up-and-comer in the district attorney's narcotics office. "We're offering a suspended sentence, no fine, zilch. But we're going to need a plea, fifty hours of rehabilitation, and a minimum of three public statements on the hazards of drug abuse, wording to be approved by our office."

Next to David, Jake Tyne, the post acid-rock singer of nasal, bittersweet love songs, returned Capinagro's smile from behind mirrored sunglasses. On the way downtown in his limousine, Tyne had fortified himself with a large, shiny black pill and several gasps on a hash pipe. It was the prescription he always used when making deals, he had told David. He said it helped him see the other guy's point of view. Two months earlier a raid on Tyne's suite at the Carlyle had netted enough acid and hash to put the singer in confinement for upward of twenty years—and that didn't even include charges of statutory rape and harboring minors which the same raid could have brought down. But Tyne had never once doubted that some sort of deal with the D.A.'s office could be struck, that a star of his status had something more valuable to offer the state than twenty years behind bars. David Debilio had been Tyne's natural choice as the man to strike that deal.

"I assume those fifty hours of rehabilitation can be scheduled around the demands of my client's work," David said.

"Within reason," Capinagro said. "As long as Mr. Tyne provides the press with photo opportunities during his therapy sessions."

That was the real point, of course. No one in the D.A.'s office truly cared if Jake Tyne gave up acid or not, but he must be *seen* kicking the habit under the auspices of some fleshy-jawed psychologist at a drug clinic. And that wasn't because the D.A. hoped to inspire acidhead kids to seek professional help themselves; no, the D.A. simply wanted to show those troubled kids that he could bring even Jake Tyne to his knees, make him play his game, fuck him. All things considered, it was a better deal than David had expected.

"I'd like to confer with my client," he said.

"I'm afraid I haven't finished yet, Dave," Capinagro said, flashing a phony apologetic smile. "There's one other item we'll need.

We'll want the name of the person or persons who supplied Mr. Tyne with his drugs, a sworn statement, and assurances of Tyne's availability for a grand jury."

David's face burned. He had dreaded this.

"I'd like to discuss some alternative possibilities," David said quickly, trying to hold the young prosecutor's eye. "My client has suggested the possibility of a television special on drug abuse, bringing other entertainers in, that sort of thing—"

"Dave, *somebody's* got to go to jail," Capinagro cut in.

"I can dig that," Tyne crooned, obviously having no difficulty seeing the other guy's point of view at the moment.

David squeezed the edge of the table between his thumb and forefinger. He had told Tyne a dozen times about the perils of finking, what the press could do with it, what his fans would think. They might catch the implied wink in his rehabilitation photos, but turning in his drug connection would not sit well with the teeny pothead set. Yet it was not Jake Tyne's career that David was worried about.

"Can I have a word with you?" David said quietly to Capinagro. The two lawyers left the room and started down the corridor of the court building. "John, I've got a conflict," David said.

"Is Tyne's connection a client?"

"No, but he's a personal friend."

"Really?" Capinagro leered at David and laughed. "You do run with a fast set, don't you, Debilio?"

"I'm going to have to disqualify myself if we can't come up with something," David went on. "What if my friend were out of the state in twenty-four hours, absolutely clean? He's nothing big, John. He just likes doing business with folk singers. He's more of a groupie than a dealer."

They were at the end of the corridor before Capinagro responded. "All right, Debilio. But you owe me one." He grasped David's arm at the elbow. "Listen, off the record, what is this kid to you?"

David looked the condescending prosecutor straight in the eye. "We roomed together at Harvard," he said.

The taxi left David at Second Avenue and he set off at a brisk pace toward Tompkins Square, ignoring the paranoid eyes of street people as he penetrated the inner sanctum of the East

Village in his coat, tie and attaché case. Since moving to the apartment on Central Park South, David rarely had occasion to come down to the Village anymore, East or West. He had participated in a Bill of Rights panel discussion at the New School the year before, and when Gwen was in town he would spend a late night or two at her Washington Square apartment, but that was about it. These days he spent more time in Los Angeles than below Fourteenth Street.

It was more than mere geography which was changing in David's life as he approached thirty-five. With Lincoln Ames's blessing he had opened up his own Madison Avenue office three years ago, and it had expanded so fast and in so many directions that half his briefs were dictated in airplanes and taxicabs. He was still known in the press as a civil liberties lawyer, and he and his partners always took on a few interesting First Amendment cases each year, but more and more of his time was now spent extracting film actors and recording stars from the binds they found themselves in: bad marriages; bad contracts; drug and sex busts; traps which could catch anyone but required a species of law and negotiation all its own when they caught celebrities. Along the way David had become rich. The first year of his own practice netted him a hundred thousand dollars; the second year more than doubled that. It was a singular pleasure when he had been able to call his father-in-law in Boston and tell him that his monthly "supplementary" checks were no longer appropriate, that perhaps they should simply be made over to the Civil Liberties Union or the Urban League. To be sure, there were many people who, some secretly and others not so secretly, accused David of selling out, of using the movement to leapfrog his way into the salons—and fees —of the radical chic. There had been a scathing article in *New Times* called, "Star F—kers of the New Left," which averred that every time David Debilio's picture appeared in the paper beside some poor black slob his fees for movie stars jumped another fifty dollars an hour. David had managed a little laugh when he read that. "My fees and their circulation," he wisecracked.

They are the cynics, David thought, the burned-out idealists of the overblown decade which had just fizzled to an end. All they have left are their embittered judgments. He was not disappointed in himself. He was content in ways no cynic could possibly be: He loved his children dearly; his daughter Ashley only four and already as pure a patrician beauty as her mother had once been, existed at the very center of his life. Even Patricia—still so much a child herself, although her oval head now bristled with stray silver hairs—was an integral part of the family portrait he cherished. It was proof of his optimism that he was still married while most of his warmhearted colleagues at the ACLU had banged and bruised their way out of their marriages in the name of "integrity," "freedom" and the holiest of new sacraments, "self-expression." Brought up in a family where he could not possibly have been understood, David was sure that self-expression was a solitary pleasure to be found in his work, travel and numberless casual affairs. It had nothing to do with family life.

Whether Pat would agree with this estimation was not clear to David. She changed. Several years ago she had insisted that they undergo marital therapy to "break the patterns" that were keeping them from "making contact." The idea had come from her friend Melissa, who was now married herself to a Jewish psychiatrist, no less, and was as firm a believer in psychological truth as she had once been in psychedelic dazzle. Twice a week for close to a year David had gone off with Pat to a therapist's office, where, like a well-rehearsed defendant, he had said as little as he could get away with. The truth—the affairs, the alibis—could only generate unhappiness. Because he wanted Pat to be happy he said he believed in honesty; for the same reason he lied to her. It was during this period that he had had his little fling with Axel's abandoned wife Despina. Somehow she had gotten to him more than the others; it was probably her intensity—certainly not her surprisingly childish lovemaking. But the absurdity of going from Despina's bed to the marriage counselor's Naugahyde lounger had finally made David clam up altogether. The therapy came to an end. And, wonder of wonders, only a week later Pat declared that she felt "liberated" by not having to go to those dreary therapy sessions anymore. She was onto something else by then.

Tompkins Square had not changed. The stoned-out hippies and freaks lolled on broken benches and the bone-hard ground as if spring were already there. It had been the first meeting place David had thought of when he got Jerry's answering service on the phone, but now he wished he had picked more neutral territory. The kids were eyeing him suspiciously: Anyone in a suit was either a narc or a private detective come to drag somebody's kid home to

New Jersey. David rubbed his hands together as he stared back at them. His son Joshua, a fourth-grader at the Walden School, had announced one day that he had tried grass and found it boring. A good sign, that, although there was rather much that the boy already found boring; he had inherited his mother's attention span. Behind David somebody was whistling a familiar tune, something from before the era of the Rolling Stones. David recognized the song just as a hand slipped under his arm. Jerry Halligan was beside him whistling "Fair Harvard."

"Perfect football weather," Jerry said with a Cambridge clip. "Did you bring the flask?"

David laughed in spite of himself. Whatever else a decade of drugs had done to Jerry's brain, it had not dulled his sense of irony. Tompkins Square as Harvard Yard—a flash of ten years in a single absurd image. Perfect.

"I'm glad you made it so quickly," David said.

Jerry looked much better than he had expected. His eyes were clear, still bright. His skin had as much color as anyone's at the end of a New York winter. His hair, though shoulder-length, was clean, freshly blow-dried, David guessed. In all it was a fair assumption to say that he looked a hell of a lot younger and handsomer than most of their old classmates.

"Your message had a certain ring of urgency about it," Jerry said, still holding David's arm. "Is there some way I can help you out, Davido?"

"Sort of. Have you had lunch?"

Jerry laughed. "Why, is it lunchtime?"

He led David toward a Polish luncheonette on Avenue A—the only one of its kind this side of the Iron Curtain, he said. It was as if his discovery of the place had caused it to exist; that, too, had not changed in ten years. Wouldn't it be wonderful if old Jerry, the prophet of change, was the one who had changed the least?

David had not seen Jerry since moving uptown. When they still lived in the Village Pat had brought him home now and then— Jerry and two or three teenage wraiths with orphan eyes in jeans and T-shirts. By then there already had been little for the two men to talk about. Of course, Jerry's name had come up frequently with David's clients these past few years. At first the pop singers and society junkies invariably referred to him with great affection; he was the prince of pushers, always fun to get high with and easy about giving credit. But after a recent string of busts some of David's clients had grown wary of Jerry—one client suspected him of being a narc, while the others just thought he was too indiscreet. It was a bad idea for a drug pusher to be a name-dropper.

David gazed across the booth at Jerry. He looked like a young page in a Shakespearean play, charmed and innocent. "I've just spent an hour downtown with the county prosecutor and your friend Jake Tyne."

"How is Jake?" Jerry said. He had not stopped smiling.

"He's feeling better," David said, looking directly into Jerry's eyes. "I was able to get him a suspended sentence."

"A suspended sentence," Jerry repeated, hitting the sibilants dramatically. "Sounds perfect for Tyne. Like limbo."

"Considering that the alternative was twenty years in jail, he thought so." David saw that Jerry's eyes had already drifted to the blackboard menu over the counter. "Part of Tyne's deal was to give the name of his connection," he said.

Jerry laughed. He had not so much as flinched.

"Funny, how you and I move in the same circles, Davido," he said. "A mystical thread binds us, you know. We must have been brothers back in Rome or Jerusalem or someplace."

David grasped the edge of the table with both hands as if to steady himself. "Jerry, you've got one day to get clean and get out of the state of New York," he said evenly. "It was the very best deal I could—" David halted mid sentence. Jerry had placed both his hands on top of his own.

"What's the matter, friend?" Jerry said quietly. "Look at you, you're still hanging onto the edge, aren't you? Still think the world is flat." He suddenly lifted one hand and touched his index finger to the center of David's forehead. "Shazam!"

David froze. Then he gently pushed Jerry's hand away. He was overcome by an awful sadness, an echo of a dimly remembered loss. He could barely look in his old friend's eyes.

"Jesus Christ, Jerry, don't you know that's all over?" he said. "It didn't work. It was bad magic. Even your good friend Timothy Leary says so. I saw him in the paper next to Eldridge Cleaver in Algeria, for God's sake, and he says it's time to quit drugs and get moving again. To *do* something." David shook his head. His mouth felt dry. The sadness would not go away. "Please, Jerry," he pleaded, "give yourself a chance. Start again. All that other stuff is over."

"Of course it is, Davido," Jerry laughed, his eyes sparkling. "Something absolutely new is happening every moment. Even now!"

29

"ON DONDER! On Blitzen! On Agnew and Nixon!"

Jerry cracked an imaginary whip in the backseat of the Checker cab. Outside New York streaked by, a light show.

"Give me a hit, would you love?"

The girl in the flasher raincoat pressed the joint to his lips like a baby bottle. Where had she come aboard? Chumley's? The Brasserie? Holding down the smoke, Jerry gestured with his head toward the cabdriver and the girl dangled the joint over the front seat while the driver took a long toke. Angelo Garcia, his hack license said. Angelo had turned off the meter a long time ago.

"Max's!" Jerry called. "The end of the line."

He patted the Mickey Mouse lunch pail on the seat beside him. Even after five stops of his grand farewell tour, the box still held six thousand dollars' worth of pure windowpane acid. Jerry was giving it away, souvenirs of the Golden Age.

"Oh God, they're exquisite." He suddenly rocked forward, pointing at a young couple in evening clothes who stood on the near corner of Lexington Avenue. "Just a quick stop, Angelo, okay?"

Jerry rolled down his window as the cab pulled up in front of the beautiful couple. He leaned out his head.

"Have you any idea how lovely you look?" Jerry smiled at both of them. "Angels! Seraphim! Can we drop you somewhere?" The couple backed away, still staring at him. "We may never have this chance again, you know. Beware lost opportunities! Missed moments!" Jerry blew them a kiss and the young woman in her satin

gown flushed in spite of herself. "Nevermore!" Jerry called as the
cab began to move again. "Nevermore!"

Oh God, it really was sad, loving the whole world so perfectly
and having to dish it out so hit or miss. All those *lives* whirring by
the window. Jerry grabbed the hand of the girl beside him and
sank back into his seat. Jesus, he'd tripped to the edge of the
universe a million times, but he was scared to death of leaving
New York City.

It was five in the morning when Angelo dropped Jerry off at La
Guardia Airport. At nine Jerry bought a one-way ticket to San
Francisco, as if he had known that was where he was going all
along.

30

JERRY SLEPT twelve and fifteen hours at a stretch in the gabled
third-floor guest room of Todd and May's Victorian house. He only
came downstairs at suppertime, cloaked in an old comforter with
tufts of cotton sprouting from its seams and clinging to his unwashed hair. "Mothman" the twins called him.

A week before he had danced in unannounced through their
front door with gifts for everyone—even the new baby. Old Jerry,
high and happy. "Just dropped in for a home-cooked meal," he
said. He had done little but sleep ever since.

"He's moulting," Todd said.

May smiled. Todd was never happier than when someone was
occupying the guest room. Since they had bought the house, the
room had had at least twenty tenants: foreign doctors visiting the
hospital; friends who had been fighting with their husbands or
wives; Axel, when he came by for supplies.

"It saves us plane fare," Todd would say. "The world visits us."

A second week passed and Jerry still had barely spoken a complete sentence. He seemed in a perpetual daze, like a child awakened in a strange bedroom. Todd asked him nothing. May made

sure his plate was always full. One evening, when Todd was taking the twins up to bed, Jerry padded up the stairs behind them. He sat on the floor in the corner of their bedroom as Todd began their story.

"Where were we?"

"Zeitman was on the China Wall," Kristin piped.

"No, it already turned into the date vine," Jan said.

"The date line," Todd said. He sat on an ottoman, big as a Buddha, while the children lay, stomachs down, on their beds, their little faces propped up in their hands. "Yes, there was Zeitman balancing on the international date line, Tuesday to the left of him, Wednesday to the right of him, and he began to teeter-totter terribly. If he fell on Tuesday, he would have to do the hardest job in the whole world—live the same day all over again."

"What's so hard about that?"

"Because then you've got to do everything exactly the same way you did it yesterday. Pick up your spoon with exactly the same fingers, put exactly the same number of Cheerios on it. Everything the same all day. And if you do just one thing differently, you have to start all over again at the beginning until you get the whole day exactly right."

"Wow!" Jan said.

"What if he falls on Wednesday?" Kristin asked.

"If he falls on Wednesday," Todd said, "he has to do the second hardest thing in the whole world—he has to live the whole day for the very first time."

From the corner Jerry laughed softly. When Todd finished the night's installment of "Zeitman," Jerry followed him back down to the kitchen. Todd poured them each a cup of coffee.

"I've been trying a little experiment in consciousness alteration upstairs," Jerry said. "Seeing what happens to the human mind if you deprive it of drugs."

Todd laughed "And your conclusions?"

"It's deadly," Jerry said, shaking his head. "God, it's deadly." He grinned. "But it certainly is *relaxing*. One thing about not getting high is that you don't have to worry about coming down."

"Newton's law," Todd said, and they both smiled.

"You haven't tried it since that night, have you?"

Todd shook his head. "Not that I haven't thought about it. I guess I never believed I could top that one time."

"Ah, but you can. You always can, Toddy." Jerry raised one finger. "Once—Christ, I don't know how many years ago—four of us locked ourselves in a house on Long Island and drank acid from a Coke bottle for two weeks straight. It was incredible. There was pure white light shining through the tops of our heads. But every time we thought we'd gotten as high as we possibly could, we'd rocket up another million miles and look back at where we'd just been and say, 'Jesus, we were only pygmies then, metaphysical morons.'"

"Sounds endless," Todd said. "It was something like that that finally made me quit grad school."

Todd popped a chocolate chip cookie into his mouth and pushed the box across the table to Jerry, but Jerry was now staring off into the dining room, the comforter pulled around his shoulders. He might have been an old woman trying to remember a day in her childhood. Neither man spoke for several minutes.

"Do you know what they call me in New York?" Jerry said, his head still turned away. "The French Chef. I concocted these marvelous menus for everybody—speed hors d'oeuvres, acid soup with mushrooms, sorbet with poppers. I was always looking for the right combination, the perfect sequence for the perfect high. I catered. People would call me and tell me just what kind of party they wanted—how much God, how much fucking—and I'd bring it all in my lunch pail. I did the punch at the Albright party on Fishers Island. I did Jake Tyne's birthday."

Jerry turned and looked directly into Todd's eyes.

"One time I catered a suicide," he said in the same flat tone of voice. "In a loft downtown. The host put all his furniture in a circle, like a theater, and then sat in the middle while I served. I wore a tux, of course, the maitre d'. Everyone was so stoned by the time our host poured the cyanide down his throat that hardly anyone saw him fall over. They still talk about that party, though. It's a famous party."

Todd held himself perfectly still, his eyes fastened on Jerry's. Suddenly Jerry was on his feet, the comforter floating to the floor.

"It's a fucking hard act to follow, Toddy," he said loudly. "Half the people I ever knew are dead or in asylums or traipsing around Nepal looking for somebody who *knows*. I'm ten years old. I've been on Mars. On the plane out here the stewardess handed me a newspaper and I started laughing so hard they thought they'd have to drop me in Chicago. That paper looked like something out of the archives to me, the Dead Sea Scrolls." Jerry's nostrils flared as he drew in his breath. "What the fuck am I supposed to do now, Toddy? Get a good job? Bake bread?"

Todd still had not moved. His shoulders ached from hunching over the kitchen table. He had no idea what he was going to say until he began to say it.

"Wait, Jerry," he said softly. "Just try to wait, I think. You're one of the most gifted men I've ever known and absolutely the luckiest. That's not going to change now. That's one of the immutables."

For a moment it looked as if tears were gathering in Jerry's eyes, but a second later he had thrown back his head and was laughing.

"You're still the holy man, aren't you, Todd?" he said. " 'Cheese is cheese and heart is heart.' I've never forgotten that one, you know." He planted both palms on the table and leaned his face into Todd's. "That Zeitman you tell your kids about—he's Tim, isn't he?"

Jerry stayed for a year. A few weeks after their conversation in the kitchen, he asked Todd if he could help him find a job, something easy, and Todd got him one in the laundry at the hospital. They drove together to the hospital and back almost every day, often talking about one or another of the books from Todd's library that Jerry had been reading. Other guests came and went, sleeping in the gabled room next to Jerry's. Once Axel called, wanting to stay for a night, but when he heard Jerry was there he hesitated and finally begged off. Sometimes, when the dining room table was full of Todd and May's friends, Jerry would regale them all with bizarre tales of Millbrook, Mexico and New York—the "cosmic capers" he called them, as if the life he'd once led was a comic strip in an underground newspaper. But there also would be weeks at a time when he would grow silent again. He seemed happiest with the children; after a while the twins only wanted Jerry to tell them their "Zeitman" stories. They said his versions were much funnier than Dad's. One day he came home with his blond hair shorn and "styled," as they now called it. May said it made him look like a movie star, but the truth was it made him look older and heavier.

The following winter the papers were full of Tim Leary's capture by federal agents in Afghanistan. Fifty policemen with riot guns were at the Los Angeles airport when his plane came down. Tim, in handcuffs, smiled over their helmets at the newspaper photographers. And in San Francisco Jerry packed his bag.

31

GREG GREGORIAN had not read a newspaper in three years. "The plot's too repetitious," he liked to say. In any case, the only English-language news that reached the island of Hydra was the international edition of *Time,* and it was printed on stock too skimpy and scratchy to be of any practical use in his kitchen or bathroom. Life on Hydra was a matter of essentials.

He had gone to Paris first, late in '68, but that place had been supercharged with expatriate success stories: Every café he visited boasted a Hemingway, Miller or Jones *table d'habitués.* From there he had traveled to Venice, but the damp made his throat sore. A woman he met in a hotel brought him to Athens, and a woman in Athens took him to Hydra for a weekend. At the harbor taverna a drunk Swede called Hydra "the last stop" and Greg decided to stay. He supported himself by tutoring English to the boys at the island's maritime academy. He started one play—about a man who has a sex-change operation and sleeps with a picture of his former self under his pillow—but after five pages he had put away his typewriter with great relief. He rarely thought about Annalena anymore.

In late winter, when the six o'clock ferry from Piraeus began delivering more foreigners than Greeks, Greg and his friend Antony sat in the port and watched the vacationers debark, enjoying the contrast between their own vision of the island and that of the new arrivals. Seen from the sea, Hydra had a dreamy look. The ferry threw up a spray which filtered the island's image, softened it, and made it float. But on the island when the sun shone every view was severe with relentless detail. The minute shadow

of a rock five miles out on the Peloponnesian shore appeared as
sharp as the crack in the window it was seen through. This was the
celebrated clarity of the Aegean sun: It attacked the eyes and then
proceeded to work over the entire nervous system.

Antony, an Australian poet who had lived on the island for over
ten years, crouched like a hunchback over his ouzo, leering at each
couple that paraded by, predicting that this pair might have hope
but that the other two would "do their nut" in two days flat and
then leave early for Florence, while those English newlyweds
heading for the *agora* would have done better day-tripping to
Brighton for all they would soak up here. Antony's judgments had
a simple moral premise: A stay on Hydra only served its purpose if
several personal illusions were shriveled in the process.

"I can't look at them, Gregimou. Those two. One day on the
griddle, that's all it will take." Antony closed his eyes as a prosper-
ous-looking German walked by with a young, exuberant woman.
"She has alibis of gossamer, I tell you. The compromises that
woman has made, poor baby. I see a tragedy of broken bones,
maybe a neck. Not a chance of a surgical separation—they're
bound with diamonds."

More often than not, Antony's prophecies proved accurate. Just
sitting in front of Tasso's café in the huge, horseshoe-shaped port—
a natural amphitheater—Greg could watch the strain begin to
take its toll on the holiday lovers. "Afternoon television," he called
the pastime. By sundown Greg would know just where to go to
seek his bedroom companion for the night.

"Hold your applause, Gregor, that was only the overture."
Antony flourished his hand. *"Voici la diva!"*

Greg squinted along the quay at the last passengers leaving the
boat: a deeply tanned woman flanked by two awkward looking
men. He recognized Despina Stenhorn immediately.

"So, what does the oracle see?" Greg said, watching Despina
walk toward them. She wore an oversized men's shirt tucked into
tailored jeans. She was barefoot and every head on the *agora*
turned as she paraded by. "A duel at sunrise? A double suicide?"

"No, no!" Antony laughed. "This one has high comedy written
all over it."

Greg smiled. Despina had slowed her pace and was now openly
studying him. Living in the sun had turned Greg's complexion the
color of brandy. His hair was much longer than it had been five

years ago; he was fifteen pounds lighter. Never mind that the last time he and Despina had seen one another—in Macy's toy department—*she* had been the one in disguise; here on Hydra she could not figure out who he was. She walked straight up to his table. "Who are you?" she said.

Greg smiled sphinxlike, feeling marvelously perverse. Next to him Antony's jaw had dropped, speechless for a change.

"I'm an old friend of your husband's," Greg said at last.

Despina's face colored. The men on either side of her—dough-colored Englishmen—smiled nervously.

"Former husband," Despina said. She suddenly beamed. "Of course. You're Gregory, the T.V. stunt man."

"Former." Greg stood and kissed her on both cheeks. "Have a seat. It's the best table on the island."

"Must be fate," Despina said, smiling prettily as she sat. "I was hoping I'd find an American to celebrate with." She held up an Athens newspaper and pointed at the lead headline. "They've done it. They've signed in Paris. The war is officially over."

"Wonderful!" Greg raised his ouzo. "Who won?"

Despina looked at him harshly for just a moment, then laughed. Her two escorts sat down tentatively on either side of her. They were journalists from the London *Times* down to do a series on "Life Under the Generals." The poor blokes were obviously waiting for her to choose between them. Antony signaled Tasso for a bottle of ouzo. Then he sat back, grinning broadly.

"I came over last April to help a friend do an article on draft evaders in Sweden," Despina said. "But I've been stringing for *Ramparts* and the *Voice* on my own ever since."

Greg nodded. He did not remember Despina having been so eager to impress, at least not in this way.

"Did you come across Axel?" he said. "In Sweden, I mean."

"Not a trace," Despina said lightly. "God knows, David—David Debilio—and I tried to find him. To sign the separation agreement. I finally had to declare abandonment." She laughed.

Greg sipped his drink. Obviously he was meant to catch the familiarity with which she mentioned David's name; no doubt the two of them had been thrown together by Axel's disappearance too. Remarkable, the way Axel had distributed the women in his life that night: his sister to Greg, his wife to David. Antony was now straining to provide his most earnest face as Despina explained the crucial role that the media had played in ending the war in Southeast Asia.

"And now there's all those poor burned-out movement kids in America with nothing left to do," she went on. "They finally all got mired in their own bullshit."

Greg looked around the table. Three grown men were nodding enthusiastically to everything Despina said. The two Englishmen had ordered plates of *taramosalata, tzatziki* and *oktapodi* in brine. This was turning out to be a regular party. While Despina chatted on, Greg gazed out at the line on the horizon that was the Peloponnes. Once again he was struck by the clarity of distances in this place, even in the setting sun. From the corner of his eye he caught a glimpse of a couple arguing outside the taverna at the other end of the *agora*. It was the prosperous German and his young woman. She had flirted with a waiter. He had refused to take her to the best hotel. Something had begun to clarify what they truly meant to one another. Greg swallowed the rest of his ouzo and turned back to Despina.

"Revolution is a state of mind," she was saying. "My God, even Marx knew that."

Greg found himself slowly rising from the table. For the first time in years he felt unbearably unhappy. It had never stopped, really; he ached for Annalena.

"Are you all right, Gregimou?" Antony looked up at him.

"Just a little overwhelmed," Greg said.

"You can't be leaving me," Despina said, but Greg was already on his way, striding along the port, his eyes stinging. Only when he had reached the far end of the harbor where the road curved away did he stop, turn and look back. He could see his table in bold relief, as if he were viewing it through a telescope. Despina was smiling animatedly at one of the Englishmen while under the table Antony's hand rested on her knee.

32

IT WAS old home week at the Starseed Information Center. That was the name Tim Leary and his new perfect love, Amanda, had given to the court-in-exile in San Francisco when he began his fifteen-year sentence in Folsom. Amanda was the queen. She'd been with Tim in Kabul when the bust came down and now she carried this carte blanche mash note from him—the "holy writ" one kid called it—which said she was Tim's voice and wisdom, the royal proxy. She was beautiful, although her skin and eyes were jaundiced to the color of lemons, and on the day she opened Starseed she picked Jerry right out of the crowd.

It wasn't hard. Jerry wore a blue Oxford button-down shirt, white ducks, and tennis shoes. He was the only man in the room whose hair did not come anywhere near his shoulders.

"Where do you connect with Tim?"

"In this life?" Jerry grinned.

The queen started to look away, impatient.

"Harvard," Jerry said without hesitation. "Where it all began."

Amanda laughed. "You're putting me on."

"No, he isn't." From the edge of that jammed office a woman's voice sang out, clear and familiar. It took Jerry a moment to find her face among all the others. It was Gabby and she saluted him with a big smile on her face. Her red hair was in braids curled on top of her head, the same way she used to wear it at the house in Newton. There was a red-haired child on the shoulders of the man beside her.

Amanda gave a yellow scowl. "For openers," she said to Jerry, "let's get the hippies and creeps out of here."

Everything tied together too perfectly to be coincidence: Tim's queen designating Jerry as Starseed lieutenant; Gabby materializing after a million years. It had only been a question of waiting. Jerry's mind was pure crystal. He looked everyone directly in the eye. The first and last order of business was to fill the war chest, to get Tim free. That afternoon, Jerry set up "The Benefit" committee. In the evening he went home with Gabby.

Gabby shared a house in Sausalito with a fluctuating group of people—more than ten, less than twenty-five. She had a man, a skinny kid in his early twenties named Bo, who had been up at the Starseed office with her. He was not the father of her red-haired little boy, though. They all ate together in a long room with a view of the harbor—brown rice and spinach, walnuts for dessert. Gabby smiled whenever she looked at Jerry.

"I can't believe this, can you?" she said.

"Absolutely," Jerry answered.

Neither of them asked the other where he'd been, what had come down. They had both survived somehow; that was enough. After dinner someone lit up a hash water pipe and passed it around. Bo took a hit and handed it to Jerry, but Jerry waved it on. Gabby smiled again. They found him a sleeping bag and a corner on the third floor. He was up at five, buzzing with ideas.

He would call the concert "Tim Leary Sets *You* Free." There would be music and a light show, of course. He'd get Ginsberg to do a poem, Ram Dass to incant the benediction. But the star would be Tim himself, Tim-behind-bars setting everybody free. Somehow, they'd have to make a film of him in Folsom. By six Jerry had filled ten pages of his brand-new notebook with lists of calls to make, procedures to follow. It was as if he had been rehearsing for this ever since Texas. Downstairs half a dozen children were having breakfast with Gabby and a couple of the other women. Jerry grabbed two of the kids around their waists.

"Who wants to hear the story of Zeitman?" he said.

The Starseed office was locked when they got there at ten. No one knew where to reach Amanda. By ten-thirty she still hadn't shown up and half of "The Benefit" committee was talking about going to the movies. Jerry led them down to the wharf to a bank of glass phone booths.

"The rooms are small," he said, "but it's the best address in town."

He bought everyone fish and chips and gave out assignments. Gabby would check out theaters—how big? how much? Bo and a kid named Willie would find out about printing tickets and posters. Mona, a dark-haired girl from the Sausalito house, would be in

charge of publicity, and Taylor, a man of at least forty who said he
used to work at the Fillmore, would be the stage manager. Jerry's
job was to get the talent.

In the early afternoon they wandered back to the Starseed office, where Amanda sat on a chair, her long legs stretched onto the
desk, a circle of young men and women around her like a wall.
Every one of them was stoned. Jerry ducked between them, all
smiles. He touched Amanda's hand.

"Just a word," he said softly. "I'll need the office key a moment
to get a dupe made. Things are popping. We'll need someone on
top of the phones all day."

The queen squinted down at him.

" 'The Benefit' committee," Jerry said, winking.

Amanda pulled the key from her bag and dangled it a moment,
eyeing Gabby and Mona and the others by the wall, before dropping it in Jerry's hand. Later Gabby whispered in Jerry's ear, "I
don't think she digs me," and Jerry answered, "She's just frightened."

By the end of the week one fact was eminently clear: To raise
money, you needed money. It would cost ten thousand dollars to
put the benefit on. Jerry started phoning New York. He was calling
in all debts, all favors. Anyone who had ever had a party catered by
the "French Chef" was on his list. In ten days' time he had checks
amounting to over eleven thousand dollars made out to the Starseed Information Center. It was all happening and everyone knew
exactly who was making it happen.

The concert was scheduled for the fourth of August at Winterland. Jerry read over the theater contract and sent it with Bo and
Willie to Amanda for her signature and deposit check. He attached a note reminding her that she would have to get moving on
the film of Tim in Folsom—only she had access to him. Jerry closed
the note, "Tell Tim we need him." He leaned back against the wall
in the long room of the house in Sausalito, his feet stretched out in
front of him. He felt positively marvelous. He was at ease in a way
he could not remember ever having been before. For years the
price for peacefulness had been paralysis—drugs' ransom—but
now he felt tranquil and *strong.* Energy surged through him from
the moment he awakened in the morning—calm energy, smooth
energy. Decisions felt right the instant he made them. Nothing
disappointed him. Again tonight about a dozen people had re-

mained downstairs after dinner—some of the kids from Starseed, others just from the passing population of the house. Most were ten years younger than Jerry, earnest and slack, kids who had become entranced with simple truths long before they ever had had a chance to ponder anything complex. They sat in a ragged circle with Jerry at its head, talking about the benefit, coming up with new ideas for it. It seemed to Jerry that all of these people were feeling much better these days too.

By midnight Gabby said she was picking up bad vibes—Bo and Willie still had not returned. Jerry reached out a hand and rubbed the back of her neck. "Don't give those vibes energy and they'll go away," he said. At one the two young men shambled into the house, zonked out of their skulls.

"Where is it?" Gabby said, shoving her hand in front of them.

Bo rolled his eyes and Willie giggled. "Hey, like where is anything?"

Gabby put her hands on Bo's belt, spun him around. An envelope protruded from the back pocket of his jeans. She yanked it out. It had never been opened—no signature on the contract, no check.

"Assholes," Gabby hissed.

Willie laughed in her face. "Dig yourself, chick. You're all hung up on a fucking piece of paper."

"Assholes!"

Jerry rose between them, smiling. He touched Willie gently on the shoulder, looked directly in his eyes. "How high did you get?"

Bo cocked his head to one side and Willie grinned. "She had pure Panama coke. Fucking dynamite."

"But how high?" Jerry demanded softly, still smiling.

Willie shrugged. Everyone in the room was looking at him.

"High enough so you never have to get high again?" Jerry said a little more loudly. "High enough so you'll stay high?"

Both boys turned away, shaking their heads and laughing.

"Because if it's just another round trip," Jerry went on evenly, "you're stuck. You're dead men. Nothing new will ever happen in your life again."

Everyone stood still as Willie turned back, his eyes slightly out of focus, his mouth open in a sloppy smile.

"Man, we heard all about you tonight, Halligan. You know what Leary told Amanda?" Willie's face was right in front of Jerry's. "He

said you were perfect for your job, man. He said like no matter
what you put in Jerry Halligan's brain, he always comes up thinking like an ad man."

Willie and Bo giggled, then some of the others joined in. Jerry's
heart thudded in his chest. His legs felt weak. Without thinking, he
reached out both arms, grabbing Willie and Bo by their hands and
pulling them toward him. He smiled beatifically.

"Perfect," he crooned. "You can always count on Tim to set you
free." He could feel pure love pouring out of him. No one made a
sound. Suddenly tears appeared in Bo's eyes.

"Jesus, man, I'm sorry," he said. "We really fucked it, didn't
we?"

"Ah, but it was worth it." Jerry touched the center of Bo's
forehead with his finger. "You just upleveled yourself into a whole
new game, my friend."

Mona was the first to join them, looping her arms over Jerry and
Bo's shoulders. Then Gabby and two of the others linked hands
around them. In less than a minute everyone in the room had
huddled in a circle, pressing, touching, trying to catch the glow of
Jerry's pure love.

In the morning Jerry went alone to Amanda's apartment. She
answered the door in her nightgown. Her skin looked yellower.
Jerry cleared a space on the table, gave her a pen and showed her
where to sign the contract and the check. He left quickly, already
thinking of the calls he had to make. At the Starseed office Gabby
said the phone had not stopped ringing since she arrived: performers, agents, *Rolling Stone* magazine, Asylum Records. Everybody
wanted to be a part of Tim Leary's benefit. By the end of the day
Jerry had added five more acts to the concert, started negotiations
on a concert album, and told three performers that his program
was currently too full to add them to it. Among those he had to
turn down was his old friend Jake Tyne. It was nothing personal. It
was just that Jake no longer had much of an audience: He hadn't
had a record on the charts in two years.

The next day the Winterland manager called at ten: The seven-
thousand-dollar deposit check had bounced. Jerry told him there
must have been some mix-up, to redeposit it. Then he called the
bank and the bank informed Jerry that the Starseed account was
empty. It had all been drawn out in cash; Jerry's eleven thousand

dollars was long gone. The word spread immediately. By five the poster studio and the printer had called demanding cash deposits, and his biggest rock groups had threatened to withdraw if Jerry couldn't guarantee the date for them. As quickly as everything had come together it was all falling apart.

Everyone was waiting in the room when Jerry arrived back at the house that evening. Mona threw her arms around him. She had been crying. Gabby's eyes were burning.

"That bitch," she kept saying.

"Shit, it fits, doesn't it?" Willie said. "I mean, Leary's defense fund going on the best dope money can buy, right?"

The air was dense with hash smoke. Gabby passed the pipe to Jerry. He held it a moment, the sweet, acrid smell stinging his nostrils, and then he began to laugh. He laughed so hard that Gabby grabbed the pipe from his hand and guided him like an invalid to a pillow against the wall. They all gaped at him as if he had freaked out.

"It's such an incredibly perfect game," he said, grinning up at everyone. "The ultimate hide-and-seek head game. Hesse would have smiled on this one." He rocked up to his feet, light as a dancer. "We've got the Feds over here, afraid if people get high they won't wear a uniform or pay their taxes or sleep with the same woman for the rest of their lives. And so they go halfway around the world to catch Tim, thinking that'll get things back to normal. Yeh, lock up Tim Leary and it's 1961 again and everybody will join ROTC and go steady and plan their retirement, just like old times. Except the thing is, of course, it's too late. The cat's out of the bag."

Jerry twirled around, one finger raised.

"But that level is nothing, right? I mean, any ten-year-old kid who's sniffed a model airplane has seen through that level. So now Tim says, 'Forget the drugs, man. That phase has served its purpose. We've *done* that. We've learned what we have to do.' And everybody runs around asking, 'Shit, he doesn't mean that, does he? Old Tim is really putting the Feds on this time, right?' " Jerry held his finger under Gabby's chin. "Wrong! Because what Tim is really saying is, 'Wait a second. Something funny is going on here. This old stuff isn't getting us high anymore, is it? All it's doing is making us pushovers and patsies. Prisoners!' Big Brother has finally realized, 'Hey, if we keep everybody stoned, they won't make any trouble and we can get on with our agenda.' "

Jerry moved around the room like a man on fire. No one else made a sound.

"And so now the Feds are really worried," Jerry said, "because old Tim has gone and trashed their game again. And, Christ, locking him up isn't going to do the trick, so what they've got to do now is make him look like an asshole. That's the game we're right in the middle of now." Jerry stopped and shook his head. "For one second there I almost fell for that game," he said, and abruptly laughed again.

Still no one else had spoken. They gazed at Jerry, dazzled and bewildered. Willie lit the hash pipe, drew on it, and smiled.

"Hey, like that's really beautiful, Halligan," he said. "But there's one part I don't get: Are you going to bring off this benefit or not?"

Jerry shook his head, the indulgent teacher. "You really don't get it, do you? The benefit *is* happening. Right now. Right here. Our energy *is* the benefit."

Gabby stepped directly in front of him, her face still drawn in anger.

"He's talking about the concert, Jerry," she said flatly. "Is there going to be a concert?"

"Of course there is," Jerry answered.

The fact was, Jerry did have a plan. It had only been half worked out a few minutes ago, but now with energy flowing through him like electricity, it was all perfectly clear. He checked his watch, then walked to the telephone in the corner of the room and dialed New York.

"Hello, Josh, is your dad in? Tell him Jerry Halligan is calling from San Francisco."

While he waited, Jerry pantomimed to Mona to get him a cup of coffee. David sounded irritated when he picked up the phone. They hadn't spoken to one another since that afternoon in Tompkins Square.

"Are you all right?" was David's greeting.

"Never better."

"I mean, are you in any trouble?"

"None at all, David. There's just something that's come up that I thought might interest you. Do you still represent Jake Tyne?"

"I suppose so. I haven't seen him in quite a while."

"Neither has anybody else," Jerry said. "And I have an opportunity for him to do something about that."

Jerry quickly described the Leary benefit, which singers were headlining it, what record company was doing the album. He told David that *Rolling Stone* was featuring it in their next issue as the ultimate sixties "Resurrection Concert." He told him that Jake Tyne had already called, asking to be on the program, but that he had had to turn him down. Now, however, he might be able to find room for Jake, even get his name on the marquee.

Jerry paused. On the other end of the line David was laughing.

"Well, Jer, you've really come home, haven't you?"

"Just doing what needs to be done. Playing my part in the metagame."

"What's it going to cost Tyne?" David asked, suddenly cold.

"Ten thousand dollars," Jerry answered.

"Tim Leary Sets You Free" sold out the first week tickets went on sale. Outside the theater, scalpers were getting twenty-five dollars a seat the night of the concert. Jerry wore white slacks and a white, collarless shirt that fluttered as he strode out to the front of the proscenium carrying the microphone like a scepter.

"Shazam!" he sang out to the crowd. "The magic is on our side!"

The audience cheered. They cheered for the Grateful Dead, they cheered for Ginsberg and Ram Dass and even, God love them, for Jake Tyne. There was only one awkward moment, late in the evening. Amanda suddenly appeared with five minutes of film of Tim in prison. Jerry saw it for the first time with everyone else at the concert, and he knew immediately that it somehow missed the mark. Tim looked flat, flatter than the screen, and when he spoke he seemed to be off by a beat. He said he was the greatest philosopher of the century. He said that the comet Kohoutek that was due next month was a sign from the higher intelligence that it was time for man to move on from his home on planet Earth. When the film clip was over, someone shouted, "Leary is dead!" and for a few moments some others took it up as a chant, but Jerry cut them off with a wave of his hand and a smile.

"Not that Tim would mind," he said into the microphone. "Last year they were saying God is dead."

Over a hundred people showed up at the party Mona and Gabby organized at the house to celebrate the concert's success. Many of them wanted to shake Jerry's hand and clap him on the back, but for the most part people became quiet when he entered a room or looked their way. Their eyes widened expectantly, as if at any second Jerry Halligan would tell them exactly what they should do with the rest of their lives.

33

WHEN DAVID told Pat about Jerry's scheme to squeeze ten thousand dollars out of Jake Tyne, Pat looked up and said, "Good old Jerry. He's loyal to Leary to the end, isn't he?"

"I hadn't quite thought of it that way," David said, smiling. Pat was always charitable when it came to judging old friends; she deserved to be an expert on loyalty.

They were sitting at the dining room table after dinner, David with his books and legal pads spread out in front of him, Pat with her slides and floor plans in front of her. Lately they had been working across from one another like this every night David was home, and he found himself happily reminded of their first exciting days in New York. He was excited now. The books in front of him were ones he had not cracked in a decade—Holmes's lectures, Berns's *Freedom, Virtue and the First Amendment.* When Lincoln Ames died that autumn, David had been asked by the Columbia Law School to take over his seminar on "First Amendment Issues," and David had accepted without hesitation. He felt honored and he felt vindicated in the eyes of his ACLU detractors, but the feeling which had taken him by surprise was his sheer joy in studying legal theory again. He devoted easily twenty hours each week to preparing his classes.

And Pat—dear Pat—was busy with her latest project, the Beardsley Gallery. Once she had come up with the idea of running her own art gallery, she had immediately dropped everything else —her dance classes, her children's-theater group, her hospital volunteer work.

"A gallery's what I should have been doing all along," she kept saying. "It just combines everything I love."

David had tried gently to dissuade her from this venture. A New York gallery, no matter how small, was a terribly complicated business; more than anything, he wanted to protect her from disappointment. But Pat had stuck with it for half a year now, rushing out every time a realtor called to say some space had fallen vacant, going to galleries and museum exhibits all over town, auditing classes in gallery management at NYU. A few weeks ago she had come home saying she had found the perfect spot down in SoHo and had already put down a binder on it. She said she had asked Jack Eagen, her father's New York lawyer, to work out the lease for her.

"I would have been glad to take care of it for you," David told her.

"Oh, I didn't want to bother you, what with your course and everything," Pat answered. "Anyway, this way Duncan gets to keep an eye on his money." Duncan and Margot had pledged a hundred-thousand-dollar "investment" in their daughter's new career.

Now David peered at Pat over his old Harvard casebook as she slipped a Kodachrome slide into her viewer and held it toward the light.

"God, this man is fantastic," she murmured. She handed the viewer across the table to David. "I'm trying to get him for our first show."

David put the viewer to his eye. He saw a very red isosceles triangle with what appeared to be a shoelace attached to its center. Good God, he feared the worst for Pat.

In the middle of the week David flew out to the West Coast for a hearing involving a Hollywood client who had been slapped with an expensive paternity suit. David took an early flight back, reworking that night's lecture the entire trip; his seminar had become a necessary antidote for all the time he spent negotiating with the victims of his wealthy clients' vices. In New York he took a taxi directly to Columbia, arriving only minutes before his classes began. The topic again was free speech versus privacy. David talked for a while about the implications of that distinction for the

Watergate tapes, then about the difference between public and private utterances.

"But where do you want to draw the line?" David asked the class. "Should someone be allowed to call you a child molester in front of one or two friends, but not in the New York *Times*?"

A vigorous discussion followed, dominated, as usual, by an aggressively bright student named Lydia Spinelli. She argued that all utterances were public, that slander in front of one person was the same as in front of a million. After class Miss Spinelli lingered with a few of the others while David packed his briefcase.

"I found a fascinating document in the stacks the other day," she said, resting one haunch on the seminar table. *"The People* v. *Calvin Monroe,* Mr. David Debilio, attorney for the defense. It was fabulous. I wish I had been there, but I was busy finishing ninth grade."

David smiled. "I don't know how I ever got the case. I was only fifteen at the time myself."

Miss Spinelli laughed, then leaned against him as she slipped off the table, one of her large, resilient breasts pressing against his arm. By the time they were outside, the other students had said good night and Lydia had slipped her arm through David's. "You look exhausted, Professor," she said.

"Totally," David said, but even as he said it he felt his pulse quickening. They were walking together down Amsterdam Avenue. Neither of them spoke for several moments.

"My apartment's right over there," the young woman said quietly as they reached the corner.

David stopped. How deliciously easy it would be to spend an hour or two with this girl, everything understood, nothing held back. Her voluptuousness reminded him of the Hoboken girls he had seduced in his brother's car so long ago, yet surely Lydia Spinelli would be more responsive than any of them had been. She was smiling expectantly up at him. Yes, it would be easy, but it also would be easy to lose that sense of contentment he had finally found with Pat.

"No one's going to call you a child molester," Lydia said, pressing herself against his arm.

"I'm sorry. I'm expected somewhere," David said. "But thank you very much."

Patricia called "Hello" from the living room when David let

himself in the apartment. He leaned his head inside the living room door. Seated across from Pat was a thin, bland-looking man and a frizzy-haired woman wearing some kind of silky garment that resembled pajamas. David managed a smile as Pat introduced the woman as Florence somebody-or-other from *ArtNews,* the man as Winthrop Rawlings. Rawlings, it turned out, was the painter of red isosceles triangles.

"I believe we were at Harvard together," Rawlings said, shaking David's hand. "I'm class of '63."

"'61," David said. "We probably passed one another in the Yard." He would not have remembered Rawlings's face, however; it was like so many others at Harvard—smooth, boyish, vaguely effeminate. No doubt he had belonged to one of the exclusive clubs, Fly or Fox or Porcellian. And now, God love him, he was resting on five generations of Rawlings's assets as he pursued the perfect triangle.

"These two are cooking up a knockout show," the *ArtNews* writer was saying to David. "Ground-breaking, really. A redefinition of geometry."

David stared back at the woman, then at Rawlings's shy smile and Patricia's glowing face. He could not, in his heart of hearts, believe that any one of them was truly serious. Yet later, when Patricia crawled into bed beside him, David surprised himself for the second time that evening. He put his arms around his wife and kissed her mouth.

"I'm proud of you," he said, pulling her fragile body against his own.

Winthrop Rawlings's one-man show opened at the Beardsley Gallery on a Thursday evening, so David had to excuse himself early from his seminar and take a cab down to SoHo. The gallery was packed by the time he arrived. At the door a young man in black tie asked to see his invitation. "I'm the father of the bride," David said, and pushed by.

With everyone juggling plastic goblets of champagne and caviar-covered crackers, there was no way of telling that this was an art show rather than a cocktail party. All but one or two of Rawlings's paintings were completely eclipsed from view by the gowns and blazers of Patricia's guests. David recognized most of the guests—couples from their apartment building; Pat's friends from her dance class and children's-theater group; the woman from *ArtNews;* Melissa and her husband—but by far most of the familiar faces belonged to Duncan and Margot's friends from Boston and Wolfeboro.

"How come you didn't have to wear a monkey suit, Dad?" Joshua edged in front of David. His brown hair hung in ringlets to the satin collar of his tuxedo. He looked absolutely princely.

"Because somehow I manage to look like a waiter in one," David said. He gave his son a conspiratorial nudge. "And we can't have that here, can we?"

"Duncan and Margot sent me over to fetch you," Joshua said. There had been a subtle change in the cadences of Josh's voice since he had transferred to the Collegiate School. He was adaptable, that boy. David had seen that he listed himself as Joshua Beardsley-Debilio in the school directory.

Duncan and Margot were in high spirits. They had Lincoln's widow, Faye, with them, as well as the Holders and Maxwells. Every one of them congratulated David on his wife's cleverness. Duncan waved a tall, silver-haired man over to them.

"I want you to meet my son-in-law," Duncan called. "Ted Rawlings meet David Debilio."

It was the artist's father, an old school friend of Duncan's it turned out. As David shook his hand he had the sensation that he had slipped into some exclusive Boston clubhouse. From the corner of his eye he saw Pat waving at him across the room. He blew her a kiss and started toward her. He had taken only two steps when he felt a hand closing around his biceps. He turned and immediately flushed. It was Lydia Spinelli.

"What are you doing here, Miss Spinelli?"

"I just wanted to see how the other half lives." The young woman gave him a teasing smile. *"Your* other half."

"I'm afraid tonight it's by invitation only," David said coldly.

"Ah, scratch the liberal and find an elitist." Miss Spinelli tightened her grip on David's arm and leaned against him. "I'll bet you still fuck like an old guinea, though, don't you, Professor?"

David's hair bristled. He felt beads of sweat forming on his forehead. He wanted to yank himself free of this girl, but he was afraid of what she might do next. Clearly she was capable of anything.

"Darling!" Pat suddenly appeared in front of them. She was

wearing a silk pajama suit which left her shoulders and neck bare. She leaned her cheek in front of David for a kiss. "It's hard to move in all this crush," she said, her eyes sparkling, "but I love it."

"Congratulations, darling," David said. "It's obviously a great success." He hesitated, his face burning. "Pat, this is Lydia Spinelli, a student in my seminar. Patricia Beardsley, my wife."

"How lovely of you to come all the way down here," Pat said. She seemed genuinely pleased. "What do you think of the show, Miss Spinelli?"

Winthrop Rawlings edged through the crowd beside them before Lydia could answer. He smiled at David, then slipped his arm under Pat's. Lydia looked from one face to the other, her hand still firmly attached to David's arm.

"Why, I'm just crazy about it," Lydia said. "I mean, all those triangles—they're so provocative." And with that, thank God, she dropped her hand and said good night.

Sixteen of Rawlings's twenty paintings were sold the first week of the show, the largest garnering twenty-five hundred dollars from the Beardsleys' friends, the Maxwells. *ArtNews* led the critical acclaim, calling Rawlings's work a "playful interplay of Buckminster Fuller spacial forms and serendipitous found objects." The *Voice* singled out Patricia in their lead paragraph for her "stylish presentation." Winthrop gave two of the remaining paintings to Pat as gifts, and she, in turn, presented David with one of them for his office. He hung it in the hallway just outside the conference room, but somehow no matter where he sat his eye would catch on the corner of Rawlings's dark blue triangle.

David was relieved when the semester ended at Columbia. For the final weeks he had found himself fleeing down the hallway at the end of each class, terrified that Lydia Spinelli's hand would reach out and grab him. She had called him twice at work and once at home. The last time she had pleaded with David to spend just one hour with her in her apartment. David had told her that he thought she should see a psychiatrist. He hated her for taking all the joy out of the class for him.

In July Patricia mounted her second major show at the gallery, and it was again greeted by the New York art world as a significant event. David was continuously amazed by her dedication and expertise and by her undeniable success. She was rarely home in

the evenings anymore, always busy at the gallery, at other exhibits, or meeting with collectors. They hired a housekeeper to look
after Ashley and prepare meals. More often than not, when David
was home he took his dinner with the children in the T.V. room.
One evening in August, when David was working late at the dining room table, Pat walked in and sat across from him without
saying a word. Her hair, which she had recently dyed a honey
color to hide the premature gray, was swept back from her face
with a comb on one side, much the way she had worn it when she
was a freshman at Radcliffe. She looked at David softly for a moment.

"I'm afraid I have some bad news," she said quietly. "I don't
really know how to say it except just to say it. I've fallen in love
with somebody else, David. It's Winthrop, actually. We'd like to
get married."

David stared back at her, not breathing.

"I never expected this to happen," she went on, "not in a million
years. I tried to keep it from happening, you know, because of you
and the children. But . . . well . . . it just did, David. It just did
and now it's done and in the end what's there to do except follow
your heart?"

David grabbed the edge of the table with both his hands. Tears
streamed down his face, caught in his throat.

"I'm sorry," Pat said, coming over beside him, touching his hair.
"I don't regret anything, you know, not a day of our life together.
Not a moment, really. But when you think about it, this really
makes more sense. I mean, I probably should have been married
to an artist all along."

"An *artist?*" David stood. His voice was an uncontrollable growl.
"You mean a dilettante, Patricia. A rich, Harvard dilettante."

On the day David moved out of the apartment Ezra Kornfeld of
the *Village Voice* rushed up to him just as he was flagging a cab.

"Glad I caught you, David," he said. "Did you see this morning's
Times? Tim Leary's making a deal with the Justice Department.
He's testifying before a Chicago grand jury, giving names, talking
about the Weathermen, the whole spiel. Can you give me something?"

David uttered a short, brittle laugh.

"I'm not surprised," he said. "All the chickens are coming home to roost. Leary's just the counterculture's Nixon."

34

TODD COULD NOT resist. For months he had been seeing posters and advertisements for Metaman Encounters, and this evening, just ten blocks away from his house, there was a Metaman lecture scheduled at the Jack Tar Hotel. How could he pass it up? Tonight's speaker was the founder and director of the Metaman Institute, Mr. Jerry Halligan.

Since that gentle year he had spent with them in the house, Todd and May had had little contact with Jerry. He would call every few months, usually early in the morning, and ask about everyone, especially the twins. And not a birthday or holiday went by without the arrival of one of Jerry's embarrassingly expensive gifts. But he never seemed to want to get together with them, and even long after his Metaman Encounters had been written up in every California newspaper, he never talked about what he did.

Todd paid seven dollars at the Jack Tar ballroom, sat on a metal folding chair, and started looking over the four-page questionnaire he had been given at the door. The first question was: "Why are you losing the game you are playing?" The rest of the questions did not get any easier for Todd to understand.

"Is this your first time at M.E.?" The young woman seated next to Todd smiled at him.

"Yes," Todd answered. "And you?"

"Third. But this is the first time I'll actually get to see Jerry."

Todd leaned his big head down. "Tell me," he said, "do *you* know why you are losing the game you are playing?"

"But I'm not," the young woman answered happily. "Not anymore."

When Jerry Halligan strode to the front of the audience, Todd

applauded along with everyone else. By God, Jerry did look good
—tall, tan and healthy. He wore a loose-fitting collarless shirt and
white pants, and his blond hair was parted in the middle. He
smiled, his eyes sparkling, and lifted the microphone.

"Head is head and heart is heart," he sang out. "And all the rest
is bullshit. Everything *is* just exactly what it *is*. Before you really
get that, you've got to clear your head of a lot of trash—drug trash
and school trash and church trash and T.V. trash. But once you do,
you can start playing the metagame to win."

The woman next to Todd burst into a cheer, and Todd rose and
slipped through a side door, trying desperately to hold down his
laughter until he was out on the street.

FIVE

1976-1977

"What was so normal about marrying you?"

"The Dutch also believe in charity," Greg said, grinning. No matter how much complaining he did, Greg could not conceal the fact that he was immensely happy, happier than he ever had been. Four years ago he had returned from Greece, surprising everyone with his moonfaced Dutch bride and her three-year-old son. He had met Saskia in Athens, where she had a job in the Benaki Museum restoring crockery from archeology digs. Her face had reminded him of Annalena, but, he'd told Todd, there had been none of the same mad passion with Saskia, just calm, comforting love. "She's a master of restoration," he'd said. "She restoreth my soul."

Todd closed his eyes. He felt a tiny glow at the base of his neck. A picture of his brain appeared in his mind; it looked like a Ming tree.

"I think it's starting," he said. "Just a twinge."

"I don't feel anything," Greg said.

"You're probably too high to begin with. Like those Indian gurus who swig down a whole bottle of LSD and never notice the difference."

"Yup, that's me, Baba Gregorian."

"I mean it. You know, I once read this long essay by an English artist from sometime in the seventeenth century, and this fellow had just had his first cup of tea—one of the first cups of tea to hit Europe from the Orient. Well, this guy was up for three days straight. Couldn't sleep for all the images that were flashing in his mind, all the colors, the incredible ideas. The man was clearly higher than a kite—*on one cup of tea!* My mother has two cups of the stuff every afternoon at four in Emporia, Kansas. Now how do you accc unt for the difference?"

"They made better tea in those days," Greg said.

"I bet that's not it," Todd said. "I bet the difference is that our whole culture is 'tea high' now. Saturated with it. And I don't mean we've built up some kind of physiological tolerance to the orange pekoe leaf. I mean that all the perceptions, the flashes, the clarity that the first cup of tea gave that Englishman are now routine parts of our consciousness. So my sixty-five-year-old mother drinks a cup of tea and she just feels normal. Her mind vorks like everybody else's in a country where they've been rinking tea for three centuries. Getting high has to be relative to

35

"HERE'S TO the rest of our lives."

"And more!"

Todd clinked his glass against Greg's and poured the sweet metallic-tasting water down his throat. He smiled happily, sitting with his arms wrapped around his knees on a blanket in MacArthur Park. They could not have been given a better day for their celebration. The air was crisp, the sun clear. Greg swirled the potion around his mouth before swallowing.

"Do you realize this is vintage acid? Nineteen sixty-four, to be exact. I'm not guaranteeing anything, pal. It may have lost its bouquet."

"Aging always brings out the subtler qualities," Todd said. He lay back and squinted up at the sun. Today he and Greg were keeping a date they had made twelve years ago when Jerry had presented them with the sugar cubes of acid for Christmas. On the advice of a Village drug maven, Greg had dissolved the cubes in water and frozen the result in his refrigerator, where it had remained all that time—even those years he was in Europe—until last month, when he moved to Los Angeles.

"You know, maybe I should have bought some fresh stuff," Greg said. "LSD isn't exactly difficult to come by in Hollywood, you know. The gesture would have been the same, don't you think?"

"Nope," Todd said, still staring at the sky. "Not after all that loving care you've given it. And all those years of anticipation. They're part of its chemistry now."

Greg laughed. "As long as it makes my hair grow back, I'm not complaining."

Todd propped himself up on his elbows and looked at his friend. Poor Greg—he'd been able to delay just about everything in his life except losing his hair and now, just in the few years since he had been married, the top of his head was completely bare, giving him a slightly comic, monkish appearance. He hated it. He called it the beginning of the end. Todd told him it was the beginning of wisdom.

"Sasky doesn't approve of this outing, you know," Greg sai "She thinks we're just inviting disappointment. Typical Du attitude. Comes from living below sea level. They've got a pression that goes 'Act normal, it's crazy enough.' "

some kind of normal consciousness. I'll bet you've got an LSD high all the time now, Greggy, so you aren't even aware of it."

"Nice theory," Greg said seriously, "but I can still remember that night in Newton and I've never had an experience anywhere near it since."

"Can you *really* remember it?" Todd wrapped his arms around his knees again and looked in Greg's eyes.

"I think so," Greg said. "Parts of it at least. And once in a while when I smoke some pot I get little flashbacks of how it felt when I popped into that state of not being me anymore. Remember? I was convinced that I could literally jump out of my skin and slip into anybody else's—yours, Jerry's, Axel's, even Leary's. I mean, personal identity was about the slipperiest thing in the universe that night. And, Jesus, what a liberating feeling that was! It's everybody's favorite fantasy, right? Not having to be yourself?" Greg laughed. "It's the ultimate stunt!"

Greg suddenly jumped to his feet, miming a microphone in one hand and freezing his face in the manic grin of a T.V. emcee.

"Good afternoon, everybody," he sang out cheerfully. "And a great big welcome to—da-da-da-daa—'The Life Exchange,' the show that gives away big bucks for the biggest stunt of them all— switching identities!"

Todd grinned up at Greg. Except for the baldness, he might still be back in college doing one of his bits in the Adams House dining hall.

"Ah, and here's our first contestant, Mr. Todd Brewster, from right here in San Francisco." Greg squinted at an imaginary cue card. "Hmmm. Married, father of three, chief honcho of the city hospital. Sounds to me like you're the perfect normal middle-aged American, Mr. Brewster. But what's that? You say you're a little bored? Well, you've come to the right place, Mr. Brewster. Who in the world would you like to trade identities with—right now, live and in color?"

Todd was laughing so hard his head was spinning. He pushed himself up onto his knees and leaned toward Greg's imaginary microphone.

"Well, there is one secret fantasy I've always had, Roscoe," he said. "For once in my life I'd like to be short. Who's available? Mickey Rooney? Toulouse-Lautrec?"

They both roared.

"You know, I'd really watch that show," Todd said at last. "I'd watch 'The Life Exchange' five days a week if it were on the tube. So would May and the kids. Hell, the world's ripe for a metaphysical game show."

He fell back onto the blanket. A cloud seemed to hang in the sky directly over his head. He felt light as air. Suddenly he was up again, pointing a finger at Greg.

"Greggy, do you remember Halligan's questionnaire? The one he gave us in the car on the way out of Newton?"

Greg nodded.

"He asked what we expected out of that night and I remember you answered that all you wanted was one terrific idea you could put onstage. Well, pal, I think you had it!"

Greg laughed, but his mood had obviously changed. "I've forgotten what your answer was—on the questionnaire, I mean."

Todd's mouth felt dry as smoke. "I said I wanted a religious experience, no less." He forced a grin. "Pure greed, huh? And the one sure way not to have anything even resembling a religious experience." He stretched out on the ground again. "You know, I think I had more riding on that night than I ever let on to myself? I had this kind of preconscious wager with myself that if anything did happen—any sign at all—I'd switch to divinity school as soon as I could. It's what I really wanted to do, but I didn't think I deserved it—not without a certified mystical experience. And then all that ever happened was my bawling over the vegetables in Leary's cupboard."

Greg had walked over and stood directly above Todd, his face looming against the cloud. "Funny, that vegetable business always sounded pretty holy to me," he said.

Todd smiled up at his friend. There was no one else in the world he could talk to with this kind of understanding. "Maybe old Jerry was a genius after all. Maybe that night was full of clues, our lives on the head of a pin." Todd laughed. "And all the rest, Greggy, all the rest has just been waltzing with the zeitgeist." He reached out his hand. "Help me up, would you, pal?"

They walked side by side in silence for several minutes, Todd resting his big hand on Greg's shoulder. "The Mutt and Jeff of post-Kantian idealism," Jerry used to call them.

"Hey, did you get high?" Todd said.

"Nope. This stuff is too ancient."

"Hell, you wouldn't know. You're high all the time, Gregorian," Todd said, and the two of them burst into uproarious laughter.

That night, when Todd lay down next to May in bed he said, "What would you think if I quit the hospital and started divinity school at the age of thirty-seven?"

"I'd wonder what took you so long," May said.

"You know what I keep thinking, though?" Todd said. "If I left the hospital, who'd send Axel his medical supplies?"

36

AXEL FILLED the radiator of his fusty Oldsmobile with bottled water while he waited for Tati outside the *clinica*. The temperature was near ninety already, although it was not even eight o'clock. He closed the hood and patted it like an animal's head. The road to Calexico would reach 110 degrees before noon.

"Ready!" Tati walked around the rear of the car, tying her hair back from her face with a red bandanna. "All babies are content. Both in or out of their mama's bellies." She smiled across the front seat at Axel. Her brown face glowed red at the cheekbones and her black eyes gleamed.

"Me too," Axel said. *"Contento,* that is."

On only two tries, the engine caught and Axel guided the car slowly along the bed of dust that was the *colonia*'s only street, but despite his care the dust rose in a fan behind them, dark as smudge. Tati leaned back in her seat.

"This feels like a trip to paradise," she said.

They rarely got to make the run to Calexico together, just the two of them. Either a patient's fever had to be watched or a young woman's first contractions of labor had just begun and one of them would have to stay.

"Let's treat ourselves to lunch at Tonello's," Axel said. "Shrimp in a basket and beer, the businessman's special."

Tati laughed. She slid over and rested her head on Axel's shoulder. *Contento* indeed.

Only three years ago Axel had still been shuttling back and forth across North America, responding without question to directives from underground commanders whose faces he no longer knew. He would mend a thigh ripped on the barbed wire surrounding a nuclear-power building site in Maine, then fly to Vancouver to deliver a baby in a Weather safe house; a month later he would be on a bus bound for Chicago because some aging draft evader or bail jumper like himself needed help kicking his heroin habit. Everyone called him "Doc" and they all somehow knew that Doc did not want to hear a word about their causes or missions or philosophies, only their medical complaints.

During that period Axel had thought frequently of turning himself in. Draft evaders had been granted amnesty, and his charges in New York had long since slipped by the statute of limitations; only the bail-jumping charge remained. But Axel was afraid of what he knew—or at least of what some government agent would think he knew about the Underground. He had heard of more than one comrade who had surfaced with a promise of immunity, only to find himself pulled in front of a grand jury or, more likely, in jail for refusing to testify before it. And, anyway, what was left for him in the "straight" world? He was too old to go to medical school now. He was a stranger to everyone he had ever known before except for Todd and Annalena. He was an expatriate in his own land—how could he come home?

In the summer of '73 he had been summoned from Eugene, Oregon, to San Diego, where he was picked up at the airport by two Spanish-speaking men in a pickup truck and driven east across the bottom wedge of California to a little corner of Arizona. Their destination was Colonia Xito, one of the hundreds of twin towns and cities that had sprung up just across the Mexican border like desert mirages of the homeland. Xito's distinction was that it was even poorer and more disease-ridden than most of the other *colonias.* Half its population were illegal aliens; the other half were children who had been born there. It had no running water, no doctor, no school, no post office. The nearest town in Arizona, itself indigent by American standards, had redrawn its county border to separate itself from any connection to Xito. It was a no-man's-land —a perfect location for a safe house.

When Axel had first seen Xito from the road, it looked like some exotic metal mobile suspended from the hill. The corrugated tin roofs of the *casitas* threw up a screen of shimmering heat that made the village dance. Closer, it looked like a garbage dump, rats scrambling on the privy roofs. Axel was led to his patient immediately, a boy of no more than sixteen with one bullet lodged in his thigh and another in his shoulder. Fortunately someone had had the good sense to clean the wounds with alcohol and bind them tightly. The bandages looked fresh. Axel gave the boy a shot of morphine and a shot of penicillin before he even washed his hands. A broad-faced Mexican woman about his own age led Axel out to the courtyard to wash up.

"He's lost blood. Too much," she said. "No one knows their blood type here. I am O positive. He'll have to take mine."

She spoke a hybrid of Spanish and English which Axel was surprised he understood so easily. Her name was Tati Marquez and she was Xito's chief midwife. Midwifery, Axel discovered later, was Xito's major industry.

"I'll be able to do something about the bullets, I think," Axel told her. "But if there is any internal hemorrhaging, he'll have to go to a hospital."

"They won't allow that," the woman answered, and she led Axel back into the open-windowed room where the boy now slept. It was understood that Tati would assist Axel. She ordered everyone outside except for two young girls. The girls were her daughters and they responded quickly and silently to everything she asked: blankets hung over the windows, freshly boiled water. Axel and Tati worked side by side for over two hours removing the bullet from the boy's thigh, deciding to leave the other buried in his shoulder. At the end Tati lay down on a cot beside the boy and Axel fed a pint of her blood directly into him. The boy's temperature began to drop at dusk; his blood pressure, miraculously, climbed to normal.

Axel ate with Tati and her children in their own *casita*—rice and beans, one carrot apiece. After dinner Tati opened a cot for Axel in the kitchen. In the morning they went together to see their patient. He was sitting up, talking with one of the men who had driven Axel in from San Diego. The boy seemed eager to be up and out already. Tati then led Axel to the maze of interconnected *casitas* where she brought infants into the world. That morning it housed three young women with newborns at their breasts. All three mothers had come across the border just to give their babies American citizenship; they would return to Mexico once Tati had secured birth certificates for them. For this they paid Tati two hundred and fifty dollars. Axel knew without asking that the money did not stay in Tati's possession long—it spread quickly through the entire *colonia*. Before sundown that night, Axel knew that he wanted to stay in Xito. He wanted to build a clinic, set up a sewage system, clean the water. He had not thought that way or felt such eagerness since he was a young man, fifteen years ago in Africa. He had not been in love since that time either.

Three months went by before anyone tried to contact Axel. He was in his clinic swabbing mites from a youngster's ear when a bearded man in fatigues walked in and presented him with an envelope. It was an order to go to Tampa to perform an abortion. Axel folded the note and placed it in his pocket before he spoke.

"I can't come with you," Axel said. "I'm staying here."

The bearded young man glared. Axel could read in his eyes that he was considering taking Axel with him by force. That was the method of the new generation of underground troops; they were more militant than American marines. Axel hesitated a second longer, then put his eye back to the otoscope in the youngster's ear. He spoke softly to the little boy in Spanish. "They are having a feast in there, Nicito. They eat better than we do." When Axel looked up, the bearded man was gone.

Xito's safe house had been occupied only three times since then, and each time Axel kept his distance. Once a young Puerto Rican who was in hiding there came into the clinic and asked to see the doctor. He complained of sharp pains in his abdomen. Axel gave him a complete workup, then delivered his diagnosis as solemnly as possible: The young rebel had ulcers.

Within months of his arrival in Xito, Axel moved from the cot in Tati's kitchen into her own bed. He had never imagined that he could love a woman so naturally, so easily. He considered Tati his wife—his first true wife—and he thought of her children as his children. He never thought of turning himself in anymore. He was a citizen of Xito. He had found his home.

Axel waited, sweltering in the car while Tati entered the Calex-ico Post Office. Once, many years ago, he had been standing in line at the general-delivery window of a Denver post office when he found himself squinting at a photograph on the wall. It was him-self, beardless and tan, in his mother's favorite photo of him. No doubt she had made a gift of it to the FBI because she still hoped to save Axel from himself. He had avoided post offices whenever possible since then. Tati appeared at the door, struggling with two large cartons, and Axel jumped out and took them from her. In the parking lot behind Tonello's Café he opened the boxes and took a quick inventory of their contents. Todd, as always, had included every medical supply Axel had requested, and then some. Axel removed a pair of envelopes before locking the cartons in the trunk.

"What are you waiting for, Axelito?" Tati laughed. They were sitting at a booth in Tonello's, almost shivering from the air-condi-tioning. "Read your letters. You can think of nothing else anyhow."

Axel opened Annalena's letter first—it had been sent to Todd only a month ago. Instinctively Axel turned to the last page; like their mother, Annalena always held off until the end to break whatever unhappy news she had. In her most recent letter she had gone on cheerfully for five pages before she announced that she had separated from Lester. Today she only added that the divorce was now final and that she was feeling more relieved than sad. Sweet Annalena. He wished he could bring her and the children to Xito to live. Surely that would be better than living forever five blocks from their parents' house in Akron. Axel opened Todd's letter.

Dear Axel,

I have resigned from the hospital. But don't be alarmed. I have made arrangements for your clinic to maintain its status as the Mayo of MexiAmerica; packages will continue to arrive on the present schedule.

What I am doing, for reasons that still baffle me, is attending S.F. Seminary. But here is the part I thought you would appre-ciate the most—God knows, I do. I am the recipient of a unique and heartbreakingly generous "fellowship" that al-lows May and me to keep the house on Russian Hill and continue to live more or less as we always have. It's a gift that

Greg cooked up with Jerry. Whatever else one might think of those two men, they are both in possession of prodigious hearts . . .

Axel folded the letter without continuing.

"You look unhappy," Tati said.

"Not really." Axel sipped the froth off his beer. "Well, maybe a little. I miss people sometimes. Some of them people I never thought I'd miss."

The moment they saw Xito on the hill in the early evening sun, Axel knew something terrible had happened. Two green vans were parked at angles next to the water drums. The entire village seemed to be gathered outside the clinic. Axel pressed the accelerator and the car bounded through the dust like a phantom ship. Everyone was screaming when Axel and Tati jumped out of the car and pushed their way to the clinic door. A man was lying like a slab on the bed and blood was pouring in a single stream from each of his legs.

"Tourniquet!" Axel grabbed one of the man's legs and reached under the knee for the popliteal artery. It was only then that he saw that both of the man's feet were gone, freshly severed at the ankle.

"How in the name of God did this happen?" Axel shouted.

The answer came from a voice in back of him: *"Bombas."*

37

DAVID HAD completed his second lap underwater when he saw Manuela's shadow on the side of the pool. He floated up to the surface.

"Telephone, Mr. Debilio," the woman said, squinting down at him. "I told him you were busy, but—"

"That's all right. I'll take it here." David vaulted out of the pool and took the towel from her hands. "Might as well have my breakfast out here too, if you don't mind." He rubbed his hair briskly before sitting in the lounge chair and lifting the phone. "David Debilio," he said.

"Shit, man, hate to take you away from your ablutions."

"Who is this?"

"Monroe. Cal Monroe. Listen, Debilio, they are really trying to pull some colossal shit on me. We need to talk."

David sat up straight and his towel dropped from his shoulders. "What's the problem, Cal?"

"A grand jury in San Diego. I'm subpoenaed for one o'clock this afternoon. They say it's about that bombing, but you know what the fuck it's really about."

"When were you served with the papers?"

"Day before yesterday."

"Why didn't you call me then?"

Monroe paused for just a beat. "You weren't my first choice, man."

Manuela set down David's breakfast tray and poured his coffee. She had started back to the house before David spoke.

"I'll meet you at my office in an hour," he said. "We can drive down to San Diego together."

David hung up the phone. He lifted the coffee cup to his lips but returned it to the tray without sipping it. His heart was racing fast enough as it was. Jesus Christ, Calvin Monroe—it was like an omen. There had not been a day in the past two months when David hadn't thought about the man. His name was everywhere, his handsome brown face on the local news every night. Monroe was running for state representative from an LA district that encompassed part of Watts. He had formed his own party, Street Corner Caucus, a blend of hokey black populism and tough European socialism that advocated, among other things, seizure by eminent domain of all privately owned shorefront property so the beaches could be returned to the people. At first no one had taken his candidacy seriously, but lately the media could not get enough of Cal Monroe, and now there was talk of his grass-roots socialism being the wave of the New Left's future. David was sure there were a great many people who wanted to stop Monroe before he got any bigger, and he knew without question that Monroe's subpoena had more to do with maligning his name than it had to do with tracking down the San Diego bombers. The only part that surprised David was that Monroe had called him at all.

David's break with the liberal establishment was made complete when he moved out to California and set up his practice in West Hollywood. He was not even on the ACLU mailing list anymore. That part of his life was over, he'd told himself, that part along with just about everything else he'd left in New York. And yet when Cal Monroe had resurfaced a few months ago in the LA *Times,* something had resurfaced in David too. It seemed to him that after all the bullshit that had passed for radical politics in the past ten years, Monroe was getting back to basics—a program for changing the system from within. A couple of times David had even considered contacting Monroe, perhaps volunteering to be counsel for his campaign, but somehow he had never found the time for it.

Cal's call *was* an omen. David jogged into the house and up to his bedroom. He hesitated in front of his bureau for only a moment before pulling open the bottom drawer and removing his faded blue workshirt.

"Man, these are the same motherfuckers who are scaring the shit out of everybody with tales of the Red scourge. 'Elect Monroe and you'll be taking orders from Moscow.' Shit, Moscow is here, man!" Monroe waved his subpoena papers in the air. "The KGB is here and it's called a federal grand jury!"

David squinted through the windshield, trying to restrain a smile. Monroe had been ranting nonstop for close to an hour, his big hands in perpetual motion. His mind had grown both keener and wilder than David remembered it, his timing and sly irony even more hilarious. It was little wonder that his course on "Black Consciousness" was so popular at UCLA, and it was no wonder at all that the media had seized on his campaign—Monroe was the best showman in town. David did not have a client on his roster of Hollywood celebrities who could begin to match his wit—the basic difference was that Monroe's humor depended on raw truth. And the truth was that the San Diego federal prosecutor was using his grand jury as a fishing expedition, resorting to the flimsiest of hearsay evidence to link whomever he wanted to with the Native American Army, the terrorist group which claimed credit for the restaurant bombing.

"They want to make us all look like *banditos*. Put us through their famous media mix: flip-flop; all feminists are bulldykes with whips; all Rican separatists are terrorists; any Indian who wants a piece of the action is a scalper. And a black politician, man, he's the worst—he's either on the take or he's part of the Big Conspiracy. Man, they've even co-opted paranoia from us."

David laughed. Once again he wished Joshua were with him taking all this in. When the boy visited last August, he had made it damned clear that he thought just about everything in his father's life was either shallow or boring or both. "Compared to what?" David had shouted in spite of himself. "Hotchkiss? The SoHo art scene?" He would give anything to have the boy in the backseat right now. The first sign for the San Diego turnoff appeared on the right. David dropped his speed to fifty.

"Cal, I'm going to go through this one more time," he said. "Anything more than your name—a grunt, a nod—and you've waived your right to silence. They'll start with innocuous questions, but soon they'll be quizzing you on everyone you've ever known. And let me tell you, they'll try anything to make you open your mouth. Anything."

Monroe nodded. He stretched out his long legs and pressed his back against the seat. "I fired two lawyers before I called you," he said, "both of them black and smarter than either of us. But I wanted you, Debilio, because I needed somebody who knows just how those motherfuckers think."

On David's advice Monroe only smiled to the gaggle of newsmen who swarmed up to them in front of the San Diego Federal Court House. "Mr. Monroe will have a statement for you later," David told them. Inside they were led to a small room with barred windows at the end of a corridor. Monroe, amazingly, slept. At four the bailiff called him. David followed to the door of the grand jury room.

"I'm not allowed any closer than this," he told Monroe, "but if there's anything you want to ask me, they have to let you out for consultation."

Monroe was back out in three minutes. He was furious.

"Well, man, taking the Fifth doesn't mean shit in there. They say I've been granted immunity already, so if I don't talk I'm in contempt of court. What the fuck do I do now, Debilio?"

David shook his head slowly. They were running out of options fast. His only chance would be with a judge. "Don't talk, Cal," he said.

The next time Monroe came out, there was a marshal on either side of him, the federal prosecutor behind him. The prosecutor smiled at David. "Judge Balthazar is waiting for us," he said.

Jesus Christ, what a well-oiled machine it was. Totally shameless. The federal judge was indeed waiting for them at his bench, a cup of coffee in his hand. The whole setup reminded David of the Southern courthouses of the sixties. David made a motion to quash Monroe's subpoena, but it was all futile. Calvin Monroe was found in contempt of court for failure to respond to questions critical to national security. He was remanded to jail until such time as he chose to cooperate or until the grand jury was terminated. One of the marshals slapped handcuffs on him.

In the corridor outside the holding cell, Monroe turned and spoke to David for the first time since they had left the courtroom.

"Just get me out of here, slick!" he said.

The sunlight pouring on the courthouse steps momentarily blinded David. A microphone was pushed in front of his face, then another. He wet his lips. He had not even begun to think of what he would say.

"This country is under threat of terrorists," he began, "terrorists with bombs and guns, and terrorists who hold the Constitution of this country in flagrant disregard. The latter are the terrorists who have kidnapped Mr. Monroe."

One of the television reporters had slipped behind David and grasped his sleeve as she pressed her microphone in front of him. "Will what happened today in any way affect Monroe's campaign in LA?"

"Mr. Calvin Monroe is still an active candidate for state representative," David answered. The reporter's hand squeezed his arm.

"Thank you, David," she said. David turned his head and Despina Stenhorn smiled at him.

38

"HEY GREG, here's one of your favorite types—a last gasper."
Reg Jarvick, the contestant coordinator for "Life Swappers,"
waved a letter like a semaphore from his end of the table. "Mr.
Arnold Morgenstern of Milwaukee, eighty-three-year-old propri-
etor of Morgenstern's Funeral Parlor, would give anything to deliver just one baby before he dies." Jarvick held the letter close to
his eyes and went on in a comic Yiddish accent. "Tell me, gentlemen, vod dere be a docta somewhere who longs to do a little
embalming?"

Greg laughed along with the others, but then he said, "Don't
toss it out, there might be something there—beginnings and end-
ings. Always look for the poetry."

Everyone nodded seriously, even young Jarvick. One of the
hardest parts of Greg's spectacular success was getting used to
people taking him seriously. He had never had that problem before. Certainly it had been considerably easier to get a giggle out
of people before he thought up the twenty-third most popular
television show in America.

"How about this?" one of the P.A.'s beamed over at Greg. "A
lady stockbroker who longs to ride an elephant into the big top?"

"Sounds promising," Greg said. "Put it in the *B* pile."

"Life Swappers" had happened faster than any show anyone in
Hollywood could remember. On the Monday after returning from
his visit with Todd, Greg had dropped in on his old game show
producer Bobby Burger and said, "Did you ever ride with a cabbie
who thinks he's a comedian? Well, what if that guy traded places
with Flip Wilson for a week and we followed them both around
with cameras? I bet we'd get a 30 Nielsen." That Wednesday Greg
and Burger had pitched the idea at NBC, and by Friday they had
seed money for a pilot. The pilot had been harder to produce than
either of them expected. They had gone with the cabbie/come-

dian idea where the cabbie actually gets a chance to do a five-minute turn in front of a Las Vegas audience, but one after another the would-be comics bombed and their failures were too painful for anyone to watch. That's when Greg had another inspiration: He hired two top comedy writers to write a monologue about cabdriving and it clicked perfectly with their next candidate, especially when they ran it juxtaposed to the sequences of Flip Wilson getting into a hilarious argument with his fare as he drives a taxi through the streets of Chicago. The NBC people had loved it. They commissioned two more shows—a baseball player/stockbroker switch and a waitress/opera singer switch—and changed the name from "The Life Exchange" to "Life Swappers," and put Burger-Gregorian Productions on standby. The next month, after three new NBC sitcoms in a row took rating dives, "Life Swappers" was plugged into the Thursday-night-at-eight spot. It was then only ten months since Greg and Todd's private party in MacArthur Park. As Greg had predicted, the first show garnered exactly a 30 Nielsen. It also got more mail than any new show that year, and by the third week it had already generated an incredible number of articles in magazines and newspapers. As just about every columnist observed, "Life Swappers" touched the most fundamental American fantasy—How would my life have been if I'd done it all differently?—and it always gave the answer that people were dying to hear: You're better off just the way you are. Several critics cited Greg for coming up with the right idea at the right time, but not once in all the interviews he gave did Gregory mention that the original idea had come to him sixteen years ago under bizarre circumstances in Newton, Massachusetts.

In less than a year Greg went from being the oldest stunt writer in Hollywood to being the man-with-the-latest-idea. He was asked to lunch weeks in advance by network executives, agency and studio suitors. "What's next?" they all wanted to know. Greg loved being a success. After years of trying to convince himself that success did not really matter, when success finally did come it grabbed him around the waist and swung him in the air. "Success has been much maligned," he now said. "In fact, it has a number of advantages over religion." Greg was well aware that "Life Swappers" was not a play or a novel—he could not call himself a "successful writer"—but, by God, the show was one of a kind, and when it really worked it did have poetic reverberations. On top of all that, he was making more money in a week than he used to make in a year. He hired a financial adviser. He moved the family to a ten-room beach house in Carmel. He constantly asked Saskia and Wim—who at eight was already devoted to a life of surfing—if there was anything in the world they wanted. "Nothing," Saskia would answer. "We have more than enough already." But one night when he asked again, she blurted, "You know what I want, Greg. I want a child with you."

It was the one thing that Greg could not bear to give her, although for the life of him he did not understand why. God knows, he had been a perfect father to Wim from the day he married Sasky; he spent much more time with the boy than most fathers did with their natural sons. But whenever Sasky suggested that they have a child together, Greg had a reason why the time was not right: It wouldn't be fair to Wim; they didn't have enough money; the house was too small. Over the years she had stopped asking—until now.

"We're too old," Greg said.

"I'm not," Sasky said. "And don't tell me this house is too small."

"But I'm busy all the time now, Sas. We don't want to bring another neglected California kid into the world, do we?"

"I won't neglect him. Or her. And neither would you, Greg. I don't understand you. We can have anything we want now. Why not this?"

"I don't know."

He truly did not know. Early in the morning Greg called Todd. "What's wrong with me?" he asked. "Just the thought of having a baby still gives me the existential willies. I'm thirty-eight and it makes me feel like my life is over."

"Kids are supposed to do that to you," Todd said. "Little jolts of mortality. Every time I see a child born at the hospital, I think about how little time I have left. You sound normal to me, pal."

"But I'm breaking Sasky's heart."

"Why don't you just do it then. Think of it as a stunt, Greg."

"Not funny."

"I'm serious. No matter how much I've loved each one of my kids, having the next one was always a leap of faith."

Try as Greg would, the faith did not come. Once again Saskia stopped asking, but this time something joyless lingered in their house and it became harder and harder for Greg to look into his wife's eyes.

When they had met in an Athens café years ago, it had been Saskia's eyes which attracted Greg. She had looked directly back at him, unself-consciously, unafraid. There was not a trace of artifice in the woman, no self-pity. She had possessed a sense of contentedness with everyday life which inspired him; he had known immediately that he could start life over with her, borrow her strength, her focus. But now that everydayness seemed to sap his strength, and her focus on the details of life made him feel myopic. She wanted less and less from him. She ground their own flour, baked their bread; he stayed late at the studio, ate out with the staff. At home he sat on the deck and stared out at the Pacific. He was afraid he had forgotten how to dream.

"Ah, here's a honey," Reg Jarvick was saying, "a librarian from Akron who wants to be a Playboy bunny."

Greg lifted his head. "How does she look, Reg?"

Jarvick leered at a glossy photograph. "She's the kind every schoolboy dreams of getting lost with in the stacks."

"Arrange a test," Greg said. "I'll come out with you."

Although Greg frequently accompanied the crew for contestant screen tests, he did not kid himself about why he had chosen to come along to Akron. He had started thinking about Annalena again. Whenever he saw a clipping of a magazine article about "Life Swappers" which mentioned his name, he found himself wondering if she had read it. Once he asked Todd if he had any news about Annalena via Axel, but Todd had managed to avoid answering—he was the last of the secret-keepers. Another time Greg decided to just call her and get it over with, but he only got as far as tracking down her number. It was almost nine years since he had heard her voice.

The Akron librarian turned out to be a real lulu. She wore rimless spectacles and, in or out of the library, spoke in a fussy whisper, but she insisted—on camera—on being allowed to wear an uplift bra under her bunny outfit. Greg gave her test an $A+$; he was sure that finding a "Playmate" to switch places with her would be a snap.

Greg left while the crew was still packing up. He had decided to take a cab directly to Annalena's house without calling ahead—

better to perceive her fresh and all at once. The cab turned onto a maple-lined avenue and slowed to a halt in front of a huge Victorian house. Somehow it all looked familiar to Greg. He pulled his Greek fisherman's cap down tightly on his head—he'd rather not have his bald spot be the very first thing she saw—and started up the front walk. God, he felt peculiar. The house turned out to have several entrances, divided into apartments. That certainly did not fit Greg's picture of how Annalena and her family lived. He paced from one door to the next on the long front porch. The last door listed ANNALENA BERGLIN as the occupant. Just Annalena, no Lester. Jesus, she was divorced, maybe widowed. Oh God. Greg sucked in his breath. Hell, hadn't he half expected that? He drew in his breath again and rang the doorbell, waited, rang again. No one answered. Greg rang one more time and then burst out laughing. Nine years and she wasn't home! He reached into his jacket and pulled out a notebook, but immediately stuffed it back. What kind of note could he leave: "I was just in the neighborhood. Sorry I missed you"?

Greg sat back on the porch railing, looping his arm around a pillar. He looked at his watch: It was just after five. She probably had a job. She would be home soon. Other cars had begun to roll up in front of other houses, pulling into driveways, stopping under sprawling elms and oaks. They were mostly men who got out, carrying briefcases and newspapers, occasionally a bag of groceries. They all looked tired. They all looked reasonably happy. There were no sharp sounds here; the slam of a car door in a driveway across the street melted in the air. It reminded Greg of the tricks of light in Greece, but there everything was made sharper; here everything seemed muffled. Greg might have lived here, he knew. If he had married Annalena, they might have found a house on this street. Maybe her parents would have helped them out. Their child would have been eight now, the same as Wim. Across the street a green sedan stopped under a maple tree and a man about Greg's age hopped out with a briefcase in one hand and a box of diapers in the other. The Life Exchange.

A car swung into the driveway beside Greg and he saw a flash of blond hair through the windshield. He held his breath. The first time he ever saw Annalena she was sitting on a stoop as he was now, waiting unexpected, unknown. It was the day that Axel had burst into flames in Macy's while performing Greg's stunt. But it was not a stunt, of course. Nothing was. The car door opened. Oh God yes, it was Annalena. Annalena! In the ocher light she looked the same as he remembered her—frail, beautiful, light as a dream. Greg slipped behind the porch pillar. Another figure was emerging from the car, a young man. No, a boy, her eldest son, Greg realized. He wore a knapsack. He carried the groceries. Now a second boy appeared from the garage with a basketball under his arm. For a moment all three were framed in Greg's eye like a photograph on a mantel. Annalena and her children. Greg's eyes filmed with tears; the image blurred. They were walking toward him. With an instinct sharp as a scalpel, Greg leapt over the porch railing and raced across the lawn to the street. He did not stop running until he turned the corner.

Saskia was pregnant before the summer came to an end. When Greg announced the news to Todd, he told his friend that he had been right—it took a leap of faith.

39

TODD TOSSED his books—Augustine's *Confessions, The Meaning of Revelation, Waiting for God*—into a locker and eased himself down to a bench in the orderly's changing room. It was his favorite part of the day, his classes over and ten minutes to kill before his ward shift began. Of all the recent changes in his life— the "regressions," as he called them at home—returning to the status of hospital orderly pleased him the most. All his responsibilities here were immediate and clear; there was nothing ambiguous about a bedpan which needed to be emptied. Going to seminary, his mind swam in ambiguity much of the rest of the day.

At first the board of San Francisco General had refused to let Todd sign on as a part-time orderly—it struck them as a bad precedent to allow a man to go from the top position in the hospital to the lowest—but in the end they had relented. Why Todd had wanted the job was another question. Jerry and Greg's "fellow-

ship" more than covered his family's financial needs. And he
hardly needed to hold a job at the hospital to insure that Axel's
medicine packets continued to be sent out. No, there was something in an orderly's routine, in the round of stretchers and bed-
pans and bloodied bandages, that Todd needed for himself.

He pulled on his white canvas trousers and reached for his
smock. *Waiting for God.* He carried the book with him everywhere recently. He stood by the locker leafing through the pages,
most of them now loose from the binding. "The danger," Simone
Weil wrote, "is not lest the soul should doubt whether there is a
God, but lest, by a lie, it should persuade itself that it is not hungry
for Him." There was no danger of that for Todd. Nothing in seminary even began to abate his *yearning* for faith. He smiled. It was
the kind of painful paradox which Weil would have appreciated: a
school of theology that increased one's hunger for God without
ever beginning to satisfy it. That was not the school's intention, of
course. The other students, most of them a good fifteen years
younger than Todd, were already in possession of a cool pastoral
certainty. They were of the new Marlboro-man breed of clergy;
rugged and handsome, they had plans of taking their parishioners
on Outward Bound treks through Big Sur to feel God's presence
among the redwoods. Todd had not missed Greg so much since
college. Seminary had also increased his hunger for irreverence.

"Todd? Todd Brewster?" A reedy voice called tentatively from
the hall door. It took a moment before Todd recognized it as
Axel's.

"Yes, I'm here. Come in! Come in!"

Axel's head appeared from behind a long row of lockers. His hair
and beard were full and woolly, sun-bleached red; his long face
was the color of copper. It was five years since Todd had seen him
last, and it was the first time that his friend had ever struck him as
handsome. He looked positively biblical. Axel quickly surveyed
the room before he walked up to Todd. The two men gazed into
one another's eyes and then they embraced, Todd leaning from
the waist so that their cheeks touched. It was the first time for that
too.

"May said I'd find you here. I'm surprised. I thought you'd be a
full-time student."

"I need this for ballast," Todd said, smiling. "Or maybe it's just
more fence-sitting."

"Maybe we both should have been doctors," Axel said.

Todd laughed. He glanced quickly at his watch. "Hey, I hope this isn't one of your famous hello/good-byes, Axe. I'm supposed to go on duty in a minute, but if—"

"My plans aren't definite."

"Hell, I've got an idea." Todd walked to the closet and pulled out a freshly laundered pair of white slacks and a smock. "Why don't you come up to the ward with me? We can talk. And you can do the bending for me."

Axel did not move.

"No one is going to ask who you are if you're with me," Todd said.

Without saying a word, Axel took the clothes and quickly changed into them. He followed Todd to the service elevator and up to the sixth floor. At the desk the shift supervisor gave Todd the day's list of special duties. Of all the hospital's employees, this woman had adjusted most enthusiastically to Todd's retrograde status at General; she seemed to go out of her way to reserve the most menial tasks for him. On today's list were five bed-scrub-bings, two involving patients over three hundred pounds who needed to be lifted into their wheelchairs. Todd was doubly glad that Axel was with him, but, as it turned out, he was hardly any help at all. As soon as they approached a bed, Axel reached for the occupant's medical chart, studied it, questioned the patient, even began examining him before Todd signaled to stop.

"The doctors here have been known to get touchy if they think anyone's giving an unsolicited second opinion. Especially if it's a nurse or an orderly."

"Sorry," Axel said. "I don't often get an opportunity to see other people's diagnoses."

At the next bed he again reached for the chart and Todd smiled and let it pass. They barely exchanged another word until they broke for dinner. Axel took a small bite out of a sandwich and set it down.

"Todd, I'm losing a patient in my clinic," he said softly. "He's slowly dying from an infection. It doesn't respond to anything I've tried."

"You'd better bring him to a hospital."

"I can't."

"Bring him here, Axel." Todd leaned across the cafeteria table. "I'm sure I can make special arrangements."

Axel shook his head. "The risk is too great."

"I thought you said he was dying."

Axel smiled ruefully. "There are greater risks than that for some people."

Todd sat back again and sighed. "What can I do?"

"I need to consult with a trained physician, preferably an immunologist. It has to be somebody you trust completely, Todd."

Todd gazed into Axel's eyes, but Axel immediately looked away. "I might as well tell you now, Todd," he went on, "the initial cause of this man's infection is that his feet were blown off in an explosion. Just that fact is enough to identify him in any hospital."

Todd drew in his breath. Yes, that was certainly enough to identify the patient. He had seen the FBI circular which had been sent to every hospital in the nation. Any man brought in with his feet or legs severed was to be reported immediately. The charred remains of a pair of feet had been discovered next to the detonator in the San Diego restaurant that had been bombed. The owner of those feet was wanted for conspiracy and murder. Todd took a sip of his iced tea. His heart was thumping. In all these years of illicitly supplying Axel with medical supplies, he had never truly confronted the reality of what his friend did. He had imagined Axel as a sort of underground Vista worker, a missionary to misfits and illegal aliens. Axel's secrecy had helped him block out the rest. Todd had never imagined anything like this. Jesus God.

"I don't have much time," Axel was saying. "Just tell me if you think you can help or not."

Todd shuddered. He leaned his big head across the table. "Isn't it time to stop all this, Axel?" he said softly. "Isn't it time to come back?"

"I can't," Axel whispered.

"I'm sure you can."

Axel did not move for several seconds, then abruptly pushed back his chair and stood. "I have to go," he said.

"No, please!" Todd was almost shouting. He stood. "I'll find someone to talk with you. It'll have to be an internist, I think. Wait here."

Todd raced upstairs and into Paul Rothstein's office. Rothstein was the young resident who signed, without question, for all the drugs Todd sent to Axel's clinic. Todd caught him just as he was leaving for home and quickly explained what Axel wanted. He told the doctor that there was considerable risk involved, but he did not tell him that the patient had lost his feet in an explosion. Rothstein did not hesitate for a moment. He asked Todd to bring Axel around to his car in the parking lot and several minutes later the three of them were in the front seat driving along Van Ness Avenue as Axel recited each stage of his treatment of his patient. Rothstein nodded, keeping his eyes on the road. He had not even blanched when Axel described the severed feet. When Axel finished, the internist said, "I'd need to see a complete blood workup before I could make any definite recommendations. But I'm afraid antibiotics can only take you so far in a case like this. I wouldn't rule out amputation at the knee, Doctor, but of course no one should attempt that procedure except under the most sterile conditions and with adequate backup."

Todd watched Axel's face as he listened. There was a look of utter helplessness in his eyes. "Thank you," he said when Rothstein finished.

They drove in silence until Rothstein dropped them back at the hospital. Axel thanked the doctor again. "I wish there were more I could tell you," Rothstein said.

As Todd and Axel entered the hospital, Axel said, "I think I'll change back into my clothes now."

"I'll come with you."

"I can find my way, Todd. Thank you for everything." Axel touched Todd's arm quickly. "I'll be in contact," he said, and turned and pushed open the door to the stairwell.

Todd held himself back from going after him. He stood, trembling in the corridor, then slowly headed for the elevator and returned to his duties on the sixth floor. For the rest of that evening while he bent and scrubbed and lifted, he thought about Axel and he thought about himself. His own life seemed puny, a series of dodges and privileges, the choices he had made not real choices at all, and his so-called spiritual agonies nothing more than a hobby, drawing room crises. He was forever buying himself off with tokens, riskless good deeds, part-time charities. Until today he had not even really wanted to know what Axel's life was like. While he wrestled with metaphysical ambiguity, he had been denying the real world.

th tears in his eyes, he begged Tati to bring a newborn infant to
s bedside for him to see. His lieutenants made weekly trips
ross the border in their vans, returning with weapons and explo-
es. They conducted guerrilla exercises on the hill below Xito
nile those children whose mothers could not stop them watched.
ventually three of the older boys began training with them. Two
the young women were sleeping with one or another of them.
cel frequently heard the men discussing plans to move on as soon
their leader was well enough to travel. Axel had devoted every
oment to trying to cure him, to rid Xito of the hideous infection
nich was killing them all.

"But I can't do that," Axel said. "I know that for certain now. I'm
t really a doctor, Todd. Not really. I can't amputate his legs, not
a tin-roofed *casita* with flies on the ceiling. But I can't watch
to die either." He shook his head. "My only hope is that if I leave,
ey will leave too. He can't live much longer the way he is. They'll
ve to take him somewhere."

Todd had hardly spoken a word since they began walking. Sev-
al times he felt tears spring from his eyes and roll down his
eeks in the dark night. He felt a torrent of love and admiration
r his friend. He felt privileged to be with him.

"I'll start back for Xito in a few hours," Axel said. "I can be there
 the afternoon and get Tati and the children to San Diego by
morrow night." He laughed softly. "How would you and May
el about having a little Mexican family stay with you for a
hile?"

"Nothing would make us happier," Todd said. They continued
alking in silence for several moments. Todd buttoned his jacket,
ddenly cold.

As they made their way back to the hospital and Todd's car, Axel
gan talking about the future. He and his family would eventu-
ly return to Xito, of course, but when they did he would have
thing to hide and nothing to fear. First he wanted to get
ramedic training in a hospital. He also wanted to find out how
ey could incorporate the village and make it part of the local
unty and its water supply. In time it would not be a place where
yone could hide. It was obvious that Axel had been thinking
out all of this for a long time.

At eleven Todd dropped his sponge and pail in the utility (
and walked to the elevator. In the basement he showered
changed. He jammed his books under his arm and left b
service door. He had only taken a few steps when a figure
peared from the darkness alongside him.

"I'll need your help," Axel said, looking straight ahead a
spoke. "I'm coming up. I'm turning myself in."

They walked for hours, striding through neighborhoods in
middle of the night which normally Todd would not have c
near even in the day. And all the while Axel talked. He tal
about the past fifteen years in a way Todd had never heard
talk before, a flood of anguish and hope, dedication and desp
coming back again and again to the two inalienable truths of
life—his love for Tati and her children, and his love of medici
He told Todd that his political ideas had not really changed sii
Africa. He still believed in *ujamaa*, of a garden that flourish
under everyone's hand, of free clinics and schools, of revolution
example. Everything else, he said, had turned out to be the polit
of terror and fear.

There had been a time, Axel told him, when he thought f
quently about surfacing from the underground, accepting wh
ever punishments were waiting for him, starting all over. Ye
Xito he had found everything he ever wanted, a family, a clini
new chance to try the experiment. For years he had been abl
disassociate himself from his old connections in the undergrou
to keep his distance from those who passed through the safe h
in the *colonia*. But all that had changed when the Man-Witl
Feet came. There were three others with him, all members (
American Indian sect whose goals were obscure but whose
presence was terrifying. The entire village had changed with
arrival. The terrorists had virtually taken over the clinic as a
mand post, the Man-Without-Feet issuing orders from his be
was an emaciated, curiously dull-looking man with a razo
scar above his upper lip like a permanent sneer. He spoke Sp
well—he had once lived in Peru. As the infection moved
legs and his temperature rose, his eyes glazed and he had
rage and hallucinations in the late afternoons. One time
dered his lieutenants to execute all the dogs in the *colonia* b
he was sure they were the source of his infection. Anothei

Todd cashed a check with the hospital cashier and gave Axel four hundred dollars. At the airport they embraced again.

"Until tomorrow," Todd said.

40

"WE DID not let you go to San Francisco to find out what you could not do."

The Man-Without-Feet's legs were streaked red all the way to his groin. His pillow was sopped.

"You need a hospital. You need a surgeon. I swear, I can do nothing more for you myself."

The Man-Without-Feet raised one stump from his bed. The room was filled with his fever, stank from his disease.

"You take them off, Doc. You cut them off, now."

41

TODD DECIDED to skip "Gnostic Origins," traded his shift at the hospital with a friend, and spent the entire afternoon with May preparing the guest rooms for Axel and his family. They brought a second dresser up from the basement. May hung a potted fern from the ceiling. Todd selected books for the bed tables—Hamsun's *Growth of the Soil*, Orwell's letters. At dinner Todd realized that he did not even know if Axel's wife and her daughters spoke English. Kristin said she hoped not; she wanted to practice her Spanish. May wondered whether Tati would want her children enrolled in school immediately. At eight the whole family sat down to watch "Life Swappers." This week a librarian from Ohio traded places with a Playboy bunny from Chicago. For the first time Todd had to acknowledge that Greg's show seemed more jokey than existential. It all looked contrived and, worse, it looked trivial. Everyone else seemed to still love it, though, and they all cheered wildly when Uncle Greg's name flashed on the screen. At nine Todd called the airport to find out when flights were due to arrive from San Diego. At two in the morning he drove out to the airport to meet the last plane coming in. Axel was not on it.

The next morning Todd called home between every class, but Axel had not arrived or called. Again Todd traded his hospital shift and came directly home. At four it occurred to him that Axel might have tried to contact him at the hospital, and he drove over and checked with the operator, then waited until eight in the orderlies' changing room. By the time he got home and found there was still no word from Axel, Todd could no longer deny that he was worried.

"I think you're getting yourself worked up over nothing," May told him. "I'm sure Axel meant he'd come up as soon as possible. He couldn't speak for Tati and the children. Maybe Tati has a patient in labor."

Todd paced around the kitchen table, shaking his head. He had not told May the complete story; in fact, he had omitted everything about the Man-Without-Feet.

"For heaven's sake, Todd, Axel has been underground for ten years. I don't think a few more days are that critical to him."

"You're probably right." Todd had considered any number of possibilities for Axel's delay, including a patient in labor, a sick child or even a broken car. It was also possible that the Man-Without-Feet had died and Axel had decided to wait for the other terrorists to leave before he abandoned the village. Or maybe Axel had changed his mind altogether. Or maybe he was being held against his will.

"I'm sure he'll get in touch with us as soon as he can," May said.

Todd spent most of Saturday in the seminary library trying to catch up with his schoolwork. He worked a double shift at the hospital, and when he came home Sunday morning he went to bed for the rest of the day. He awoke at dusk, his whole body bristling with sweat. He knew he could not wait any longer.

He pulled on a pair of jeans and a checkered shirt. In the bathroom he considered dropping his razor and toothbrush into an overnight kit but decided against it. May and the children were eating supper in the kitchen when he came downstairs. Todd took a plate from the cabinet and sat down with them.

"You missed a whole day, Pop," Jan said. "Like it never happened."

Todd smiled. "I've been a day behind for years," he said.

When they finished eating, Todd took May by the hand and led her into the hallway. "I'm going down to Xito," he said.

"Are you sure Axel would want you to do that?"

"I'm not sure of anything, May." He kissed her on the cheek. "I'll call you tomorrow."

There were no direct flights leaving for San Diego until eleven, so Todd decided to take the shuttle down to Los Angeles and make connections there. The moment he buckled himself into his seat he began to have second thoughts. Even though May did not know about the terrorists, she might be right: He could be overreacting. He really didn't have that much information to go on. Axel's version of what had happened in his village was muddled in his mind with newspaper accounts of the San Diego bombers, and those accounts themselves were only speculations leaked from the grand jury which was convened there. When he had walked with Axel through the streets that night, it had seemed as if Axel had held nothing back, but now it seemed as if he had left out everything that was truly important. Damn it, was he in danger or wasn't he?

The plane raced down the runway and lifted into the air. Where did this overwhelming sense of urgency come from if not from Axel? Or was Todd simply enlisting in someone else's war again, seeking another shortcut out of the shadow of halfhearted faith? Todd closed his eyes. In the name of God, please, he was making this trip to save Axel, not himself. As soon as he got off the plane Todd called Greg. "I need to talk," he told his friend.

"Are you all right, Todd? Is May all right?"

"Yes. Can you meet me at the airport, Greg? I'd rather talk here."

"I'll be there in forty-five minutes. There's a bar on the upper level. Is that good?"

"Fine."

When Greg jogged into the airport bar, he was breathing hard.

He put his hands on Todd's shoulders before he could rise and he kissed his cheek. "Tell me everything," he said.

Todd began by swearing his friend to utter secrecy. "I'm breaking a trust I've held for over ten years," he said. "It's about Axel."

Greg sat down.

Todd started by reciting every contact he had had with Axel over the years, the medical supplies he had sent him, the life he had once imagined Axel living. Todd slid from his chair to the one next to Greg.

"Last Wednesday Axel turned up at the hospital," Todd said softly. He recounted every detail he could remember of that day. "He didn't act like he'd have any problem getting away from that village, Greg. But, my God, these are the people who bombed that restaurant. And this man who's dying seems capable of anything. We didn't make any plans, no contingencies for if he didn't show up . . . how long I should wait . . . nothing . . . Jesus, I don't know how I let that happen, Greg. Axel would never ask me on my own to make plans like that, to take any risks myself." Todd took a deep breath. "There's no way to find out why he hasn't come—no phones, no telegraph—no way except by going down there. But if I do go, that might be just the thing that sets these people off. They don't know who I am. For Christ's sake, they all walk around carrying machine guns."

Greg grabbed Todd's forearm with both hands. "I don't know what the hell you're talking about," he said loudly. "You can't go down there, Todd, but somebody sure as hell has to. Of course Axel's in danger. The police should know about this, Todd. Maybe I don't understand something, but I don't see anything confusing about that."

Todd held perfectly still. For a moment he did not breathe. "I'm . . . I'm not sure Axel believes in that," he finally said.

"Then he's crazy!" Greg said. "You're both crazy! Jesus, I don't think we should let Axel risk his life because we can't second-guess his goddamned principles." Greg stared at Todd. "This isn't Harvard, pal."

Todd slowly nodded his head and Greg rose from his chair. "I'm going to call David," he said. "He'll know how we should do this."

42

DAVID AND DESPINA were sitting up in bed, his arm looped over her shoulder and his fingers idly revolving around her left breast as they watched themselves on "California Roundtable." The program, taped that morning, was about grand jury abuse and Despina was by far the most aggressive of the news panelists interrogating David.

"Let us imagine, Mr. Debilio, that the mayor of Los Angeles has been kidnapped and the kidnappers have given him a day to live," Despina was saying on the T.V. set at the foot of the bed. "And the only lead the authorities have to go on is a man whom they *suspect* knows the kidnappers. Now, if this man refuses to answer their questions on the grounds that they're trying to malign his good name, are we to simply pat him on the head, show him the door, and wait for the gun to go off?"

In bed David pinched Despina's nipple, while on the screen he fumbled for a moment before saying, "A man can always refuse to talk, Fifth Amendment or not, Ms. Stenhorn. Are you suggesting that under extenuating circumstances *any* means should be legally permitted to get him to talk? Hot pokers? The iron maiden?"

In the bed both of them jiggled with laughter. Calvin Monroe's imprisonment for contempt of the San Diego grand jury had put the two of them on television regularly over the past month. Despina's reports for her San Diego station had been picked up several times by CBS National News in New York; there had already been inquiries from network headquarters about the extraordinarily sharp and beautiful reporter. And David's outspoken critique of grand jury abuse, what he called "judicial terrorism," had catapulted him once again to the forefront of civil liberties law. It had galvanized him, made him feel on top of things again. Even Joshua seemed to have regained respect for his father; he called from Hotchkiss every time David appeared on national television. But it was Despina, marvelous Despina, who deserved the credit for goading him to make grand jury abuse a national issue, the new McCarthyism. She was good for David. They were together all the time now, and she challenged him in everything they did.

"It's no secret that Calvin Monroe's political campaign has virtually come to a standstill with Mr. Monroe behind bars." It was Hollins from the LA *Times,* and David's back tightened, just as it had in the studio that morning. "Tell me, Mr. Debilio, is there any truth to the rumors that Monroe is seriously considering finally cooperating with the grand jury so that he can get back to the business of running his campaign?"

"No truth at all," David said on the screen.

Beside him Despina nudged his ribs with her elbow. "Cross your heart?"

"Absolutely," David answered. He was lying to both of them. Since the beginning of that week Monroe had been threatening to break his silence.

"Shit man, like I got nothing to tell even if I do open my mouth," he'd told David. "All my pals from the old days are either dead, in Africa, or got Jesus. I don't know any bombers anymore, just slick Italian lawyers."

"If you talk now, the press will kill you," David had answered. "It doesn't matter if you recite Mother Goose in there, you'll be called a fink and you won't be able to get yourself elected dog-catcher."

"Well, you're the fucking expert on the press, aren't you, Debilio? You're the fucking expert on everything except getting me out of here!"

On Friday Monroe had put David on notice that he was going to talk to the grand jury if he was not out of jail by the end of next week. They both knew that it was David whom the press would really crucify.

The moderator of "California Roundtable" was summing up when the phone rang. David reached behind Despina and picked it up. "Hello?"

"David? This is Greg Gregorian. Sorry to call you so late and so out of the blue, but I'm afraid it's an emergency. Todd's here with me. We need to speak with you right away."

"My God, Greg Gregorian. It must be something like ten years, isn't it?"

"Yes. Can we come right over, David?"

"Can't we make it ten years and a day, Greg? I'm kind of tied up. How's lunch tomorrow?"

Despina pulled the phone from David's hand. "Greggy?" she said, laughing. "This is Despina. Despina Stenhorn. . . . Sure, you can always find me at David's when I'm in LA . . . Why don't you come right over, okay? Do you know how to get here?" When she hung up, she kissed David on the cheek. "We didn't have anything else planned, did we? I mean, except for the 'hot poker!' "

David forced a smile. "I didn't even know you knew Gregorian."

"Oh, we're old friends." Despina swung her feet out of the bed. "We even had a delicious little rendezvous in Greece."

David turned quickly so she could not see his face. She loved dropping little bombs like that and watching his reaction. She seemed to have had "a thing" with half the people he knew.

It was almost midnight when Greg and Todd arrived. They were still as comical-looking a pair as they had been in college, perhaps more so now that they were both losing their hair. Despina gave Greg a big hug and said something to him in Greek, but David was pleased to see that Greg seemed more embarrassed than flattered. The truth was, both he and Todd looked dazed. Todd immediately asked if he could use the phone and a moment later returned to the living room shaking his head. "May still hasn't heard anything," he said quietly to Greg.

Greg was standing by the wall, rubbing his palms as if he was cold. He looked at Despina. "Would you mind if we spoke with David alone?"

"Oh, come now, Greggy, we don't have any secrets between us, do we?"

Greg clenched his teeth, his eyes cast down for a moment. "Please, Despina," he said.

Despina smiled. "Maybe we can all have a little drink when you're finished," she said, and gracefully left the room.

Todd moved his chair next to David's. The two men had not had a word of contact since college, although David had heard somewhere that Todd was a steady family man with some kind of unimportant job.

"This is all confidential," Todd said quietly.

"Of course."

Todd leaned his big head only inches away from David's. "I know where Axel is," he said. "Our Axel. And I think his life is in danger there." He leaned even closer. "I think he's being held by the people who bombed that restaurant in San Diego."

"You know where the bombers are?"

"Yes."

"How?"

"I saw Axel last week."

For one dizzying moment David closed his eyes. Then, as calmly as he could, he put his pen onto the coffee table. "I don't think I should record this," he said. "Now tell me everything you know, Todd."

While Todd spoke, David tried to keep his mind from racing ahead. He kept thinking that the moment Cal Monroe had called last month he'd known it was an omen. First Cal, then Despina, now Greg, Todd, Axel. All the chickens coming home to roost. All the ghosts coming home.

"I'm still not absolutely sure we should tell the police," Todd was saying.

"I don't think we have any choice," Greg said.

David paused a moment. "I agree with you, Greg," he said quietly. "We have no choice." He looked Todd directly in the eyes. "And there's something else you ought to know, Todd. Apart from any danger Axel may be in at the hands of these terrorists, he's at a tremendous risk with the U.S. Government simply by being associated with them. From what you've told me, he's not only harbored known criminals, he's voluntarily given them medical aid. He could be found guilty of all kinds of complicity. I don't know how he expected to come out of hiding now without having to spend much of the rest of his life before grand juries and in jail. Thank God, we can probably keep any of that from happening." David stood. "I don't think we should delay this another minute. I have to make a couple of calls and then you can drive me to the airport."

Todd suddenly shot out his hand and grabbed David's sleeve. He was trembling. "For God's sake, David, make sure they'll be careful."

"The following are my conditions for releasing this information," David said.

Across the table from him, Farley, the San Diego grand jury prosecutor, and Malone, from the FBI, poised their pens above their pads.

"First, no one outside this room is ever to know where the information came from.

"Second, these men are holding a captive by the name of Axel Stenhorn. He must be guaranteed immunity from any prosecution for aiding or abetting the criminals. I don't want him used as a witness, no grand juries, nothing."

David paused, savoring the moment.

"And, lastly, I want Calvin Monroe's subpoena dropped and I want him released this morning."

David could not hold back his smile. All coming home.

43

AXEL LIFTED the thermometer from his patient's mouth and held it in front of the oil lamp.

"One hundred and one," he said out loud in Spanish. "A full degree below what it was yesterday at sundown. You are well out of danger now."

The Man-Without-Feet laughed. "It is touching to see how eager you are for me to recover."

Axel shook the thermometer and returned it to a glass filled with alcohol. "You are incredibly lucky," he said without looking up.

"No, no," the Man-Without-Feet answered. "It is you who are lucky, Doc."

Axel said nothing. He looked at his watch. "I will prepare your injection," he said finally.

In the corner of the room Billy rose from his chair and slung the strap of his rifle over his shoulder. He snapped on a flashlight and played the beam at Axel's feet as he followed him to the courtyard behind the clinic, where a kerosene generator kept a small refrigerator running. Axel filled a pan with water from a jug, connected the hot plate to the generator and set the pan on it. He dropped the syringe and needle into the water, then rolled down his sleeves and buttoned them. The evening air was cool again. He searched the sky for the moon. A bright crescent was just beginning to rise over the courtyard wall. Tati and the girls would be eating supper now. He had not seen them since the operation.

When Axel had refused to perform the amputation, the Man-Without-Feet had ordered Tati and the children back to their *casita* under guard. "You and I are not leaving here until it is done," he told Axel. "And no one is leaving Xito until I am able to."

Axel had taken a day and a half to prepare for the operation. They had allowed Tati and the girls to assist him, scrubbing every surface of the clinic, stretching plastic tarps across the windows and doors, suspending every flashlight in the *colonia* from the ceiling and walls. He had enough sodium pentothal to anesthetize the patient and he refrigerated five pints of blood for transfusions, but he did not have the tools—the surgical knives and saws—to make a clean separation at the knees. They sterilized kitchen cleavers and a plumber's hacksaw. Axel studied his medical and anatomy charts through the night.

The next morning he performed the entire procedure in under four hours. Miraculously the patient's heart did not falter once; no blood was lost, none clotted in the veins. Within twenty-four hours after the operation his temperature began to drop. Each day since, it had dropped by increments. The infection was gone, removed and buried with the rest of the village's garbage, but still Axel was kept sequestered in the clinic with his patient and his bodyguard, Billy. No one came or went except to deliver food and messages. The Man-Without-Feet spoke of leaving the *colonia* by the end of the week. Axel counted the hours.

There had never been a chance of simply picking up Tati and the girls and taking them back to Todd's. How in the name of God had Axel ever deluded himself into thinking he could? They had only let him go to San Francisco because Tati had stayed behind, a tacit hostage. Axel had succumbed to the soft logic of Todd's civilized world, where the hardest thing a man had to do was make up his mind; for a moment he had even convinced himself that the

Man-Without-Feet would see the light and go to a hospital. It seemed as if Axel's whole life was strewn with muddled misjudgments like that, each one taking him further away from what he truly wanted to do. Even now, did he truly think he could surrender himself to the authorities with impunity, no questions asked? By now even Todd must have realized how absurd an idea that was. Surely he no longer expected him.

Axel lifted the syringe and needle from the boiling water with a pair of tongs. He screwed them together, then opened the refrigerator door and removed an ampule of tetracycline. He inserted the needle through the cap and pulled the yellowish liquid into the syringe. He nodded to Billy and the two started back into the clinic. Axel had just passed through the door when they heard the whoosh and smack of bodies leaping over the courtyard wall. Billy spun around and fired one shot. Floodlights blinded them both. A single shot fired back at them and Billy dropped to the ground, dead.

Inside the clinic the Man-Without-Feet screamed, "Diablo!"

"Get him!" a man behind Axel shouted.

Someone pinned back Axel's arms in a half nelson. The hypodermic needle dropped from his hands and shattered. Three other men bounded inside with their weapons held straight in front of them.

"Diablo!"

Axel heard the oil lamp crash to the floor. A muffled cry. Silence. The entire village seemed to be holding its breath.

Handcuffs snapped on Axel's wrists behind him. A rifle butt nudged him forward. He stumbled through the clinic door. He felt numb except for a searing pain where his heart was. The entire room was white with the light of high-powered floodlamps. The Man-Without-Feet was sitting straight up in his bed, his hands in the air. A commando stood on either side of him, one with a pistol at his head. Still no one spoke; still the village was silent. Not one of the Man-Without-Feet's men had appeared. But he was smiling.

"You are Axel Stenhorn, correct?" the commando behind Axel said.

Axel tried to answer, but his jaw would not move. He nodded his head.

"*Serpiente!*" The Man-Without-Feet hissed at Axel.

"I'm afraid we'll have to keep you handcuffed until all of this is over, Stenhorn." The commando behind Axel pulled him back through the door to the courtyard. They both stumbled over Billy's ankles. The moon was now high above the wall and Axel could see the man standing beside him. He was young—no more than twenty-five—and had light skin and blond hair which had been darkened with soot. He was looking directly into Axel's eyes.

"My name's Bellows. I'm FBI," he whispered. "Now how many of them are there, Stenhorn. Where are they? What kind of weapons do they have?"

Axel stood paralyzed. Billy's pupils had rolled up into his skull and the whites of his eyes gleamed. A moment ago it had been Billy's gun that was pointing at him; now it was the FBI's. Axel knew where at least one of the other terrorists was: Moon was in his *casita* with Tati and the girls.

"Go away," Axel whispered, his breath quavering. "Leave Xito alone."

"Don't be stupid, Stenhorn. Tell me where they are. It's your only chance. For now and for later too. Especially for later."

"Just go away," Axel pleaded. There were tears in his eyes. "Please just go away before it's too late."

One of the other FBI men appeared at the door.

"Nothing," Bellows said to him, gesturing with his head toward Axel. "He's with them."

The man at the door lifted a walkie-talkie from his pocket and pulled out the antenna. The radio crackled. "Harper," he said into the mouthpiece. "We've taken the clinic. The one without feet, Stenhorn and another one who's dead. One shot. Stenhorn won't talk." The radio crackled again and the man put it to his ear. Axel could hear nothing. They pushed him inside the clinic again. The man with the radio strode to the center of the room.

"All right," he said, "I want you to listen carefully. This entire village is surrounded. We've got eighty-five men out there totally armed. We have five helicopters. We have flares. It's all over, you see? I want you to tell the rest of your men to walk slowly to the center of the village with their hands over their heads. There is absolutely no reason for one more shot to be fired, do you understand?"

He looked from Axel to the Man-Without-Feet. The Man-Without-Feet was laughing. "It is *you* who is surrounded," he said, lowering his hands to his sides. "Why do you think no one came running when a shot was fired? What kind of fools do you think we are?" He laughed again. "There are explosives planted in the ground like corn all over this hill. Bombs. And every one of them will go off in just five minutes. Sooner if another shot is fired. The clock was set when I yelled 'Diablo!' The entire village will go. Two hundred people. Mothers, children, all in flames."

Axel was quaking, sobbing.

"Throw your guns out the window. Call your friends on the radio and tell them you are hostages. Then handcuff yourselves in a circle. Only then will I call the bombs off."

The three FBI commandos stood absolutely still. Then the one with the radio raced out to the courtyard, again pulling on the antenna. Axel fought to keep down his sobs, to catch his breath, to listen. The man holding the radio rushed back in.

"Give us an hour," he said. "We need an hour to move the men back."

"You only need a minute to get rid of your guns and handcuff yourselves. You only have three minutes left. Maybe two. You cannot stall me."

"In the name of God, do it!" Axel wailed. "Do it!"

The man next to the bed suddenly pressed the barrel of his revolver against the Man-Without-Feet's head. "Call it off!" he shouted. He pulled back the hammer with his thumb. "Call it off or I'll shoot!"

The Man-Without-Feet burst into diabolical laughter.

It was over. It was over. It was all over. The cry exploded from Axel's mouth as he ran through the door to the street in front of the clinic. "Tati! Tati! Tati!"

The first bomb went off directly behind Axel. He spun around, his bound arms swinging up behind him as an orange ball of fire spun in the sky like a comet. People on every side of him screamed. They were all in the streets now. One of the FBI men stood in the door of the clinic with his rifle raised, but no one saw him or heard his commands. The next group of bombs went off all at once. A blast of heat seared Axel's skin. The flames were everywhere. Xito was burning. Axel knew this fire. He had seen this fire before.

Above him helicopters fluttered on angels' wings, casting down perfect columns of yellow light, spumescent Jacob's ladders. Yes, he knew this fire. He had been waiting for it to come again. The heat enveloped him in a coat of fleece. A spark lighted on his beard like a butterfly and suddenly it was ablaze, licking his neck. He yanked at its tip and miraculously it came off in his hand, but underneath was another beard and it was on fire too, and he yanked again and again and again, his head twisting back and forth, while above him the camera's eye shone down in a perfect column through a wreath of Christmas lights. It was over, it was over. He fell to his knees, clutching the child to his chest, feeling the heat of his skin burn his own, grafting their skin together, black and white, charcoal and ashes. He had seen this fire before. He knew this fire like a lover. He knew her fluttering veil, her glowing skin, her laughter. Oh God, yes, it was the fire he had yearned for, the lightning thaw, the Light. A hand reached through the smoke and touched his own. "Easy," the young man said. "It's not happening to you. Not to you, my friend." Jerry's long fingers closed around his wrists. "Just let it go. Pass through it." And Greggy laughing on the couch, goggle-eyed, waving his fuzzy head back and forth, pointing his finger straight at him, and David by the window, flat as glass, the flames reflected in his eyes; he sees the fire too. Axel fell backward on his wrists. A blanket of black smoke floated in the air above him. He held his breath. The flame inside his head flashed red, now blue, now pure white light shooting through the center of his forehead, a perfect column spinning heavenward. And hovering at the end of the light he saw the face, the beatific smile, the incandescent eyes.

Axel screamed.

Timothy Leary looked like the Devil.

Epilogue

TODD TURNED UP the collar of his jacket against the drizzle falling outside the Greyhound terminal. He felt as if he had passed through half the world's latitudes in the past ten hours, on and off buses from Calexico to LA; the air-conditioning on the cruiser up from San Diego had been subarctic. He leaned against the concrete wall, stretching his back. Jerry had offered to send his private plane down to Xito to pick him up for the birthday celebration, but Todd had not been able to accept. Since coming to live and work in Xito, he only traveled by bus. Todd peered up the steamy street. After all this he certainly hoped Jerry remembered which terminal to come to.

Part of Todd had been reluctant to come tonight at all. It was not that he anticipated another painful meeting—the last time all four of them had been together was at Axel's funeral two years ago, a day so raw with sorrow and shared guilt that Todd had kept away from the others as much as he could. But all that was long past now and, as with everything else in Todd's life since they had buried Axel, the past was not what mattered. No, what worried Todd about tonight was that Jerry had poured so much into the preparations that he may have made it into an event of impossible expectations. Todd shook his head, smiling. Jerry Halligan, the most illustrious of them all, the millionaire wizard of Metaman Encounters, throwing his own fortieth birthday party just for his old college pals. He was the last one any of them would have expected to be smitten by middle-aged nostalgia.

A long midnight blue limousine pulled up to the curb and the rear door swung open. "Toddy!"

"Hello, Jerry. Happy birthday, old friend."

The two men embraced on the sidewalk, then stepped back and looked at one another. Except for the ruddy mustache and the deepened lines in the corners of his eyes, Jerry still looked like a twenty-year-old. He was wearing a tuxedo.

"I hope we aren't going to the opera," Todd said, pulling at his windbreaker. Along with his chinos and white shirt, he was wearing the best of his current wardrobe.

"We *are* the opera," Jerry said, grinning.

A round, almost completely bald head jutted out the car door. "Name tags," Greg piped. "I told you we should have worn name tags. How do you expect anybody to recognize me?"

Todd stooped over and threw his arms around Greg, dear Greg. They had corresponded frequently these past few years and spoken on the phone several times when Todd was in Calexico, but this was the first they had seen one another since the funeral. Greg was more nervous about this moment than he had realized, afraid it would re-ignite the horrible sense of complicity they both had felt when they heard about the siege of Xito. It had changed Greg too, that explosion on a remote hilltop near the Mexican border, though not as dramatically as it had Todd.

"Okay, it's true, I'm shorter," Greg said as Todd straightened up. "All my height was in my hair."

Todd squeezed Greg's shoulder and laughed.

"Enter to grow in wisdom." Jerry flourished his hand like a magician and they all got into the back of the limousine. He pressed a button on the partition that separated them from the driver and said, "Courthouse next."

"Ah, so the mystery is solved," Greg said. "You're throwing the party in night court, right?"

"Not even close, Gregorio," Jerry said. "That's where Debilio wanted to be picked up." He pulled up the jumpseat and sat across from Todd, gazing into his pale gray eyes. Lately he found himself thinking about Todd often, mostly memories of when he had lived with him and his family in San Francisco. In some way he had never felt more content than that year he spent cloaked in the moth-eaten blanket telling "Zeitman" stories to Todd's children.

"So, tell all," Jerry said. "How's everything going? Is it true that you actually deliver little babies down there?"

"Not if I can help it." Todd smiled. He had taken a concentrated paramedic course before moving the family down to Xito to help the survivors rebuild the *colonia,* but, fortunately, once they were there May and Tati made most of the medical decisions. "I'm still basically a bedpan man," he said. He looked quickly from Jerry to Greg and back to Jerry again. "By the way, everyone wanted me to thank you both for your checks. The water tanks were delivered last week. We've named them Greg and Jerry."

"Immortality at last," Greg said, and they all laughed.

They rode in silence for several minutes. Outside the heavily tinted windows Los Angeles looked positively picturesque. The rose-colored glasses of the rich, Greg thought. He could not help wondering if Jerry truly believed all those hip parables and "metagame strategies" that his Institute put out. Somehow both Jerry and he had ended up in the business of changing lives. Last year, however, with a mixture of relief and fear, Greg had sold his share in "Life Swappers," fixed up a room in the attic, and started again to write plays. Miraculously, with the constant tumble and chatter of children around him, the writing was going better than it ever had.

"So, where *are* we going tonight?" Todd said as the car began to slow.

Jerry beamed. "Ah, now I'm happy," he said. "Even old Toddy is curious."

The limousine came to a stop and Jerry pushed open the door. It took a few moments before any of them spotted David in the cluster of young people standing near the entrance of the court building. The young people all wore large red buttons on their lapels and David seemed to be lecturing them on something. When he saw Jerry waving, David handed his briefcase and some papers to a woman at his side and started toward the car in a little half-sprint. He looked very much indeed like a winning candidate. Just three weeks before, a caucus of California Democrats had nominated him for State Attorney General.

"Happy birthday, old man!" David gave Jerry's hand a quick, vigorous shake, then pulled a small gift-wrapped package from his suit coat pocket and handed it to him. "A little something for auld lang syne," he said.

Jerry immediately opened the gift; it was a photograph of David and himself standing side by side in front of Thayer Hall in the fall of 1957.

"I'm the one on the right," David said, winking.

From inside the car Greg and Todd watched tears appear in
Jerry's eyes as he and David locked in an embrace. Greg smiled at
Todd and lowered his eyes. Maybe spending the evening with
David would not be so bad after all. The last time he had seen him
—at Axel's funeral with Despina in I. Magnin black at his side—
Greg barely had been able to contain his disdain for either of
them. Their grief had been too public, too chic; somehow Despina
had even managed to appear as if she were Axel's bereaved
widow. But perhaps all that had been just more of Greg's own guilt
spilling over. God knows, David must have suffered too. Greg
shook his hand warmly as he entered the back of the limousine.
Then David took Todd's hand and held it a moment in both of his
own. He looked at Jerry, smiling.

"Jesus, this is the best idea you've had in twenty years, Halligan!" David said.

"Eighteen," Jerry said. "It was just eighteen years ago in June."

"I stand corrected," David said and laughed. God, he felt happy
tonight, fulfilled somehow. He looked from face to face. They had
all mellowed, it seemed, even Greg. He was sure he could feel
their pride in his success. These were, after all, his enduring
friends, his true friends. His Harvard friends.

"Proceed," Jerry said into the chauffeur's phone. He wagged his
eyebrows fiendishly as he pressed a button that lowered a black
shade on all the windows in the car. He flipped on the interior
lights and pulled open the bar. A bottle of champagne appeared in
an ice bucket, now in four glasses. He *was* a magician. David raised
his glass.

"To you, Halligan," he said, "our eternal leader."

"No, no—to us," Jerry said urgently, earnestly. "All of us. Axel
too."

He also raised his glass. It was clear to them all that Jerry had
rehearsed this moment a great many times, word for word.

"There were never any like us, before or since, not at Harvard
or any other place," his toast began. "We were on the cusp, the
edge of things to come, freaking ourselves out before anyone
knew what a freak-out was. We were the original psychedelic
virgins and we've spent two decades trying to recapture that moment when the whole world changed for us."

They all sipped from their glasses, then fell silent in varying mixtures of embarrassment and love. Todd was shaking his head back and forth, his eyes twinkling.

"Actually," he said, smiling, "if you think about it, we're just another bunch of middle-aged Harvard grads. We all got to where we were supposed to. We just took some detours."

Jerry cocked his head to one side, hiding the flinch that crossed his face, then burst into a beautiful grin. "I'll drink to that," he said.

The car had come to a halt. Jerry put his hand on the door handle.

"Gentlemen, the party begins!"

The door swung open and they all gazed out. They were parked in front of some kind of a nightclub. Greg leaned his head way down and looked up at the marquee.

"Improvisation Club" the sign read. And underneath, "Tonight's Featured Comedian—Dr. Timothy Leary."

Good God! They filed out onto the sidewalk behind Jerry.

"How's this for symmetry?" he said. "Tim was just forty himself back then—you know, on the night in Newton."

The manager of the club obviously had been waiting for Jerry's party. They were led to a table at the very front of the club. The place was crowded and smelled of beer and cigarettes, perhaps a hint of marijuana. Greg had been here once before, long ago. It was just off Sunset Strip. Young comedians who wanted to be seen tried out their acts here for nothing. The lights faded. In the dark a voice came over the loudspeakers.

"Ladies and gentlemen, after years of silence, it gives me great pleasure to present to you Dr. Timothy Leary."

The spotlight flashed on.

Standing at the microphone in pale gray flannel slacks, tennis shoes and a robin's egg blue V-neck sweater pulled over an oxford cloth button-down shirt, loose limbed and cool, the white, close-cropped hair still thick, the ironic smile still responding to some private, no doubt *cosmic*, funny business, Timothy Leary looked— by God, there was no better word for it—he looked *collegiate*.

"I . . . I'm not really a comedian," he began, squinting into the spotlight. "I just issue reports on the incarnations of the human spirit." He scratched behind his ear in mock befuddlement. "But then, of course, there's nothing quite so comical as the human spirit."

Around the small nightclub only a few people laughed. At some tables guests were still talking among themselves. At Jerry's table they neither laughed nor talked. They all—Jerry, David, Greg and Todd—gazed dumbfoundedly up at Leary as if he had just materialized by magic, as fresh and sneaky as a hallucination.

ACKNOWLEDGMENTS

I never cease to be impressed and touched by how generous people are in helping me prepare and write my books.

In particular, I was dependent on other people's knowledge and experience for the section on Tanganyika (Tanzania): Dr. David Lippman, who practiced psychiatry there, and Kate Wenner, whose marvelous book *Shamba Letu* details her experiences as a teacher in a small Tanzanian village.

I also want to thank the librarians of Simon's Rock College and of the Widener Library, Harvard, for aid beyond the call of duty; Douglas Ferguson and Fred Rutberg for graciously letting me pick their brains; and Julie Michaels, who gave up vacation time to read my first draft.

I am indebted to Susan Schwartz, my editor, for her abiding faith in this book and in me.

Finally, it is no exaggeration to say that I would not be able to write a chapter, let alone a book, without the emotional support and incisive criticism of my wife, Freke Vuijst.

DMK
Great Barrington
Massachusetts